KWEK

A Ghanaian At Boa

1960s and '70s Britain

MICHAEL A PEPERA

A catalogue record for this book is available from the Ghana Library Authority

ISBN 978-9988-53-216-1

FIRST EDITION

Dedicated To My Parents

Kwabena Pepera

&

Beatrice Pepera

PREFACE

On passing the milestone of another decade in 2018, I received another reminder that my let on this earth is, so to speak, not freehold but strictly leasehold. Becoming a fully-fledged member of the society of sexagenarians in 2019 triggered an impulse in me, rooted in interest shown by others in various topics broached in casual conversation over the years, to recount parts of my life's experience. I have chosen to do so in this book vicariously through a fictional character, Kweku, who is loosely based on me.

I hope the reader finds the book, my first attempt at one, of some interest, and is not put off by the many chance digressions into the fields of human motivation or rudimentary political thought. It is a fact that politics influences more aspects of our lives than we are often comfortable acknowledging. For many of us it seems "uncool" to obsess too much about how we are governed, until, that is, the possibility of extraordinary disruptions to an acceptable existing lifestyle catches our attention. Things do change over time – sometimes too slowly for the impatient human spirit – and opportunities for growth, health and prosperity are influenced by the quality of political and moral leadership in the big and small societies within which we interact with others.

Custodians of leadership are always temporary, identity habits and cultural attitudes more enduring. The value of learning is priceless, the cost of ignorance and hypocrisy potentially infinite. With deference to the central tenet said to have been propagated by the brilliant but humble ancient Greek philosopher,

Socrates, I am happy to concede that I am always learning, and shall forever battle against ignorance, including my own, for as long as there is life in me.

Michael A Pepera

Accra, Ghana

7th January, 2020

CHAPTER ONE

Wheels Up

September 1964

It was a humid, overcast Friday morning in Accra, Ghana. Kweku had endured a sleepless night, nervously anticipating a day that would take him from the only home he had known since birth far away to the home of his country's recent colonial masters, where his parents dreamt he would have access to the best possible education in the world.

Inside the long terminal at the international airport, the tannoy was in full swing, reverberating around the hall with a series of flight and information announcements.

An hour and a half earlier, at home in Cantonments, Kweku had swallowed the last spoonful of his favourite all-day home brunch of steamed rice, spicy red and green *kpakpo shito* pepper and sardines. He bade a tearful goodbye to his nanny Tina as Victor, the driver, loaded a smart new suitcase in his favourite royal blue colour into the car boot. His parents sandwiched him cosily on the back seat. Tina, who doubled as the house cook and made herself generally useful, swung the gate open to disgorge the car into the world outside, its black wrought-iron leaves closing firmly behind them as the car turned on to the road.

For the short journey to the airport Kweku sat mute and apprehensive. An array of thoughts swirled inside his head. He wanted to be positive, to imagine that everything was going to be all right. Mummy and

Daddy couldn't be wrong about sending him off to boarding school in England at the age of just six? After all, they were his lynchpins to reality, his reference points for validation of everything. They showed concern for his well-being every day, forgiving light transgressions like raiding the kitchen larder at home between meals, punishing more serious ones like engaging in fights at nursery school.

To boost his self-confidence for the challenges that lay ahead, he batted away negative thoughts as irritating intruders trespassing on his crowded mental space: he would have no problem sleeping in a strange house, in a strange land, eating strange food, with strange people watching over him, he imagined, willing himself to believe it but not quite succeeding.

Other times, bringing himself back down to earth, he chose to dwell on practicalities, developing them into what-if scenarios… 'What if the flight is cancelled?... What if Auntie Emily isn't there to meet me at the other end?' he wondered.

The giant billboards along the highway alternately loomed large and small, the 3-dimensional cut-outs tantalising the senses with their proximity. A lifelike bottle of orange Fanta, another of Pepsi-Cola, a smiling mother stooping to deliver into the eagerly outstretched hands of her beaming son a hot drink, wisps of steam rising from the mug, an outsized tin of Ovaltine slanted diagonally across the top right hand corner – all seemingly appeared from nowhere, waxing bigger and bigger till he could almost touch them, before shrinking back into the distance, out of sight and out of mind. Kweku knew he wouldn't be seeing these dream-inspiring pictures again for a long time.

In less than fifteen minutes they had arrived at the airport and were climbing up the gentle slope towards the terminal. He could now hear the roar of plane engines thundering on the runway, parking, idling. To the right the tail of a plane, with white cross painted on a deep red background, caught his attention. The car finally came to a halt opposite the terminal entrance.

As they alighted, a porter in bright red uniform came rushing up out of the shadows, swinging into position by the car boot a huge trolley at the ready. Victor waved him away: 'It's just one bag,' he said, 'We only need a small trolley.' With glum resignation, the porter swung back 180 degrees and beckoned to a rival. A small, rickety trolley which, like its handler, back bent with age, had obviously seen better days, was shuffled into place.

Once inside the terminal, Kweku, his parents, and the hunched porter, the blue suitcase in tow, went straight up to the Swissair check-in desk. It was manned by a tall, handsome man with slick black hair, dressed smartly in company uniform with no frills. His attire matched perfectly the mechanical efficiency of his demeanour. Announcing themselves, Kweku's parents, Kojo and Deborah Mensah, explained to him that they were there to escort their son Kweku into the airline's care for the flight to London.

'Thank you, Mr and Mrs Mensah,' he said. 'And this is Kweku, is it?' He peered down to get a closer look at their young charge.

'Yes,' Kojo affirmed, Kweku and Deborah nodding silently in turn as they watched on.

Handover documentation was briefly reviewed, endorsed, exchanged, and the blue suitcase was taken airside for loading.

'The flight is on time, Mr and Mrs Mensah. We'll let you know when we're ready to board. Thank you.'

'Thank you very much.'

With that, the Mensahs turned to head for the designated waiting area. The porter, relieved of baggage and anxious for his tip, reminded Kojo with the affected clearing of an unblocked throat that time waits for no one. Quickly getting the hint, Kojo reached into his pocket and stuffed a folded note into the porter's hand. 'Sorry, there you go!'

Opening his hand to get a closer look, the porter beamed back at him. Even though the note was in a low denomination, it amounted to double his usual takings for a single trolley run. Affecting to doff a non-existent hat in appreciation, he exclaimed: 'Thank you, Sir, Madam! Have a blessed day, and safe trip to the young man!' before quickly melting away into the throng with his trolley, casting around for another catch.

Kojo and Deborah searched the waiting area for a section of three unoccupied seats in a row. Kojo spotted one:

'Ah, D, have you seen? Over there.' "D", short for "Darling", was how Kojo and Deborah sometimes addressed each other, although Kojo used it much more often; Deborah usually preferred to call Kojo by his first name. Amongst the Akan ethnic group in Ghana, both men and women have different forenames corresponding to the days of the week on which they were born. Kojo was the name for a male born on a

Monday. Deborah's day-name was Adjoa, for Thursday-borns, but she settled on using her Catholic name and married name.

'Well spotted, Kojo,' Deborah said. 'Come on, Kweku, let's go before someone else takes them!' They went over and sat down. It would be his parents' last chance for words of advice to their son before he left their care. They knew that and certainly made the most of it. His mum delivered her full repertoire on the importance of smart dressing and staying warm. His dad listened in, hovering, waiting to chip in whenever a gap appeared momentarily in her delivery. It was like a tag team, two against one!

Mum: 'Don't forget, Coco, England can be cold, even in June. Make sure you always wrap up warm, indoors and outdoors.'

"Coco" was how Kweku used to pronounce his name when asked for it as a two-year-old. His parents liked it so much that they decided to adopt it as their own intimate name for him, however old he got. Kweku found it embarrassing, but in deference to his parents decided to keep that embarrassment to himself and learned to accept it as a sign of their affection.

Dad: 'Tina did pack your pullover in your satchel, didn't she, just in case?'

Kweku half swung round and unzipped the top section of his satchel to check for himself. To his relief, the jumper was there and he gave a confirmatory nod.

His dad then asked, 'Have you checked the small side pocket of your satchel?'

'Huh?' Kweku was puzzled.

'Go on, open it, check! …'

‘Kweku unzipped the side-compartment of his satchel and stuck his hand inside. He hit what seemed to be a plastic pouch of something. He pulled it out to check and to his delight it was a bag of honey sweets from the new confectionery plant his dad had recently set up with a Swiss partner. He recognised the red and blue ‘Sonimo Mim’ logo, named after the town of Mim in Brong Ahafo, half way up the country to the west where the factory was located, and the Honimo brand name in a russet brown colour distinguishing the honey sweets from the rest of their confectionery.

‘Ohh, thank you so much Daddy!’ Seeing his mum looking a bit left out, Kweku quickly added: ‘… and Mummy!’ His dad chuckled. He loved treating people to unexpected surprises.

More cautionary advice followed from both of them on manners, discretion, respect and personal hygiene – the kinds of things it would be almost unthinkable for youngsters to listen to patiently nowadays.

One piece of advice from his dad caught Kweku’s attention: ‘Don’t forget, Son, when in Rome, do as the Romans do.’ In later years, he was to reflect that it was probably the most important all-encompassing guidance anyone can receive when going to a new country.

After what seemed like half a day but in reality could not have been a minute more than half an hour, Kweku suddenly became aware once again of the sound of the tannoy. It was now addressing them directly.

‘Passenger Kweku Mensah and his guardian, please proceed to the Swissair check-in desk.’

Kweku leapt to his feet, his parents flanking him on either side as they made their way back to the check-in desk. Halfway there, they noticed a stewardess approaching. She was dressed smartly in the airline's red apparel, white piping at the borders of her blazer and knee-length skirt. The clicking of the heels of her buckled, glistening red shoes against the terminal's freshly polished terrazzo flooring seemed in perfect consonance with her immaculate, clipping gait and confident smile.

'You must be Kweku Mensah's parents,' she said, shaking their hands warmly and flashing a smile evincing complete spontaneity despite being honed by years of painstaking professional training.

'Yes,' they replied, almost simultaneously, relieved to see that they would be entrusting their son into the personal care of someone so well turned out. Appearance still spoke volumes in those days, first impressions all the more so.

'I am Gitte Rohner,' she said, pointing to the name emblazoned in bold on the company badge attached to the left lapel of her blazer.

'And what is your name?' she asked, moderating her voice with the usual lilt that adults apply when introducing themselves to babies or young children in the presence of their parents. She maintained her broad smile as she stooped to Kweku's level, hand fully outstretched to meet his tentative greeting.

'Kwe-ku.' Embarrassed by the attention, Kweku shyly articulated his name slowly, lingering on the first vowel.

'Well, you can call me Miss Gitte, and I will be taking care of you from now on all the way to

London!' Her arm extended gracefully upwards in a sweeping gesture as she gave full vent to the word 'all'.

Brief, nervous chuckles bubbled up in unison from Gitte and Kweku's parents.

Kweku remained po-faced, looking up at his mum, then dad, for confirmation that it was safe to part.

His dad nodded approvingly. His mum stood silently by his side, tears now welling up in her eyes. Kweku had always slept in the nest that was home to all of them. Now he would be flying for the first time, up and away into the hands of people who could never understand him like she did, who wouldn't be able to give him the attention she had lavished on him for the first six years of his life. But they were now in public, and her traditional upbringing had taught her to control personal emotions in public. Appearance was key, and Accra was such a small place… you never knew if someone who knew you would be watching, unseen, from a distance and later revel in peddling stories at the hairdressing salon about what they had witnessed, complete with fictitious embellishments to make their gossip juicier.

Kweku lifted his arms to hug his parents for the last time. His eyes moistened but he had to control himself. A quick embrace first with dad, complete with firm handshake on release. As young as he was, Kweku already understood that boys shouldn't wear their hearts on their sleeves in times of crisis. For young girls, this was OK – even becoming … not so for tough boys. And Kweku was determined to show his dad he would be tough enough for the challenges in front of him.

'Goodbye, Son,' Kojo said. 'Be good… Let Auntie Emily call me or Mummy after you land so we can talk.'

Kweku turned finally to his mum, arms outstretched as she swept him off the floor into her tight embrace, his feet paddling the air momentarily before finding the floor again. All the while Gitte kept a respectful distance, appreciating their need for privacy in their last moments together. After what seemed like an eternity, Deborah released Kweku. His hands dropped to his sides. He gave a short tug to swing his satchel back into place over his shoulders.

'Bye-bye, Mr and Mrs Mensah' Gitte said, her head half-tilting to the left in empathy as she added: 'Don't worry, Kweku is in very good hands.'

'Thank you,' his parents said in turn, nodding in appreciation as they spoke.

With that, Gitte clasped Kweku's left hand in her right before marching him off briskly in the direction of the boarding gate. As they turned the corner going out of sight, Kweku looked back to see if his parents were still standing where he had left them. They were, his mum now dabbing her eyes with a handkerchief as she watched him go, his dad also now looking on with watery eyes. They exchanged last waves and then were gone from view.

The realisation finally sank in with Kweku… that night, for the first time in his life, he would be sleeping alone, separated from them, in far-away Britain, the *Aburokyire* or 'white man's land' he had heard and read so much about, home of many of the business friends of his dad who had visited the house in Ghana. But first, Kweku had a plane journey to survive.

By now tears were streaming down his cheeks as Gitte whisked him past long queues of passengers right up to the front desk at the boarding gate. He pulled himself together again as she handed over his shiny new passport and air ticket. Both were promptly stamped. She muttered something to the airline official at the desk and they both giggled. Kweku imagined it must have been something quite innocent, as Gitte smiled at him and tugged him closer immediately afterwards.

Soon they were off again, past seated passengers waiting their turn to board the bus to the plane, Kweku with his shorter strides struggling to keep up. Into a corridor, down the stairs at the end, stepping briefly on to the tarmac and then climbing on to the bus parked opposite the boarding gate. Some mothers with babies and toddlers were already on the bus. They were joined moments later by a few suited professionals and casually dressed elderly couples.

The doors closed and the bus set off, hugging the perimeter of the terminal wall before making a sharp turn to the left. In less than a minute it pulled up opposite what seemed to Kweku like a stairs car which had just moved into place against the plane's front door on the left-hand side. Looking up, Kweku realised that the plane was the same one he had seen some two hours earlier as he first approached the airport in the car with his parents and Victor. He was so excited. This was not at all like the Dinky toy VC10 his parents had given him the previous Christmas. This was enormous, the real thing, engine roaring, at times reaching a high-pitched shrill – like an imaginary lion alternately growling baritone and shrilling soprano.

As they climbed to the top of the stairs, Kweku clinging firmly to Gitte's hand, he saw the elderly couples and suited business types turn left. He, Gitte and the mothers and toddlers turned right to sit in the front rows of the adjacent cabin.

Gitte asked him: 'Do you want to sit next to the window? That way you'll be able to get a better look at all the sights on the way.'

Delighted to be given the option, Kweku instantly piped up 'Oh, yes please, Miss Gitte!' nodding so vigorously as he spoke that he almost felt his neck snap. He removed his satchel and leapt into the window seat.

Gitte strapped the seatbelt firmly around his waist and put his satchel away in the stowage locker above. 'Your satchel's up here. If you need anything from it, call me and I'll bring it down for you.'

But Kweku wasn't listening. He was already peering through his porthole, turning to check whether the one in the row behind was the same.

'That's funny,' he told Gitte, 'it looks like there are two windows in each hole everywhere – one on the inside and one on the outside.'

'Yes,' Gitte chuckled. 'These are special windows for planes, to keep us all safe.'

'All right, Kweku,' Gitte continued, her finger moving to a yellow button under the right arm of his seat. 'Press this button if you need anything. I'll be just here,' she said, pointing to the staff service area in the middle immediately in front of them. 'Otherwise I'll be passing by to check on you from time to time.'

'Thank you,' Kweku nodded in appreciation. He looked around. As the aeroplane took on board more and more passengers with their overloaded hand-luggage, he saw stewards dressed like the man at the check-in desk earlier and other stewardesses dressed just like Gitte. After about half an hour, he realised that he had forgotten to ask Gitte something.

Catching her attention the next time she walked past, he asked 'Oh, Miss Gitte, how long will it take before we reach London?'

'Oh… the flight will take about six and a half hours,' Gitte replied. 'And if you need the toilet, it's just over there.'

'And how far is it to London?'

'About three thousand miles.'

'Woooww, three thousand!'

A man's voice came over the tannoy, identifying himself as the captain and announcing that take-off was imminent. Within minutes all passengers and flight crew were seated. The aircraft was fired up and thundering down the runway. But take-off was much more of a struggle for the plane than Kweku had thought it would be. He had imagined the plane lifting itself effortlessly into the sky, just like a bird. Instead he heard it grumbling and groaning before finally, just before the end of the runway, it went wheels up, seeming almost immediately to dip and nearly crash back to the ground before suddenly catching a swirl of air underneath with increasing speed and being pushed up by the air into the sky. He had no idea how the plane's aerodynamics worked, but was just relieved to be airborne.

Kweku couldn't believe how quickly everything on the ground shrank as the plane climbed into the sky. Storey buildings, the odd skyscraper, houses nestling blue swimming pools, roads and moving cars all now looked like toys he could play with – if only he could reach out to them – before they finally disappeared below layers of clouds like puffs of intervening smoke.

The plane shook as it was buffeted by the clouds, before finally settling at a steady altitude. A bell pinged – the same pinging sound that Kweku had earlier heard immediately preceding tannoy announcements in the airport terminal. After this there was a scattered chorus of clicking as passengers unlocked their seatbelts, cabin crew began circulating, smokers who had grown increasingly fidgety for twenty minutes during taxiing and take-off, could finally light up, some blowing long plumes or smoke rings to celebrate like inmates walking through the prison gates free after serving their time. Cigar smoke wafted through from the first class cabin ahead.

Kweku was struggling to keep his eyes open. He didn't want to miss any of the fantastic sights now filling his window. Clouds had always been far away up in the sky, unreachable, untouchable… now he was able to look down at them. It seemed really weird.

After an hour, he could faintly smell food of some kind being prepared in the service area and the pop and swish of fizzy drinks being poured. Nature was calling. He fiddled around with his seatbelt to find the catch, took it off and dashed to the washroom. Coming back out again into the aisle, he saw stewards and stewardesses pacing up and down placing lunch trays on tables extending from the backs of the seats in front.

Kweku was born with a healthy appetite. It had been somewhat blunted by the nerves surrounding the parting from his parents and this first ever flight, but he had been anticipating lunch on the plane with considerable curiosity and expectation. He sat back in his seat and slid his seatbelt clasp back on, clicking it into place.

Gitte suddenly appeared in front of him with a smile, the same smile she had worn when they first met, now clearly on display as the reflexive accompaniment to her opening pitch to conversations with all passengers on the flight. She was holding his lunch tray, and placed it with a flourish in front of him. He looked down and saw that it encapsulated one boiled egg, a piece of toast, and a Coca-Cola.

'Will that be enough for you?' she asked, without a hint of sarcasm.

'Oh yes, that's fine,' Kweku replied, determined to blend in with the crowd, as it seemed from the absence of any audible complaints that everyone else considered the food plenty enough or, if they didn't, were too polite to complain. 'Thank you,' he added. Secretly, his thoughts flashed back to the brunch he had eaten that morning. He thanked his lucky stars that his mother had had the foresight to hedge against the unknown, ensuring his stomach had been stuffed for the day before they left the house.

A few teaspoonfuls of egg and bites at the piece of toast later, and lunch was gone, washed down by the much-appreciated Coca-Cola. As the last drop of Coke passed his grateful lips, his sleepless night suddenly caught up with him. He fell off an imaginary cliff into a deep slumber.

He woke up just before landing, rubbing his eyes to clear his blurred vision before gazing out of his porthole to marvel at the sheer size of the airport and runway complex below. This must be London airport, he thought. It was a huge spread. Planes below seemed like milling ants everywhere, before taking on their fuller size as his plane made the final descent.

The plane touched down with a soft jolt, but everything seemed so quiet. Then he realised his ears were blocked. He stuck his little finger down one ear and shook vigorously to see if that would help. No change. He then instinctively tried yawning. He heard a pop in one ear, then the other. He could see Gitte trying to explain something to him, but wasn't able to make out what. Forcing more yawns, more pops followed, until one ear was finally clear.

He could now hear what Gitte was saying. 'Kweku, one of our London airport ground staff will be here shortly to take you to meet your aunt Tulver in the arrival hall. We just have to wait for the passengers in front to leave first.'

'Here's your satchel,' she said, bringing it down from the stowage locker.

'OK, Miss Gitte.'

'OK, I'll be back soon.'

After the first and business class customers had left the plane, right on cue, a portly, bespectacled middle-aged man with fair hair and medium build came into the cabin. As mothers and toddlers at the front of the cabin walked past him to disembark, he looked at cabin crew and asked, with a slight cockney accent,

'Master Kweku Mensah?'

Gitte came forward, pointing to Kweku, still waiting in his seat, his seatbelt by now unfastened. 'That's Kweku!' she said. 'And you are…' looking at his badge, she continued 'Martin Jones! … OK Martin, here are the papers… Can you sign there please?' Jones already knew exactly where to sign on the form and promptly initialled it. Gitte tore off her copy. Handing the rest of the papers back to Martin, she added, looking at Kweku, 'He's been good, no trouble at all... Kweku, this is Martin.' She gestured to Martin, who came forward and stood by Kweku. 'Martin will take care of you from now and take you through to see your aunt Tulver.'

'OK, let's go now, Kweku,' Martin said, glancing at passengers trapped standing in the aisle in the rows behind them during this brief handover, who were by now signalling their irritation at being kept waiting.

Kweku quickly rose from his seat, swinging his satchel round on to his back. 'Bye, Miss Gitte. Thanks a lot for everything.'

'Bye-bye, Kweku, hope to see you again soon on Swissair!' Gitte replied with her trademark generous smile. With that, she gave Kweku one last hug and he stepped off the plane with Martin.

They joined the first of the waiting buses outside. The ride to the terminal lasted much longer than the one in Accra from the terminal to the plane. Martin held his hand. Once inside the terminal, they headed for the special immigration queue for airline staff.

Everything was in order, and they were soon through into the baggage hall.

Within minutes, Kweku spotted his striking blue suitcase from a distance. 'Oh look, there's my bag!' he shouted, pointing it out.

They went over and Martin picked it up. Kweku's parents had neatly labelled it. He loaded it on to a trolley and they headed into the arrival hall. Martin had been given a rough description of Kweku's guardian, his 'aunt' Emily from the documentation. He guessed that Emily Tulver, a white English lady whose deep wrinkles around her eyes suggested that she was at least in her early fifties, was not actually Kweku's aunt.

In fact, she was a professional childminder, contracted to look after him during exeats and holiday times around his schooling in England. She had been asked to come to the airport with photo ID and address confirmation to facilitate the handover. Finally she would have to call Mr or Mrs Mensah for them to speak with her and confirm before Kweku could be released by the airline into her care. Kweku himself had absolutely no idea what she looked like.

In the front row of people behind the rope at the arrival hall, Martin noticed a late middle-aged woman with greying hair, a plain-looking wine-red handbag slung over her left shoulder, holding up a board with Kweku's name in block capitals.

'Mrs Tulver?' he asked.

'Yes, Emily Tulver… and is that Kweku?' she looked down at the young child walking alongside him.

'It is indeed… I'm Martin Jones, airline ground staff. Please come with us to the desk.'

Martin and Mrs Tulver exchanged small talk on the short walk to the Swissair ticketing desk. Everything went smoothly. Documentation was routinely exchanged and signed, and a call was placed by Martin to the number in Ghana for the Mensahs on the form. Mrs Mensah answered almost straightaway. She had been waiting anxiously by the phone for over an hour.

'Hello?'

'Hello, is that Mrs Mensah?'

'Yes, this is Mrs Mensah ...'

'Martin Jones, Swissair ground staff.'

'Oh… Is Kweku there with you?'

'He is indeed, Mrs Mensah. He's arrived safely and our colleagues on the flight said he was no trouble at all.'

'Ohh, thank you,' Kweku's mum replied. She was embarrassed by the compliments, however much motivated by diplomatic niceties. But any embarrassment was far outweighed by her relief at Kweku's safe flight.

'In fact they loved having him on board, Mrs Mensah. He's here. Would you like to speak to him?'

'Yes please.'

'OK, I'm passing him to you now.' Martin handed the phone down to Kweku.

There was a crackling sound on the line, but Kweku was still able to make out his mum's familiar voice clearly enough.

'Hello Coco.'

'Hello Mummy.'

'Well done! So how was the flight? Did you get enough to eat? Is everything OK?'

'Yes, Mummy, everything's fine.' Kweku dared not complain – least of all with Martin standing right beside him – about the spartan nature of the plane lunch.

'Anyway, is Auntie Emily there with you?' his mum continued, equally sensing the need to move on in the absence of any notable hiccups.

'Yes, Mummy.'

‘OK good. Auntie Emily will cook you a nice English supper when you get home.’

‘And how is the weather?’

‘It’s fine, Mummy, cooler than in Ghana, but it’s all right.’

‘OK, so now Auntie Emily will take you home to the flat. Be good and we will chat again later. Your daddy is still out but I’ll tell him once he gets home.’

‘All right, Mummy.’

‘Bye-bye then, Coco. Be good, and listen to Auntie Emily. Wrap up warm, too; soon winter will come and it will be much colder. OK, please let me speak to Auntie Emily.”

Kweku held the phone out towards Tulver. Taking it, she said, in her best Queen’s English: “Hellooo, Mrs Mensah… And how are you and Mr Mensah?’

‘Oh, we’re fine, thank you Emily. Thank you so much for looking after Kweku for us. Please take good care of him. Do let us know if there is anything he needs or you need, or anything we’ve forgotten.’

‘I will, thank you, Mrs Mensah. And please don’t worry, I’ll look after Kweku and make sure he has everything he needs.’

‘Thank you, Emily. Can I speak with Martin again please?’

‘Yes, just a moment.’ She passed the phone back to Martin.

‘All right, Mrs Mensah, so everything’s fine and Kweku seems to be in good hands. Thank you for trusting us with him. He’s a good young lad.’

‘Thank you so much. Everyone has been so wonderful and we really appreciate it. Thank you.’

'Not at all, Mrs Mensah, and please do not hesitate to contact Swissair again any time Kweku will be travelling alone.'

'All right, we will. Thank you.'

'Goodbye.'

'Bye.'

With that, Martin hung up and turned to Kweku:

'Cheerio, young man,' he said, signing off on their encounter with a wave. Kweku waved back. Tulver took Kweku's hand and they left the terminal straight into a waiting taxi, at the head of a queue of black taxis of the same shape and design. Kweku marvelled at their uniformity: in Ghana, taxis could be any model of car, the only distinguishing features were that sections of the car had to be painted alternately in yellow and one other colour – typically white, black, blue or dark red. The taxi driver loaded Kweku's suitcase into the boot and off they headed into London.

Kweku was curious about the inside layout of the taxi, the sliding window separating driver from passengers, the pull-out backward-facing folding seats. He sat with Tulver on the cold, but bouncy, leather rear bench seat.

As they left the airport, his attention was gripped by the music playing on the radio. He recognised two of the tracks instantly: *I Want To Hold Your Hand*, a hit from his favourite pop band, The Beatles, and Millie Small's sugar-coated *My Boy Lollipop*. Only this time he wasn't having to sneak into his parents' record collection while they were out and play the singles on their record player in the living room back home. Here it looked like the latest international popular music was being broadcast freely over the airwaves. It seemed such a relief from the excruciatingly dull news, documentaries and cultural programmes force-fed on the airwaves back home by the government's Ghana Broadcasting Corporation, BBC's World Service or the Voice of America.

The driver was the chatty cockney Sid James type with cloth cap, large wrinkly eyes and a big grin. He attempted friendly conversation:

'Did you come from far then?' he asked, looking up at Tulver through his rear-view mirror. His innocuous query was met with a stony silence. Now that the obligatory niceties of the handover had been completed, she was in no mood to waste the effort of additional courtesies on someone she correctly calculated she was unlikely to cross paths with in her lifetime ever again. For her, politeness was stress-inducing and had a price. And so it shouldn't just be given away freely.

The driver, ever-ready to cash in on his natural proclivity for casual conversation, knew that in his line of work being polite could make the difference between having an OK day and having a very profitable one. September had only just begun, but he was already saving up for Christmas shopping. So he tried once more, in case his question had been missed, this time addressing his question directly to Kweku in order to hedge his bets. Tulver was English, he assumed. So maybe she had only come to meet Kweku off the flight rather than travelling with him. There had only been one suitcase after all.

'Have you come from far, young man?'

Tulver didn't flinch.

Courteous by nature and uncomfortable at the direction of the conversation, after a quick glance at a still unresponsive Tulver, Kweku decided to try to ease the growing tension in the atmosphere by answering: 'From Ghana.'

'What was that you said? Where was that again? Guyana?'

Kweku looked quizzically at Tulver, having no idea where in the world the "Guyana" was that the taxi driver had just mentioned.

Tulver finally decided to pipe up. 'No, that's Ghana in West Africa. It used to be called the Gold Coast.'

'Ahh, got you now. From Africa then…'

'Yes,' replied Tulver with firmness, hoping that would be the end of the conversation.

'Lucky you with all that sun!' the taxi driver continued. 'Anyway, can't complain, I suppose. We've had a good few days of sun ourselves here this week. Planning to go down to Brighton Beach on Sunday with the family. Bet it rains all day, knowing our luck with the weather!' He burst out cackling.

Kweku was absorbing all the sights and sounds accompanying his new adventure. He didn't think it was his place to try to converse with the taxi driver. His experience was that, if adults wanted to talk to you, they would signal it by looking down at you, using simple words and inflexing them with a tone they thought appropriate for child language, one step up from baby talk.

Meanwhile Tulver remained stony-faced, staring blankly out of her window.

The taxi driver finally took the hint. Antagonising a reticent customer could shrink any possible tip even further, so he decided to keep his natural curiosity in check for the rest of the journey.

But Tulver's abruptness and its marked contrast to her smiles and chuckles so recently on display during the handover at the airport and the phone call to his mum had not gone unnoticed by Kweku. The change slightly unnerved him. This was the person he would now be on his own with until the start of school on Sunday, so he would have to figure out a way to make things work between them somehow… His parents couldn't be wrong about her either, he once again tried to reassure himself.

A pang of hunger streaked across Kweku's stomach. He realised that it must be because of the unexpectedly frugal lunch he'd had on the plane. He suddenly remembered the small bag of Honimo sweets his dad had slipped into his satchel. Luckily the satchel was right beside him and not in the boot. He unzipped it at the side and there was the bag of Honimo, none the worse for wear. He opened up a section at the top, removing one of the honeyed sweets. As he unwrapped it, Tulver noticed its peculiarly attractive scent. Kweku saw her looking on, intrigued.

'Do you want some, Auntie?' he said, readying himself to dip his fingers in and pull one out for her.

'What's that?'

'It's a honey sweet… from Daddy's factory in Ghana.'

'Do they make honey in Ghana? I didn't know that.'

'Oh yes… They sell English honey in the shops, in jars, but the colour is usually much lighter. The Ghanaian one is darker and has more flavour. It makes a great sweet – at least that's what Daddy and Uncle Adrian thought when they set up the business.'

Kweku offered her one.

'Here you are, Auntie, try one.'

She removed the wrapper and, after scrutinising it like a cat sniffing around and poking new food offered by their owner before tasting it, she looked at it from above, underneath and all around before suddenly popping it into her mouth.

'Mmmm,' she said, rolling it around and sucking on it as it melted inside her mouth. 'It really does taste like honey, but somehow with an even richer flavour.'

Kweku laughed. 'Yes, Auntie Emily… that's because it's Ghanaian honey. Here… you can have another one if you want.'

'Well, it tastes really good,' she said, wolfing down a second Honimo sweet. 'Your daddy ought to try selling it here. I'll suggest it to him sometime.'

'Would you like some more, Auntie?' Kweku asked her politely, praying secretly she would say no.

'No, that's all right, Kweku… Thank you for sharing it.'

Kweku was palpably relieved and greedily popped two more sweets into his mouth at a go, his cheeks bulging on either side as he savoured them while taking in the sights of a new country. But moments later Tulver added, unable to resist:

'Actually, do you have a last one, just for me to remind myself of the difference in taste with Ghanaian honey?'

Kweku nodded and swiftly gave her another.

'Thank you.' Tulver took it and left Kweku to enjoy the rest of the bag on his own.

Kweku smiled broadly. He felt pride at being able to showcase something produced entirely in his home country that it seemed English people really liked – well, at least the English lady sitting beside him.

***

Gazing wide-eyed out of the windows on both sides of the taxi and in front for most of the journey from the airport, Kweku's attention was especially drawn to the redbrick nature of most of the houses. It was a change from the almost ubiquitous use of cement in buildings in towns and cities across Ghana, although in rural areas such buildings were only occasionally to be seen, in between, and sometimes as extensions of, simpler structures of mud huts and thatched roofs.

He saw the big red buses, giving off the appearance of moving houses, with people sitting upstairs and downstairs, advertisements emblazoned on their sides promoting celebrities, food and drink. After no more than a boiled egg and a piece of toast on the plane for lunch, his stomach had been burping and growling on and off for a couple of hours now. He salivated at the images of tasty hamburgers, frankfurters and fizzy drinks springing up here and there on billboards.

Everywhere the roads were bigger, wider than in Ghana, not a pothole in sight. Buildings seemed so much taller, landscapes busier. Technology yelled out bright, flashing neon lights. Fast-moving trains sped through fields in the distance beyond, compact office and housing developments mostly obscuring his view of them.

There seemed to be a much bigger variety of shapes and sizes of cars and trucks, and so many of them.

Everyone seemed to be in such a hurry to get somewhere or do something, their attention laser-focused on their missions as if their lives depended on it. Not here the '*abotare ya*' or 'take your time' mentality advocated by some back home in Ghana. His thoughts flashed back momentarily to the hunched porter at Accra airport and his smartly dressed colleague, always on the lookout for a fresh catch. They would have been right at home here.

It was good news for him, too, or so he thought. His mum had been fond of telling him that he had been an impatient child from birth. Within months, he was falling out of his pram in his eagerness to walk… He told her he could see everyone else around him doing it, and so didn't know why he shouldn't have a go too. And falling over on to the floor had proved no bar to his dusting himself down and having another go! Once, his mum said, when she was spoon-feeding him, irritated by the delay in travel time of the food from the bowl to his lips, he just snatched the spoon from her hand and started feeding himself directly from the bowl. At first startled by the audacity of this move, his mum's thoughts quickly turned to relief on realising that it meant feeding him was one labour of love she would no longer have to endure!

So Kweku had always been in a hurry. If things moved faster in England, he reflected, that might give him some comfort to compensate for the shock of other novelties.

After about 45 minutes, they reached the apartment block in Sloane Square, South West London, where his parents had rented a flat.

Tulver guided the taxi driver for the last bit of the way:

'Just up to the front door over there... Here will do fine.'

The driver brought Kweku's bag from the car as they alighted and returned to his seat. Tulver gathered Kweku's suitcase, reminding him not to forget his satchel on the seat. The driver pointed to the amount displayed on his meter:

'That'll be five pounds, two shillings and tuppence please.' Tulver removed her purse from her handbag, counted out five pounds three shillings and handed it over. The taxi driver rummaged around for the change in a plastic pot to his side, checking it and looking up to Tulver as he handed it over. Tulver collected it, but remained at the front window. The taxi driver gave her a puzzled look.

'Receipt?' she quizzed tersely.

'Oh, sorry, gotcha! Just a moment.' Humming to himself, he opened his glove box, reached for a small notepad and hurriedly scribbled out a receipt, tearing it off. 'There you go, madam.' He peeked at Kweku, standing patiently beside Tulver, satchel on his back and pulling at the straps. 'See you, young man! Hope you enjoy your time here.' Kweku watched the taxi as it chugged off.

***

By now it was 8 o'clock at night, yet the sun had only just set in an orange sky. In Accra, the closest city to the centre of the world, the sun virtually rose and set between 6 o'clock and half past 6, morning and evening, all year round. So Kweku was perplexed:

‘Do nights always start so late here, Auntie Emily?’ he asked excitedly. He calculated that, if it was always daytime up to almost 8 o’clock in England, then adults wouldn’t be able to tell him, as they did in Ghana, that it was time to go to bed at 6:30 … That would give him more than an hour extra before bedtime every day!

‘You should have been here in midsummer, just after the middle of June,’ Tulver responded dryly. ‘It doesn’t get dark until after 10 o’clock then. But it’s all downhill from there … gets dark again earlier and earlier.’

Kweku’s face dropped, his shoulders sagged.

‘Come on now you, stop dawdling!’ Tulver said. ‘Let’s get inside.’ She lifted Kweku’s arm in one hand, picked up his suitcase in the other and headed for the entrance to the block. ‘By October’s end, there’ll be more night than day. The weather will turn too. You’ll soon see!’ As she finished speaking, she added a half-evil chuckle and a shake of the head.

They crossed the floor of the lobby and entered the lift. Getting off on the third floor, they walked down a corridor, turning right, then left, before coming to a halt opposite a door, the number 8 in bronze fixed in the centre of its upper panel. By now beginning to pant audibly under the weight of carrying Kweku’s suitcase, Tulver brought out from her handbag and jangled a huge bunch of keys resembling a jailer’s set. She selected the right one to insert and turn in the lock. A slight push and the door swung open to small hallway. Tulver set Kweku’s suitcase down to catch her breath.

A short corridor led to a door on the left. Another short corridor to one on the right. Directly ahead of them seemed to be a living room area. Inside it, Kweku could spy an occasional table, a two-seater sofa with adjacent armchair and a dining set beyond.

'You'll be staying in this room,' Tulver said, pointing to a door at the end of the corridor to the left. She picked up his suitcase, opened the door and set it down.

'You do know how to unpack, don't you?'

Kweku took Tulver's question to be a rhetorical one and dared not answer no for fear of ruffling her feathers:

'Yes, Auntie Emily.'

'OK.' As she came out of Kweku's new bedroom, motioning him to follow her, she added: 'The bathroom is the first door on the left just there and the living room is next. Let me know when you've finished.'

'OK Auntie.'

Kweku was struck by the cramped nature of his room: a single bed, made up with a thick blanket; a small gap around the bed, past a wardrobe to the window at the rear; a small bedside table on the other side, a tiny lamp perched on top of it.

He popped back out into the corridor and went through an open door to the bathroom. Again, it was purely functional, much tighter for space than he was used to back home in Ghana.

Tulver suddenly re-appeared in the hallway as he came out of the bathroom.

'Oh, I nearly forgot. You must be hungry now? ...'

Her words came as music to Kweku's ears, temporarily distracting him from his disappointment at the tightness of his surroundings. The sweets he'd had in the taxi hadn't blunted his appetite for long; he was starving once again.

'Yes, Auntie, I am,' he quickly answered.

'All right then, I'll cook you up a nice supper.'

'Thank you, Auntie.'

Kweku began fantasising about the kinds of food he had seen displayed on buses and billboards on their way from the airport. As he unpacked as best he could, he smelt what he thought were the beginnings of a good meal coming together. He was sure it wouldn't be as good as mum's home cooking – nothing could better that. But at least it would be a big improvement on the plane lunch.

After unpacking and changing, he went to the living room. He could hear sounds coming from the kitchen and walked closer, the floorboards creaking as he reached the doorway and popped his head round. Tulver swung round and saw him:

'Ah, you've finished?'

'Yes, Auntie.'

'OK, it'll soon be ready.'

Returning to the living room, Kweku sighted a smaller armchair: this would be cosier for his diminutive frame than the big one next to the sofa. He looked around the room: just as in his bedroom and the bathroom, no space was wasted, gaps between furniture items had been kept to a minimum. He noticed a solitary place setting at the side of the dining table sharing a wall with the kitchen.

A small television stood on a sideboard positioned centrally on the longest side of the living room. To the left of the sideboard as he faced it was a small desk with a phone on top, a huge telephone directory next to the phone. He decided to wait until Tulver had finished cooking before asking her to switch the TV on. Her seemingly irritable disposition acted as a positive disincentive to the impulse to engage in the casual experimentation common for children Kweku's age, so he dared not try to switch it on himself, in case anything went wrong.

Minutes later, Tulver shouted from the kitchen: 'OK, supper's up now,' entering shortly afterwards with a tray carrying a bowl filled with a creamy white concoction, wisps of steam rising from it.

Setting the bowl down carefully on the table mat, she announced triumphantly, like a chef confidently presenting a culinary pièce de résistance of a meal to an Egon Ronay: 'There you go, some lovely hot chicken soup! That'll warm you up against the elements.' She returned to the chicken, feeling very satisfied with herself.

But, far from tucking into the soup straightaway, Kweku seemed mystified at what he saw in front of him. He had always associated chicken soup with a reddish, tomato colour, whole parts of chicken visible in it. He poked around the creamy concoction, checking to see if the chicken portions, even if they weren't full-sized ones, were submerged somewhere in there. But, for all his efforts, he could only come up with small bits, tiny scattered cubes of an indiscernible composition. He decided to try one of them. It was more pasty than meaty. Could this be the chicken? he wondered. Surely not. There must be some mistake.

From the kitchen, Tulver thought she could hear him sniffing. She came through to see how he was getting on. He wasn't. Tears were rolling down his cheeks, snot running from his nose. When he saw her, he quickly grabbed the serviette to wipe the snot from his nose and tidy himself up.

'What's the matter now, then?' Tulver queried testily.

Kweku looked up at her 'Nothing, Auntie, it's OK.' Through sniffles, he asked:

'Please Auntie, when is Mummy coming?'

'Your mummy? I'm afraid you won't be seeing her for a long time now. So you'll just have to manage with me!'

Tulver's answer was blunt, but entirely consistent with her style. She was never one to mince her words and, despite her professional qualification as a childminder, could struggle to make exceptions for addressing children, if she didn't feel in the right mood. It was the cue for Kweku to break out in a long bawl.

Tulver threw her hands up in the air, exasperated:

'For heaven's sake! I can't do anything about that! … Anyway, why aren't you having your soup? Don't you like it?'

Kweku looked at her, shaking his head as he continued crying.

Nonplussed, Tulver barked:

'Why? What's the matter with it?'

Kweku stared back at her, petrified to ask. In the end he summoned up the courage:

'Auntie, you said this was chicken soup but, well… Where's the chicken?'

'What do you mean, "where's the chicken", you ungrateful child? There's lots of chicken in there.'

‘I mean… where are the pieces of chicken, the leg, thigh or wing or something?’

As he was speaking, Tulver, tossing her head and rolling her eyes to the ceiling in frustration, disappeared into the kitchen. She returned seconds later, holding up inches from Kweku’s face an opened can on which he could make out the words “Campbell’s” at the top and “Chicken Soup” at the bottom.

‘There! That’s chicken soup the way we make it here in England. I have absolutely no idea what chicken soup looks like where you come from!’

‘But… Mummy’s chicken soup has chicken in it. This one doesn’t.’ Kweku didn’t want to sound ungrateful and possibly risk the retribution of outright starvation in an act of vengeance from someone whose limits he didn’t know. He couldn’t work out what he was saying wrong to upset Tulver so much. Out of the corner of his eye, he thought he could see Tulver raising her right hand behind his head, bringing it down to clip him round the ear, before suddenly changing direction on the downward swing and lifting it again to run her fingers through her greying hair... No, he must have imagined it – or so he thought!

An awkward moment of silence followed in which Tulver took a deep breath to muster her self-control. ‘OK, I know what I’ll do. I’ll rustle up something else for you,’ she said, carefully removing from the table the still full bowl. ‘But you will have to wait a while.’ She added under her breath, in a mutter Kweku could hear as she went back to the kitchen, ‘Silly child! What a fusspot!’ Fresh tears rolled down his cheeks.

Next he heard her switch on what sounded like a radio, a voice delivering a soliloquy with perfect English diction. Must be the day's news or some other boring adult information, he speculated … definitely not anything for kids!

His eyes wandered to a small cuckoo clock above a bookcase behind the TV. It was already 9 o'clock. This had been an inauspicious start. He still dared not ask Tulver to switch on the TV, so he just took off his new slippers and rolled up on the sofa, feeling chastened.

In between the sizzling and popping sounds of frying coming from the kitchen, he could hear Tulver still muttering to herself intermittently. But he was too far away to make out what she was saying over the sound of the radio, and thought that was probably for the best.

A little over half an hour later, Tulver returned with a plate which she slammed down with authority. 'There you are! That's the best I can do for you. Eat up! It's well past your bedtime now.'

Kweku got up and walked the short distance to the dining table. As he sat down and looked over the objects piled carelessly on the plate – he couldn't yet call them food until he had identified them – he recognised potato chips, hewn crudely in huge blocks from fresh potatoes and speckled with black bits which had survived the peeling and cutting process. Battling with these for space were two fried eggs, burnt at their base, and a chipolata, incinerated black and shrunken to the size of a large kidney bean. Hungry as he was, he struggled to finish what was in front of him.

When supper was over, it was mercifully time for bed and a retreat to the sanctuary of his own little new private corner of the world. He climbed slowly into bed, feeling depressed and disoriented, apprehensive about the days ahead at a new school, far from home across the seas. Buckets of tears later, after a few hours tossing and turning in his bed with anxiety, he finally drifted off to sleep.

He woke up in the middle of the night, feeling that he wanted to use the bathroom. He heard the pitter-patter of raindrops on his bedroom window. He walked out of his room. He was all alone. Tulver was there, but she wasn't anyone he could count on. He didn't think she wanted to be his friend. She had just been pretending at the airport. He could hear her snoring loudly, he lost his way in the corridor. Everywhere seemed dark and unfamiliar and he didn't know where the light switch was. In the end he found his way back to his bedroom without finding the bathroom, got back into bed and, sobbing at his helplessness, fell asleep again.

***

When Kweku woke up the next morning, the sun was shining through the curtains. It put him in a completely different mood, reminding him of the weather in Ghana and everything else back home. In a surge of optimism, he felt fearless, ready to face the world and anything it could throw at him: his best times were ahead of him! Soon he heard the shrill sound of the phone in the house ringing. He thought he could hear Tulver speaking to someone down the line, punctuating her sentences with nervous laughter and feigning what he now knew to be a courteous tone out of step with her true character. After hanging up, she sashayed into his room, swinging his curtain open with a flourish.

'Time to get up, Kweku!... Come on, it's half past seven. Lots to do today. We have to go the outfitters to get you kitted out in your new school uniform. Come on, can't laze around in bed all day!'

'OK, Auntie Emily.' Kweku croaked back, slowly cranking himself up in bed, rubbing his eyes and yawning at the same time.

'Come on, wash your face, brush your teeth and get ready for breakfast. I'm preparing a nice English breakfast for you. I'll put it on the fire when you come through.'

But Kweku's experience with Tulver's food the previous night was still fresh in his memory. It filled him with dread, so he took his time washing and getting dressed, like a condemned prisoner trying to stretch out his last walk to the scaffold. When he finished, he sat for a few minutes at the bottom edge of his bed. Gazing out of the window, he could see people busying themselves in kitchens in flats opposite. He imagined a whole gamut of activities underway behind cover of the drawn curtains in the rooms beside the kitchens. Some, he speculated, would be mundane, others less innocent.

Half an hour later, as he came through to the living room, his eyes lit up when he saw a packet of Kellogg's Frosties standing tall on the dining table. He instantly recognised its blue colour theme with a grinning tiger staring straight back at him: all the Kellogg's cereals were big favourites in the well-to-do Ghanaian society Kweku came from.

'Where have you been, Kweku? What took you so long?' Tulver asked, frowning a little.

As most human beings learn to do from a very young age, Kweku chose to lie diplomatically: 'I was getting ready, Auntie ... Sorry ...'

'Oh, never mind, come and sit down!' He noticed that her mood, like his, seemed totally different today, although he couldn't imagine that the same reasons lay behind the change in both cases.

Rushing to his seat, he tilted the cereal box and began emptying its contents into his bowl, piling a heap before she intervened: 'That's enough, Kweku!'. He came to his senses and put the box down. Next, she pressed and removed the silver foil cap from the milk bottle and poured half of its contents out over the Frosties. Kweku snatched at his spoon. Plunging it into the bowl, he started munching and gulping away, asking for and receiving a second helping.

Before long, a plate arrived with a fried egg, not burnt this time, sandwiched by 2 rashers of streaky bacon. A small bottle of ketchup, toast and butter, Robertson's Strawberry Jam and hot chocolate were added.

When he finished, Kweku sighed with the relief of a refreshed wayfarer. Breakfast had gone down much better than the previous day's supper. He continued to guess at reasons for the change in Tulver's attitude that morning. She had a much more sympathetic look on her face. She was welcoming, wanting to please. He wasn't sure if this was because she had received some good news, or had realised somewhere along the line that the possibility existed that he might be a little bolder than she had given him credit for and, if asked later by his parents how he had enjoyed his time with Tulver, might actually tell the truth?

His suspicions deepened later when Tulver asked him whether, once they had finished at the school uniform outfitters, he wanted to have lunch at a snack bar instead for a treat. If he was a good boy, she would take him to a nearby Wimpy Bar American-style fast food restaurant. Kweku responded with alacrity 'Oh, yes pleeease!' His mind went to the phone call earlier that morning. He now recalled that Tulver's distinctively courteous phone voice and mannerisms were identical in tone to what he had witnessed at the airport the previous day when she was speaking to his mother.

He had cracked it! His mum must have been the caller who rang the flat that morning. Maybe she had discreetly reminded Tulver to make his arrival easier, as he was very young and would take time to get used to his new surroundings?

They caught a taxi to the outfitters, Kinch & Lack in the City. On the way, he continued to marvel at the colour and variety of London's historical landscape, resplendent in the sunshine of a bright September morning.

But his excitement came crashing to a halt when they arrived at Kinch's. The building was neat, inside and out, in keeping with the smartness of the immediate vicinity. Much to his chagrin however, he found the visit there arduous and very tedious.

The outfitters were insisting on perfection. For each article of clothing, he was in and out of the changing room until they were satisfied they had found just the right size. Meanwhile Tulver seemed to be exercising extraordinary patience through all the tries and re-tries of the various items. In the end, school blazer, tie, cap, jumpers, trousers and satchel were all secured, white shirts, black shoes, brown shoes, plimsolls, sportswear, slippers, even socks and underwear added. Kweku marvelled at the thick padding of the slippers – a soft woollen wall sewn on the inside to hug the feet in winter. These were nothing like the Bata sandals or *chale wote* flip-flops back home.

Next the outfitter brought out a large rubbery rectangular pouch with a rubber cap at one end.

Examining it closely, Kweku asked Tulver: 'What's that, Auntie?'

'That's a hot water bottle.'

'What's it for?'

The outfitter intervened: 'Well, young man, when the weather turns cold, which it will do soon, you'll be needing this to keep you warm in bed.'

Tulver took over: 'They'll let you fill it up with hot water, and you can take it to bed with you and cuddle it to stay warm.'

'Ahh,' Kweku responded, apprehensive at the thought of the imminent onset of colder temperatures but comforted that some protection was being planned against them.

The full uniform, kits and all boring bits finally out of the way after a full two hours, they walked to the local Wimpy Bar and sat down for lunch. Staring open-mouthed at the tantalising pictures protruding from the laminated menu, Kweku's eyes settled on an option labelled "King-Size meal". Above it was an image of a hamburger, beside a frankfurter curved in a circle around half a tomato, a fried egg cooked in a perfect mini circle, and straight-cut chips. A trio of milk shakes in different colours to the side completed the presentation.

A short, dark-haired, moustachioed waiter approached their table. 'Are you ready to order?' he asked.

Kweku looked at Tulver. 'Yes,' he said quickly, nodding vigorously and swinging his legs in excitement under the table, just missing Tulver's shins.

'Well, go on then,' Tulver said. 'You tell him what you want. I'm not having any of this American so-called "fast food".'

'OK, then I'd like a King-Size meal with, err… strawberry milk shake!' Kweku's big smile had returned and he began swinging his legs excitedly again.

'Very good, young man,' the waiter said. Turning to Tulver, he added, 'And you, madam, what about a drink? Are you sure you don't want anything? Maybe a cup of coffee?' He attempted to flirt with Tulver, flashing a toothy grin.

But she waved her hand, shook her head and pointed at Kweku: 'Nothing for me thanks, just him.' The waiter's grin quickly evaporated.

'OK, so that's one King-Size meal with strawberry milk shake coming right up.' With that, he gathered the menus up, tapped them a few times on the table to align them correctly, and headed straight to the cook standing in front of a huge griddle. Kweku's eyes followed him as he went, settling on the cook. Sporting an enormous chef's hat, he resembled a musical maestro conducting an orchestra, his steel spatula his baton as he played all the ingredients of a Wimpy meal, flipping a burger here, cracking an egg into a circular stainless steel egg-fryer there, swivelling round to empty and shake out chips from a deep fat fryer behind him. It was Kweku's first taste of fast food and, like almost all kids, he loved it.

As they left the Wimpy, Tulver had one more surprise for him.

'Kweku, have your heard of The Beatles?' she asked.

'Oh yes, Auntie, they were playing one of their songs on the radio in the taxi we took from the airport yesterday. And… and I've been seeing them in big pictures in the streets and pictures on taxis and buses everywhere since yesterday. Paul and Ringo are my favourites.'

'Well, they're all the rage here now. They've just released a new film called *A Hard Day's Night* and it's on now at the Odeon Kensington, near our flat.'

'Really, you mean it? Wow! … Then can we go?' Kweku asked, blinking expectantly and tilting his head to one side in an earnest appeal.

Tulver looked at him for a few seconds, then smiled and turned to glance at her wristwatch:

'OK, I don't know if there's still time. The next showing is at four. If we take a taxi straight there, we might make it… All right, let's try.'

'Yay!' Kweku exclaimed.

Tulver flagged down a taxi. 'Taxi! Odeon Kensington please, quick!'

'All right, darling, I'll do my best,' the taxi driver said with a thick cockney accent, reaching behind through his open window to open the door for them. He drove like an old hand, turning on a sixpence in places, narrowly missing cars and kerbs like an expert geometrician. In less than twenty minutes they were outside the cinema.

Thankfully the queue was short, and they were soon inside, cosily ensconced to one side, next to an aisle. The Pearl & Dean adverts were running and the auditorium was almost full. Moments later Kweku noticed an usherette down in the corner to the left, box in front slung around her neck, selling popcorn and ice cream.

'Oh, can I have a strawberry ice cream too, Auntie, and some popcorn?' he asked.

'Yes, all right... Here, take this.' She gave him a one pound note. Kweku sprang up from his seat, stepping impatiently around Tulver's legs as she tried to swing them out of his way. 'Don't forget to bring back the change!' she added. Her eyes followed Kweku as he ran down to the usherette. She had mixed feelings as she looked on.

Her mind went back to an occasion almost forty years ago. Her dad had taken her as a special treat to watch a pantomime at the London Palladium. It was a fun day she never forgot … She then reflected that later, as an adult in a difficult, tension-filled marriage that had lasted 12 years before an acrimonious divorce was finally settled in the courts three years earlier, her husband had only ever taken her twice to the cinema. On both occasions it was as part of an attempted reconciliation after a big slanging match. Before that, once, during the six-month period of courtship before their marriage, he had taken her out to watch Humphrey Bogart and Ingrid Bergman in *Casablanca*. But he nodded off soon after the opening credits, snoring loudly long before Sam played it again! Nudging to wake him up only resulted in his coming to and rolling his eyes for a fleeting moment, before crashing out again and resuming snoring at an even higher level of decibels. He finally woke up amid the frenetic scenes and gunshots at the end of the film.

She envied Kweku's innocence. At the same time her envy was mitigated by sympathy that tomorrow he would be at boarding school at the age of just six, in a foreign country. She was still lost in these thoughts as Kweku walked back up the aisle and into their row, grinning contentedly from ear to ear, ice cream in one hand and popcorn in the other.

'Excuse me Auntie,' he asked as Tulver swung her knees to allow him to walk past and resume his seat on her right. 'Oh, and here's the change. See, I didn't forget,' he added, patting himself on the back.

The film was everything Kweku had dreamt it would be. Along with other children in the audience, he rocked and swayed noisily in his seat, tapping along to the music. He could have sworn that at one point he saw Tulver swing her head gently from side to side in rhythm with the music for a brief moment, before recovering her default, stiff-upper-lip posture. Many of the songs were new, and Kweku was enthralled. He was so grateful to Tulver for taking him. He couldn't wait to tell his mum and dad.

For supper that evening, he noticed that Tulver had taken markedly more care in preparing the food. The chips had been cut much smaller and straighter than the ones the day before. Beside them on the plate were two whole pieces of fried chicken fully recognisable as coming from a chicken – a drumstick and a thigh.

Dessert was a tub-like section of vanilla ice cream surrounded by an outer lining of jam cake. Kweku found it yummy, and asked Tulver if she had made it herself. She owned up that she hadn't. She had cut it from a packet of Bird's Eye Arctic Roll. She showed him the packet. Homemade or not, it tasted delicious.

As he finished supper, the phone rang. Tulver got up from the sofa and walked over to pick it up. Kweku could only hear Tulver's side of the conversation:

'Oh, helloo, Mrs Mensah! And how are you today? … Oh, fine thank you… Everything is fine here, Mrs Mensah…Yes, we got all his uniforms at the shop yesterday... And Kweku has been a pleasure to look after. I think he's really been enjoying London… Shall I get him for you?... OK, just a moment please.'

Tulver beckoned Kweku over: 'Kweku, it's your mummy!' She passed the handset to him.

'Hello Mummy.'

'Hello Coco…'

'Mummy, I've had so much fun today. We went to the cinema and they were showing The Beatles! It was so funny, and everyone was laughing, singing and dancing in their seats.'

'Slow down, Coco, first things first. Auntie Emily told me you got all your school uniforms today?'

'Yes Mummy.'

'OK good… Phew! So, what was the film called?'

'*A Hard Day's Night*, like their song.'

'OK yes, that's great to hear, Coco. So Auntie Emily has been looking after you well then. And how's the weather?'

'Well… it's colder than in Ghana, but everyone here's saying it's warmer than it usually is around this time of year.'

'OK, I hope you're putting on your jumper whenever you're outside, so you don't catch a cold? Has it been raining much?'

'No, not much.'

'What about the food? It's different isn't it?'

'Yes Mummy, it is.'

'But I don't think it's better than in Ghana, is it Coco?'

'No Mummy... But… well yesterday, after I got my school uniform, Auntie Emily took me to a nice bar…'

'She took you to a bar?!' asked Mrs Mensah, horrified.

'No!' Kweku chuckled; his mum Deborah had completely got the wrong end of the stick. 'I mean the place is called a Wimpy Bar, and they make hamburgers and frankfurters and milkshakes and so many things there.'

'Aahh, OK, I understand.' Deborah sighed with relief.

'Yes, and everything tasted really nice.'

'OK, that's good. So, are you all set for school tomorrow?'

'Yes, Mummy.'

'All right, Coco. Your daddy and I are really proud of you, so please keep it up. The minicab driver Uncle Bill will be there by 1 o'clock in the afternoon to take you and Auntie Emily to your new school… Oh, your daddy has just walked in. Hold on and speak to him.'

'Hello, Son!'

'Hi Daddy.'

'I hear everything went smoothly with the flight and you've settled in at the flat with Auntie Emily. Well done, Coco, we're really proud of you!'

'Oh, and Daddy, I saw a Beatles film today. It was called *A Hard Day's Night*. It was really funny and the music was really good'.

'Oh, that's great... So tomorrow you'll be starting your new school. The driver will be there by 1 o'clock to pick you up...'

'Yes Daddy, Mummy told me.'

'OK, Coco. Then we wish you a safe journey. Be good, and let us know if there are any problems...'

'OK Daddy, I will.'

'By the way, the school said we shouldn't call you for the first week of the term. They said it's one of their rules, to help you settle in... So I hope you'll understand if we don't call you for the first week?'

'Huh? OK Daddy, I didn't know.'

'Yes, but even with what they say, if you have to call us about anything, you must. But don't call unless something really bad happens and you really need to. Above all, don't forget, when in Rome...'

'... I know, do as the Romans do.'

'OK.'

'Well done Coco. Bye... bye.'

'Bye Daddy.'

'Oh, are you still there?'

'Yes.'

'Your mummy wants to speak to you again... Hold on.'

'Hello Coco.'

'Hello Mummy.'

'OK, so be good and if there is anything, don't be afraid to call us... And remind Auntie Emily to give you her phone number as well, in case the international lines aren't working and you can't reach us.'

'OK Mummy.'

'Bye Kweku.'

'Bye Mummy.'

'Bye-bye.'

CHAPTER TWO

New School

It was drizzling outside when Kweku woke up the following morning. This was it. By the end of the day he would be lying in his third different bed in four days. But tonight's would be the most daunting experience. He had no idea what to expect. Bill Young arrived with his minicab fifteen minutes early. He decided it would be polite to wait until closer to the scheduled time before ringing the doorbell. Kweku was all washed and packed up. He'd just eaten a shepherd's pie for the first time in his life for lunch and Tulver was helping him put on his school uniform.

Ten minutes later, they were in the hallway, suitcase and new school satchel at the ready, all set. Kweku took one last look around the flat, committing its features to memory as his first base in his new country. He had left his old satchel from Ghana behind in his bedroom cupboard to mark his stake to the small territory comprising that bedroom. Just then the doorbell rang. They went out, down the corridors and into the lift. As they came out on the ground floor, Bill's car was waiting opposite the entrance.

'Hello Bill,' said Tulver.

'Good afternoon, Mrs Tulver.' Bill bent down to offer Kweku a warm handshake: 'And good afternoon to you too, young man, all set for school then are we?'

'Yes thank you, Uncle Bill.'

'OK, in you get.'

Kweku looked at his bag as Tulver brought it closer to the car.

'We'll stow that nicely away,' Bill said, lifting it and locking it away in the car boot.

Kweku slept through most of the journey to his new school. By the time he woke up, they were no longer on main roads, but wending their way through narrow country lanes, ensconced in woodland. The drizzling had stopped. The sun peered through gaps in the canopy of ash and chestnut trees lining the road on either side. As they emerged into a clearing, Kweku could see to his right a train running for a while almost parallel to the road, the railway tracks bringing it at one point within 100 yards of the road before it swung back away into a tunnel and out of sight.

The car began its descent down a long hill. At the bottom was a walled entrance, the words "Ketlers Hill School" painted in silver-grey on a metal signboard to the left. By now the adrenalin was racing through Kweku's young system. His heart was pounding so heavily it felt like it was going to pop out of his chest at any moment. He quietly took a deep breath in an effort to calm himself. Through the gates they went, down a short way to a car park on the right-hand side.

Alighting from the car, Tulver and Kweku saw a typed signboard saying "New Boys Welcome", an arrow at the bottom pointing back towards the "Main Reception".

'OK Bill, wait here for us,' Tulver said. 'We'll be back in a second.'

'No problem.'

They walked up to the door. Once in, they could see a small crowd of children and parents milling in a hall to the right. Tulver walked up to the front desk. Within the class-conscious British society of the time, she was cognisant of her status as working class or at best lower middle class. She knew she would have to affect the very best elocution of the English language she could muster until free once again of the school's environment.

'Hellew,' Tulver began.

'Hello,' the receptionist beamed back, adding as she looked down to Kweku, 'And who have you got there?'

'This is Kweku Mensah,' Tulver replied.

The receptionist looked at Tulver: 'And you are? ...'

'I am Mrs Emily Tulver, his guardian.'

'All right then, let's see now... Kingsley, Lambert, Makin... Ah, there it is! Mensah, Kweku Mensah!' She marked a tick beside his name.

'Welcome to Ketlers, Mrs Tulver, Kweku. Now then... Kweku is in Willow House. Do you know the way there?'

'Erm... sorry, no, I don't,' Tulver replied.

'Don't worry, I'll show you. Follow me.' They walked back out through the entrance and turned left. As they passed the car park she pointed to a mansion, about 50 yards behind the car park to the right, a neatly trimmed hedge dressing its front entrance.

'There's Willow House, you see, Mrs Tulver, just there.'

'Oh OK, yep. Thank you very much.'

'Then I'll see you back here at Main Reception soon.'

Tulver turned to Kweku: 'All right, Kweku, let's go and get your bag and satchel first.'

Entering Willow House, they were met at the door by a youngish lady in her thirties.

'Hello, I'm Laura,' she said, ushering them in with a welcoming smile. 'Mrs Tulver, isn't it?'

'Yes, that's right.'

'My husband is the Housemaster, David Hurst. He's otherwise engaged right now, so I'm assisting.'

Looking to Kweku, she continued: 'And you must be Kweku?'

'Yes,' Kweku confirmed, shyly.

'All right then. Let me show you to your dormitory.' They began walking. 'So, Mrs Tulver, I think you have come from London? How did you find the journey down here? I hope you didn't get lost; it can be quite tricky taking all the right twists and turns first time around.'

'Actually the directions the school gave were very helpful, and we had an experienced driver with us. So we came straight here really, didn't get lost.'

Mrs Hurst walked through to the last dormitory on the right. There were six iron beds with spring bases and mattresses, made up, one small bedside table by each, and three cupboards. She pointed to the second bed along from the right, in the first corner.

'That's your bed, Kweku,' she said. 'For now, you can just stow your suitcase and satchel away under it and make your way back to the reception. We'll see you back here later, OK?'

'Thank you very much, Mrs Hurst,' Tulver replied, seeing Kweku gawping at his new surroundings in silence.

'Will you be OK finding your way back to the reception?'

'Oh yes, thank you, we'll be fine, won't we Kweku?... All right, Mrs Hurst, bye for now then.'

The lady at the reception welcomed them back.

'All sorted at Willow House now, I hope?'

'Yes, thank you.' Tulver replied, Kweku nodding in confirmation.

'That's good. Please feel free to go through and mix with the other new boys and parents and some of the teaching staff. And there are lots of sandwiches, tea, coffee and biscuits… The Headmaster will be through shortly to give a welcome address, but I'll still be here in case you want to ask about anything.'

Minutes later, a man in his late fifties, with a square-jawed face, dark, bushy eyebrows and short-cropped hair greying at the fringes, breezed through the main door straight into the hall. He walked up to the front and turned to address the waiting assembly.

'Good afternoon to all of you and welcome to Ketlers Hill School. For those of you who don't know me, I'm the Headmaster, Roland Docherty. I hope you've not had to come from too far to get here and that no one got lost on the way!' [cue polite laughter from the parents].

But Kweku wasn't paying attention. Weighed down with anxiety about his new predicament, he was lost in his thoughts, trying to steel himself up for the challenges ahead. Tulver had been difficult to warm to but at least, over the two days since he arrived in England, they had begun adjusting to each other. Now he would have to start all over again – with so many strangers all at once.

At the end of the Headmaster's address there was stunted, polite applause. Docherty hovered from group to group for a few minutes, like a bee bumbling erratically through clusters of bluebells. Then he vanished in a swirl, leaving his staff to continue fielding the bulk of parents' questions. Tulver felt out of her depth in the smart gathering she had been thrust into. Embarrassed by her social standing, she was petrified to mix in and risk being exposed as 'not belonging'. So she floated on the periphery of various conversations in order to appear sociable, while secretly desperately hoping that none of the participants would actually try to draw her into any of the discussions.

Kweku had by now retreated into his own shell and was just waiting for Tulver to pull the curtain down on the ordeal so he could escape. After five minutes, which seemed more like fifteen, a rather kind looking man in one of the groups turned to Tulver and said: 'What do you think?' Startled, Tulver turned to Kweku, pretending to respond to an imaginary question that he hadn't actually asked. 'All right Kweku, yes, let's go and do that.' She then swiftly turned back to the man, summoning up her best diction to announce rather tersely: 'I am sorry, I have to go…', leaving him totally nonplussed.

Kweku felt temporary relief, imbibing through dilated nostrils the cool evening air as he and Tulver walked the short distance together back to Willow House. Mrs Hurst greeted them on their return. They went straight up to his dorm. Tulver, somewhat unnerved by her recent awkward experience in the hall, had now reverted to her default, businesslike mode. She gave Kweku a quick pat on the shoulder.

'All right, bye then Kweku. Be good, won't you?'

'Yes, Auntie Emily.'

'Oh, I nearly forgot to give you my number.'

‘Oh yes,’ Kweku said, keeping to himself his embarrassment that he had so soon forgotten that his mum had asked him just that same morning to make sure to get it.

Tulver reached into her handbag for a notepad, wrote her number down, tore the sheet off and gave it to Kweku.

‘There you go, Kweku. Let me know if there’s anything you need. Otherwise, best of luck! Cheerio!’

‘Bye.’

With that she was gone.

***

Other new boys entered the dorm where Kweku was now starting to unpack. One had a brother in a senior dorm who came to make sure he was OK and show him the ropes. Another seemed to originate from the Far East, although Kweku had no idea which country. Two chatted ten to the dozen in bursts… no doubt to distract themselves from first day nerves. Making his way to the washroom, Kweku noticed that the other dorms were by now full of boys of various ages, arranged by year group. Many were conversing animatedly about where they had gone for the summer hols, the films they had seen, latest toys and games, crazy stuff.

Soon a prefect came to each dorm telling everyone to assemble in the common room for an address from the Housemaster. Kweku followed the chatting throng into the common room, where a young, smart but simply dressed man sat at a table at the front. Once it seemed to him that everyone was there, Mr Hurst rose to speak, introducing himself to the new boys.

Mercifully, like the Headmaster before him, he kept his address short. He welcomed the new boys to Willow House, got them to stand up and introduce themselves in turns. Kweku learnt that the Asian boy in his dorm came from Japan.

The Housemaster went on to introduce his wife, the house matron, house prefects, more senior school prefects and their roles. He then ran through a list of key rules about activity times, paying attention to bulletin boards, security of the building and other administrative matters whose relevance went over the heads of Kweku and most of the other new boys.

Minutes after everyone returned to their dorms, the bell went off in the house for school dinner in the main hall. Kweku's verdict on the dinner, which he kept to himself, was that it was miles better than Tulver's first supper, but worse than her second and light years worse than the meal at the Wimpy. But nerves had in any case dissipated his appetite. He nibbled at the edges of the food on his plate and made little effort to join in the conversation with the other boys at his table.

Forty-five minutes later, all the Willow House boys were back at the house, those in the junior dorms preparing for bedtime. In his own dorm, after lights out, most boys exchanged few words on that first evening together. Kweku noticed the Housemaster popping his head around the door later to admonish the two chatterboxes with a 'Shhh! Go to sleep!' Meanwhile the rest of the dorm were already in the land of Nod, a place of anguished exile rather than tranquil sleep – or, like Kweku, on their way there.

CHAPTER THREE

Tough Start

For the first two weeks at Ketlers, Kweku cried constantly whenever alone. He missed Ghana, his mum's home cooking, the spice and variety of Ghanaian food, friends' birthday parties, movie nights at home. He also thought of his friend Kwesi Osei, who lived in a flat in an adjoining neighbourhood in Accra and shared his passion for a football knockabout in the street with others in Kweku's neighbourhood.

And the rooms were so cold. He would lay shivering in his bed at night, amid the howling sounds of the cold winds leaping opportunistically into the dormitory through gaps along edges of the window frames in the years before double-glazing was popularised.

His body still hadn't adjusted to the lower climatic temperatures. 60 degrees fahrenheit was still 20 degrees lower than the 80 degrees fahrenheit of Ghana's cooler rainy seasons – talk less of the 85 degrees and more which the temperature in Ghana normally was for most of the year.

As the weather turned colder with the onset of autumn, Kweku hoped the school would finally switch on the radiators dressing the walls everywhere, to convert them from mere decorative accessories into the functional heaters they were designed to be.

But even in late September, as outside temperatures plummeted, the radiators were left off. Kweku learnt that, barring a cold snap, they would only be switched on in winter, in January, next term. At least he had his hot water bottle to cuddle at night and boy, did he now appreciate the need for it!

There were four Africans at the school in other houses already when he came. Three were from Nigeria, one from Sierra Leone. Kweku had heard that an Organisation of African Unity had been set up to bring together the continent's newly-independent countries. He had no idea what it meant, but it sounded grand and suggested that Africans were coming together to help each other in some sort of brotherly context. But from where he stood, there seemed to be no great affinity between the African pupils beyond realising that they were all from Africa. Moreover, these other boys were much older than Kweku and, in the harsh environment then fostered by the school, it was every man for himself.

***

At Ketlers, a sense of abandonment left Kweku constantly distracted, unable to motivate himself to pay attention in classes, performing very badly academically as a result, disinterested in sports and generally feeling sorry for himself. His time there resembled a nightmare and passed in a blur.

His mornings would usually come alive with the "whoosh" of a birch, whistling as it swung through the air before making contact in the form of a painful thwack across his backside.

'Come on, get going!' came the shout from the austere PE teacher, Mr Mason. Kweku knew straightaway that meant he was now last in the caterpillar-like chain of boys crawling across the fields and wooded landscape on the daily cross-country jog.

The only way to escape the recurring lashes from Mr Mason's birch would be to launch a sprint to overtake the boy in front, and then summon up reserves of oxygen from his lungs to propel himself to overtake one more boy to provide a cushion. Before long he might hear the short shriek of the first boy he had just overtaken and soon after the muffled shriek of the second one. He knew he had to continue swivelling his head round and back over either shoulder to make sure that, if one boy got past him, a second one didn't in the same move. And on it went.

The regular morning jogs were truly a baptism of fire. On the bright side however, the body heat they generated acted as a useful antidote to the lack of central heating in the dorms and classrooms.

Kweku learnt to sing innocently along to new songs, whose true meaning he would only discover to his embarrassment many years later. The lyrics usually involved subjects that are taboo in today's much more sensitive, politically correct times.

One particular favourite used by everyone to pick someone to perform a task, going by who the rotating pointed finger settled on when the last word was uttered, was the jingle which ran:

"Eeny meeney, miney mo
Catch a nigger by his toe,
If he hollers let him go
Eeny, meeney, miney mo."

'Nigger' sounded to the young Kweku like 'knicker', as it was sung, 'hollers' like 'hollows'. To ask why a knicker should be a 'he' rather than an 'it', what the meaning of someone 'hollowing' was, or not to realise that the song was founded in the racial discrimination of the slave-era Southern United States, was to anticipate too much analysis in those days for all but the most precocious six year olds, whose number certainly did not include Kweku.

These were days when Robertson's Golden Shred Marmalade jars would be put on breakfast and supper tables with labels attached depicting a Golliwog. They were also days when a clip round the ear or a good spanking were accepted remedies for performance below expectation, or failure, intentional or otherwise, to follow prescribed rules.

The punishment at Ketlers for coming bottom of the class was to have that same part of your anatomy spanked in front of the whole school at the end of term. Kweku regularly came bottom of his class, and consequently returned home at the end of each term with a very sore backside, sitting rather gingerly on furniture for the first couple of days.

Things came to a head in the last week of the summer term in his second year. A fight had broken out in the main school yard. Kweku had been sucking slowly on sweets from a bag of Fox's Glacier Fruits he had bought at the Tuck Shop the day before. As he removed the bag from his pocket to pick his favourite strawberry-flavoured one, a classmate, Ralph Hillier, snatched it from his hand. Reacting instinctively, he snatched it right back, and Hillier punched him in the chest.

As they rained blows on each other, a crowd of other boys surrounded them in a matter of seconds, not to intervene, but to watch, shadow-boxing enthusiastically as they shouted and cheered on one side or the other. Here was some real excitement for them to banish the boredom of the school grind. Unfortunately for all of them – but fortunately for the combatants' physical health – a teacher who had seen the fight develop from a window overlooking the yard opened it and yelled:

'Heyy! Stop fighting down there!'. Mr Mason heard the shout and came rushing out of the Administration block. Seeing what was happening, he began blowing his whistle furiously. The crowd parted as he sprinted up and jumped to insert himself between the sparring duo, pushing them apart with a single breaststroke thrust which sent both of them sprawling to the ground.

Recovering his footing first, Hillier shouted, pointing at Kweku,

'He hit me first!'

Kweku fired back as he stood up: 'No I didn't, you liar!'

But Mason had already heard enough: 'All right, not one word more from either of you! Go to your houses now! You'll be hearing from me.'

Kweku stared at Hillier, who avoided his gaze. Both turned to retire sheepishly to their houses.

***

The next morning, Kweku's housemaster Mr Hurst called him out of his class to tell him the Headmaster wanted to see him in his office at the end of the class. Kweku's pulse immediately raced into overdrive. He knew that an invitation to the Headmaster's office was never good news. Good news was usually restricted to posts on school billboards or announcements in assembly. For senior boys, good news could be whispered in their ears by a master. An invitation to the Headmaster's office on the other hand was guaranteed to end with a spanking from a special cane he was known to keep, steel-tipped at one end to deliver maximum pain.

Kweku had to think on his feet. For the remaining fifteen minutes of the lesson his thoughts raced around the impending encounter. His priority was to lessen the pain that he was convinced would shortly be delivered to his backside… He needed protection. If he tore off the cardboard backing from the rear of his exercise book, that would surely absorb most of the impact, he thought.

At end of the class, after the teacher and all the other boys had left the room, he stealthily tore off the cardboard backing, folded and tucked it into his blazer pocket and raced to the toilets. There he took it out, bent it slightly at the sides so that it wouldn't stick out, and then stuffed it down inside his pants, praying that Mr Docherty wouldn't notice. Then he raced towards the Headmaster's office.

He knew where it was. He had often seen people, masters and boys, closing the door behind them as they left it, often looking chastened, rarely smiling. Once, as he approached the door in the passageway, he had heard the sound of a lash followed by a boyish shriek of pain, and Mr Docherty shouting: 'Now get out, and don't do it again!' The door had opened as he walked past. A boy had sidled out gingerly, rubbing his backside vigorously to soothe the pain. Slowing down to get a good look inside, Kweku had glimpsed in the background a large mahogany desk, a brown leather desk chair behind it, a bookcase to one side stuffed with large tomes, cabinets on the other side and a large bay window directly behind. Dark red wallpaper gave the room a sombre appearance. It was not a room he had ever wanted to get to know any better, but fate had now determined that he would see it up close and personal.

He knocked softly on the door.

A voice sounding exactly like Mr Docherty's barked from the other side of the door:

'Come in!'

Kweku crept in slowly, closing the door gently behind him. Mr Docherty looked up from his desk, putting his reading glasses down:

'Ahh, Mensah isn't it?'

'Yes, Sir.'

'Come closer, dear boy.' Docherty beckoned Kweku forward, raising his hand for him to stop once he was close enough. 'Hmmm… I was just glancing through your half-term report… Doesn't look very good, does it, eh?'

Kweku couldn't answer. By now his gaze was transfixed by Docherty's short but famously lethal cane, which he had just spotted beside the ink-pot near the front edge of his desk.

'Can you not hear me, young man?... I said, not very impressive, is it?' His voice had by now reached a pitch that would have been audible in the corridor outside.

Kweku's eyes darted away from the cane back to Docherty. 'No, Sir.'

'You mean you can't hear me?'

‘No, Sir, not that…’

‘Then what?’

‘I mean, the report… that it doesn’t look very good, Sir.’

Calming down, Docherty continued: ‘Are you happy here, Mensah?’

Kweku held his tongue… If he told the truth, it would likely only add another lash to the total he was about to receive. He decided to lie: ‘Yes, Sir.’

‘Well, it doesn’t look that way from what I'm reading…’ Docherty looked up and squinted his eyes in closer scrutiny of his prey. ‘Aren’t you the fellow who’s always coming bottom of the class since he came here?’

Kweku had no answer.

Docherty continued: ‘Anyway, I’ve called you here because I got a report that you and another boy were fighting in the school yard yesterday… Is that true?’

‘Yes, Sir.’

‘So, what do you think I should do with the pair of you? Eh?’

Kweku stood there in silence, crouched forward slightly. By now Docherty had got up from his chair and walked round to the front of his desk, reaching for his instrument of choice for dispensation of instant justice. It confirmed Kweku’s worst fears about what was about to happen.

Snatching up his cane from the desk and tightening his grip around it, Docherty moved alongside Kweku.

‘Now bend down, dear boy.’

Kweku bent over. Docherty lifted his cane and was about to spank his bottom when he noticed a rectangular outline protruding from inside Kweku's trousers.

'Ahh, I see. Think you're clever, do you, boy?' he exclaimed, reaching down into Kweku's pants to remove the intended padding and tossing it disdainfully across the room. 'Some of you boys think I was born yesterday, eh?'

The cardboard removed, Kweku instinctively put his arm across his bottom to provide some sort of protection, hoping it might soften the blow.

Thwack! The first blow came, Docherty accelerating on the downward swing. The cane's steel tipping ripped across the outer skin of the fingers on Kweku's left hand, and he let out a shriek just like the one he had heard emanating from the same office as he walked by six months earlier.

He quickly removed his hand before the next lash came down. Three more followed, Kweku groaning as he felt the excruciating pain coursing through his buttocks. He awaited a sixth swing of Docherty's cane. Instead, he felt Docherty's hand pull his left shoulder back up and say:

'It's all right, you can go now.' Even through his pain, Kweku felt a flood of relief envelope his whole frame. 'But don't let me catch you here again. Understood?'

'Yes, Sir.'

Kweku rushed out of the room. It was an experience he would never forget.

***

At the end of term, Kweku was bottom of the class again. Once more he received a hiding from his form master's birch. It was the last straw. While he was on the phone to his parents with Tulver at Sloane Square at the start of the summer holidays, they told him a famous Headmaster had been in Ghana promoting a new school in the neighbouring county to Ketlers', in Kent. The Headmaster's father had been a senior British judge in colonial West Africa, so he had long had a connection to the African continent.

Anxious to find a new school for their son, as things clearly didn't seem to be working out at Ketlers, Kojo and Deborah had met the Headmaster at a presentation and he had invited them to make an application for Kweku's admission to the school. Kweku was overjoyed. Any change would be better than none. A new school beckoned, and he could dream of better times. He had felt the steel tip of Mr Docherty's cane for the last time.

His parents then gave him the news that he would be spending the summer holidays back home in Ghana for the first time since he left two years earlier. Kweku danced a jig for joy, handing back the phone to Tulver with a flourish.

CHAPTER FOUR

Back Home At Last

July 1966

Catching Up

It was mid-July. The BOAC plane touched down at Accra Airport. For Kweku, the flight had evoked memories of his first with Swissair two years before. But while he had been well looked after once again, and lunch this time had been more expansive than the boiled egg and solitary piece of toast of that first flight – it had even included a spicy tomato and onion sauce – no cabin crew member had kept a special eye out for him: at 8 years old, he was now expected to get a lot more done by himself.

A blast of close, tropical heat struck his face as he exited the plane's air-conditioning into the Accra night air. He stepped down the mobile staircase, accompanied by one of the Accra airport ground staffers sent to assist him and three elderly, wheelchair-bound passengers. The stifling heat of a tropical evening was suffocating his breathing, but for once he was glad to be suffering. He knew it would not take long for him to acclimatise.

'It's great to be home!' he told his handler.

'Home, sweet home!' the handler echoed, chuckling.

***

Soon they were through immigration, baggage hall and into the arrival hall, where Kweku's parents embraced him like a long-lost puppy. His dad hurriedly signed the handing-over papers and tipped the handler. The driver Victor, giving Kweku a wink and a wave, took the trolley with his bags. Kweku smiled and waved back at him.

'Welcome home, Coco!' his dad said.

His mum quickly added: 'And how was the flight?'

'Fine thank you Mummy.'

'We've really missed you.'

'Me too.'

'Auntie Emily told us you bumped into the corner of a bedpost and cut your lip at school. Let me see now.'

She bent down to examine his wound more closely. Seeing that his upper lip was a bit swollen, she sympathised:

'Oooo, sorry Coco.'

Kweku was relieved his mum had made no mention of the schoolyard fight. He started wondering, had the school kept this a secret from Auntie Emily and his parents? It would be great if they had – that way he wouldn't have to explain to any of them why he had lost his cool, and that he had been sent up to the Headmaster for a spanking afterwards.

He had to think fast. 'Yes, and the swelling's worse because of the raw onions they gave us for lunch on the plane this time, Mummy,' he said. He hoped that for now that would throw them off the scent… It seemed to have worked, as there weren't any follow-up questions from his mum!

***

Minutes later, they were in the car driving the short distance home. Victor blew the horn as the car rolled up to the gate. The night watchman opened it and Kweku saw Tina, waiting patiently on the front verandah. As he got down from the car, she came forward to give him a big hug.

'Ei, Mister Kweku, welcome back!' she said, adding teasingly with a wink: 'So now you are an Englishman! Look at you! Very smart!'

Kweku felt embarrassed. 'Thank you, Tina.'

'Ei, we've missed you oooo!' she continued. 'Anyway, for your *akwaaba* meal to welcome you home, we've made you one of your favourites, *banku* and fish stew. Don't worry, we've taken out all the bones. And then for dessert, some *kelewele and tatale*.'

Familiar scents of Ghanaian cooking he had missed for two years wafted on to the verandah as she spoke. He salivated at the thought that he would soon be gorging on the enthralling sweet and sour taste of *banku*, fermented corn mixed with doughy cassava starch into a hunger-satiating white ball of starch, and *kelewele* and *tatale*, made from sweet and spicy fried plantain.

'What about *kenkey* and sardines?' he asked Tina, expectantly.

'Ei, *abotare ya*, be patient! We've already lined that one up as a special treat for you tomorrow morning. We'll be getting the kenkey from the kiosk in Osu across the road from Modern Bakery. Theirs is the best!'

As all they walked into the cool of the airconditioned sitting room, Tina suddenly remembered… Adrian had sent a radio message shortly after they had left for the airport to meet Kweku. He wanted to speak to Kojo. She turned to Kojo:

'Sir, we received a message for you from Mr Adrian while you were out.'

'Ah, did he say it was urgent?'

'I don't know, Sir.'

'OK, I'll try and get back to him now… All right, Coco, welcome home. So, enjoy yourself and I'll catch up with you later.'

With that, Kojo disappeared into the study.

Deborah continued:

'OK, Coco. Now, go upstairs, unpack, have a bath and then come back down for supper… Tina, go with him to help him… Oh, by the way Coco, we've put you in a bigger bedroom now, as you're a growing boy. Your room is now the one at the far end upstairs.'

'Oh, thank you Mummy.' Kweku was excited. He followed Tina up the stairs and into the corridor.

His eyes widened as he put his bags down in his new, bigger room. But he couldn't resist rushing out again briefly to take a peek inside his old room. He wanted to remind himself where he used to be. With the much bigger room set to be his new base, he was amazed how he could have managed in that smaller room. He had grown taller, everything around him looked a bit smaller, and his new bedroom was perfect for his increased size.

Within a jiffy, he had unpacked with Tina's help, bathed, put on t-shirt and flip-flops and was back down for supper. The banku, fish and kelewele tasted sweeter than ever, his appetite for them sharpened by the intervening years of deprivation.

That night, he slept the sleep of a freed man; in his own bed, surrounded by familiar smells and cocooned in love and comfort. He was home.

***

The next morning, his dad had already left for work by the time he woke up. Tina brought him his kenkey and pepper, as promised. He was floating on air. As he ate, his mum came down the stairs:

'Ah Coco, that's good. And how are you finding the kenkey?'

'Mmmm, it's really good, thank you Mummy.'

'Don't forget to close your mouth while eating. It's good manners and nowadays I want you to behave like an English gentleman,' Deborah cautioned.

'Mummy? ...' he asked, before swallowing another mouthful, 'Can Victor please take me to Auntie Sheila's place in the afternoon so I can play football with Kwesi?'

'Yes, all right, Coco. But mind you don't stay too long over there and worry Auntie Sheila. As we told you on the phone earlier this year, Kwame Nkrumah has been overthrown by the military. There is a new government in power. So, as always, be careful how you behave in public, you never know who might be listening or watching, and whatever you say or do can come back to us: people can think we are the ones teaching you those things. So never speak badly about the government – any government – in public. Remember that people can't speak as freely in Ghana as they can in England.'

Deborah was referring to the overthrow in a military coup in February 1966 of the socialist-leaning government of the country's first President, who had come to power as a democratically elected civilian leader and accelerated the first transfer of European colonial power to an independent African state in 1957, but later turned the country into a one-party dictatorship under his rule as President for life. He was overthrown by a western-leaning group of soldiers and police officers, acting with the support of civilians and chiefs who had lost power in the process of Nkrumah's centralisation of power under his rule.

The specifics of Ghana's politics were of course beyond Kweku's comprehension, as he prepared to visit his friend Kwesi Osei, but he understood his mum's general advice and promised to try to remember not to talk politics outside the house.

***

Osei was thrilled to see his new 'been-to' friend – 'new' because he had now been to London, and anyone who had travelled to white man's land, particularly Europe or North America, was affectionately termed a "been-to" on their return home to Ghana. The nomenclature automatically gave them a higher social status than those who had been stuck behind in Ghana all their lives. As far as concerned travelling to most other countries in Africa, although that was rare, that didn't count to elevate anyone to 'been-to' status. These countries were considered to be struggling to develop every bit as much as Ghana was – even more so – so going there was viewed as nothing to write home about! So much for African brotherhood, but true!

Osei's dad was out at work, but he and his mum Sheila were dying to hear from someone with first-hand topical knowledge about life at boarding school in England. After the experience Kweku had just endured at Ketlers however, English boarding school life was the last thing he wanted to talk about. As he began speaking of his time in England, the phone went off. Sheila went to answer it.

Kweku continued, explaining to Osei how extensively built up and densely packed the cities were, how modern everything was, how many roads, planes, cars, buses and trains there were – even ones running in tunnels underground – the neatly trimmed hedges and farm boundaries. On school life, Kweku spoke laconically, steering the conversation back to generalities any time Osei wanted him to go into specifics such as how the facilities were, how the teachers treated the boys, what school outings they'd been on.

He did allow Osei some glimpses into the reality of his tough experience at Ketlers: new boys were given a rough ride by more senior boys, the teaching staff were very focused on discipline. And English winters were bitterly cold; he had never seen snow or hailstones before and there were times when the wind-chill cut through to his bones like a knife through thin air. But Kweku let Osei know that he was much more anxious to talk about what he had missed in Ghana.

They went outside to kick a ball around in the yard behind the flat. Well, he hadn't missed much, Osei told him. He and the rest of their classmates at Nursery

School were now at primary school, not far off the bottom rung on the ladder of seniority and having to take orders from anyone older – just as Kweku had described in outline about school in England. To Kweku, it sounded like there was only one difference in their daily routines, but it was a big one – in Ghanaian primary schools, pupils got to have supper and sleep at home every night. Kweku envied that.

Her long call over, Sheila brought out some Muscatella, Kweku's favourite soft drink, homemade cup-cakes and later some delicious Milo hot chocolate drink. They munched and sipped, chatted about old friends, music and films, had a laugh about things in Ghana and England. Before long, Victor was back at the flat to take Kweku home for supper. Kweku thanked Sheila for everything and he and Osei said goodbye to each other, certain they would be able catch up again but unsure when; that would depend on the adults.

***

Kojo had promised to take his son on a trip up to the factory in Mim the next day. Deborah would join them. On the way up, they would pass through Kojo's hometown, Abetifi, the highest habitable point in Ghana. Kweku was really looking forward to the trip. He loved the adventure of long-distance rides on roads taking him into a nature-filled world, up the dangerous escarpments of hills, with surrounding trees and vales and vast rural expanses cooling the environment.

Meanwhile Deborah continued plying Kweku with his badly missed favourite Ghanaian foods. Their taste reminded him of life as it had been before he had flown to England. But exposure to more than one culture was giving Kweku a fresh perspective on life. He could more easily distinguish strengths and weaknesses between the two cultures from direct experience, without having to rely on reports from others. Ghanaian food was still the best in his opinion, the rich tastes and diversity of its offerings far surpassing that of English food. But a much greater variety of technologies attractive to children was available in England. The television programming, particularly cartoons, extensive amusement parks and fast food restaurants all pandered to the uncomplicated desires of a young child. Travel around London on underground trains and on the upper floor of double-decker buses added to the excitement.

After a kenkey breakfast, Kweku spent the morning playing football with neighbours' kids whom proximity had turned into a network of friends.

For lunch his mum made sure Tina had all the ingredients to make his favourite fufu with palm nut soup, including goat meat, smoked fish and pigs' trotters with *okro* or okra. The gardener, Robert, slipped out of the side gate as soon as he heard the call go up for him to come and help pound the fufu. Today he was exhausted with mowing, weeding and trimming and needed a break. He would pick things up again in an hour's time.

So Victor got landed with the job of helping Tina. Fufu is the favourite staple food of the ethnic group to which Kweku's mother belonged, the Asantes or "Ashantis". It is as much of a staple as fish and chips in the UK generally or pie and mash to a cockney.

The fufu is made from boiled plantain or yam and cassava, allowed to cool, then pounded for up to half an hour for the smoothest finished texture by two people. One kneads the fufu by hand in a large wooden mortar base, while the other pounds it using a long wooden pestle in a constantly alternating process which essentially has changed very little over the centuries – just as with baking bread in the Middle East and later across the rest of the world.

Actions of kneader and pounder must be perfectly timed. If either of them gets momentarily distracted or loses their rhythm, a kneading hand could easily be pounded or otherwise disfigured in the mortar bowl. Ouch!

Kweku heard them pounding the fufu. Pounding fufu was normally the last stage of meal preparation. It meant the soup had already been cooked, so Kweku knew that food would soon be ready. He couldn't resist going out through the kitchen trap door, and down the steps into the yard where they were doing the pounding to get a closer look. After marvelling at their perfect alternating timing for about 5 minutes, Victor pounding the fufu with the pestle and Tina kneading the fufu in the mortar, he asked Victor:

'Can I have a go?'

Victor scoffed that the little sprite could imagine he could even hold a pestle, let alone pound with it. Facing rejection, Kweku turned his attention to Tina, his head tilting and eyes appealing for her intervention.

She was too kind-hearted to reject his plea. 'Let him have a go,' she said. Reluctantly Victor offered the pestle to Kweku, still keeping a strong grip on it, and together they pounded the fufu, at a snail's pace, 10 times before Tina called time on the lesson:

'All right, Kweku, now go back inside. We'll bring it soon, OK?'

'OK, Tina, thank you.' Kweku rushed back inside the house. Thirty minutes later, Tina brought the fufu and soup in. It was something he had been dreaming about on and off ever since he left for England two years earlier. His mum said she would eat hers later. This freed Kweku from any concern about the mess he was creating as he tucked in. Kweku gorged himself on it greedily.

After lunch, he felt drowsy. He made his way slowly upstairs, intending to take a nap. But as he closed the door behind him at the top of the stairs and entered the corridor, his eyes fell on the main bookcase opposite him to the right. He didn't know why he hadn't noticed the books it housed before now. He decided to cast his eye over them to see if any were in his league.

First he saw the huge tomes of an Encyclopaedia Britannica in white hardback cover with dark red print: these would be beyond his capacity to handle, let alone try to read. Next a collection in scarlet hardback cover of classic novels by illustrious authors like Harding, Austen, Bronte and Dickens. He didn't feel confident enough to attempt these yet – he was sure that most of the nuances and lessons about the world they contained would entirely escape his naïve and inexperienced mind.

He had almost given up when, in a small corner of the bottom shelf of the bookcase, at ankle level, he caught sight of some paperbacks. Moving closer, he saw that they were children's books: a series of stories by Enid Blyton. Beside these was a stack of large colourful cartoon booklets, with the words "Hergé's Adventures of Tintin" emblazoned across the top. Ahh, these would be much more down his street! He delved into them and they were to eat up huge chunks of his spare time for the rest of the summer holidays.

Later that afternoon, Deborah popped her head round his bedroom door. Seeing he was awake, she came forward to hug and congratulate him, passing on the great news they had just received that his application to transfer from Ketlers to Glenwood School in Kent had been successful. She said she was now off to visit her close friend Susan Carreira for tea.

She asked Kweku if he wanted to join her, but he politely declined. Auntie Susan's daughter was too young for him to play with, and he understood that his mum saw these visits as her chance to entertain herself with the latest on the grapevine in trusted company. He knew that in such situations he would consequently be excess baggage for most of the time, the unwanted third person crowding out a company of two.

So Kweku was happy to stay at home and take refuge in the world of fiction presented by his new literary finds, a world he could close the door on and return to reality from at any time – just as he could emerge from a zany dream or nightmare – with all the familiar support structures of his life still intact around him.

Besides, he had movie night to look forward to that evening. Dad had promised taking out another movie from the American Embassy's publicly available film library for them to watch. Kweku was hoping it would be another Charlie Chaplin silent or Laurel and Hardy talkie. They loved all those vintage comedies, and Dad would be leading the way as they rolled around in stitches.

Dad came home, showered and had supper. It was now movie time and everything was set in the living room. All that was left was the projector. Dad went upstairs to bring it down. Ignoring his mum's pleas to sit tight and wait, Kweku rushed upstairs after him. As his dad brought it out, still in its box, Kweku insisted on carrying the box down the stairs. Kojo told him no, but Kweku insisted, rapidly escalating the issue to one of trust between them through a combination of earnest appeals and assurances.

Kweku actually had no idea at all how heavy the projector was. He had only seen how easily his dad always lifted and carried it around in its box. Based on these untested observations, he made huge assumptions, dismissing any concerns about its weight and his own capabilities. He was now a strapping 8-year-old, he thought: surely he could do the same as his dad. Hearing all the kerfuffle, Deborah came to the bottom of the stairs and looked up. But Kweku sounded so convincing and was so insistent that Deborah looked the other way and decided to hope and pray. For the same reasons, his dad also decided to risk it…

To Kweku's utter shock, the moment his dad handed the box to him, it slipped from his fleeting grasp and the projector fell out of it straight on to the steps below, smashing into several pieces. Kweku was aghast and immediately began sobbing, frozen where he stood. Kojo and Deborah held their heads in their hands, then rushed to comfort him, stepping carefully around the broken pieces.

The next morning, his dad gave the shattered projector to a senior technician working with the main government engineering company in town, who somewhat implausibly vaunted that he would have his boys start work on it right away and get it fixed in no time. Kweku prayed that a miracle would happen and the man would be successful… But no one ever saw the projector again.

In later, more cynical years, Kweku imagined the technician had probably flogged off any components that were still functioning for a small fortune, and had the rest melted down as scrap.

The incident ended the tradition of family movies at the house. Kweku felt so guilty and crestfallen that his recklessness had deprived the family of a key source of entertainment and relief from their daily routines. But he had at least now learnt one lesson which repeatedly falling out of his pram when a baby had failed to teach him: that, if others are liable to pay the price for the recklessness of your decision, you have no right to involve them in such recklessness unless with their informed consent, devoid of emotional blackmail of the kind Kweku had used in this case.

***

As Kweku continued his love affair with home-cooked Ghanaian foods for the rest of the holiday, his mind went back to his first English supper with Tulver and what the British called chicken soup. He reflected how Ghanaians preferred soup with real meat inside rather than flavouring – real chunks or pieces of chicken, beef, sheep, goat, game, grasscutter, snails, rabbit, even cats and bats for some. He had already been conditioned by his middle-upper class English upbringing before ever travelling to England to stick to the conventional stuff: goat and offal stood at the furthest end of the scale he would venture to, even though on the other hand in all honesty rabbit, snails, sheep and pig's offal, frogs and even horses were and still are acceptable fare in many parts of Europe.

And so meat or fish of some kind were always a necessity with Ghanaian cuisine, often combined with strong-flavoured smoked fish and offal, including pig's trotters, gizzard and intestines. He could already imagine, if this food was cooked in England, most of the neighbours complaining of the strong-flavoured smells. But essentially this was no worse than what Louisiana Afro-Americans tucking into their rice with black-eyed peas and filé gumbo would call their 'soul food'.

A popular staple in the evenings on his holiday were the stews – chicken, fish, beef, corned beef, with an accompaniment of rice, boiled yam or plantain. Most times these stews wouldn't contain green vegetables: for Kweku, as for most children, all vegetables still smelt and tasted like medicine. He made one exception: boiled spinach leaves. He would happily eat these – cold with red pepper, fish, fried yam and *apem* (green plantain), or stewed hot with beef or smoked fish to make his second favourite food after fufu and soup, palava sauce. For Kweku, spinach was delicious. Besides, the cartoon character Popeye validated it in pictures and on TV everywhere as muscle-giving: so somehow it didn't count as a vegetable!

His favourite desserts were his mum's hot homemade vanilla and strawberry Madeira cakes. Enticed by the smells of the cake mix in preparation, he often used to sneak into the pantry to scoop some from the bowl and eat it off his fingers when his mum wasn't looking.

In the late afternoons, if not playing games like hide-and-seek with neighbours or at friends' birthday parties or other functions, if his parents weren't at home, he would rummage through their record collection in the downstairs living room. Letting himself go while he thought no one was looking, he would seize the opportunity to play and dance expressively to favourites such as the Beatles' *Twist and Shout*, Rolling Stones' *Route 66*, or Trini Lopez's *La Bamba* alongside calmer tunes like *Wimoweh* from the Bert Kaempfert orchestra's "A Swingin' Safari".

***

August 1966

Trip Up Country

It was another sunny morning. Today Kweku and his parents would be leaving Accra to visit the factory in Mim, passing through Kojo's house in the mountains at Abetifi and sleeping overnight at Deborah's house in Kumasi on the way up. Kweku would also get to meet in Mim Kojo's Swiss partner in the confectionery business, Uncle Adrian. It was four years since they had last met, and Kweku only had a vague recollection of him.

They set off around 9 o'clock. As they began the dangerous ascent on winding roads to Abetifi, only thin metal barriers protecting a recklessly speeding driver from a likely fatal fall into steep ravines and valleys below, Kojo thought it was a good time to distract his son with a little history lesson about his paternal roots.

He explained that Abetifi was located in the part of the Eastern region of Ghana settled by Kwahus. The Kwahus were known locally as "the Jews of Ghana" because of their predilection for trading. They were Asantes who had grown tired of the endless cycle of war, conquest and imperial domination being practised by the Asantes in much of the area comprising today's Ghana. Instead they just wanted to live a peaceful life engaged in merchandising and commerce. They began migrating eastwards in the 16th century and retained a reputation for interests in trading, wholesaling and retailing.

Moving to personal family history, Kojo told Kweku he had been baptised a Roman Catholic as his mum was one. Kweku looked at Deborah: 'What about Dad's religion, why am I not baptised in that one too?' Smiling back at him, Deborah clarified that the rules of the Catholic Church were that any child should be baptised a Catholic if either parent was one. Kojo resumed the thread of his lesson, explaining that he and his traditional family were brought up as Scottish Presbyterians. The Basel Swiss missionary Fritz Ramseyer had built a mission in Abetifi in the 1870s which still stood, and the Presbyterian Church of Scotland had taken over the missionary work when the Swiss left. The mission had made the town famous internationally.

In truth, Kojo wasn't sure how much his son was taking in. Deborah encouraged Kojo to give it a break; she was sure he was probably only confusing their son. Kojo acknowledged the likelihood that a lot of what he was saying was floating over Kweku's head. But Kweku seemed so attentive and genuinely interested to find out answers to everything, as if each answer was a piece in the jigsaw puzzle of life that he would one day finally solve and never be confused about anything again. So Kojo carried on. He explained what Abetifi was most famous for nationally:

'Coco, did you know Abetifi is the highest habitable point in Ghana?'

'The highest what?' Kweku asked.

'The highest habitable point. That means the highest altitude or highest place you can live at in Ghana.'

'Wow.'

‘Because it’s so high up, the weather is cooler than it is in much of Ghana all year round. During Ghana’s two rainy seasons – the main one from April to June and the milder one from September to October – temperatures in Abetifi can even drop as low as they are in autumn in England. On some evenings you need a jumper at night to stay warm. And with the cold winds blowing, you certainly don’t need any air-conditioners to stay cool like you do in Accra. In fact, we Abetifi folk refer to the cold winds at such times as “God’s air-conditioner”,’ Kojo chuckled.

As his son’s eyes widened with astonishment, Kojo continued: ‘Rumours were that, after the Second World War, the colonial administration sanctioned an experiment…’

‘“sanctioned an experiment?”’

‘… sorry, approved a trial by the Food and Agriculture Organisation – that’s part of the United Nations – to grow potatoes in Abetifi. But the experiment was abandoned when trial marketing of imported potatoes at exhibitions in Accra confirmed that the majority of Ghanaians were unlikely to ditch their long-held love of yam in favour of potatoes. The taste and use of potatoes as a starchy food was just too close to yam to make growing them on a large scale in the mountains of the Kwahu ridge worthwhile.’

After three hours on the road, they finally reached Abetifi. The staff at the house were delighted to see Kojo and to meet his son for the first time. In later years, Kweku would more cynically view this glee as their happiness at having another opportunity to prove their continued usefulness and justify year-round full employment for only part-time work. But in those relatively gullible years, Kweku was more often than not ready to take people at face value.

For lunch, smoked tuna with palava sauce, the *kontomire* or spinach stew that is the staple food of the Kwahus, was brought to Kweku's delight. Boiled yam and apem were added as starch. His dad opted for fufu with *ebunubunu* or "green green" a kontomire-based soup with goat meat and snails, while his mum chose fufu with chicken light soup.

After lunch, they were sitting on the upstairs front verandah, enjoying drinks – soft drinks for Kweku, water for Mum and post-prandial port for Dad. Suddenly Kweku noticed what he thought were puffs of smoke coming towards them. Rushing to the edge of the balcony, he asked:

'Daddy, why is that smoke coming so near us. I can't see any fires burning nearby.'

Carefully putting his book and port down on the side-table, his dad rose to join him. 'Oh that!' he said, chuckling. 'That's not smoke… those are clouds!'

Kweku gasped, amazed at what he was witnessing: 'Clouds? Here?'

Just then, the clouds started passing through them. Up to that point in Kweku's life, clouds had always been things that belonged in the sky, things he could see up close from inside a plane, but never actually touch or smell. Curious to the point of distraction, he took a deep sniff to check the smell, grasping at them at the same time. It was a smoky, chemical smell. As he rubbed his hands, he felt a soapy film on them and literally saw bubbles floating by just as with, say, Fairy washing up liquid.

‘Wow! I never knew clouds were like this,’ Kweku said.

It was a surreal and unforgettable experience. For Kweku, Abetifi would always seem closer to heaven after that.

***

An hour later, after some rest and time enough for Kojo to give some parting instructions to staff on hand, they were back on the road. The journey from Abetifi to Kumasi took two hours. They stayed overnight at Deborah’s house near the town centre. Kumasi was much closer to sea level, more humid, greener, with a beautiful variety of flora. It had earned its status within Ghana as the “Garden City” and capital of the Ashanti Region. But the machine-powered cold air-conditioning in the house certainly came in handy there to ensure a peaceful night free of mosquitoes. Once again, staff were thrilled to see them and they were spoilt for choice with food.

The next morning, they set off for the most challenging part of the trip in terms of road surface. Leaving the outskirts of Kumasi, a bumpy drop in the road just after Abuakwa announced their car’s descent on to the untarred roads that would dominate the rest of their journey. As they headed north in the direction of the Brong Ahafo regional capital, Sunyani, Kweku tried to peer through the dense forest on either side to catch glimpses of the animal and plant life they were hiding. A left turn at Tepa junction before Sunyani took them west towards the Ivory Coast border, through Akyerensua, Hwidiem and Nkaseim.

The sight of large mounds, which Kojo explained to a puzzled Kweku were actually elephant droppings, signalled that they were nearing Mim. The area was then known as a transit point for elephants criss-crossing to Ivory Coast and back, blissfully unaware of any man-made borders. Before long they had reached Goaso, the district capital.

A right turn northwest at Goaso put them on the last 9-mile stretch of untarred road towards Mim. This road, with open ditches on either side, could be quickly navigated in the dry season, but turn treacherously slippery and almost impassable in the rainy season. Fortunately, Kojo's Land Rover was an all-wheel drive vehicle and, as it was still only August, the second rainy season was yet to arrive. The roads became fully tarred again as they finally entered Mim, their tarring a legacy not of government action but by courtesy of social infrastructural investment by the main privately-owned timber company in the town during the previous decade.

They drove straight past Sonimo's factory buildings. It was early evening, so they would tour them tomorrow. For now, they would visit Kojo's partner Adrian at his bungalow to announce their arrival and then take supper at the Mensah family bungalow.

***

As they parked up in Adrian's yard, he came out to welcome them. Kweku observed that he was a bit taller than his dad but a carbon copy in so many other ways: a little gruff on the exterior, but approachable to those who made the attempt – polite, slightly chubby and cheerful. And they both had a wicked sense of humour about the hypocrisy of politicians and of human behaviour. It was little surprise they seemed to get on so well together.

As Adrian led them into his bungalow, Deborah asked him how his wife Eva was. After glancing at Kojo, who nodded understandingly, he replied with a chuckle: 'You know how Eva hates travelling, Deborah. So we agreed between us that it's really best that she stays at home in Zurich, while I mind the shop down here and fly back whenever I can.'

They sat down in the living room, made, as were the living rooms in all the senior management bungalows, with full-length glass windows, giving those inside a direct view of nature and the plant life and forests beyond. Mahogany cabinets and room dividers, tongue and groove ceiling panelling and beautifully polished solid wood parquet flooring rounded off the cosy look and feel of a country hideaway.

As a domestic assistant introduced by Adrian as Ruth served them drinks, Kweku sensed a friendliness in interactions between her and Adrian possibly indicative of more than a strictly master-servant relationship; but he dared not pry further. His attention was rather caught by a large room with glass walls and roof extending out from the bungalow to the right. Pointing at it, he asked:

'Uncle Adrian, what's that room over there?'

'Oh, that's my laboratory' Adrian replied. He was a biochemist by profession. 'That's where I test the ingredients and formula for production of all the sweets at the factory to ensure that their taste is absolutely right and meets the standards of the Food and Drugs Board – that's the government's food quality inspectors if you like. I also store some hibiscus samples there.'

'What?'

'Hibiscus. It's a plant, one of the key ingredients for our very popular honey bonbon, Honimo.'

'Oh yes, I know Honimo, Uncle Adrian. It's my favourite.'

Adrian smiled contentedly, then turned to address Kojo. Deborah gestured to her son to allow the adults time now to chat on their own for a while. Kweku resorted to quietly sipping and savouring his Fanta orange drink.

Kojo and Adrian spent the next 20 minutes chatting about some key issues affecting raw material supply. The local bee farmers' collective, seeing rising demand from Sonimo for their honey, and claiming higher costs of imported hazmat-like protective gear for their members, were seeking a supplementary price increase ahead of the annual round of price negotiations.

The Secretary of the Brong Ahafo Regional Association of Beekeepers and Bee Farmers had made an unannounced visit to the factory the previous week and complained that local versions of the protective gear they had been getting custom made in Sunyani were developing cracks. Angry bees disturbed in the hive were slipping through these cracks and seizing the opportunity to deliver vengeful stings to the farmers' noses and other facial organs under their masks and at other joints.

Consequently their work was becoming increasingly hazardous, and they had registered a rising toll of injuries. Three farmers had even lost their lives to bee stings over the preceding twelve months, which was a record. Apart from that, the rising costs of fuel and bee smokers were eroding all their profits.

Adrian said he told them he had taken note of their concerns and asked them to return to the factory the following week, when his partner would be able to meet them and engage in more in-depth discussions. He explained to them that his own focus was on production and technical issues, while Mr Mensah was the one in charge of administration and local issues. In response, the Secretary had agreed to return with a full delegation, and the meeting had been set for tomorrow.

Winding up his discussions with Adrian, Kojo turned to Kweku and explained that Brong Ahafo was the heart of Ghana's bee farming industry: that was the reason he and Uncle Adrian had decided to site their business at Mim, then an upcoming town in the region.

***

The factotum at the Mensah family bungalow, Augustine Owusu, a staffer highly valued for his horticultural and culinary brilliance and given added responsibility for supervising all domestic staff at the senior management compound, gave them a warm welcome. Together with Victor, he brought in all their luggage as they settled down with drinks and coffee. He showed Kweku to his own ensuite bedroom next to his parents' master bedroom.

The entire bungalow was centrally airconditioned, the full-length glass panes in the main reception room allowing those inside to see through a transparent viewing screen the lush greenery and well-manicured lawns, to watch nature at first hand while nestled indoors, safe from dangerous predators like cobras, pythons and other reptiles living in the forest beyond the borders of the garden.

The ubiquitous terrazzo floor and cement walls, decorated with traditional artwork and paintings, and generous use of hardwood in ceiling and wall panelling and room dividers gave the rooms a cool, alluring atmosphere. Augustine's dinner was a *tour de force*, combining rural delicacies like antelope soup with traditional British fare such as roast beef, homemade Yorkshire pudding and gravy with a salad made using tomato and vegetables grown in the garden.

***

The next morning after breakfast Adrian came round to offer them a tour of the factory. Deborah had seen it all before, so she preferred to stay indoors with a pot of tea and some books she had brought up with her for the duration of the trip. But Kweku leapt at the opportunity to join his dad and Adrian for the tour.

First, they stopped at the two main warehouses. Both were ventilated and regularly swept for pests. In the first one, Adrian pointed out large yellow tubs containing natural dark Ghanaian honey. Kweku was given a teaspoonful to taste. Apart from having the appeal to all children of tasting sweet, it had a rich body. He lapped it up. Adrian explained that the honey was trucked in by company contractors from bee farmers in Brong Ahafo as well as further afield in the Ashanti Region.

Suppliers were paid cash on delivery, once the quality and weight had been assessed and certified by the company's experts on hand. Only first grade product was accepted. There were occasionally disputes with new suppliers unaware of the company's stringent quality standards or trying to sneak a substandard batch in. Much of the rest of the storage space in this first warehouse was taken up by large stocks of sugar for the manufacturing process.

In an adjacent second warehouse, apart from more stocks of sugar, lemons were stacked in one corner and cans of concentrated milk in another, beside containers of cinnamon cassia powder imported from China. Along one side was a locked, air-conditioned room. Inside this room, hibiscus flowers were carefully stored. In a large refrigerator dominating the room were hibiscus juice filtered in the factory and fruit essences imported from Switzerland – apple, orange, strawberry, blackcurrant and lime.

A small building to the left of the warehouses housed the diesel power generating station providing electricity to the factory and staff residential areas. In front of that were large water tanks connected to 2 drilled boreholes, from where filtered water was piped into the production machinery as part of the manufacturing process as well as to the senior residential compound. The dimensions of the stocks and equipment were a lot for Kweku to take in, and he remained open-mouthed for most of the tour.

As they walked round, Kojo keeping a close eye on his son to ensure that he stayed within the safety lines out of the way of moving pallet trucks, senior and middle level production staff kept interrupting Adrian to get approvals for releases or confirmation of production priorities. Whenever Adrian was distracted for longer periods, Kojo would step in to explain things to his son, while waving and chatting to staff who were also welcoming him and his son to Mim.

Inside the factory proper, Adrian first pointed to a train of large vats dissolving sugar in water or milk for the honey and other flavoured sweets and toffees, according to the end product. Essences, flavourings including hibiscus and cinnamon, starch and food colouring were added in line with the product recipe.

The resulting syrupy mixture was boiled until it reached the required sugar concentration. A higher temperature was needed for hard candies and a lower one for soft candies. Kweku was shown how the sugar concentration affected the texture of the mix, and how it increased as the water evaporated.

Heavier lifting work, including handling, stretching and folding on the rollers and kneading tables, was exclusively done by men, but women were heavily represented when it came to sorting, wrapping, packaging and quality control, where they generally seemed to have a more critical, selective eye than the men.

It was Kweku's first time visiting the Sonimo factory, and Kojo could clearly see that his son was blown away by the expanse of it all. At the end of the tour, Adrian gave Kweku a large sample bag full of every flavour of sweets the factory produced, including his favourite Honimo. Kweku couldn't believe his eyes. He thanked Adrian and grabbed at it with both hands.

In the car on the way back to the bungalow, with an eye to protecting his son's dental health, Kojo took over the bag, promising to give his son the sweets but gradually over a period – not all in one go. He told him he was sure that was what Uncle Adrian had intended. He also reminded Kweku to share some of the sweets with his mother. While happy to share the sweets with his mum, Kweku was slightly disappointed that they had effectively been confiscated by his dad for piecemeal distribution over time. But he was in no position to argue with his dad. And knowing Kojo's generosity, he trusted he would not hold back whenever he needed any. In the end he was grateful he could look forward to getting so many sweets to savour over the coming weeks.

Kojo dropped him back at the bungalow to rest and spend some time with his mum, while he prepared with Adrian for the meeting with the Bee Keepers and Bee Farmers Association.

***

After lunch, Kweku was anxious to explore his new surroundings at the family bungalow, so Augustine took him on a tour of the garden to see the wide range of subsistence plants he was cultivating – plantains, bananas, yams, cocoyams, mangoes, pineapples, tomatoes, cucumbers and lettuce. He even showed Kweku how to plant some more. He promised him he would mark their position in the garden, so that Kweku could check on their growth on his next trip to Mim and on until they were ready for harvesting. But Augustine warned Kweku that, if he wasn't around when they were ripe, then they would eat them to stop them going to waste and hope he would be around for the next crop.

An interest in farming was beginning to take root in Kweku. He loved the idea of nature's agents – the sun and rain or, in the absence of the latter, harvested rainwater – producing something out of planted seeds alone. He was too young to understand the pitfalls of farming – the need for high yields and risk of disease necessitating endless maintenance and expenditure on fertiliser, pesticides – not to talk of financing during the long time lag from planting to first harvesting for many crops or more complex concepts way over his head such as the opportunity cost of the land.

***

The next day, Deborah joined them as they toured local spots, picnicking on a nearby hill accessible in normal footwear. The view at the top of the hill was spectacular. On one side, beneath sheer slopes, forests stretched for miles into the distance and landmarks more than thirty miles away were visible. On the other side the factories, including Sonimo's, and the sprawling township developments where staff and their families lived, were clearly distinguishable but from the distance resembled matchstick toy models.

Afterwards they visited the Mim industries' common clubhouse for lunch. Later they had a go at badminton on the court situated beneath the clubhouse. Unfortunately the game never really got going, as Kweku literally couldn't get the hang of the shuttlecock in the air. From there they took a dip in the Olympic-size swimming pool beside the badminton court.

Later in the afternoon, Deborah took Kweku with her to the local market. There were large quantities of fruit and vegetables on display, some colourful cloths, beads and souvenirs, but Kweku was honest with his mum that they were much smaller than the markets in Accra and Kumasi.

***

On their last day in Mim, Kojo had an appointment with the new District Commissioner for the area in Goaso. The Commissioner had actually been at post for almost a year, but clashes in their schedules meant a meeting between them hadn't been possible before now. Kojo took Kweku along for the ride, as the plan was that from there they would go on to visit a cocoa plantation, for him to show his son the crop his country was most famous for.

The country's first government following independence, under Dr Kwame Nkrumah, had been heavily in favour of state ownership across key sectors of the economy. But even after the overthrow of this government in a military coup 6 months earlier, sale and marketing of cocoa, the country's main export cash crop, was still being monopolised by the government.

Kojo dreamt of the day when he would be able to purchase dried beans from cocoa farmers and process them locally into semi-finished chocolate products for export to the large international confectioners, adding value and employment numbers domestically in a win-win-win for manufacturers, employees and also government through increased tax collection, instead of continuing to send raw beans overseas for other countries to add those benefits to their economic numbers.

Kweku stayed in the car chatting with Victor, while Kojo went into his meeting with the District

Commissioner, Yaw Frimpong. Mr Frimpong was the pragmatic type, short, thin-faced – a man of few words but courteous and intelligent. He rose from his seat as his secretary ushered Kojo into his room:

'Welcome, Mr Mensah, to my humble office.' They shook hands warmly.

'It is hardly a humble office, Sir,' Kojo replied.

'Ha ha, if you must say so. Please, have a seat.'

'Thank you, Yaw – or should I say Mr Frimpong?'

'Yaw will do just fine, Mr Mensah.'

'Then so will Kojo.'

'What?... Oh, I see yes. Got it!'

'Yaw, if you don't mind my saying so, I know you are appointed by the Head of State and can report directly to him on any local matter without necessarily having to pass through the Regional Commissioner, so I am aware of the power of your office.'

Frimpong nodded and smiled as Kojo spoke, impressed that Kojo knew that in his position he did indeed have the direct personal ear of the Head of State. Over coffee and biscuits, Frimpong acknowledged the huge support Sonimo was making to the District in terms of taxes, growing employment and corporate social responsibility – particularly in the areas of education and sanitation.

He knew there was a demanding section of the District's population, who felt that the company's construction of schools, boreholes, lavatories and positive responses to many other ad hoc emergency requests were the minimum it should be doing anyway, judging by the profits it was making. He wanted to assure Kojo that such ingrates did not reflect the views of the majority, including himself, who were aware that the company's social investment went well beyond any fair reading of its moral obligations to the district.

They had a wide-ranging conversation about topical issues in international politics, which Kojo always loved to discuss, while steering clear of any mention of local politics in case they were overheard.

As Kojo left his office, Frimpong raised his index finger, indicating he had one thing more he wanted to tell him:

'You know, Kojo, with your business acumen, I want you to stay where you are and continue expanding the business with Adrian and helping our community. But did you know that your sense of altruism and pragmatic approach to analysis is exactly what we need more of in politics? It's such a refreshing change from the business leaders who, even though they are doing comparatively little, far less than you I might add, always think they are doing the community a favour. In doing so, they forget the benefits of all the infrastructural resources and indirect benefits provided to them, and the ease of doing business offered by myself and my predecessor.

If ever you feel your business is in safe hands and you are looking for another challenge, why not give politics a try? It might fulfil you in ways you may not have imagined yet.'

It had never crossed Kojo's mind to think of entering politics to represent an electorate. He often found it a hard-enough task trying to explain himself to company staff or propose straightforward alternative solutions to problems. Wouldn't it drain all his energy, if he had to deal around the clock with people who didn't understand how fast he wanted to move, or who might blame him directly for obstacles that other politicians were putting his way?

He finally piped up: 'Well, Yaw, I once heard it said that politics is an ungrateful business; it always ends badly…' Realising what he had just said, he hastened to add: 'But I'm sure that won't happen in your case!'

'Oh, don't worry!' Frimpong chuckled. 'I hadn't taken it that way anyway… Anyhow, give it some thought will you Kojo?' Drawing Kojo closer and whispering in his ear, he added: 'God knows I could do with some saner people around here!'

Kojo laughed out loud, adding diplomatically: 'OK, I'll think about it,' without having any real intention of doing so.

On their way out of Goaso, Kojo reflected on what the Commissioner had just told him. Despite his love of news and political debate, getting involved in it personally as a public representative did not appeal to him, for the reason he had given the Commissioner. He thought he was too old to start anyway.

He did however harbour ambitions for Kweku one day to be a political leader, to have a way of paying back into society at a higher level than by building schools and public amenities here or there, as Sonimo had been doing. As a member of a National Assembly, for instance, Kweku would have the capacity to impact positively potentially thousands of lives at the same time over an electoral area and beyond.

But such dreams were for the future, and Kojo was never one to get ahead of himself.

***

The afternoon trip to the cocoa plantation near Tepa turned out to be another eye-opener for Kweku. They stopped by the roadside at a farm a few miles down the road. Victor was on friendly terms with one of the farmhands, and he had been waiting for them. They got down and stood at the border of the farm, while the farmhand went into the plantation to lop off a ripe yellow cocoa pod from one of the trees. He brought it back and sliced the head off in their presence.

Kojo reached inside with his fingers and tore out one of the beans, which he bit and savoured. He then offered the pod to Kweku to remove a bean for himself and taste it. Although slightly sour, the bean was sweeter than Kweku had expected for a raw plant, and the unique taste which lay at the heart of all finished chocolate confectionery was clearly discernible.

The next morning, as the Mensahs bade warm farewells to Augustine and Adrian, Kweku reflected on the mind-boggling experiences of the last three days. Mim had at once been everything and nothing he had expected.

***

The day after his return from Mim, Kweku was anxious to make the most of the little time he had left before returning to the rigours of English boarding school life. He asked his mum to let Victor take him round to his friend Osei's place one last time. She agreed. Kweku and Osei first went to Can's Bakery in Osu for hot bread fresh from the oven and Fan ice cream. From there they went with Victor to the open-air Orion cinema near Kwame Nkrumah Circle to see the latest Roman gladiator film, a popular movie genre amongst the Ghanaian public alongside biblical films, romantic Indian musicals and Chinese action films.

The film was made in Italian, but dubbed in English. In practice that made very little difference, as the audience – most of whom had come there only to see the swashbuckling and gore, the good inevitably winning out melodramatically over the bad – shouted in rhythm as blows were rained. They then immediately broke out in noisy chatter all the way up to the next fight. That meant no one who was actually interested in listening to the plot, as Kweku was, could hear it to enjoy its intricacies or properly judge whether it held any useful lessons about life.

Osei on the other hand fully cast his lot in with the noisy majority. This difference between him and his Accra-based friend struck Kweku on that day. He wondered how it had never occurred to him before. But he tried not to read too much into it: he was after all on holiday. They gorged on soft drinks and biscuits, laughed as children do – especially in the case of slips, trips or falls – at accidents experienced by the characters in the film and cheered lustily as the hero got even with all the villains, one by one.

At the end Kweku dropped Osei off back home. They'd had fun, but Kweku couldn't help reflecting on some gratuitously gory scenes where his friend Osei had revelled in the carnage, cackling wickedly more than many even in that plot-averse audience. It slightly unnerved him. They shook hands as they said goodbye – no cuddles between boys in those days: it was viewed as a girly thing to do. Kweku promised getting in touch on his next trip down to Ghana scheduled for the following year.

***

It was a sunny Friday morning, the start of the last weekend of Kweku's Ghana holiday. On Sunday he would be flying back to school in England.

As he sat down to his usual kenkey breakfast, he noticed the skies suddenly darkening outside, the winds stirring. They were the harbingers of an oncoming storm. He rushed out on to the verandah. He had been at school in England during the main rainy season from April to June. Since his return to Ghana in mid-July, there had been no rain. He was convinced that the huge cloud approaching ominously overhead heralded the start of the year's milder rainy season for the next two months. He did not want to miss out on this one, too.

Deborah, still upstairs, rang the bell for Tina. She climbed the staircase and knocked on her bedroom door.

'Madam, I'm here.'

'Tina? Come in… Please close all the windows, it's going to rain… Has Kweku had breakfast?'

'He's eating now, Madam.'

'All right.'

Tina went back downstairs to the dining room, but Kweku was nowhere to be seen. She called out his name but there was no answer. Then she spotted him near the front wall of the verandah, looking up at the sky.

Just then a dervish of fresh winds waved in an exhilarating scent of oxygen-rich air pushed down from the ozone. It was confirmation of nature's signature announcement for a tropical shower. Flaring his nostrils as wide as he could, Kweku drank in the fresh winds as if it were heaven-sent nectar, the interaction with nature stimulating his cluttered mind. A myriad of pleasant thoughts criss-crossed his imagination, giving him a 'natural high'.

But all too soon, the descending rains chased this special scented air away. First a few drops here and there, pattering on rooftops and windows, accelerating in a matter of seconds through drizzle into heavy showers, then ferocious torrents. Sharp cracks of lightning streaked across the sky as clouds collided, followed by stunted peals of rolling thunder from the same collision event, sound travelling much more slowly than light.

And then, after a downpour of just 15 minutes, almost as suddenly as it had appeared, the storm vanished. This was different from the monsoon-like showers of the main rainy season, when the ferocity of any deluge would be sustained for hours on end. It was as if nature's rain-god had suddenly lifted its foot off the pedal, ushering in a lull, followed by victoriously re-emerging sunshine.

The wet patches on the ground and recycled raindrops falling intermittently from roofs and trees were left as the only empirical evidence that a storm had taken place at all. September's climate in Ghana was every bit as changeable as the British weather in June.

***

It was now Saturday afternoon. Kweku was on cloud nine. He had just learnt that he would not be travelling alone back to England. His parents had decided that this time his dad would accompany him to his new school, combining his trip with an important business meeting with buyers in Holland, while his mum held the fort at home. The daughter of a cousin of Kojo's, Daisy, would go with them to help with cooking and housekeeping.

Not only that, but Deborah felt her son had suffered enough while she allowed a stand-in mother, Tulver, to look after him on holidays. She knew, without having to ask Kweku, that he would prefer his real mother to be with him instead. What child wouldn't, what mother of an only child wouldn't? And she and Kojo were now wealthier. Against a background of accelerating market demand – especially for its signature Honimo product – Sonimo was now able to retain enough cash after covering business and social responsibility costs to make substantial payments to its owners.

Consequently Kojo and Deborah had decided between themselves that, in every school year from then on, she would travel to England to be with Kweku for the short holidays lasting just over three weeks which followed the Winter and Spring Terms, while for the longer summer holidays Kweku would fly down to Ghana unaccompanied.

For unaccompanied flights, Bill Young, the minicab driver, would collect him from school to the airport at the end of term, and pick him from the airport and return him to school for the start of the next term. Three weeks of holiday time, taking into account days needed to adjust and acclimatise before and after travel, were considered too short to justify a 6,000-mile round trip down to the Equator and back. But

Tulver would still be needed to take care of him during the much shorter exeat weekends and half terms.

Kweku's thoughts switched to Tulver. The changes meant that from now on he would only ever be stuck with her for relatively brief periods. In one sense, he was relieved; in another, he felt sorry for her that her work doing something he guessed she was only going through because she felt compelled to – judging by the uncharacteristically super-courteous phone voice she would suddenly adopt whenever his parents called – would in future be severely curtailed.

The reason Tulver was desperate to portray a happy environment whenever Kweku's parents called was of course for the money – the same reason the minicab driver 'Uncle' Bill was picking him up and taking him to school and back with a ready smile; the same reason countless others performed mundane tasks daily to keep the world going round. But in the artificially happy world that adults build around children to protect them from the embarrassing ugliness of the mercantile reality underpinning most human interactions, this necessary – although by no means always exclusive – motivation was disguised under a cloak of altruistic sacrifice for the sake of their well-being.

Santa Claus, whose existence Kweku was by now becoming suspicious about but hadn't quite yet stopped believing in, was a myth constructed to disguise the reality of the Christmas present giver having to use money to buy the presents ostensibly gifted by Santa, and in this way protect children from the scarier reality that – except in the few cases of charitable donations – no Christmas presents come without cold, hard cash being paid by someone.

CHAPTER FIVE

All Change

September 1966

Arriving back in London with his dad and Daisy, Kweku was shocked not to be taking the usual route from the airport to the flat in South West London but to be heading elsewhere in London. With the continued expansion of the confectionery business, his father had been able to move from the small flat in Sloane Square to a semi-detached house in Highgate.

Kweku was delighted with the much bigger space of his new bedroom and surroundings. The next day, as he sat, legs folded, on the carpet in front of the television, watching intently his favourite cartoon programme, "Atom Ant", he saw during a commercial break an advertisement for a beautiful red model Dinky Toy car. The shout went up from the advertiser: "On sale at Toys Toys Toys in Swiss Cottage. Buy now before it's too late!"

Ignorant, as many young children are prone to be, that going to school was in his own best interests rather than for his parents' or society's benefit, Kweku wanted the toy so badly that he decided he would simply refuse to go to school without it. At first his dad underestimated just how fixated his son was on getting that toy. Surely, Kojo thought, it was just a momentary fad? Kweku's attention would soon be distracted elsewhere. And anyhow there wasn't enough time to make a special trip towards the West End of London, with all the likely attendant traffic chaos, just to buy this toy his son was harping on about. They had only just arrived the previous day from a long journey. He had important business meetings scheduled for later that week. His son, he was certain, would appreciate that preparing for his new school, after his failure to excel in either academic or sporting areas at his previous one, was far more essential than a toy which could only ever amount to a passing obsession.

By the evening of the start of the new term, Kweku still clung desperately to his dream of buying that toy car. He had now seen the same advertisement on television twice more. With his Sisyphean endurance at Ketlers Hill still fresh in his memory and fearing a repeat at his new school, he was determined that the long, sleek and shiny red toy should operate as a tangible dream, a readily available analgesic against the punishment of boarding school life.

Somewhat optimistically overestimating his son's maturity, Kojo tried to appeal to a sense of pragmatism. He told Kweku he had seen in the regulations for his new school, spelt out clearly in black and white, a warning to parents that any pupils arriving with toys would have them immediately confiscated to storage and only returned to them when leaving the school. Unfortunately however, Kweku wasn't listening to such rational advice. Even if what his dad was saying was true and not an adult ruse, he was prepared to wait until the first exeat weekend to play with the car, so long as he got one before they all sold out. Otherwise he could miss out on his only chance in life to own one, which in his small world would be a calamity.

***

The following morning, with a stubbornly impudent Kweku still refusing to back down, his father finally relented. The minicab driver Bill was asked to come to the house an hour earlier, so that they could head towards the West End to Swiss Cottage before continuing to Kent. As luck would have it, by the time they got to Toys Toys Toys, to Kweku's unmitigated delight the toy was still available in stock. They quickly bought it. His dad had brought a camera along for the day, to capture for posterity historic moments of Kweku's first day at his new school, Glenwood. Kojo decided that the detour to buy this toy in order to satisfy Kweku's obsession was definitely worth a snap and asked the shop assistant to take it for him.

As they left the shop, the large toy box straddling Kweku's upper body as he jealously grasped it at both ends, Bill asked Kweku to turn round to have his picture taken. He happily swung round, beaming a satisfied grin from cheek to cheek that elicited instant chuckles from his highly amused dad and Bill. He had finally got his pound of flesh, and was in cloud cuckoo-land. As soon as he was in the car, he greedily opened the box and marvelled at the car's beauty from every angle all the way down to Kent, distractedly numb to any anxiety that he was about to start life at a new school.

***

They were now minutes away from the school. Kweku packed the toy car back into its box and his dad now gave him the kind of pep talk any child might expect from a parent on their first day at a new school.

Exhortations to good conduct, following the teacher's instructions, smart dressing and cleanliness were all aired to a quietly receptive Kweku. Now that he'd had his way and got his toy, he regretted the emotional blackmail he had felt compelled to use and was anxious to evince a guilty gratitude before parting ways with his dad.

***

Happily, Kweku's first impressions at Glenwood were strangely positive. He couldn't quite put his finger on it, but from the welcome of the Headmaster and Elm House Housemaster and greater expanse of the school grounds to the more settled disposition of the boys, everything just seemed calmer, more relaxed than at Ketlers. He speculated that maybe the softer landing at his new boarding school was down to one of his parents being there with him on the first day. The welcome tea party and introduction to the school certainly seemed a less tense affair than the new boys' function at Ketlers had been with Tulver.

In fact, the general atmosphere in the country seemed brighter than when he left it for his summer holidays in Ghana. Little more than a month earlier, England, a football-loving nation, had won the world cup for the first time, beating in the final, of all teams, the same country it had defeated with Allied help in the Second World War just over two decades before.

Kweku's first few weeks at Glenwood were in many ways a re-run of his first weeks at Ketlers, but in a gentler environment. With two years of boarding school life now behind him, he felt like an old hand among the eight-year-olds in his year group experiencing the shock of its deprivations for the first time in their lives.

***

Kweku was beginning his fourth week at Glenwood on a glorious autumn day in Kent. The school had a quaint feel about it, nestled comfortably as it was amid playing fields, freshly mown lawns, neatly trimmed hedges and colourful flower beds in a clearing hemmed in by woods. Enthroned in cloudless blue skies, the sun illuminated the beauty of nature's offerings as an escape for senses dulled by the monotony of daily routines.

Sitting at his desk during English class, Kweku looked up. Instinctively, he knew that the words 'of course you wouldn't know about that sort of thing', which had just been uttered by the teacher, Mr Simmonds, were directed at him. He nevertheless shuddered at the casual brutality of the smear. This wasn't a case of physical harm being applied, as at Ketlers, but the words used were designed to prick and embarrass him and did so. It was one of the phrases lazily tossed in by Mr Simmonds to punctuate his descriptions of traditional British life as part of a systematic effort to remind Kweku that he 'didn't belong' and embed in his psyche a sense of alienation and inferiority.

It did not seem to matter to Simmonds that, as a subject of Ghana, which had gained independence less than a decade earlier after almost a century of British rule and whose official language was and still is English, and as a two-year veteran already of English boarding school, Kweku was as familiar as his classmates with many of the British idiosyncrasies under discussion. As some of the other boys turned round to look straight at Kweku – a few sympathetically but most nonchalantly, some even staring strangely at him in consonance with the tone of Simmonds' query – his eyes met the disdainful stare of Simmonds. Satisfied that his barbed comment had left its intended sting, Simmonds turned away, pouting his lips smugly.

But these were the times when the first of the post-World War Two baby boomers had reached adolescence. Emboldened by the inability of the "grown-ups" in the two immediately preceding generations to deal with the continuing teething problems of societal development without resorting to costly global wars, they were determined to question long-held orthodoxies and seek their own solutions to life's challenges. Never again would age automatically be taken to imply better judgment.

Winds of change were blowing across Europe's remaining colonies worldwide. The Allies' fight to topple the hegemonies of Hitler, Hirohito and Mussolini had ironically provided the justification for the struggle against the continuing dictatorial hegemony of colonial empire, to which the focus of innovative political thinking shifted after the defeat of the Axis powers.

After the Second World War, the Soviet Union, the great power in Eastern Europe, had no compunction in continuing with its pre-war crude tools of imperial control, managing satellite states through installed puppet regimes appointed and protected by the centre of power in Moscow. The hypocrisy of a foreign power continuing to rule others by diktat could however not survive the logic of the new world order being trumpeted in countries following the political paradigms of "the West". The great powers in the

West, led by the United States and including countries geographically located in other parts of the globe attempting to follow a democratic model based on imperfect, but best-in-class models of universal suffrage and an independent media and judiciary, found themselves compelled by the lessons of the Second World War to invent more subtle strategies to exert continuing dominance.

The solution was to present the appearance of complying with new global regulatory frameworks, while seeking to retain indirect influence and control through a process sometimes described as neo-colonialism or, more simply put, a new form of colonisation. The model frequently involved deployment of superior financial investment muscle on a bilateral or multilateral level – either directly on a government-to-government level, or via multinational companies headquartered in their jurisdiction – in order to pressure the debtor country into selling income streams based on its natural resources many decades into the future at below-market prices dictated by the lender.

This would sometimes be combined with the hidden hammer of military bases, established ostensibly for the protection of the target country but in reality for the protection of its compliant government or prevailing political system.

The flip side of the same strategy included destabilisation and overthrow of autocratic governments viewed as unfriendly to the investing companies – often, it must be said, encouraged by the popular support of the indigenes being oppressed by the autocratic government, although such concern for the well-being of indigenes hypocritically did not extend to situations where the autocratic governments were compliant with the profit-seeking or military objectives of the western government or its associated multinational companies.

In England, as elsewhere, corporal punishment, a cornerstone of discipline not only in the home generally but particularly at school – notoriously so in boarding school and other closed lodging environments – was gradually phased out on the basis that it was counter-productive, a form of abuse encouraging the abused to become future abusers. Awareness was evolving of the potentially pernicious effects of bullying and discrimination, and their prevalence across and within all the cultures of the world to varying degrees.

A few days prior to Mr Simmonds' barb at the start of that fourth week, the Headmaster, Mr Bairstowe, an extrovert and mercurial young rising star among contemporary headmasters, had enquired directly from Kweku how he was settling in at Glenwood. Startled and impressed that his opinion as an 8-year-old mattered, Kweku mulled over whether to mention the sustained ridicule he had been enduring at the hands of his English teacher in those first few weeks.

As one of the first wave of young Africans to enter the British private boarding school system, he had quickly developed a thick skin in what might be interpreted as an example of rapid application of Darwinian natural selection instincts in order to survive! He had learnt to try to view opportunistic insults launched in his direction as "water off a duck's back", telling himself in such instances to ignore mere words and 'get on with the job at hand'.

Indeed, as is well known, victims of verbal and physical abuse of the era were by no means limited to people of a different ethnicity. This is of course still the case. Anyone even within the same ethnic group or gender was 'fair game' for targeting by those in positions of authority over them or even on a peer-to-peer basis. And so Kweku was used to an unspoken code of the era: internalise your suffering, don't complain, and above all don't be a sneak. The code is powerfully and accurately illustrated in Thomas Hughes' epic Victorian novel, *Tom Brown's School Days*, where it forms a recurrent theme.

Then again, Kweku pondered, if he did spill the beans and the gamble paid off, Bairstowe would hear him out and at the very least he might gain clues to help solve the puzzle which had been clouding his thinking since his very first English lesson: Why was Simmonds constantly singling him out in this way?

After a silence which must have seemed like an eternity to Mr Bairstowe, Kweku looked straight up at him. Detecting a look of genuine empathy on Bairstowe's face, Kweku decided to respond to the open invitation to talk which he had just received from the adult in the very highest position of authority at the school. He went for it, expatiating on Simmonds' repeated slurs towards him in open class, including regular references to monkeys, bananas, jungle habits and the like. 'Ahh, Simmonds!' came Mr Bairstowe's reply. 'Don't take any notice of him. He still hasn't got over losing family members in Kenya during the Mau Mau crisis!'

Although generally aware of the recent independence of Ghana and its West African neighbours, Kweku knew nothing of the struggles against British colonial rule on the other side of the African continent, in the East. He had no idea about the bloody brutality of the Mau Mau Uprising in Kenya, in which, as he would discover in later years, unspeakable atrocities were committed on both sides in the indigenes' fight for self-determination.

Mr Bairstowe promised having a word with Simmonds. Crucially however, as he had by his bold action seized the initiative to confide in Kweku on the likely motivation behind Simmonds' insults, Kweku would now be better equipped to handle them should they continue. In the event, the rate of Simmonds' insults fell off a cliff soon after Bairstowe's intervention. By force of habit, Simmonds could not bring himself to eliminate his provocative barbs altogether from his lessons; but they became far more muted in their delivery and from then on virtually always aimed at imaginary third persons, rather than directly at Kweku himself.

In large part thanks to the feeling that the individual at the top of the tree at his school had his back, a reinvigorated Kweku began to blossom, performing well both academically and on the playing fields. Mr Bairstowe's protective interest was by no means a given in the still relatively harsh context of a period, even though one in flux, when conspiracies of silence and inaction in response to reported complaints were still the norm rather than the exception. But being taken seriously gave Kweku fresh confidence to try to be exemplary in his own conduct.

***

Kweku's newfound inner equilibrium was however to be disturbed just one month after his chat with Mr Bairstowe. There was an infamous violent bully at the school, a fourth-year pupil called J.J. Harrison. An effete-looking boy with long dark hair, which he would alternately flick forward to hang loosely over his face and then, tossing his head backwards, tuck behind his ears again on either side, he had the exaggerated strut of a prize gamecock constantly marking out the borders of his self-proclaimed territory.

Known to everyone simply as 'JJ', often in the short break before afternoon tea he would square off around an area just beyond the Elm House courtyard, shoulders back and chest out in military fashion, looking for unsuspecting prey to ambush. That day he spotted Kweku walking back to his dorm from lessons and decided it was his turn to be reminded who was boss.

The first Kweku knew of anything, pebbles were showering around his ankles and shins. He looked up and saw a senior boy stooping to grab another handful to launch in his direction, using a low-trajectory sliding action that a Major League Baseball pitcher would have been proud of.

He yelled "Dance, you fool, dance!" as he threw the stones at Kweku, his shouts interspersed with the cackles of a demented hyena encircling its trapped quarry. Kweku remembered being told by other boys of a school bully operating in this area; how he would begin by aiming projectiles low and then, whenever the fancy took him or he felt that his target hadn't reacted with enough fear and panic, emotions which were the big turn-on for him to arouse in his chosen victims, he would aim higher, at the upper body and head.

Kweku had taken some painful stings to his leg but realised he might only have seconds left before things got out of hand. Armed with his new spiritual self-confidence, he switched rapidly to defending himself. Starting in Harrison's direction, he gathered a few pebbles and launched them right back at him, following through on the swing with all the strength he could muster.

In the time-honoured fashion of bullies – good at dishing it out but not so good at taking it – Harrison seemed bewildered that anyone would dare throw stones back at him. He briefly lost focus but, after recovering his composure and shovelling a bucketload of stones into his huge goalkeeper-like hands, he rained a storm of stones higher up, slamming them into Kweku's torso. Realising he was outgunned, Kweku at last took to his heels and ran for cover inside Elm House. In the relative safety of his dormitory, schoolmates who had witnessed the incident remarked what a swine Harrison was and how unfair it was that he was always getting away with it.

As every other victim of Harrison's bullying before him, Kweku said nothing to any house prefect, not only because of the culture of silence which still prevailed in those days, but also on the assumption that any senior, on being told the story, would automatically side with Harrison as their fellow-senior. Beyond prefects, the thought never crossed Kweku's mind to report Harrison to the Housemaster, the strict and highly organised Mr Holman. He did briefly toy with the idea of apprising the Headmaster, whose ear he seemed to have. But he quickly reasoned that would be overkill: it would be better to reserve requests for intervention from that high a level to things that really were a matter of life and death or at least serious injury.

Curiously however, he had no further encounters with Harrison, nor was there any chatter doing the rounds on any fights involving Harrison after that date. Months later, Kweku reflected that any one of a number of possible scenarios could have occurred. At the most improbable end of the spectrum, Harrison could have experienced a "road to Damascus moment" after that day and undergone a personality transformation. Almost equally unlikely, perhaps one of the witnesses had subsequently reported the incident to a prefect or Mr Holman. At the most likely end of the spectrum of possibilities, matron, Mr Holman's wife or Mr Holman himself had witnessed the incident and decided to rein Harrison in.

The next year, which should have been Harrison's last, he was nowhere to be seen. Kweku could not recall any gossip among boys or announcement from the Headmaster or Housemaster about his exact fate. Everyone just assumed that he had been quietly withdrawn from the school at the end of the school year following a discussion with his parents. It was the way things were done in those days. Using a metaphor from the theatre, a hook would be extended slowly from one of the wings, its handler invisible to the audience – in this case the rest of the boys. The hook would then lock around its target's neck and in one swift move the target would be yanked offstage, never to be seen again. From the boys' viewpoint, that is how the vexatious problem of Harrison came to a sudden end.

***

The evening before the end of term, Kweku was thrilled to get a call from his mum confirming that she had flown in from Ghana and would be coming to school the next day with Bill Young to attend the Carol Service and take him home to Highgate.

The following morning, Deborah and some other parents were already seated in Assembly for the Service when the boys started coming in, shepherded by masters into rows, form by form. Deborah saw Kweku as he walked in. He hadn't spotted her yet. She could have sworn that he'd added a couple of inches to his height since she last saw him at the end of the summer holidays. Her immediate thought was that it was a good sign that they were feeding him well. She watched him chatting animatedly with other boys to his left and right and was happy to see him looking contented.

After the Service, Elm House Matron Erica Fallstrop and her assistant Rose were on duty at the house to sign everyone out. Erica greeted Deborah with a warm smile as she walked into the reception. She had a thick overcoat on and handed her the obligatory Christmas cards for house staff, including her. They made polite chatter introducing themselves, while Rose went to call Kweku from the common room. He came rushing out to the reception:

'Mummy!'

'Yes, I'm here!' she said, giving him a bear hug. Goodbyes were hurriedly exchanged. Kweku slung his satchel over his shoulder and Bill took his suitcase and a large envelope, which Kweku said contained his holiday project work. They walked out into the crisp December air. As they set off, Deborah had Bill tune the car stereo to Radio London, so that she and Kweku could enjoy the latest pop tunes.

Deborah had an eclectic taste for music, which she had passed on to her son. She loved everything from traditional Asante *adowa* and *kete* rhythms to Ghanaian Highlife and Gospel music, jazz, pop and classical. But she was Beatles more than Stones, Beach Boys more than The Who, The Supremes more than The Animals.

She was curious about the new friends Kweku was making. She asked him if the boys she saw him chatting with before the service were friends. Kweku couldn't recall who she meant. Like almost every other mother, she was protective of her brood and hungry for the comfort of assurances that her son was mixing with friends who would be a positive rather than negative influence on him. She was concerned that, being an only child, he should make friends at the school who would be as constant with him as real brothers. She left the topic for another day.

Once they got home, as Kweku unpacked and watched TV while she cooked lunch, he began to smell delicious flavours coming from the kitchen. They weren't the same as the ones in Ghana – it seemed like a different version of excellent. As he spread himself out on the sofa, he sighed with contentment that he would no more be at the sole mercy for holidays in

England of Tulver, her mood swings dictating how much effort she put into preparing his meals. For Kweku, as for everyone lucky to have a mum around to support them in childhood, mum's cooking was always the best.

His favourite in England was her chicken stew with steamed rice. It was beautifully spicy, heavenly. He didn't know all the ingredients she was using, but a couple of times when he sneaked into the kitchen to try to make out the source of the savoury smells reaching his nose, he did see on top of the sideboard a half-empty packet, with "Oxo Chicken" in white letters against a bronze background, some cubes wrapped in silver foil still left inside it. Sometimes he would see her crushing and sprinkling the cubes into the boiling stew below. Spicing helped a lot, but he was sure that as big a reason for the alluring taste was the source of meat itself.

All her meats – chicken, pork, lamb and beef – were bought from the local specialist purveyors of meat and poultry, Tom's Butchers in East Finchley. Unlike packaged frozen meats in the supermarket, theirs was always fresh. Kweku would be striding proudly alongside his mum as she walked on shopping rounds between East Finchley and Muswell Hill, pushing her shopping cart along. If the cart was full, he would help by taking a light carrier bag. As his strength grew with age, he would carry more of the weight to ease the burden on her or give her a break pushing the cart.

On the way they would sometimes chat about life back home in Ghana. Things were going well with Dad and Uncle Adrian's confectionery business. The new government had declared itself to be a friend of the private sector, including businesses like his dad's company, and was still finding its way. In fact, Ghana had been an independent country for less than ten years and so was still trying to find its way.

But mostly Deborah would ask him how things were at school, encouraging him to work hard to reciprocate the sacrifices she and Kojo were making to give him such a privileged education in the UK. Sometimes she would suggest he invite one of his friends round to spend the day, but Kweku was too shy to do that. Anyhow his friends' homes were scattered all over the country. Some even lived abroad. His best friend Chris McNulty's parents lived in India, for instance. If one of them lived in London or nearby and was inviting him to a party, fine. Otherwise he was reluctant to appear desperate, as he far preferred her company anyway.

There was the occasional birthday to attend for children of friends of his parents living in London. It gave him a chance to mix outside of school with others his own age. But they would never be together for long enough for friendships to develop, and he was always happy to be returned at the end of the day to the familiarity of his surroundings at home.

***

Shortly before Christmas, Deborah took him to Marylebone Road near Baker Street in the West End. First they went to The Planetarium, where Kweku was introduced to the magic of astronomy, of science fiction turning into fact. Less than three years later, as it turned out, the United States would actually land men on the moon. From there they went next door to

Madame Tussauds, where history and the present were brought to life through a clever arrangement of wax models of historical and contemporary figures, and enthralling re-enactments of battles, speeches and other important events in rooms including a frightening Chamber of Horrors.

Kweku stumbled around, fascinated and sometimes lost in that historical Arcadia as he criss-crossed the expanse of time. He recoiled in shock at the waxworks which he kept mistaking initially for real people, so lifelike were the figures which had been expertly sculpted. Even The Beatles were there and, unlike in real life, he could actually get up close to them and stare, mesmerised, before being hustled along by others behind them impatient to get their turn.

At the end of the Easter holidays Deborah took him to Billy Smart's Circus, under a huge tent. Apart from clowns and jugglers, they had performing elephants, mischievous monkeys, daredevil tight-rope walkers and acrobats. Kweku joined other children bobbing up and down excitedly in their seats, his heart in his mouth as he watched daring stunts, followed by moments of comic relief provided by clowns and animals forced to perform routines for the laughter of the audience at their expense.

On the last Saturday they went to the Battersea Park funfair in South West London. Beyond the entrance gate Kweku discovered a true children's wonderland. He had never seen anything like it. He didn't know where to start. He wanted to go on the dodgems, on the big dipper ride where he could see people enjoying high-speed thrills as they whizzed up, down and around the tracks in their carriages. But Deborah couldn't bring herself to trust that nothing would come loose or fall off at those speeds. And she couldn't let Kweku go on his own: he was too young for that. Kweku was disappointed but, with the fickle attention of a child presented with a myriad of attractive options, his mind quickly veered to the next adventure platform appearing seemingly out of nowhere.

She joined him for the spinning wheel, merry-go-rounds and other gentler rides, and they watched pantomime acts, magicians, jugglers, while vaudeville music played in the background, its merry tunes sucking children deeper into blithe insouciance. The hot dogs were mouth-wateringly huge, garnished with tomato ketchup and relish, the hamburgers appetisingly thick. Sweets on offer included different-shaped cones mounted with whippy vanilla ice cream and chocolate dressing, and fruit-flavoured iced lollies. By the late afternoon he was so exhausted that he slept that night like a baby.

***

In those early years, Deborah couldn't spoil him enough when he was under her care. Sometimes she would just hug and cuddle him quietly for a short while, pressing him closer, then letting go, saying how sorry she was that she and Kojo had sent him to boarding school so early in his life. Kojo especially had thought it would be the best way to introduce him to world-leading education. In Kojo's view, throughout modern history, great thinkers and political leaders in the most advanced countries had undergone such training from an early age. It had given them a strong start in life, teaching internal strength and independence. It would help ensure Kweku would always be able to stand on his own two feet, no matter what – God forbid – should happen to his parents in future.

She'd had her doubts, but had gone along with the decision out of respect for Kojo, praying things would turn out well. She had since had regrets, but Kweku's improved posture and the pick-up in his self-confidence since he started at Glenwood had made her think that maybe in the end it was the right choice after all. Nonetheless, she confided in Kweku that, if she had the same decision to make again, she would insist that they wait till he was eight or nine years old before letting him go to boarding school alone like that. Even then, she admitted, she still might have had some doubts about it. But she was delighted with the way things were going now, so he should keep it up.

***

Whenever Kojo was able to come over to England to join Deborah for the school drop, they would squeeze in time to take Kweku somewhere for a treat. A memorable occasion was when they took him for lunch at the restaurant on the revolving top floor of Post Office Tower. Kweku was agog at the startling panoramic view it gave of central London below, including famous landmarks like Hyde Park and Trafalgar Square with Nelson's column.

At other times they would relax by going to watch a film at the local cinema – the Odeon in Muswell Hill or Rex cinema in East Finchley. They all loved comedies. Kojo was a big fan of the comic actor Norman Wisdom, frequently playing the hapless but sympathetic Norman Pitkin with his boss Mr Grimsdale in slapstick comedy that would have everyone rolling in the aisles.

At home they would watch quiz shows like *Double Your Money*, talent programmes such as *Opportunity Knocks*, both hosted by Hughie Green, or game shows like the warmly absurd *It's A Knockout*. Deborah's special favourites were historical or biblical films, about any period in history, ancient or modern – especially those with a didactic message – and cultural films. Kweku shared her interest for epic movies. Kojo couldn't go a day without watching or listening to several news broadcasts and catching up with the newspapers. As Kweku grew, he was able to share his dad's passion for current affairs, and comment more knowledgeably on issues of the day, enjoying the political presentations in the end almost as much as he did.

CHAPTER SIX

Climbing the greasy pole

Year by year at Glenwood, Kweku slowly climbed the hierarchical ladder of authority. As at all boarding schools of the day, seniority was based on longevity of attendance. By his second year at the school, he had informal power to instruct and advise those in their first year; by his third year, those in their second year as well. His main observed 'weakness' identified in school reports was that he was overly inclined to be patient with junior boys, even when such empathy had not been earned, and always took time to listen to both sides of any dispute before reaching a judgment. Careful analysis was not always valued in an era when dispensing swift justice – even under the influence of bias or other extraneous considerations – and moving forward was more highly prized than spending time to ensure a fair and robust outcome that would stand the test of time.

Kweku observed almost imperceptibly that, as he rose through the ranks, he continued to be promoted to positions of authority based on his academic and sporting accomplishments, but whenever masters felt that a situation warranted tough administration of discipline, another boy at his hierarchical level would quietly be given the metaphorical rod to apply so that fear of authority was not undermined.

Somewhat paradoxically in other circumstances though, Kweku had no problem intervening swiftly to discipline any senior below his rank that he saw unjustly bullying junior boys – there were times when speed in applying discipline was necessary to prevent deterioration in a developing situation. At other times there was scope to allow deliberation to sift out a more defensible sanction. Trying to ensure balance seemed more important to him than applying discipline as a reflex instinct, and this was to govern his approach to assessing fairness in later life.

As all schoolboys, Kweku had a best friend from his very first year: an English boy, Christopher McNulty. Chris' father had been a civil servant in India in the years when it was still a British colony, and stayed on after the country gained independence. Chris was born there and would regale Kweku with stories of eating his favourite mulligatawny soup, or *khisiri* far tastier than the kedgeree served at Glenwood for breakfast on Fridays, and encountering tigers and snakes in the wild near Assam. Kweku would respond with stories of delicious Ghanaian food, of fufu with palm soup and banku with fish stew, and outings to Labadi and other beaches further down the coast to the west.

They would swap and compare observations on other boys, on staff; play harmless pranks on other boys like hiding their satchels away in a cupboard after school and watching them go berserk before mysteriously magicking the satchels back on to the wall a couple of hours later shortly before bedtime. Once or twice they were caught out and had to do detention.

They loved exploring the school grounds together. Visiting the school Tuck Shop on Saturday mornings to buy sweets was a necessity. Kweku's favourites were the square Assorted Spangles with a dimple in the middle, coming in a variety of fruity flavours like strawberry, orange and lime. Also Opal fruits 'made to make your mouth water', as the jingle on TV proclaimed. Other favourites they shared were Crunchie, Toffee Crisp, Rolo, Aero, Trebor mints, Foxes Glacier Fruits and the obligatory Smarties. But Kweku hated liquorice; he couldn't understand why anyone liked it. Chris loved it.

Over ninety percent of the school were Protestants. There was a Church of England Service in Assembly on Sunday mornings, and brief hymns and prayers every Monday morning. Kweku and Chris were among the five percent of boys who were Roman Catholics, so on Sunday evenings they were taken by the Deputy Housemaster, Mr Latimore, in a minivan to Mass in nearby Tunbridge Wells. Predictably, the most exciting part of the outing for them was the trip itself to and from the Church. It resembled the glimpse of ordinary life a prisoner gets when being shuffled from court to jail, a different world.

As the two friends grew older together, almost inevitably competition came into play. Leaving the school a year before Kweku for a public school, Wetherton in Sussex, whose facilities he described tantalisingly as better than any other public school's, Chris urged Kweku to follow him there the following year. Kweku gave it serious thought, but in the end decided he wanted to be closer to London. So he chose to explore other pastures. To his great regret in life, he never saw or heard of Chris again after he left Glenwood.

***

Deborah came over to be with Kweku for the Easter holiday. They chatted as Bill drove them back from school to Highgate. However, the conversation changed as Kweku got older. Even at an early age, he didn't feel he should tell his mum everything. As everyone said it wasn't good to be a sneak, he stayed mum, so to speak, about anything that was happening which he felt he could handle. That trend worsened with the passage of time. He became incrementally discreet about what he could discuss with her: there was no sense in involving Mummy unless things were out of control and he had nowhere else to turn. He didn't want to have the tag of being a "mummy's boy", one which children with no siblings were especially prone to be saddled with.

He tried to show his gratitude for the sacrifices his parents were making by joining in with most of their interests. But there were some pursuits – such as shopping in his mum's case – that he just couldn't find the stomach to continue pretending past a certain point that he was enjoying. Frustration would invariably set in by the start of the second or third hour of shopping, whether this was window shopping or real shopping. As neither his dad nor any other man or boy he had come across by that tender age had quite the same patience for staring at dresses and other knick-knacks for hours, he concluded, without any intention of chauvinistic bias, that the activity of shopping must be something females were better suited to indulging in than males.

He was very happy to join his mum when it came to shopping for food: he could see the necessity and urgency of that. But he could not bring himself to assign even a near-equivalent level of urgency to hours spent window shopping and returning home virtually empty-handed.

And so Kweku was mightily relieved when, some months after he reached the age of twelve, his mum finally felt safe enough to leave him at home alone – home alone to watch his favourite cartoons and adventure films, to raid the larder for crisps, biscuits, afternoon cereals and any other snacks he could lay his hands on to savour while watching TV. Bliss!

On other occasions, for his penance he would willingly accompany Deborah to visit a cousin of hers in Finchley Central. She had a daughter around the same age as Kweku. Like him, she was shy, and he felt a natural affinity towards her. Sitting in front of the TV, they would politely exchange small talk, punctuated by long and nervous silences, in a family room, while in the main living room their mums swapped stories delivered with varying levels of intensity according to their novelty or capacity to shock.

***

In the summer before his final year at Glenwood, Kweku was to his surprise promoted directly to school prefect, skipping the usual obligatory trial period of apprenticeship as a house prefect. It was a prestigious appointment. The school prefects, a maximum of twenty at any one time out of a total of 440 boys, were the school's praetorian guard. Distinguished not only by special neckties but blazers bordered with pale blue piping, they were ambassadors for the school and primary arbiters of policy implementation. The boost the appointment gave to Kweku's personal self-esteem provided an essential countervailing balance to his nagging insecurities.

Despite this, the prefects' most valued privilege came far lower down Maslow's hierarchy of needs than self-esteem – in fact, all the way down to the entry-level physiological need of food. The school's Board of Governors held meetings twice every term. Their meetings would be followed by a lunch prepared by the school chef which was the stuff of legend – a clever move designed to ensure favourable last impressions about their visit.

Immediately after the last Governor had left the dining hall, the school prefects, led by the head boy, would be invited to help themselves to the leftovers. The first time Kweku got his chance, he and his fellow-prefects went in like grateful scavengers. Without waiting for a second invitation, they swooped down on the huge table boards supporting Nebuchadnezzar-like culinary presentations straight out of fantasy-land: ham legs and other whole roast joints on beds of colourful salads, a generous assortment of accompanying vegetables, including golden roast potatoes and colourful rice combinations, exotic fruits artistically assembled in mouth-watering combinations, and on and on.

It was scarcely possible for Kweku and the other school prefects for whom this was their first invitation to grasp that the same school chef was responsible for outputting the stodge that boys were served daily and the half-eaten treasures that now stretched out before them into the distance. Talk about double standards, eh?

Kweku attributed his surprise appointment as a school prefect to his improving performance in class, where he was now topping in many subjects. He was most at ease learning foreign languages, enjoying his French and fascinated by the treasure trove that was Latin. In those days Latin was still a compulsory subject for all pupils, despite or perhaps propelling the increasing popularity of the humorous jingle:

"Latin is a dead language,
As dead as dead can be,
It killed the ancient Romans,
And now it's killing me!"

But for so many pupils it was Mr Bairstowe, who apart from being Headmaster also taught Latin, who brought it to life by reinventing classic phrases. "*More potato porter*" did not represent a request by a hungry English traveller to a station luggage handler for additional servings of mashed potato, but was Latin for the rather more humorous and embarrassing "When the custom has been drunk, I may be carried away!"

Kweku's introduction to Greek culture was through the fantastic tales that were the Greek myths. Their Old Testament-style uncomplicated stories of vengeful immortals and struggling mortals served for him as a formal initiation into the mysteries of human behaviour, with exaggerated brushstrokes for the callow student.

There were tales of Prometheus, the immortal Titan who stole fire from the lightning bolt of the king of the gods, Zeus, to give to humans and was tortured by Zeus for the theft of something the gods wouldn't miss instead of being rewarded for the gift of something badly needed by humankind; of Scylla and Charybdis, the six-headed monster and whirlpool – navigating through them represented the real world equivalent of being caught between the devil and the deep blue sea; and of Sisyphus, whose futile efforts endlessly rolling a huge rock up a hill only to see it roll back down just before the summit perfectly symbolised the cyclical hopelessness of so much human endeavour.

It did not matter that these stories were on their surface utterly implausible. Indeed, their implausibility was what gave their authors free rein to explore the power of allegory, in the process providing a gateway for the exhilarating escape from a real world burdened by earthly constraints to one where anything was possible.

CHAPTER SEVEN

A Sense of Belonging

The next term, at the start of the new academic year, Kweku was taken aback and not a little embarrassed to learn that he had been made head boy. On receiving the news of his second successive promotion, this time all the way up to the top of the tree, he guessed that Mr Bairstowe, as principal, would have had the most influential role to play in the decision. Next in terms of clout would have been his Housemaster, Mr Holman, as the teacher best-placed to assess and report on his conduct in residential surroundings outside of the classroom.

Kweku surmised that character in the home – when we are usually less guarded, allowing more of our natural personality to be revealed, as the metaphorical mask we instinctively cloak ourselves in daily for self-protection is allowed to slip – must have been an important criterion in the decision-making on his appointment. The implication that he had passed the relevant test came as further ammunition for him to use against his insecurities.

His parents were so proud when he rang them to give them the news. They advised him not to let the appointment get to his head. He assured them there was no chance of that. He would simply do his best to justify the confidence placed in him by the school's authorities and exercise power and consult as fairly as he could.

***

As Kweku sat one Tuesday lunchtime at the head of the elevated table in the dining hall reserved for school prefects, he picked nervously around the edges of the toad-in-the-hole on the plate in front of him. Garnished with onion gravy and three balls of scooped mashed potatoes (quite lumpy in truth, but who was there to complain to?), it was usually one of his favourites. In Rugby trials the day before, he had been rotated in various positions, from second row forward ('lock forward' in today's parlance) to wing three-quarter. Towards the end of an exhausting afternoon, he had managed to grab hold of one knee of a speeding opposing outside centre. As the centre kicked out to break free, Kweku's grip slid from his knee to the sharp edges of his boot. Hanging on as if his life depended on it, Kweku barely hauled him to the ground, the ball spilling forward from the centre's grasp as he fell.

The tackle had prevented a certain try, as there was an overlapping sprinter on the wing totally unmarked who had called for the ball. Around the time of the tackle, Kweku vaguely recalled hearing the word "tackle!" being yelled by one of the constantly barking teachers on the touchline. But he couldn't remember if it had been shouted in urging before he made the tackle or in approval afterwards. Either way, Kweku prayed that his efforts had been noticed.

People had started peeling off from the lunch to prepare for afternoon classes when the school gossip, Ollie Bendridge, came rushing into the hall from the corridor. Amid the hubbub that suddenly sprung up around him, Kweku could hear him saying to boys in turns, 'You're in!', 'I didn't see your name' or 'No, you didn't make it!'. Everyone rushed past Bendridge into the corridor to check for themselves. Kweku got up and walked slowly into the corridor, still praying with his every step.

By now among the tallest students at the school, as he neared the front of the sea of boys gathered expectantly around the bulletin board displaying various team selections, Kweku made out his surname on the list for the school's Rugby 1st XV. He had made it! He was so excited, and simultaneously relieved! First team players, particularly for Rugby and Cricket, not only had elusive cachet but, more importantly, on weekly trips to play away matches, they could escape the school's confines and explore other towns and schools in a travelling group much like holidaymakers, leaving envious schoolmates behind staring wistfully as the coach rolled out through the parted front gates.

Now he would finally be one of those on the coach, singing boisterously as they were driven away on adventures for the day, with the ebullient Mr Bairstowe leading from the front in his Mercedes. Temporarily unshackled from the conventions of their usual environment and any uncomfortable memories still lurking there, boys felt free to express themselves as tourists do, without having to look over their shoulders to see who was watching or listening.

Even the teachers supervising such trips acted as if the boys were no longer schoolboys subject to the strict discipline operating within the confines of the school grounds. It was like a Speakers' Corner or House of Parliament, where any allegation, no matter how outrageous, could be made about any other boy or member of the teaching staff, and, even if overhead by a teacher, no one could be held to account for making it.

The spirit of camaraderie was unique. Especially when they won away matches, they sang on the coach all the way back to the school and were treated to a surfeit of tasty snacks along the route. The songs were the traditional, catchy rugby ones, occasionally interspersed with Chaucerian language, whose x-rated jokes and double entendres flew over the heads of many of the pre-pubescent boys in the group including Kweku. He nevertheless sang along heartily, parroting word sounds exactly as he heard them, sometimes remaining blissfully unaware of the full implications of their composition and meaning. Examples were:

"Dana, Dana show us your leg,
show us your leg,
show us your leg.

Dana, Dana,
show us your leg,
a yard above the knee!"

and,

"We'll drink a drink a drink
To Lillie the pink, the pink, the pink,
The saviour of... the human ra.. a.. ace,
For she invented
Medicinal compound
And now she's moving round
On wheels!"

The period Kweku spent in Glenwood's Rugby first team was a godsent opportunity to experience the jollity of group bonding in a rare setting. He'd had a best friend, who had left the school at the end of the previous term, but this… this was different. It was like inheriting several friends at once through shared experiences in the course of which the conventions and daily norms governing life within the school's boundaries could be temporarily forgotten.

***

The team was hammered by a wide margin in the first away match of the season at Wellsdon, then the national under-14 school Rugby champions. They later lost by a narrower margin in the return game at home, and at Milton, an internationally renowned specialist school for sports. But they won all their other matches that season.

One game in particular stuck out in Kweku's memory – a home match against Arkley School. From his position at right wing three-quarter, he had already scored two tries in the first half of the match. While the Glenwood team was receiving the usual half time pep-talk from their coach, Kweku happened to overhear the coach of the other team urging his opposite wing three-quarter to 'let him know you are around'. It had been a mystery to Kweku what that meant until, some 10 minutes into the second half, he found himself once more on an overlap, making a beeline in a diagonal direction for the try-line.

As he dived over the line, he felt the impact from underneath of a full punch to his stomach. Feeling as though his guts had just been hollowed out, he collapsed over the line, still clutching the ball to ensure that it was grounded properly and the try would count. But, as he turned round to look up from the ground, still winded, he was sure he could make out his opposing number, grinning with evident satisfaction at the damage he had just inflicted. He rose unsteadily to his feet, initially seeing stars, but soon recovered his balance and stayed on the pitch. In those days, there were often no ready substitutions available to jump in to replace injured players. The 'walking wounded' were expected to get back on their feet and get on with the job – unless their injury truly was a stretcher case.

For the rest of the game Kweku felt drained and exhausted, only half as effective as he had been in crashing through tackles before that first introduction to the world of dirty fouls. It was a lesson which Kweku would have done well to heed for later life but sadly often forgot: that many live by the principle that subterfuge is fine, so long as you can get away with it: the ends justify the means. The Arkley winger did indeed get away with it – there were no assistant referees in those days!

***

Kweku received a huge, unexpected consolation in Assembly on the Monday after the game. After the usual morning prayers, an announcement was made on those who had been awarded 'colours'. Typically, only half of any first team were awarded colours in a season. Colours for cricket and rugby were especially prized. One by one, winners were called up by name and applauded in front of the whole school as they were presented with the colourful pale blue, yellow and green striped tie against a black background denoting school colours. Recipients were allowed to wear them in place of any other ties at any time, and they carried huge prestige. Kweku was at the same time embarrassed and exhilarated when his name was called out. It represented a final coming of age for him. He only wished his parents had been there to witness the event.

***

Pricking Kweku's curiosity on the academic front at Glenwood was a decidedly exceptional character in the same school year, Sean Gower. Here was a rebel who revelled in all the connotations of the tag. His hair was always unkempt, an invitation to visit the school barber viewed by him almost in the same way as a condemned prisoner would view an invitation to proceed to the scaffold. On its worst days, it looked like a beehive, the dandruff visible from close up resembling pollen stored as food for the hive.

In the true style of an iconoclast protesting against the school's dress codes, the top button of his shirt was always left purposely undone, his tie hung loosely around the collar, his shirt untucked at front and back, its tails fluttering at the mercy of the winds. His guiding principles could reasonably be summarised in seven words: "Trust no-one, believe in nothing, question everything!"

Staff openly referred to him as "the mad Irishman". Yes, those were still times when a teacher, appointed to lead by example – conduct that could fairly be assumed to include eschewing casual verbal abuse – could call a boy that in public with complete impunity, provided the target would be "a sport" and not object. Slurs of this nature would not elicit the silent glares or scowls of disapproval typical of today's much more politically correct world.

At the same time, the hypocrisy of political correctness, when practised by individuals only paying it lip-service without genuinely believing in the moral superiority of the relevant words or behaviour expressing it in each case, should not be overlooked. In today's world, an individual privileged to be a fly on the wall present at expressions of both the public and private personae of another might be surprised to see that other person treading eggshells in public to avoid offending anyone, and then giving themselves free rein to air longstanding beliefs much more frankly in private in the company of souls considered like-minded and therefore comfortable with whatever deep-seated prejudices they harboured. To an extent, no one is immune from such conduct, and the best antidote against prejudice is education based on observable facts.

It is not wrong to judge others for who they are or what they do or between different options for what they offer. Judgment and analysis – even if sometimes necessarily coloured by an instinctive sense of right and wrong – should rightly be the basis for the decisions we are called to make constantly in our daily lives. What is wrong is to pre-judge people or things without bothering first to establish the facts about what they are being accused of, or judging them by different standards from those we apply to ourselves or our favourites, and not caring about the resulting double standards.

Kweku's impression was that, in Sean's case, unquestionably the main driver for his tolerance of the repeated "mad Irishman" jibe was that he himself wore it as a badge of honour. Sean, he felt, must have reflected that after all, throughout recorded history, radical new thought had often initially been associated by the "unenlightened majority" with insanity.

The Greek astronomers, philosophers and other travellers of the 6th and 5th centuries B.C. are thought to be the ones who first propounded the idea that the earth was round. But such a theory would have been considered lunatic heresy by technologically undeveloped cultures further to the north in Europe at the time convinced for millennia that the earth was flat. And the expected punishment for holding such beliefs would have been to be burnt at the stake for witchcraft. Against such a background, the tough-skinned Sean probably viewed merely being called a 'mad Irishman' for making off-the-wall propositions as coming with the territory.

Living at the zenith of the counterculture and political cynicism made more acute by events such as America's expansion of its war in Vietnam, Sean seemed to believe in virtually all the conspiracy theories doing the rounds among mature political thinkers of the day. Ones on the origins and reasons for the assassinations of JFK, MLK, RFK, the prosecution of the Vietnam War, the Cold War and neo-colonial interventions in newly independent countries around the world. He even had detailed theories on the origins of the Biafran War – the Civil War being fought at the time in Nigeria, a country neighbouring Kweku's own – and the real objectives and motivations of the leaders on both sides.

Sean was indeed a precocious talent. He regularly won prizes at the school for English literature. At the same time he was very poor at maths. Kweku attributed this to his likely disinterest in the iterative monotony of the computations that maths consisted of at that early stage.

No one knew what his sources were for all the information he stored. He could not have guessed at all that he knew. His theories and sometimes rudely curt explanations of his reasoning were no accident. As his propositions were always well-constructed, complete with logical inferences culminating in rational conclusions, he must have been blessed with a passion for understanding human behaviour in a political context, a questioning mind nurturing a sceptical approach to orthodoxy, and of course a facility for prolific reading. But beyond such innate attributes Kweku assumed that a parent or other mentoring relative must have fostered the atmosphere for the innovative analysis of current affairs that was Sean's hallmark.

Now, those used to ridiculing all conspiracy theories might snort dismissively, ignoring the facts that some, rooted in eyewitness testimony, have a greater degree of plausibility and empirical backing than others which originate from mere political propaganda based on zero evidence, and that not all are equally implausible. But Kweku thought it extraordinary how, over time, so many of the ideas floated by Sean, ostensibly crazy at the time, were subsequently validated by evidence and eyewitness testimony presented to investigative commissions years, sometimes decades later.

And so it was indeed many years later, during his university days and afterwards, that Kweku learnt the stark truth about so many of the political events on which he had so confidently challenged Sean. Some of the weirdest concerned the coming together of strange bedfellows from political establishment and criminal worlds to organise regime-change in foreign countries in order to perpetuate control over valuable natural resources or strategically important geographic locations. In those casual discussions with Sean at Glenwood, Kweku had been open to new ideas. Despite that, he found himself far more inclined to believe in orthodoxies regurgitated in the broadcast media than in fringe theories denigrated at the time by the majority of political commentators and society.

In those later years, although he had not been quite as gullible as others who had fully espoused viewpoints being propagated regularly in the established media, Kweku still felt very naïve that he had delayed for so long a receptiveness to listening to unorthodox theories. He had allowed himself to be guided by a natural humility and respect for entrenched orthodoxies for the sake of stability and security in a fast-changing world, a world that eventually turned out to be replete with charlatans. To borrow from the terminology of the great French novelist André Gide's *Les Caves du Vatican*, Kweku had been a "crustacé", a crustacean or conformist, while to his great credit Sean had been a "subtil" like the novel's lead character Lafcadio, a free-thinking non-conformist unbound by conventions.

Despite the continuing dominance of conventional thinking and conservatism among the Establishment of the time, Glenwood's teaching staff did a good job of trying to keep the syllabus relevant and up to date. Even in Kweku's final year, with the increasing use of automation in the workplace already a topical subject, almost 50 years ago now, pupils were being asked to speculate on its likely huge impact in displacing manual labour at factories and offices as well as in the home in future.

***

Kweku won an open scholarship to Huntsmere School in his last term at Glenwood. Journalists from the Kent & Sussex Courier came round to Glenwood to take photographs and interview him. He made the newspaper's front page the next day. He broke the news to his parents over the phone. They were thrilled and couldn't wait to see him for the Easter holidays. At the end of term, he and other school leavers received a sentimental send-off from friends and staff alike. Kweku was gaining in self-confidence every day.

CHAPTER EIGHT

Don Boater

April 1972

Huntsmere's Summer Term would be starting in a week's time. Kweku reflected that it was curious that in British schools the whole term was called "Summer", while half of it actually takes place in Spring-time – a bit like the "Spring" term from January to March, most of which actually takes place in a period conventionally classed in Britain as Winter-time. Anyhow, he put these down to the idiosyncrasies which can occur in any culture.

Today Kweku's parents would be taking him to visit the school outfitters in Huntsmere Town, Gieves and Hawkes, to get kitted out with his new uniform. He sensed the shop staff's astonishment that an African would be entering the school the following week. However, although visibly bewildered, they did very well to hide it. Indeed, apart from asking Kweku's parents where they came from and struggling with the reply, mistaking as usual Ghana in West Africa for Guyana in the Caribbean, they made every effort to show that, as far as they were concerned, nothing was out of the ordinary. 'If only I could be a fly on the wall here ten seconds from now,' Kweku mused, smiling as he left the shop.

The Bluer jacket distinguished Huntsmere's uniform from Glenwood's. Tailcoats, waistcoats and striped trousers he had seen his father and others wear before, although rarely. But what especially caught his eye was a brimmed straw hat with dark blue band encircling the top. Kweku saw from the list that it was called a 'boater'. His immediate impression was that it would look really smart and enhance his appearance. Little did he know the trouble it was to give him!

***

The skies were clear blue on a sunny morning in Highgate a week later. Kweku woke up early. Today would be his first day at Huntsmere. His mum cooked him a hearty English breakfast, the full works – fried eggs, Walls pork sausages, Danish back bacon and Heinz baked beans with ketchup and 2 slices of Mother's Pride toast. But by the time lunch came around, his appetite had been blunted, apart from the heavy breakfast, by a sudden onset of nerves.

He wondered how he would manage the transition from being head boy at the very top of the ladder at his prep school the previous month to just another newbie on the very bottom rung of the ladder at his new school. Ever since February, his parents had the thrill only a proud parent could enjoy: when asked by friends in Ghana and the UK what school in Britain their son was attending, they were able to say he had just won a scholarship to Huntsmere and would be starting there in April. Their shock on hearing this was palpable.

It would soon be time to set off. As usual, Kojo was fully dressed and all set well in advance, the product of a lifetime's habit of being ready to do business at any time. Deborah had spent an hour in front of the dressing mirror, experimenting, as the fairer sex routinely do to a greater extent, with make-up, dresses and different poses. Kweku had dressed up in his new school uniform as best he could. Once Kojo and Deborah had sorted themselves out, their attention turned to their son. They made a fuss to nip, tuck, adjust and re-adjust in turns, with an almost obsessive precision, every item of his uniform. A final pat on the shoulder signalled their satisfaction with the end result.

Bill the driver was on time. It was a relatively short journey northwest across London through Kingsbury and Kenton to Huntsmere. Kweku's nerves jangled as the minicab climbed the hill on the final approach to The Mount, his house. Huntsmere was steeped in 400 years of history, a history enriched by the achievements of many famous students. It was well respected in the UK and internationally.

New boy welcomes were arranged by the houses individually. Kweku and his parents entered The Mount's front door and followed the signs down the stairs and through to the garden below. They were welcomed by a rather cheerful looking gentleman with silver hair and a warm handshake. He introduced himself:

'Hello, you must be Mr and Mr Mensah,' he said.

'Yes,' Kweku's parents replied, 'Kojo and Deborah.'

He turned to Kweku: 'And you must be Kweku!'

'Hello Sir,' Kweku answered tentatively.

'I'm Roger Ventham, the Housemaster.'

'Very pleased to meet you, Mr Ventham!' Kweku's parents said, smiling politely.

'Roger's fine, Kojo. We are really looking forward to having Kweku with us. It's the first time the School has had anyone from Africa. "About bloody time too!"

I told the Headmaster.' Ventham chuckled. He seemed so friendly and affable that Kweku and his parents took to him right away.

'Now then, we've got a second-year boy lined up to be Kweku's "steer" – that's our word here for a kind of mentor to help guide a new boy through his first year, you know, someone who will show him the ropes, that sort of thing. Kweku's steer is Nick, Nick Ralston… He was here just a moment ago… Ah, there he is!'

Ventham called out to an older boy standing closer by: 'Jason, can you go and get Nick Ralston? He's standing over there you see.'

'Right you are, Sir!'

Ventham explained to the Mensahs: 'That's Jason Mortimer, one of our house supers… That's what we call prefects here, "supers", from the good old Latin word "*supra*" meaning above. They supervise the boys and see to their pastoral care, while co-ordinating with members of staff on problem-solving and improvements.'

Mortimer returned, leading Ralston.

'Thank you, Jason…' Ventham gestured to Mortimer that he was free to pick up again where he had left off.

'Ah Nick,' Ventham continued, beckoning him closer, 'come and meet Mr and Mrs Mensah and Kweku… Wonderful family, they're from Ghana… You're going to be Kweku's steer.'

'Well, Sir, provided that's OK with Kweku and Mr and Mrs Mensah,' Nick chuckled.

'Oh, that's fine with us,' Kojo and Deborah quickly added, looking at each other, and then Kweku. 'Thank you rather'. Nick's hair was slightly longer than they were used to, but he had a genial disposition. They were impressed by his apparent good manners and intuitive diplomacy.

Kweku nodded affirmatively, smiling and looking at Nick. He instinctively sensed that Nick was the straightforward, easy-going type, collaborative rather than hierarchical or judgmental. He felt 'This is someone I think I can really get along with; we seem to be on the same wavelength.'

Nick quickly resumed the dialogue with another cheerful chuckle: 'All right, Kweku, it looks like you're stuck with me then! … But don't forget, I've only been here a year longer than you, so I'm still learning things myself!'

Polite laughter ensued all around.

'OK, Nick, that's great!' said Ventham. 'Then can you show Kweku to his room so he can put his things down and then we'll see you back here later?'

'Yes, Sir.'

Turning to the Mensahs, Ventham motioned to a long table with white tablecloth, a waiter and waitress standing behind it serving tea and coffee with assorted snacks:

'Kojo and Deborah, can I interest you in some Darjeeling tea, or would you prefer an Earl Grey or just a regular tea… Or coffee perhaps? … And we've got some sandwiches – salmon and cucumber, roast beef and horseradish – oh, and wonderful scones prepared by our chef with clotted Devon cream and Fortnum & Mason strawberry preserve … Anyway, do feel free to indulge yourselves and I shall catch up with you in a bit.'

‘Thank you, Roger,’ Kojo and Deborah replied, starting off in the direction of the refreshments.

Another new boy with his parents were just coming through into the garden, and Ventham’s attention had switched to them.

‘Ahh, Mr and Mrs Hunter-Jones… and Tristan, so good to see you again! And this must be Tristan’s younger brother Edward. Yes, I remember him when he came with you last year for a tour of the house. I could have sworn he’s grown an inch or two taller since then!’

‘It’s great to be back on such a glorious day, Roger,’ Mr Hunter-Jones replied. His wife added: ‘Yes, a wonderful day, isn’t it? And how’s Marjorie?’ Ventham leaned in closer and whispered to them: ‘Actually she’s feeling a bit off colour today, you know. But I’m sure she’ll be right as rain tomorrow. Thank you for asking though …’

Meanwhile Nick and Kweku had gone back into the house, then out to the street to see Bill to collect Kweku’s bags from the car and back in again. They climbed up one flight of stairs and entered a room with three beds. Assorted posters were plastered all over the walls – racing cars, musical innovator Eric Clapton, his fingers contorted freakishly around his guitar strings in a way that allowed him to generate impossible sounds, an androgynous David Bowie in psychedelic costume, screaming out at the top of his lungs, his face twisted expressively with emotion, and a bikini-clad Cheryl Tiegs.

The boys in these rooms were clearly adolescents wishing to give controlled expression to the joys of discovering puberty and the counterculture launched in the previous decade against the pressures of sustained conformity. It dawned on Kweku: no wonder staff were happy to keep parents away from the rooms that first day. Their boys were entering a new phase of their lives, which the school understood well but which some parents might feel uncomfortable discussing with their children. The school were ready to help fill the gap and, despite appearances, that bit of tolerance devoid of hypocrisy and humbug served a useful purpose in releasing tension, provided it was not abused by the boys.

Nick instinctively sensed that Kweku was a little disappointed he wouldn't be having a room all to himself. In their house in Highgate, he now had his own room, and even though he was still in his first year as a teenager, he somehow felt he had earned the right to that privacy.

"You'll be sharing the room with two others…' Nick began.

'OK,' Kweku quickly interjected, pretending not to mind and hoping the speed of his positive reaction to this discovery would disguise his disappointment.

But Nick wasn't fooled; he had felt no different himself in his first year: 'Don't worry,' he told Kweku, 'in second year you'll only have to share with one other person – and you'll each get the chance to choose who with! … You might finally get a room to yourself in third year, but if not then you'll definitely be flying solo in fourth year.' Then the thought suddenly struck Nick:

'Anyway, you're a scholar, aren't you?'

‘Yes,’ Kweku replied, wondering how that would change things but assuming from Nick’s tone that it would do so for the better.

‘Ah, then you lucky bugger! You’ll definitely get your own room in third year. And you’ll be going straight into the Removes Class this term. You’ll skip the Shells… There’s a special Remove class for scholars, and, if you keep things up, you’ll be sitting your A-Level exams in just over 3 years from now. That means you could have the chance to finish here in three and a half years, if sitting entrance exams for Oxford or Cambridge, instead of the usual four and a half.’

Hearing that gave Kweku a thrill. He had all the respect for Huntsmere, but leaving there would put him a step closer to his ultimate goal of entry into the big wide world, where he would be able to experience forbidden fantasies incognito, and be taken more seriously – or at least be able to pretend to strangers ignorant of his age to have the right to be taken more seriously.

‘That’s your bed,’ Nick said, pointing to the one bed left in the room with nothing on it yet.

Kweku noticed that, as the nearest one to the window, it would be closest to the winds on a cold night. But he no longer cared. He was somehow more acclimatised to Britain’s colder weather than the six-year-old who had first arrived in England seven years earlier. He quickly put all his things down on top of the bed. As they walked out of the room, Nick pointed to the left:

'Oh, I nearly forgot… The loos are down the corridor to the right… and for the bathrooms you just go straight on up to the end.'

With Kweku sorted out, they headed back towards the reception. The continuing hubbub emanating from the garden as they neared it, punctuated by occasional cackles and uproarious guffaws, signalled that many parents were still enjoying the beauty of a rain-free English Spring day outside interacting closely with nature.

Nick made a beeline for Kweku's parents, who were by now chatting animatedly with one of the teachers.

'Mr and Mrs Mensah, …' he began.

'Oh, Nick, please, you can just call us Kojo and Deborah.'

'Thank you,' Nick chuckled. 'Anyway, I've brought Kweku back to you in one piece! He's comfortably settled into his room and is all now set.'

'Thank you so much, Nick, we're really grateful.'

The teacher chatting with the Mensahs addressed Nick:

'Ah, you're going to be the one showing Kweku the ropes are you, Ralston?'

'Yes, Sir.'

'Then Kweku is in good hands,' he said, turning to Kojo and Deborah.

Kojo turned to Kweku: 'Son, we've been having a really good chat with Mr Morris Bellington here. What a small world! He was out in Ghana shortly after the Second World War. In those days Ghana was still called the Gold Coast, you know …'

Bellington interrupted Kojo:

'Don't worry, Mr and Mrs Mensah. I'll be able to have a chat with him later… Oh, I must remind Roger about something… Goodbye for now then Kojo, Deborah, really pleased to have met you both. Maybe we can continue our discussion another time? …'

'That would be lovely, Morris, thank you,' Kojo said, Deborah nodding in agreement. Bellington turned to Kweku:

'Kweku, I'll see you in class.'

'Yes, Sir,' Kweku replied.

'Are you all right now then Kweku?' Nick asked.

'Yep, thanks.' Kweku purposely kept his reply short. He was already trying to sound more adult and assured.

'OK then, I'll catch up with you later for supper. Don't forget, supper's at 6:45. There'll be a bell and a roll call.'

'OK, thank you.'

Nick looked at Kweku's parents:

'Kojo, Deborah, don't worry, I'll look after Kweku. It's been really good meeting you both. Bye for now then.'

'Bye-bye Nick, thank you so much once again, we really appreciate it,' Kojo said. Deborah added coyly: '… and we're very happy you're the one who will be looking after Kweku.'

'No problem at all, you're welcome!' Nick was flattered by the compliment. 'Bye-bye.' With that, Nick sought out Ventham, then left the party.

Kojo and Deborah turned to Kweku, asking him alternately to confirm things to them directly, now that they were alone:

‘So, Coco, is everything OK in the room? ...’ ‘Are you all set? ...’ ‘Is there anything you’ve forgotten?’ The questions from his parents were tumbling into Kweku’s ears one after the other without pause; he wasn’t quite sure who was asking which question. He decided to respond with a collective reassurance.

‘Yes, everything is fine, Mum, Dad. Don’t worry, I’ll be fine.’

He followed them outside and up to the car. As they reached the car, his mum spoke first.

‘Coco, we fly to Ghana on Friday, so if there is anything you need, do let us know before then.’

‘OK yeah, I will.’

‘Well, Son,’ his dad hugged him, ‘Auntie Emily will be with you for half term, and then we’ll see you in Ghana for Christmas!’

His mum finally took over for her own hug. The tears were welling up again, as they had done before their first parting at the airport in Accra almost eight years earlier.

‘All right, Coco, then see you, be good,’ she said.

‘I will, Mum, don’t worry.’

She hugged and swayed him in her embrace for a while, then let go.

Kweku waved them off until the car turned the corner out of sight.

***

He went back to his room and started unpacking his things. He had almost finished when a loud bell rang continually for about ten seconds. Kweku knew it must be the bell for roll call before supper. Boys streamed out of their rooms from several floors, moving downstairs into the dining room. Kweku blended in with the surge and sat at the table for new boys.

Mr Ventham took the roll call. By the time they reached his name, Kweku had worked out that the answer was simply 'Sir' – not 'Yes, Sir' or 'Yes, Mr Ventham', and definitely not 'Yes, Roger'. There was one new boy who had got carried away by the informality of the reception in the garden earlier and addressed the Housemaster by his first name, to stifled tittering from other newbies. It earned an inquiring smile from Ventham, but a dark stare from the senior boy standing beside him. Kweku later learned from Nick that the senior boy glowering at the cheeky boy was Richard Miller, one of the two school supers in the house. He had a long memory, and Nick pitied the boy who had just got on his wrong side and would undoubtedly be marked out for closer scrutiny.

After supper, Kweku's two other roommates nattered away constantly about films, foreign trips and concerts they had enjoyed during the holidays. Once Kweku had finished unpacking, he just wanted to sleep. Eventually the other two tailed off and croaked out. The next morning Kweku didn't need the alarm clock his mum had bought for him. His roommates saw to that, shouting and throwing pillows at each other by 6 o'clock.

Breakfast wasn't the Savoy, nor had he expected that. But it was fine: cereal followed by a sausage and two pieces of toast with marmalade. Afterwards Kweku dressed up in full uniform, picking up his boater for the first time. It began to dawn on him what a nuisance this particular item of school apparel might be for him. But it was only when he had actually put it on a few times, felt its sharp edges and saw what it did to his curly malleable African hair, giving it the shape of a second boater underneath made of his black hair, that he came to a full realisation of what a disaster it was going to be.

Every time he removed the boater, he was going to have to struggle to pull out the flat-topped, round-edged shape it had given to his hair with and restore his coiffure to its original shape. It wasn't a question of vanity – he just didn't want his exposed head after removal of his hat to be shaped like a pie… Surely, no reasonable person could criticise anyone for seeing the humour in that? On the other hand, Kweku reasoned, why should Huntsmere have to dispense with such a distinguishing feature of its school uniform as the boater in order to suit the quirks of its first African pupil? Short answer: it shouldn't.

Kweku reckoned one solution might be for him to carry a small comb around with him everywhere, to return his hair to its normal shape every time he took his boater off. He tried doing that for a day, and then decided it wasn't his style – too vain.

Although sharp to touch, the boaters were light and brittle – easily falling apart due to their straw composition, unless well varnished. Some boys would double and triple varnish repairs to reinforce them, making them potentially lethal – like the hat of "Steed" Patrick Macnee in *The Avengers* or of "Oddjob" in the Bond film *Goldfinger*.

In time, Kweku grew to hate his boater more than anything else at the school. It was to be a recurring nuisance, mitigated only when his hair was trimmed short, leaving little to be re-shaped by the boater.

***

Not many boys in Kweku's year had chosen to do Greek. His very first session with the Classics teacher, Morris Bellington, consisted of a one-on-one exploratory conversation. Recalling they had met briefly at the new boys reception, Kweku sensed an instant familiarity as Bellington looked into his eyes. It was as if their paths had crossed in another life.

Bellington revealed to Kweku that he had taught Classics at his country's then only University at Legon, Accra, in the early post-war period. In those days Ghana was still a colony, named the Gold Coast by the British and earlier colonists after the imperishable resource which first brought them to its shores in search of wealth. The British had taken over from the Portuguese, Danish-Norwegians and Dutch, following them in realising that there were even greater riches to be amassed from trading in the most lucrative resource of all – human beings.

And so, although the British were by no means the first to export slaves from Africa, in order to satisfy the high demand for forced labour in the developing frontiers of the new world in the Caribbean and on the American continent, they were the first to seize the opportunity to turn the trade into a ruthless export machine, along what was euphemistically termed "the middle passage".

The middle passage represented the middle leg of a 3-legged journey for ships leaving Europe with manufactured goods, swapped in Africa for slaves purchased from warrior chiefs or private kidnappers, who were brought to the Caribbean or the American

Continent and in turn exchanged there for raw materials needed in Europe such as cotton from slave plantations for processing at the Lancashire mills.

The voyage across the Atlantic was consequently the second leg of the triangular journey. Huge fortunes were there to be made, and huge numbers of lives lost through sickness and appalling conditions at sea. The trade affected most cruelly the slaves chained from limb to limb and packed like canned sardines on the ships' lower decks. Although life expectancy for the ships' crew was higher, many of the sailors also lost their lives during the sea voyage in the wicked trade. Such was the desperation of the times.

Kweku felt an immediate affinity for Mr Bellington. He told Kweku that, apart from being Classics Professor at the University for a short time, he had also been instrumental in the establishment of the University's first comprehensive library. An extremely modest and self-effacing person, it was only in later years that Kweku would learn that Bellington's brother was the British hero who retrieved the Enigma machine and codebook from a sinking German U-boat in World War Two, enabling the team led by Alan Turing at Bletchley Park to crack the code and hasten the end of the war by at least two years according to many estimates, with millions of lives saved as a result.

Nor did Bellington divulge to Kweku that as a young marine he had himself been part of the team cracking Japanese codes at Bletchley Park during the war. However, what stood out for Kweku in that first conversation with Bellington was a comment Bellington made, which Kweku surmised had been prompted by the fact that he was in the company of the school's first ever African boy: 'You know, Kweku, Hitler made the great mistake of thinking that races were pure. He thought the British were pure… But of course, no race is pure. We in Britain for instance are a mix of Celts, Angles, Saxons, Vikings, Franks and so on beyond Europe's shores.'

It was a profound comment; one calculated, Kweku was sure, to console him that there was nothing impure about his own ethnic make-up, and that the world was really one big melting-pot. Kweku recalled these words years later. Glancing through an article in *The Times* on popular English surnames, Kweku observed that Smith, an Anglo-Saxon name, was the most common in England – no surprises there. But the second most common name in England, Jones, was actually Welsh – i.e. Celtic – in origin, as was the seventh most common name, Roberts. Another common surname, Robertson, meanwhile, was typically Scottish, and so again Celtic. Bellington's words were validated.

***

In moments during those early weeks of his first term, Kweku reflected that, if Glenwood had been disciplined and hierarchical, then Huntsmere was unashamedly even more formal in its structures and processes. Roll calls were conducted thrice daily, to ensure that no one slipped through the net. Deference to fellow pupils who had been at the school even one term longer was presumed, and, if not given, a grudge would be harboured for exaction of vengeance at a time when maximum impact could be attained.

It did not take Kweku long to register that he really was the only black student at the school. However pompous or presumptuous it might have been of him to think it, he now felt himself a constant target of judgment – real or imagined. He would have little control over whether such judgments would be fair or prejudiced; he could only do his best.

His mind went back to one of his parents' favourite mottoes: 'When in Rome, do as the Romans do.' This was advice they had not intended to connote any racial, ethnic or cultural undertones. And it had nothing to do with abandoning Ghanaian customs and culture. They did not expect him to do that and neither would they on their own trips to England... No, it was more to do with not imposing his Ghanaian culture on others if that jarred with extant norms where he was. If there was to be change, it should evolve, approved by the will of the majority of the existing inhabitants of the relevant area as expressed in a plebiscite or in their established local customs and common law, not be imposed arbitrarily by a minority, and certainly not imposed by agencies – national or international – based outside the area.

Huntsmere had its own governing structures, codes and procedures. It even had its own language. Teachers were "didacts" – you had to cap them if you passed them in the street. Prefects or "supers", as in other schools, were the co-ordinating link between didacts and boys, consulting with didacts, monitoring and supervising boys. Their most visible or memorable impact for boys came in the implementation of discipline, house supers in each House, school supers across the whole school.

Individuality and creativity had their place in academic thought, art, poetry and musical composition. But there could be no subjective interpretation of school rules. Respect had to be earned by being respectful to the status quo. The power to make suggestions to didacts for change was the preserve of the supers, unless other opinions were expressly sought. As the only African at the school then, Kweku found himself an unwilling pioneer in many different ways, but he soon realised he had better toughen up fast!

***

His first big challenge came in his third week. Walking between classes, he noticed a tall boy, a foot and a half taller than him, approaching with a lanky gait. He was red-faced, and his hairstyle resembled a circular saw collapsed from the centre into the shape of a dome around his head. By the time he neared to within twenty paces, Kweku sensed that for some reason he was bearing straight down in his direction.

To test his theory and reassure himself that he was only imagining it, he veered slightly to his right, nearer the edge of the pavement. Straightaway, he spied the other boy veering to his left to re-align himself on the same path, all the while keeping Kweku firmly fixed in his gaze. Well, Kweku resolved, good conduct is one thing, but he had never been one to run prematurely from any confrontation.

As they were about to cross, Kweku saw the fellow make a guttural sound to collect saliva in his mouth and, propelling his head forward in the same gesture, expel a huge gob of phlegm, not down on to the pavement, as Kweku had expected to maybe signal his disgust at something he had said or done which, unknown to Kweku, had offended him, but directly into Kweku's face.

As the globule of warm spit landed on Kweku's left cheek, slithering down, he felt a rush of adrenaline, his pulse quickening as he prepared to defend himself. With a supercilious backward flick of his head, using his right hand to comb his hair back into position, the boy continued past Kweku, in silence, without breaking his stride.

Still in a state of shock at the unprovoked nature of the abuse, Kweku removed a handkerchief from his breast pocket to wipe the spit off. He was faced with an instant dilemma: Should he run after this tall fellow? … He looked at least 2 years older than him. In a system where seniority was so heavily predicated on longevity at the school, there would be no possibility that his word would be accepted over his attacker's. Ah, but what if someone had witnessed the incident? He quickly cast around. He saw groups of two or three boys walking in both directions, engrossed in hurried discussions punctuated by giggles and chortles. Those walking on their own seemed to have their gaze fixed firmly on an indefinable space in front of them.

Out of the corner of his eye, he noticed a boy on the other side of the road slowing his stride, staring in his direction. Kweku adjusted his gaze to meet his. It was a young boy of Kweku's height, with the same slightly lost look that all newcomers to an institution have before experience boosts their self-confidence. Unfortunately for Kweku however, the moment their eyes locked, the boy hurriedly turned away, looking down. At best, he thought, this boy would be a reluctant witness; at worst, he would deny he had seen anything at all. As a new boy, Kweku concluded that for now he would rise above the affront and move on. He continued his walk to the next classroom, itching to tell his best friend James Sharpe and get his reaction to it all.

***

When he reached the classroom, the teacher hadn't arrived yet. A murmurous hubbub of schoolboy chatter criss-crossed the airwaves, occasionally interrupted by laughter.

Leaning in as he sat down next to James, Kweku began:

'You'll never guess what… I was going up the hill. Just as I passed Vale House this really tall, red-faced bloke, gangly gait, haircut just like Henry V at Agincourt, spat directly into my face. I couldn't believe it!'

'Oh, crap! What did he look like?' James asked.

'Er… OK, as he got closer, I noticed he had a broad nose, not as broad as mine of course, and thick red lips, not as…'

'Yeah, yeah, I get it!', James interjected. 'Ohhh, sugar! That must be Dennis Fletcher… Everyone knows him, he's a real bastard, a thug. Best just steer clear.'

'Really?'

'Yes,' James said, looking straight at Kweku. 'His family were out in South Africa, strong supporters of the apartheid regime… He's probably shocked to see a black guy at the school and wanted to let you know how he feels about it.'

'Hmmm,' Kweku's shoulders sagged. After a pause, getting himself back together, he sat back upright.

James continued: 'But he knows too well that, if he's caught doing anything unprovoked, they'll come down on him like a ton of bricks. So he's really sly. He usually takes a good look around first to check there are no didacts or school supers around before he does anything. A really sneaky bugger! Next time just cross the road, he's not going to go out of his way to follow you that far.'

'I see,' said Kweku, mortified that it seemed nothing more could be done but trying hard not to show it.

Just then there was a vigorous jerk on the door handle. A hushed silence suddenly took over the room, as the English teacher, Mr Lyme, who always looked as if he had just changed out of thespian clothes and a wig, swept in. He was decked in a flowing gown, a large tome and some loose papers tucked under his arm. Everyone quickly returned to their seats, and the lesson began with Mr Lyme, pacing up and down in front of the class, nose in the air, face puckered with the satisfaction of knowing what his students could not possibly yet know, plunging into a discussion of Shakespeare's Hamlet.

Fifty minutes later, the lesson was over. Kweku had enjoyed Lyme's exploration of human behaviour and motivation. But the encounter with Dennis Fletcher was still fresh in his mind and, in the vacuum after the lesson, it returned to the forefront of his thinking as he packed his exercise book and prep away in his satchel and removed his boater from the storage shelf under his desk.

As he walked back down the road outside to his next class on the other side of the hill, he drew comfort from James' advice that Fletcher had not behaved like a bastard only to him. He was thoroughly unpleasant to anyone who didn't think like him or, as in Kweku's case, look anything like him. In one sense that meant Fletcher's hatred of him was indeed personally aimed at him, in another it meant that his malign instincts targeted anyone who ruffled his highly irritable feathers, and so on that basis were impersonally aimed.

By the next day Kweku had banished the experience to distant corners of his memory. As he walked to a French lesson with a group of classmates, he heard a voice behind him calling out: 'Takoradi Mens!' He recognised the name of his country's major seaport and wondered who on earth among his classmates could have heard of or know about it.

He turned around to see that it was Andrew Bacon, who beamed back at him. Andrew had won an open scholarship to Huntsmere a year ahead of his age group and had opted to wait a year so that he could go through school with other scholars in his age group. Kweku was fascinated that one of his classmates knew anything about Ghana. He waited till Andrew had caught up with him. Andrew began:

'My dad ran quite a big construction business in India and the Far East. Later he set up businesses in Nigeria and Ghana…'

'Wow, really?'

'Yep. The business in Ghana didn't achieve the desired success, but Nigeria turned out to be a complete disaster. He lost all his equity out there.'

Even though Kweku came from Ghana and not Nigeria, he felt more than embarrassed – vicariously guilty of collapsing a classmate's father's global business empire. He was surprised, after his dad had undergone such an experience at the hands of Africans, that Andrew was still disposed to talk to him and get to know him. Here was someone, like him barely a teenager, with the maturity not to tar everyone from a broad ethnic group with the same brush. It was the opposite of the experience he'd undergone with Mr Simmonds, who had blamed him for losses suffered by his family in a country on the other side of the African continent from Ghana during the Mau Mau crisis.

They walked the rest of the way together up to French class chatting about Ghana and life at school generally and remained good friends from that day on.

***

"Boy! Boy! Boooyyyy!" The shout went up from the top of the stairwell at one end of The Mount. All the new boys knew what that meant. The last one to arrive would get whatever task a super had decided to assign. Fagging – a system under which supers could get new boys to act as their lackeys for virtually any job they pleased, frivolous or otherwise – was still rife. Today the last to arrive was Kweku.

'Ahh, Mensah!' the super said, grinning as he handed him a cassette tape in its case. 'Take this tape over to the head of house at The Hectare.' The other boys, relieved to have dodged the bullet on that occasion, lifted their hands to their mouths to hide smirks or stifle giggles as Kweku received the tape in silence.

He walked out of The Mount in the direction of The Hectare on the other side of the hill. As soon as he was out of sight, he couldn't resist opening the cassette case to take a peek at what kind of information on it warranted all the yelling and sprinting that had just occurred. He sighed as he read the label: the subject was no urgent school administration issue – just Elton John's *Honky Château*.

Although himself a big fan of Elton, in the absence of an official school purpose for the assignment he had been given, he had difficulty squaring the implication that the super's time was intrinsically more important than the new boys'. He didn't know it then, but happily, in large part thanks to the efforts of a later head boy at the school, the fagging system would soon be abolished.

***

Days after his first fagging errand, Kweku had to endure an unsavoury incident. It didn't involve anyone at the school, rather a family passing through the school. As the father drove his Triumph convertible sports car through the hill, the soft roof fully drawn back on a fine Spring day, his wife in the passenger seat and two young children at the rear, he sparkled with joy as he surveyed the school's historic buildings.

Suddenly his face went white with shock, as if he had just seen a ghost. His car decelerated. He asked out loud, his question clearly audible to Kweku, turning round as he passed Kweku to check from the front that he hadn't just passed a white Huntsmere boy dressed in blackface but a real live negro: 'What's that black wog doin' at 'untsmere?'

In that moment, a mixture of emotions darted across Kweku's mind. The brutality of the comment caught him off guard, coming out of the blue as it had. In an instant, he decided it wasn't worth rising to the bait of the provocation. The other occupants in the car glanced round briefly to see what the father was fussing over, saw Kweku, and quickly swivelled their heads back round to face the front, unsure what to make of what they had just seen or how to respond to their father's consternation. The father's neck meanwhile remained cricked, fixated on Kweku as his car continued rolling down the hill and out of sight. Kweku knew he had inadvertently ruined the person's afternoon enjoyment of Huntsmere, but the man only had his own bigotry to blame for that.

Kweku didn't bother reporting the incident to the school authorities… What did it have to do with them? It was just symptomatic of what was going on in the wider society. In any case, even at a young age, Kweku's exposure to life on both sides of the fence had already shown him that discrimination was not limited to white versus coloured. It was alive within even the smallest communal settlements, wherever sweeping prejudicial assessments about differing personal attributes could be made, not limited to skin colour.

***

After the half term break, Kweku was going downstairs to supper one evening when he couldn't help overhearing a conversation between two boys walking in front of him. One was saying he had been on the big dipper roller coaster at Battersea Park funfair the previous week. It had been a real thrill, but the devastating news about a fatal accident there had really shaken him. Kweku caught up with them:

'What? Did you say the big dipper at the Battersea funfair? I nearly went on that some years back!' he said.

'Some years back? My dad took me there just last week!'

'So, what happened?' Kweku asked him.

'Haven't you heard? Where have you been? You should thank your lucky stars – I know I have! There was a serious accident there last Tuesday. Apparently a rope snapped when they were hauling the train up the first slope at the start. It rolled back down, crashed into another train and left the tracks. At least five kids died, several more were injured.'

Kweku went numb with shock. His mind went back to the time his mum took him there but stopped him from going on the roller coaster because she was worried and thought he was too young. He felt desperately sorry for the children who had lost their lives in the midst of having so much fun, in such a colourful wonderland. It was an early reminder to him of the ever-present role of luck in determining the course of people's lives.

***

The next term a second African, a Nigerian, Chikwe Nwaike, joined the school. He was in a different house and form to Kweku and they rarely met. But he was a superb athlete and quickly became a sporting hero.

Kweku's own sporting record at Huntsmere was nothing like it had been at Glenwood. Now severely myopic, he needed to wear glasses all the time. He experimented with contact lenses, but they were made of perspex, a hard plastic, and if he forgot to take them out and fell asleep with them on, the inside of his eyelids were so sore the next day he couldn't wear them at all. If that happened, wearing spectacles the next day would be useless, as his eyes needed at least a day to re-focus to the greater distance to the correcting refraction lens.

In his beloved sport of Rugby, he tried to resume his place on the wing. He was selected once for the school's Colts 1st XV, but it was hopeless, as he couldn't see far beyond his nose, and he was substituted at half time.

With sports now off the menu, to while away his afternoons he taught himself chess. He enjoyed analysing the moves of the greats like Capablanca, Alekhine, the creative genius Mikhail Tal and the new kid on the block Bobby Fischer, the cocky American whose recent defeat of Boris Spassky at the world championship in Reykjavik had been viewed by the Soviet Union as a national disgrace. In time-honoured fashion for the ruthless transactional style of totalitarian governments, Spassky had been driven to the event on the first day in a Rolls Royce with all the trimmings but, following his defeat to a citizen of his country's nemesis, was left to find his own way back home using public transport.

***

No longer engaged in regular physical activity, Kweku was struggling to maintain his weight. Added to his problems, his antipathy towards his boater led indirectly to the one occasion, in the Lent term of his second year, when he was fined. Fining was a sanction only school supers could dispense – for failure to adhere to dress codes or any other adjudged misconduct.

In Kweku's case, he was spotted carrying his boater under his arm, instead of wearing it. He was on a short walk between two classrooms and he thought he would be able to get away with it. Unfortunately for him, his shirt had also fallen out at the back, making the shape of a tail visible under his blazer. The hanging shirt tail caught the attention of a school super, who appeared seemingly out of nowhere:

'Hey you, what's your name?' the super demanded.

'Mensah, Sir.'

'Who?'

'Mensah, Sir. Kweku Mensah.'

'Can you spell that for me?' the super said, removing a pen and small pre-printed notepad from his inside breast pocket. He wrote on it in designated spaces as Kweku spelt out his entire name.

'Sunday! Be there!' he said, tearing off the note. He thrusted it in Kweku's direction and pointed to a location opposite Assembly identified in a stamped logo at the top of the note. Kweku received the note gingerly as the super marched off. He looked at it. He could see his name and the time of his appointment but couldn't see any amount indicated as the fine.

He dreaded his trip to the supers' office. He had described the super who fined him to his steer, Nick Ralston. As he was the only one of the twenty school supers who wore glasses, Nick told him it must have been Chris Parkinson. Kweku told Nick that no amount was shown on the docket. Nick shrugged his shoulders. He told him that, for the offences shown on the note, his fine shouldn't exceed five pounds. He added a warning that fining was a demonstration of discretionary power over the boys which some of the school supers enjoyed exercising. So, when he went to their office, he should make sure not to do anything cheeky, otherwise he could easily be fined again and it could end up as a revolving door situation for him.

On the Sunday Kweku put on his tailcoat, pin-striped trousers, white shirt and an immaculately buttoned white collar, ensuring there was no sign of his shirt below the border of his waistcoat. Finally donning his boater full square, he set off for the supers' office. He was now running slightly late, as he'd had to request fresh directions on the way due to wrong information he'd been given by another boy, he was sure unintentionally. He reached a small door in the complex adjacent to the entry to Assembly. A metallic dark blue nameplate mounted at the top was inscribed with the words "Supers' Office". This was the right place. One other boy was waiting outside. Kweku didn't recognise him.

'Is someone in there?' Kweku asked him.

'Yeah… he's been in there for ages. Quite a lot of shouting going on… sounds pretty bad… What did they get you for?'

‘Not wearing my boater – I had it tucked under my arm.’

‘Ha ha! I know, they’re such a nuisance.’

‘Yeah, but at least they can’t put your hair out of shape. You’re lucky, you can just shake your hair out when you take it off. In my case when I take my boater off, I’m left with a mini-boater of fuzzy hair!’

‘Ha ha! Fair point there.’

‘It’s not funny actually; it’s a real pain.’

‘Sorry.’

‘My shirt was also hanging out at the back. Actually I reckon that’s what first put him on to me.’

‘Uh-oh, some of the supers are quite strict on that one.’

‘What about you, what are you here for?’

‘Oh, I was running late for Spug’s lesson last Monday and in the rush forgot to put on my tie. Mostyn’s the super who got me.’

‘Oh yeah, everyone’s heard of him. A real stickler, quite trigger-happy… Anyway, my name’s Kweku, Kweku Mensah… And you?’

‘Roberts, Cornell Roberts… I know what you’re thinking ...’

Kweku had to restrain himself from smirking.

Roberts continued: ‘Whatever you do, don’t call me…’

‘Yeah I know.’

‘Don’t call me “Corny”.’

Kweku couldn’t resist a brief chuckle. Fortunately, Roberts had a sense of humour and smiled. At that moment it occurred to Roberts that there was nothing routine about Kweku’s name either in an English context.

‘What about your name then? Mensa? What’s that then?’ he added jokingly. ‘Latin for a “table” or what? Like “Mensa, Mensa, Mensam, Mensae, Mensae, Mensa? Eh? Or does it mean you’re a member of Mensa?” He burst into a full-throated guffaw, before Kweku pointed to the door of the office and raised his index finger to his mouth: ‘Shhh!’

They were now joined by a third boy.

Looking at Kweku, Roberts continued: ‘Anyway, about the boater, I hear they’re going to be relaxing the rules on that soon.’

‘Really, when?’ Kweku asked.

‘Could be next year, I think. I hear you might be able to get away with not wearing them in the afternoons and at weekends – except Sunday mornings of course … But you’ll still have to carry them, and you’ll have to raise them to cap any didacts if you’re passing them …’

Just then, the door finally opened. A boy looking surprisingly quite senior sidled out, appearing shell-shocked, face flushed bright red from the ordeal he’d just been through. Kweku caught a glimpse of a super at the head of the table shouting ‘Who’s next? Come on, hurry up!’ He recognised the head of school, Charlie Reeder-Taylor. He had always seemed to Kweku quite reticent when seated in Assembly, but he was obviously now more relaxed, with his peers, in their own space, so to speak.

‘Good luck!’ Kweku whispered to Roberts as he knocked and went slowly in.

Roberts wasn’t in there for long. All too soon, before Kweku had been able to rehearse and act out various scenarios to cover every eventuality, the door opened again. Roberts emerged looking decidedly relieved. 'Just be nice to them,' he whispered to Kweku. 'Anyway, it worked for me. Best of luck.'

'OK next!' The bark came from inside the room.

Kweku knocked softly and entered. Reeder-Taylor beckoned him forward. As he approached their table, he felt the eyes of all twenty school supers following his every move. He had no time to observe the décor of the room and kept his gaze downward to avoid any of them thinking he wanted to challenge their authority.

'And you are? ...' Reeder-Taylor began.

'Kweku Mensah, Sir.'

'Come again?'

'He's mine, Charlie, wasn't wearing his boater, shirt untucked at the back.' Kweku recognised the super who had fined him.

'All right, Chris. Then you handle it.'

Parkinson gave Kweku a long stare. After a while, he asked him: 'So, you heard what I said earlier. Do you have anything to say for yourself?'

'No, Sir.'

'Well, here we care a lot about dress code. We want the right thing to be done.'

Another pregnant pause followed, which Kweku felt prompted to fill with a formulaic 'Yes, Sir!'

Parkinson continued: 'So you don't get to dress just anyhow and think you're going to get away with it.'

'Yes, Sir… I mean, No, Sir… I mean…' Some of the supers burst out in laughter at Kweku's hapless confusion.

But Parkinson, starting to feel some sympathy for him, was in a mood to move on.

'OK, so that'll be four pounds,' he said.

Their “takings” for the day – fines paid – were piled up in the middle of the table in front of Reeder-Taylor. Kweku didn’t have the exact amount. He had a five-pound note, two one-pound notes and one of the decimal fifty new pence coins. Paradoxically, he now desperately wished his fine had been one pound more, at five pounds. It would have meant one pound less for tuck, but at least that way he could have just put his fiver down to settle things and hastened the end of the nightmare.

The supers were silent, just staring at him. He felt like an actor left alone on stage to deliver a soliloquy, only in this case the last thing that was expected from him was a performance. Scrutinising more closely the pile of notes and coins on the table, he spotted a few one-pound notes. He put down his fiver, picked up one of the one-pound notes and was about to put it in his inside pocket when Parkinson yelled:

‘Heyy! What do you think this is here? Some kind of casino, or what?’

Kweku froze momentarily. Then, recovering whatever composure he could, he replaced the one-pound note on the table and turned towards Parkinson, stumped and looking earnestly at him for a lifeline. Another awkward silence ensued before Parkinson put Kweku out of his misery:

‘All right, Mensah. Go away and come back next Sunday with the correct amount. We’re not bankers here, eh? We don’t give change. Understood? … Do you want me to give you another ticket to remind you?’

‘No, Sir.’

'OK… Make sure you're here next week – same time – with the exact amount.'

'You can go now.' Reeder-Taylor uttered the final words freeing Kweku from his torment, allowing him to taste the freshness of the Spring air outside. Kweku resolved never to get into trouble with the supers again once the current tribulations were over, hopefully in a week's time.

The following Sunday he was back at the supers' office, on time, with the exact amount of the fine. Feeling a bit of a veteran, he even had time to coach a Shell new-boy who had just been fined and was as ignorant of the arcane mysteries of the intimidating appearance before the supers as Kweku had been the previous week. It was the first time Kweku felt he had earned a rite of passage at the highest levels of discipline at the schoolboy level not involving didacts, and he emerged gratefully battle-hardened from the experience.

***

An Awkward Encounter

May 1973

In the summer term of his second year at Huntsmere, Kweku was the on the receiving end of a surprise visit of a figure from his past. As he approached The Mount on his way back from classes for lunch, he thought he saw in the distance someone looking like Mr Simmonds, his English teacher at Glenwood. Initially, he ascribed this sight to a wayward imagination trying perversely to scupper his efforts to achieve precious mental equilibrium in his new environment. He was shocked to realise, as he got closer, that it really was Simmonds, and that he was looking directly at Kweku, remorse seemingly etched all over his face.

'How are you?' Simmonds began. Kweku was caught unawares. He paused before responding. He had not expected he would ever cross paths with this particular person in his life again and was unsure how to react. Should he exact a high price for his forgiveness, if getting that was indeed why Simmonds was there? … It just wasn't in his nature to be vindictive. He rationalised that the best way to leave that whole experience in the past was not to pick it up again:

'I'm fine, thank you.'

'And how are you finding it here?'

'It's OK, everything is OK.'

'You know, I am so sorry for what I put you through during your time at Glenwood. I have come to realise it wasn't at all fair on you. I was still going through some personal issues at the time... I was very bitter about something that simply wasn't your fault.'

'It's OK Sir, don't worry.'

Simmonds stood there watching Kweku, unsure what to say next. But Kweku was as stuck as he was. Both of them knew what an awful experience Simmonds had repeatedly put him through, and Kweku knew that it was only the intervention of the Headmaster, Mr Bairstowe, which had repaired, partly, the wounds of his punctured confidence with the English language.

A long silence followed as Simmonds continued staring wistfully at Kweku, unable to say any more. Kweku decided to wrap matters up. 'Don't worry, Sir, it's OK.' He motioned to the front door at The Mount. 'I've got to be going, Sir. Thank you for coming.'

Simmonds nodded. As Kweku turned away, he noticed Simmonds' eyes watering and could see him reaching into his pocket. Simmonds had behaved appallingly towards him for a protracted period at Glenwood. Kweku felt sorry for him and had forgiven him, but now he had his own life to try to live as best he could. He entered the house without looking back.

***

Late one night, as Kweku was cramming for mock exams at the start of his third year at Huntsmere, he heard a loud bang. The mirror came crashing down from his window sill. Soon word was going round. Alarms were sounding off and there was a hive of activity around the building adjacent to The Mount. Boys emerging from their rooms were told by the

Housemaster and supers to get back inside and stay inside.

By the next day it was confirmed that the Provisional IRA had detonated a bomb in the bedroom of the son of one of the didacts, Lt. Colonel Daniel Engman, who ran the school's Combined Cadet Force. The bomb had been placed on a timer after careful observation by the bombers of his and his son's routines. By a lucky twist of fate, Engman and his son had moved out of the house the day before. So the bombers missed their targets.

All the boys nicknamed Engman 'General Dan'. He had a halting gait, which according to the word on the grapevine was likely due to an injury received while on active service. With his towering height, wide arm-span, massive hands and commanding demeanour, Engman reminded Kweku of a famous Rugby number 8 forward of the day, Wales' Mervyn Davies or 'Merve the Swerve', to use the sobriquet popularised by everyone's favourite rugby commentator of the day, the 'Voice of Rugby', the great Bill McLaren. Kweku had always thought the 'General Dan' nickname was a joke. He only found out from school gossip after the bomb that Engman had actually had a distinguished career in the Army and this, as well as his leadership of the school's CCF, could have made him a prime target.

***

July 1975

Kweku came out of his last A-level exam, French written, quite satisfied. The earlier French oral exam accounted for one fifth of the marks. He thought he had done OK in that one. But this one had gone even better; he spent the last 20 minutes of the exam looking around the room wondering why most pupils were still writing. It was only during the usual post-mortem discussions with other boys outside the classroom and into the street that he realised he had misread the instructions on the front page of the exam paper and answered only 3 instead of 4 questions.

He was crestfallen. The minimum requirement for entry to Oxford for his chosen course was 3 A's. Now, no matter how well he had done in Latin and Greek, he wouldn't get in. It ruined his post-exam celebrations. As he walked listlessly back to The Mount, disheartened, he heard Steve Harley & Cockney Rebel's *Make Me Smile* blaring out of one student's window. It seemed to be played just to mock him. He returned to his room and removed from his suitcase a bottle of Dry Sack sherry. He had bought it with his pocket money during half term from a local off-licence in Highgate, posing as an 18-year-old even though still only 16, and smuggled it into school, hidden under old clothes.

He flew home to Ghana in mid-July, relieved to be able to escape to a new environment to house that post-exam/pre-results vacuum, where you feel helpless to change a fate already in motion. When the results finally came out in a telegram received in mid-August, he was stunned: 3 A's! He thought there must be some mistake – particularly with the French result – but dared to hope that there wasn't.

His parents were ecstatic. His dad straightaway took to ringing round friends to share the good news. His mum cocked her head with a big smile and embraced him. It brought home to Kweku how much it all meant to them. He felt a measure of self-fulfilment and above all relief that he had been able to reward in some way their enormous sacrifices on his behalf over many years.

For the first time since he won that scholarship to Huntsmere three years earlier, Kweku felt special, and for the rest of the holiday, he could do no wrong in his parents' eyes. His dad doubled his allowance for outings with friends to the beach and cinema, and his mum stuffed him full of his favourite foods, no holds barred. At the same time he felt embarrassed, as we often do when unexpected success comes our way. And in a sense he also felt somewhat of a fraud, because of the French result, which he still could not quite believe. He was afraid there would be a follow-up telegram correcting the result to a B or C instead.

In the first French lesson of his next and final term at Huntsmere, the famously sardonic and dismissive head of French, Nigel Walbrook, remarked, looking directly at him, then chuckling, that there was one person in the form who had only bothered attempting 3 out of the 4 written questions and still managed to get an A. Only then did Kweku realise it must be true.

Walbrook added: 'Well done!' Kweku was struck, as this particular teacher was highly regarded and known to be extremely sparing with any kind of commendation for anyone or anything. The talk among the boys was that he had played a heroic role in problem-solving with the intelligence services behind the scenes during World War Two. Even though a few brilliant students in the class had been congratulated by him more than once, it was the first time Kweku had been complimented by Walbrook. It inspired in him a confidence with French that he would never lose.

***

Kweku didn't make it into the Olympus Club for the school's top sportsmen. Although he won some academic prizes, he failed to motivate himself sufficiently to climb the sporting and prefectural heights which he had attained at Glenwood. His short-sightedness did hold him back in his favourite sport of rugby, but it was no excuse for a failure to get to grips with wearing contact lenses and trying a racquet sport or having a go at cricket, for instance. In many ways his failure at sports was a self-inflicted one possibly grounded in an innate and lingering embarrassment about being too successful. It was as if he preferred always to fly just under the radar, sampling beautiful views from invisible heights below the parapet.

His Housemaster, Mr Ventham, told him that if he was prepared to stay on for another year and leave the school at the more usual 18 years of age instead of 17, then during that last year he would be under consideration for appointment as a school super. But Kweku's successful admission to Johnston College, Oxford brought with it the tantalising prospect of a "year off", a year in which he would be free to explore the world on his own (subject to receipt of enough travel and pocket money from Mum and Dad, of course!). During such an extended hiatus, he would be unfettered by adult oversight for the first time in his life, have the space to "find himself" in the common parlance of the day – to do something wacky like sheep-farming in Australia on the other side of the globe.

In his thinking at the time, he didn't wish to sacrifice an opportunity to explore more of the world outside the confines of school or parental supervision for the comparatively mundane purpose of rising through the ranks to earn his turn to lord it over or sanction more junior boys for peccadilloes. But it turned out to be an immature choice: a precious opportunity was lost to reinforce the grounding in the ropes of shouldering the burdens of fairness, responsible exercise of authority and self-discipline which he had first encountered while head boy at Glenwood.

CHAPTER NINE

No Guardrails

December 1975

For Kweku, leaving Huntsmere was like walking into a three-dimensional blank canvas, paintbrush in one hand, palette in the other, free to choose the brushstrokes and colours to create snapshots of his life's odyssey from then on, with no one – and nothing but his own conscience – to watch over or judge him. Before the year was out, he would turn 18, the age society had set for personal responsibility, although 21 was still recognised as the age of maturity, and 25 by wily older folk as the true age of first understanding of the map of the adult world and its workings, as in the brilliant Victorian novel, Anstey's *Vice Versa: A Lesson To Fathers*.

Intoxicated by the bliss of unsupervised freedom, he wanted to go everywhere, experience virtually everything, although his conscience did place some restrictions on his self-indulgence. And he could not bring himself to demand too much from his parents to cover the expenses of his voyage of self-discovery, even though he was an only child and, in economic terms, could have exploited his scarce supply to bid up his price. A lifetime of care and sacrifice on their part deserved better.

So he would choose 3 cities to explore outside Ghana and UK – Rome and Athens, modern capital cities that had been homes for the legendary figures, classical arts and thinking that had fascinated him since his youth, and Paris, a celebrated magnet for romantics and culture vultures like him.

In Rome, he was amazed at how much of the ancient world was still left standing through all the intervening wars and pillage, even though now in ruins, no longer intact. The Colosseum, where gladiators had literally fought for their lives just to entertain the public; the Forum, where market dealers traded their wares and people gathered to gossip and peddle theories about everything and nothing.

He noticed that almost every grown-up around him was smoking. These were days when the potentially very harmful effects of smoking were being debated but not yet settled. He decided to try a cigarette, coughed when he tried to inhale his first two, and afterwards began to get the hang of it. He quickly found that cigarettes gave an adult flavour to the atmosphere and provided an alternate crutch to a drink. Cigarettes and alcohol seemed to go hand in hand. He had left school, so was an adult now, nothing was forbidden. At the time, he was OK with that.

***

Grovel
June 1976

Kweku returned to London in June to see a furore in the papers over comments made by the English cricket captain, Tony Greig. He suggested that the West Indian players had a soft underbelly and said he intended, with the help of teammates, "to make them grovel" in the forthcoming Test series. The headlines "I Intend To Make Them Grovel" or "Grovel!" screamed across the front and back pages of all the popular daily tabloids.

Even though Kweku was not a West Indian, as virtually every other black person in England those days, he was proud of the incredible bunch of cricketers the West Indies had become under the captaincy of the legendary Clive Lloyd. Batsmen like Roy Fredericks, Gordon Greenidge, Alvin Kallicharran and the great Viv Richards, who demonstrated that you could chew gum and execute a brilliantly-timed cover drive at the same time, lined up alongside gifted pace bowlers like Andy Roberts and Michael Holding, who were every bit as terrifying for batsmen at the crease as Thommo and the great Dennis Lillee were.

Kweku couldn't resist the chance to see if Tony Greig's highly provocative taunt – calculated, Kweku and others were sure, to ensure maximum publicity for the tour and ultimately successfully achieving just that – would be metaphorically rammed straight back down his throat. He bought tickets for the last day of the Second Test at Lord's, just half an hour down the road by bus from his parents' Highgate house.

There was an electric buzz all around the ground as he queued to go through the turnstiles and took his seat in the stands near the Nursery End. The beer was cold and English and West Indian fans sparred vicariously with good humour through their sporting heroes on the pitch.

English fans naturally presumed that Kweku was a West Indian, too. To avoid complications, Kweku played along with this fallacy for short conversations.

After all, he was there to watch cricket, not to tell his life story. But, if anyone did ask where he came from, he told them straightforwardly that he was from Ghana. As mentioned, it didn't really matter to either side, as all black people of the day adopted that incredibly successful West Indies team of the 70s as their own – along the lines of that famous saying about success having many children and failure being an orphan, or words to that effect.

Viv Richards wasn't playing that day, but the mixed roars and groans from the crowd as Andy Roberts mopped up England's tail enders before Fredericks had a good knock were confirmation enough that – glad, sad or mad – everyone had been entertained. Eventually the match ended in a draw, but for Kweku it was money well spent. It was now time for him to return to Ghana for the last leg of his extended holiday.

***

Deborah met Kweku at the airport. As they embraced, he noticed she had an unusually anxious look on her face. Victor shook his hand and they began walking the short distance to the car park.

'So, Coco, how was the flight?' Deborah asked.

'Fine thank you, Mum. But Mum, what's wrong?'

'Wait till we're in the car.'

In the comfort and relative privacy of the car, she broke the news to Kweku.

'It's your Uncle Kwame up in Pepease, near Abetifi. His wife Auntie Mavis phoned your dad from the post office at Nkawkaw late yesterday to say he'd not been feeling well for a fortnight. At first they thought it was just the usual malaria, so she was giving him quinine tablets. But he wasn't getting better so she took him to the local clinic. The doctor there didn't know what it was either but thought it could be malaria. They took some tests which haven't come back yet and in the meantime gave him a big anti-malarial jab in case. But yesterday evening he took a sudden turn for the worse, so Auntie Mavis rushed him to the District Hospital at Nkawkaw. It's only then that she told your dad about it.'

'Oh no!' Kweku exclaimed.

'Your father straightaway wanted to arrange an ambulance to bring him down to Accra, but he couldn't get hold of anyone as it was night. The business has been going well, so we have two drivers nowadays. But the new one, Justin, whom we're still trying out anyway, had already closed from work and gone home. So your dad drove himself up to Nkawkaw overnight. I wanted him to wait and leave with Victor early this morning. I mean, you know how dangerous night-driving can be here with poor street lighting and broken-down vehicles left on the roads unattended. But your father insisted and well, you know what he's like once he's made his mind up! He rang from Nkawkaw early this morning to say Uncle Kwame's condition had worsened. His BP is sky high and they want it to stabilise before they try moving him anywhere.'

'Oh my God.'

'Anyway, we decided not to tell you, as it was the night before your flight, and there was nothing you could have done about it anyway.'

By now they were outside the gates to the house. Victor honked the car horn. The night security peeped through his side door to check and opened the gates. As they drove in, Kweku saw Tina walking up through the verandah towards the car, fighting hard to hold back tears. He feared the worst.

'Madam, Papa just called,' she told Deborah as they alighted from the car.

'Yes?'

'He's gone… Uncle Kwame has gone.' Tina, ever genuinely empathetic, let out an anguished wail.

'Oh noooo!' Deborah said.

Sobbing intermittently, Tina continued: 'So Papa said when you get back you should call him please. He is at Nkawkaw. He said he gave you the number for the hospital already yesterday but asked me to write it down again in case. Here it is.' Tina handed Deborah the note and she rushed straight over to make the call. The receptionist answered the phone and asked an assistant to call Kojo to the phone. He came on the line, pausing intermittently to gather himself as he spoke:

'D, oh, D … if only they had told me earlier that he wasn't well.'

'Ohhh, I am so sorry Kojo… But why did they leave it so late before telling you?'

'They didn't think it was that serious… Mavis is beside herself with grief.'

'So, what was it in the end?'

'They don't know yet… By the time I got here, he had already lost consciousness. They did their best to bring him round but it was too late.'

'Ohh, D, I am so sorry.'

'I'll be here with the family for a while… As the eldest of the siblings, they are looking to me to supervise everything… you know, getting a death certificate, moving the body to a morgue and funeral arrangements. Anyway, the first of the funeral ceremonies to organise, as by tradition, will be the One-Week celebration, a week from today.'

'All right Kojo. Ohhh, I'm so sorry. But please take care over there. Do you have everything you need?'

'Yes, D... Please, don't worry, I'm fine; it's the least of my concerns.'

'But D, I have to worry. No matter what else is going on, you must take care of yourself too.'

'Did Coco arrive safely?'

'Yes, he's fine. We just got back from the airport. Here's right here. Please hold on and speak to him.' She handed the receiver to Kweku:

'Hi dad, I'm so sorry.'

'Well, Son, man proposes, God disposes… It's tough, but there you are… So how was the flight?'

'Everything was fine, thank you Dad.'

'OK, at least that's good to hear…'

Kweku heard someone calling his father in the background.

'All right, Son, I have to go now. Say bye to your mum for me will you? And I'll see you both up here for the One-week.'

'The One-week? What's that?'

'Don't worry, Son, your mum will explain it to you. Bye for now.'

'Bye, Dad.'

'Mum, he said he's been called away and to say goodbye to you. But Mum, what's a One-Week? He said you'd explain it to me.'

'Ah, let me tell you. It's about time you understood more about our traditions here; this is stuff they can't teach you in England…'

'But I've always been ready to learn more, Mum.'

'I know, Coco, it's not your fault. Actually, look, you've just got home from a long journey and it's late. I'll tell you everything tomorrow. For now, rush upstairs, have a bath and then come back downstairs for supper. We've made garden egg stew and kontomire with fish, yam and rice.'

'Thanks a lot, Mum.' Both of them knew that, with the news just in, he wouldn't be able to enjoy his food in the same way.

Kweku started upstairs and Deborah headed for her usual armchair in the living room. Then she suddenly turned round and called after him. He stopped at the top of the stairs. 'Ah, Coco, I nearly forgot to ask: did Bill not give you any mail at the airport for us?'

'Oh, yes, sorry Mum, it's in my hand luggage. Tina's already taken it upstairs so I'll get it later.'

'And then did you remember to get the Toblerone for your dad as well?'

'Yes, that too. I also brought some Matchmakers mint-flavoured chocolate for you.'

'Oh, isn't that sweet of you to think of Mummy too!' She cocked her head and smiled, gratified to be appreciated by her son without having to ask for it.

'All right Mum, I'll be back soon.'

The following day, after a breakfast of kenkey, red pepper, shito black pepper sauce, sardines and a boiled egg, his mum sat him down to explain more to him about Ghanaian funeral traditions. He already knew many of them vaguely, but as a younger child had been given a pass on having to attend the full length of funeral ceremonies. Now he had come of age and was about to go to University. He also had increased stamina for the slog of attending traditional observances. And this time the deceased was a close family member – a real uncle, no less. So Deborah felt it was time he learnt more. She began:

'Here, when someone dies, it sets in motion a whole chain of events in terms of ceremonies. The first is the One-Week celebration…'

Kweku interrupted, puzzled: 'Celebration when someone has died? That doesn't sound right.'

'I know, maybe it doesn't sound right, but that's our tradition. The idea is that we celebrate someone's life rather than mourn their death. Their death, well, once it's happened, we can't do anything about it… But we can do something about how they are remembered… Now, that doesn't mean funerals are about merry-making. Not at all. A seriousness rooted in respect must be maintained until after the body has been buried. But then again, there can be happy reminiscences and jokes exchanged about the deceased, without indicating a loss of respect for them.'

'I see.'

'The One-Week Celebration is usually held at the last known residence of the deceased exactly one week to the day from their passing, although it can be postponed beyond a week to facilitate attendance by important family members or prominent friends of the deceased. Short public announcements of the person's passing may be made in the media, once close family members have been informed and have agreed the text, but the occasion of the One-Week marks the official confirmation of the death by the family to the outside world.

Every deceased person must have a religion attached to them, even if they were non-observant while alive. After brief religious prayers officiated by a person of the cloth from the deceased's religion, a spokesperson for the family provides a rough narrative of what has transpired and how the person died…'

'You mean, even if the circumstances of their death are embarrassing?'

'Well, not as such. For now, any controversial aspects are glossed over, and the focus is on the basics. For instance, you can just say the deceased was taken ill without specifying the illness, even if you know the reason. Of course, there can be exceptions where the principal family members who cared for the deceased while they were alive agree.'

‘OK.’

‘Now, if, in the period since the person died, the family has been able to agree on a date for the funeral weekend, then this is communicated to well-wishers attending the One-Week as one of the principal purposes of that ceremony.’

Deborah would go on to explain that funerals traditionally took place over a whole weekend. The funeral weekend for deceased Christians would typically begin on a Thursday or Friday evening with a wake-keeping, where the body is laid in state for people to file past and pay their respects, before a burial service on a Friday or Saturday morning respectively, followed by interment – which often only family and very close friends are invited to attend – and then final funeral rites, the main traditional ceremony where the family are seated to receive the respects of well-wishers, including any donations. On the Sunday, there is a Thanksgiving Service in the morning followed finally by a family gathering at the family home. The family gathering is a lavish, informal affair where well-wishers are treated to a full buffet of assorted dishes, accompanied by a pig, sheep or goat roasted on a spit and a generous variety of drinks.

***

In the event the funeral for Uncle Kwame was fixed for the last weekend in August. It turned out that he died from a salmonella infection. He was fond of eating takeaway snack foods while doing his rounds as a sales manager for a drinks company, and there was speculation that he had picked it up from either chicken or fish eaten at one of those food joints. However, the true source of the infection was never determined.

The wake-keeping was to be held on Friday night. It had been decided that Victor would bring Kweku up from Accra to Abetifi the day before, as Kojo was trying out the other driver, Justin, with him in Abetifi. It was an opportunity for a now 18-year-old Kweku to chat with Victor about the world in a way he hadn't been able to during all those years growing up as a kid and being told that so many subjects that he wanted to delve deeper into were taboo, to be explained to him one day. Now he was able to discuss things on the same level as adults and wanted to be taken more seriously.

Victor for his part was anxious to hear from Kweku all about life in Europe. He had an aunt who'd had a chance to go to London to work as a nurse 10 years earlier. But, once there, with few exceptions for major family events, she hadn't really bothered keeping in touch with any of her relatives back home in Ghana, preferring to focus on her 'new life' instead.

Apart from the different weather, infrastructure and surroundings on display in the UK, Kweku filled Victor in on the typically greater formality and distance in social relationships in the UK. Unlike in Ghana, for example, you couldn't just turn up at a friend's or relative's place uninvited at odd hours and expect to be fed and entertained.

Against this Kweku balanced the similarities between Ghanaian and British versions of local neighbourhood characters – the gossiping mums and old ladies at children's parties and tea parties, the beer-swilling dads at sporting events and men's clubs. It was the same difference, really: different cultures and different styles, costumes and diets, but at root – beyond colour, facial appearances and differences in language and gestures accompanying speech – the same personalities and same types of activity.

As there were no formal funeral events taking place until the wake-keeping the next day, Kweku, the strictures of boarding school now a past chapter in his life, was ready to explore the world. He asked Victor what was happening in town that evening. Victor's eyes lit up. Being quite a sociable person himself, he was delighted to see that Kweku was up for a bit of socialising. He could show Kweku around. Who knows, he thought to himself, Kweku might do the same in London for him one day?

Cruising around, they spotted an advertisement for a disco night at the Community Centre with free admission before 7 pm. It was 5:15. As they parked outside and walked up, they could hear the DJ already blaring some James Brown classics to warm things up like *Cold Sweat* and *I Got The Feeling*. They went in past the doorman. Inside, the organisers had arranged coloured bulbs criss-crossing the room as you would do for a street party. There were no white lights, so the place had a dim hue. A few other partygoers were there early.

Everyone's eyes suddenly turned to a solo dancer making amazing moves on the dance floor with a highly flexible acrobatic figure to James Brown's *Super Bad*. It encouraged Kweku to start nodding and swaying, cutting some less frenetic moves of his own as he approached the bar. Within seconds he had an attack of guilt: a voice reflecting his inner conscience told him 'How can you be enjoying yourself like that, if your uncle hasn't been buried yet? Isn't that a bit heartless?' He stopped swinging to the music and they leaned against the bar.

Victor ordered a Coke – no alcohol for him, as he had to be ready to be called on assignment at any time. He struck up a friendly chat with the barman on the latest village gossip and politics. It had been a hot day.

But Kweku, shy by nature, needed something to loosen himself up. He ordered a beer. Now 18, he would no longer be denied alcohol in England. There, even though the legal drinking age was generally 18, it was as low as 16 if you were taking alcohol with meals. The condition of taking meals at the same time was often fudged in a typically British way. So Kweku was by now well acquainted with the properties of fermented sugar but careful about its effects. He ordered a packet of cigarettes from behind the bar. Victor was shocked:

'But Sir, when did you start smoking?'

'A few months ago, Victor, around the time I started drinking.'

'Does Papa or Madam know?'

'No, they have no idea, and I would appreciate it if you don't tell them.' Kweku lit up and inhaled deeply.

Victor raised his eyebrows in disbelief, but Kweku told him not to worry about it.

'I'm not a child any more, you know?'

'I know, Sir, it's just that… Never mind.'

They sat down at the bar, agreeing to go Dutch. Around 6:30, the place began filling up. Local farmers and young professional types had closed from work and were venturing into town in couples and groups. The DJ realised that he now had an audience to perform to and began showing off his skills. Looking at his tinted glasses, Kweku wondered how he could possibly know which songs he was playing on the turntables in front of him. His wig, made from matted blond locks, bobbed up and down on his head and swept across his shades like windscreen wipers as he writhed and swayed suggestively in sync with the music.

Kweku ordered a second beer and lit another cigarette. He cast around for someone who would catch his attention. His gaze landed on a lady, part of a group of two women and a man who had just walked in. She seemed alternately vivacious and coy, swaying her head in response to the intricacies of the varying chords. Although there were three of them, Kweku saw from the affectionate touching the other two were engaging in that they were a couple. Eventually, when the lady also cast around the room for something to catch her eye, she noticed Kweku's stare. For a moment their eyes locked. She looked away, then back. Kweku now did the same. She smiled on realising Kweku was interested in her, then laughed at a joke from the couple she was with.

Kweku turned back to the bar. He tried to barge in on Victor's lively conversation with the barman, but sensed from their sudden shift to long silences, exchanging knowing looks, that they were discussing private stuff they would prefer he wasn't part of. Kweku took one last drag and stubbed out his cigarette in a nearby ashtray. He picked up his beer and decided to circulate alone.

It was now 8 o'clock and the place was packed. The DJ morphed further into a version of the frenzied Muppet, "Animal", as he played the latest hits from Europe, including Boney M's *Sunny* and *Daddy Cool.* Kweku decided it was now or never. He looked in the direction of the lady… but they had moved. In the swelling crowds, his mental map of the place had changed.

For the next 10 minutes he moved around the room, occasionally swaying to the hits, trying to spy her out. He was about to give up when he saw her right in front of him, dancing with the couple. Summoning up his best dance moves, he sashayed up to her, smiling and pouting in an exaggerated manner to get her attention. He sensed that, like him, she had a good sense of humour, so he wanted to make her laugh to break the ice. It worked and she peeled off to start dancing with him. Kweku milked the situation, and she responded, moving effortlessly in harmony with the music. He was impressed by her sense of rhythm. At the end of the song he followed them off the dance floor. As he thanked her for the dance, she seemed pleasantly intrigued by his English accent.

Kweku asked her:

'So, what's your name?'

'Veronica. And yours?'

'Kweku.'

'Kweku who?'

'Kweku Mensah.'

'Wait a second, you mean Mensah Mensah? One of the Mensahs?'

'Well, my dad is Kojo Mensah.'

She recognised the name instantly and seemed embarrassed. She introduced him to the couple she was with.

'Oh, so you're a Mensah then?' the man said, winking at Veronica. His partner, who had ignored Kweku up to that point, suddenly gave him a welcoming smile. The man introduced himself and his partner, but Kweku wasn't paying much attention.

'Veronica, can I buy you a drink?' Kweku ventured. She looked briefly at the couple, they seemed fine with it. She answered: 'Yes, I'd like a beer.'

Turning to the couple, Kweku asked: 'And you?'

'No, we're fine, thank you. You guys go ahead.'

Kweku extended his hand to Veronica and they went off together in the direction of the bar. Victor saw them approaching. He winked at Kweku, but Kweku pretended he hadn't seen. He didn't want Veronica to think she was part of any bet or the object of a game or something. After they got their beers, they found a corner of the room and began chatting.

She wanted to know all about him, why he was there, how often he would be coming. She looked a little older than him, but he didn't care. Her witty, alternately bubbly and coy personality excited him, and as an adolescent curious about sex he was trying his best to remain cool, attractive.

It worked, and they left the disco together, Victor dropping them back at Kweku's lodgings with a parting wink to him. They were hand in hand as Kweku took her upstairs to his room… A couple of hours later, after the act, Veronica surprised Kweku by withdrawing suddenly within her shell. It was almost as if, given their difference in social status, she felt she had let herself be used, had given herself up too easily. He didn't see it that way at all. He wanted to exchange numbers and meet her again. But she felt so embarrassed, upset with herself. She dressed up and left the room, barely saying goodbye.

Kweku sat on the edge of his bed. He had mixed feelings. Thanks to Veronica, he finally knew what it was to experience the celebrated love act. But the person he had joined in such an absorbing adventure didn't see herself as being any part of his life beyond the hours they had just shared together.

Vacillating between contentment and puzzlement, he eventually crashed out. When he woke up the next morning, slightly hungover, he first lay in bed exploring how it felt to be no longer a virgin, to have ticked that one off his bucket list. In a moment of cold, dispassionate analysis, he acknowledged that the experience, hyped up so much by all his contemporaries, seemed in some ways to have been a bit of an anti-climax. He felt satisfaction and was intrigued about his state of mind, but couldn't honestly say the act had taken him to a different stratosphere. He put this down to Veronica's curious withdrawal from enjoyment after the act. It had deprived the whole experience of a key ingredient to make it special and memorable – the unrestricted participation of both parties in the before and after as well as the during.

After half an hour, he found the energy to get up. Lodge occupancy was full, so he had to wait his turn to use the bathroom. From there he went to the main house to link up with his parents. As he approached, the place was a hive of industry. Black and red marquees covered the area on the lawn in front of the house. Inside the house, the covered forecourt on the ground floor was being prepared for the wake-keeping. The area where his uncle's body would be laid in state had been marked out, the chairs positioned around it where the family would sit to be greeted by sympathisers after they had passed round the open-top coffin. He saw Tina coming down the stairs. She told him his parents were on the upstairs verandah with some family members, so he should come and greet them. Afterwards she would bring brunch to the dining room for him – some *ampesi* with yam, plantain, cocoyam and palava sauce with fish stew.

The gathering on the verandah was fairly lively. All the key relatives were there. Careful to skirt the periphery and avoid inserting himself into the potential quicksand of the discussions, Kweku went round shaking hands. Handshakes when meeting someone in any circumstances was much more commonplace in Ghanaian culture. And if there was more than one person in a group to shake hands with, it had to be done anti-clockwise, from right to left. It was a custom originating in days when the back of a right hand moving clockwise to greet could conceal a knife, which would be visible if the palm of the hand was rather moving anti-clockwise to greet.

Affecting polite laughter, Kweku parried away the predictable ribbing he was used to getting – especially from extended family – about the Englishman he was turning into:

'Don't forget your culture!'

'No chance!' he would quickly assure them. Outwardly his parents would chuckle diplomatically through any such exchanges. At the same time inwardly they would ignore them, convinced of the wisdom of the long-term strategy of exposing their son to a British education that was commonly viewed at the time as being competitive with the highest possible level of academic training for his future. For them, this was the best investment they could equip him with. Unlike money, which could disappear as a result of one or more bad decisions taken in life, education, which could equally be used to create value, would be inseparable from his person for as long as he lived.

Happily for Kweku, there were by now no visible traces of his previous day's exertions and he made it through the gauntlet of the rest of the family examination without any hiccups. After brunch, he sat down in the drawing room to read one of the books in the bookcase there, a book on African Development written by a friend of his father's.

After a couple of hours, Tina told him his cloths and sandals were in, and it was time to try them on. The exquisite skills involved in weaving cloths – especially the silk and cotton *kente* cloth hailing from Bonwire in the region of Asante close to his mum's birthplace, Ejisu, home of the warrior Queenmother, Yaa Asantewaa – were world-renowned. Indeed, the unique kente motif was being successfully worked into clothing styles all over the world, and Kweku admired its incorporation in à la mode designs for jackets, trousers, stoles, ties, gowns and other items of apparel. For him, it was great to wear kente in this way.

But Kweku did not like wearing any full traditional cloths, even those made of kente. He found them so impractical. His assessment of the traditional sandals that had to be worn in combination with traditional cloths was even more adverse. He often found himself obliged to hide all these negative feelings to avoid offending and being offended.

Before the region known today as Ghana became a British colony and western attire began influencing dress styles, cloth, known locally as *ntoma*, and sandals, known as *ahenema*, were the usual smart wear in much of country. In parts of the north following the Muslim faith, traditional wear for men and women included embroidered robes and headwear to protect the skin and head from extremes of sun and dry desert winds from the Sahara. Cloth and sandals are in fact still worn commonly by men right up to today in many communities, including the Akan communities to which both Kwahus and Ashantis belong, especially when attending customary or religious functions, women most often wearing full-length formal dresses made from traditional cloth, and shoes instead of ahenema sandals.

For every day of his uncle's funeral, Kweku would have to wear a black cloth, along with a red head band to signify that he was a close family member of the deceased. The only exception was Sunday, when black and white cloth would be worn for the Thanksgiving Service in Church in the morning. The cloth for a man is literally a rectangular piece of cloth. The wearer first drapes it over his shoulders on either side, more on the right side than the left, then brings his left hand in front of him while still holding one side of the cloth, brings his right hand still holding the other side of the cloth forward and over his left shoulder, folds with his left arm on to the top of his left shoulder and finally adjusts everything straighter manually at front and back.

The problem is that the cloth does not stay in a fixed position and safety pins obviously can't be used! With every move of the hands, arms, or body, the cloth slips a little out of place here and there and needs re-positioning. This was a recurrent activity while wearing cloth, even for experts, and, if anything irritated Kweku about cloth, apart from the key fact that it had no pockets, which in itself was a disaster for men, it was that.

Trying on next the ahenema, the open sandals, Kweku found these every bit as cumbersome as the cloth. They were certainly nothing the wearer would be able to escape quickly in if, say, there was an unexpected downpour of rain or other sudden emergency, without running the risk of the sandals flying off the wearer's feet with any stride.

The two black cloths, to be worn alternately, one black and white cloth for Sunday and the two pairs of ahenema sandals fitted perfectly in terms of size. He wore them at the Wake-keeping that evening, the Burial Service in Church the next morning, the graveside, the final funeral rites back at the house and the Thanksgiving Service on the Sunday. Each time he put them on, he honestly couldn't wait to get out of them and back into more convenient clothes and footwear.

For Kweku, it wasn't a matter of cultural patriotism nor indeed of tribal loyalty, an even bigger issue in today's twisted politics: it was simply a matter of pragmatism and convenience. He felt strongly that all customs should be open to honest scrutiny, and subject to change in the form of amendment or discontinuation. The only proviso was that the change had to be subject to the consent, as evidenced by common practice, of the majority of the stakeholders in the culture originally following the custom, rather than imposed by an extraneous authority.

As an illustration, Kweku was fond of highlighting that, before the arrival of the Romans to colonise Britain in the first century – a colonisation which lasted over 350 years and brought Britain, a civilising force of later centuries, itself into the civilised world for the first time – the inhabitants of the island were largely illiterate, although the Celts were skilled artists and sculptors. The same could be said though of Africans, who were also skilled artists and sculptors before the arrival of European colonisers.

Among several changes adopted by the colonised indigenes, the Roman colonisers gave Britain its alphabet and the etymology for one fifth of the words still in use in the English language today. It also taught Britain Christianity, which still underpins so much of British culture, however much Sunday churchgoing and other observations may have been on the decline for decades.

Boudica, the great Celtic warrior, would have appeared to the Romans every bit as much of a savage and barbarian as Yaa Asantewaa, the great Asante warrior, did to British colonisers almost two thousand years later. Acknowledging the superiority of Roman learning, architecture and technology, the indigenous people of Britain adopted them over time.

Indeed, the Romans themselves began their history as barbarians before subsuming those elements of Greek culture and learning which they deemed more fit for purpose than their own.

And so for Kweku there was nothing unpatriotic about his opinions on funeral sandals and cloth; in his view, they could simply be more fairly described as pragmatically progressive.

Over the course of the funeral weekend, any time someone from his traditional family or one of the locals teased him for being rusty with the local Akan Twi language because of all the time he'd spent in the UK since childhood, Kweku reflected that, for all of Africa's vaunted independence, the official language of many of the continent's constituent countries was still the language of its European colonisers – in Ghana, English. This was the result not only of the convenience of the colonisers' languages in terms of international prevalence and the better access to learning and international communication they provided, but because the local languages or dialects in the colonised states were multiple.

For instance, in the colonised Gold Coast and in Ghana since independence, local languages were and still are at least a dozen or more. For one – or even up to three of these, as in Switzerland – to be adopted as the official language of the country to the exclusion of the others would be viewed as insulting and unacceptable by the large swathes of the population whose languages had been left out of official recognition.

This is the real reason English is Ghana's one official language and will remain so for the foreseeable future. It was and remains nothing to do with kowtowing to British imperialism. It is more to do with all ethnic subgroups within the country uniting around and adopting a single common language originating from an outside culture with no prior shared history with any of the local subgroups and de facto inherently devoid of local bias.

The outcome is that, across the length and breadth of a country of different dialects, no ethnic subgroup is left with the feeling that that their own dialect has been relegated in importance. Cultural pride survives in the continued written and oral practice of the different dialects by the various ethnic subgroups, but the full context and reality of English language dominance should nevertheless be appreciated without pretending that it doesn't exist.

At least as far as traditional funeral wear was concerned, thankfully for Kweku, as time passed, fewer and fewer customary occasions demanded the wearing of ntoma and ahenema. Black shirt, joromi or bubu, black trousers and black shoes, all of them ostensibly far more convenient apparel, were increasingly permissible and are today commonly accepted alternatives in all but the most traditional circumstances. Nonetheless, cloth and sandals continue to be widely used on customary occasions in Ghana.

At the various funeral functions, Kweku took his place near the front rows in the churches and under the canopies. His deceased uncle's local tribal chiefs, widow, children, brothers and sisters sat in the first row and, apart from the widow, who is traditionally excused, were obliged to shake hands with all sympathisers who queued to greet them. Kweku and other nephews, nieces and extended family sat in the second and other rows further down, where they escaped the unending trains of well-wishers, although they could not escape the constant sound of the drumming.

Kweku had some quiet moments during the functions when he reflected on his few memories of his uncle and prayed that, if there was a better place, he would be there. That said, he was quite honestly relieved when it was all over and he could head back to Accra to prepare for a new phase of his life at Oxford.

CHAPTER TEN

Matriculation

October 1976

By early October, Kweku was exhausted from almost a year of carefree exploration. He now yearned for the restoration of a measure of the discipline or routine that all but the most anarchic among us need to help preserve our sanity. Oxford beckoned. He took the fast train direct from London Paddington. As they neared Oxford, he caught a stunning glimpse of Arnold's "city of dreaming spires".

He tried not to feel daunted by the experience. Unlike the case at Huntsmere, he would by no means be the first person from Africa entering the celebrated institution. Africans who had broken the mould before him included a former Ghanaian Prime Minister, Dr Kofi Busia, who had famously distinguished himself academically there, eventually becoming a don. So there would be no strange looks questioning why he was there – or so he thought.

The journey had taken just over an hour. He struggled to get his large suitcase and hand-luggage off the train just before the doors were slammed shut for its onward journey to Birmingham. Outside the station, he hailed a taxi.

'Johnston College please.'

'On Stuart Street?'

'Yes.'

‘All right,’ the taxi driver said, lifting Kweku’s suitcase, ‘let’s get this loaded… Crikey, what have you got in here then, gold bars from Fort Knox or what?’

‘Sorry,’ Kweku tittered with embarrassment at the comparison, ‘just a few books I bought and some clothes.’

‘There we are.’ He stowed Kweku’s suitcase into the boot, collected his other bits – mainly carrier bags full of sundries – shut all doors and off they went.

They were now travelling through colourful streets inside the portrait Kweku had viewed on the train from a distance through the window of his carriage. They passed a mixture of medieval, later period and modern college walls occasionally decked with neatly trimmed foliage around windows or apertures, interrupted by shops, bars and restaurants. Church spires and bell towers dominated the skyline along the route. Eventually they came to a halt midway down a street in a piazza-like area where it bulged widest, opposite tall, wrought-iron gates in a distinctive dark blue hue.

‘This is Johnston College right here, sir,’ the driver said. He got down to help Kweku remove his things from the boot.

Kweku thanked the driver, tipped him, and entered the College through a small side-gate that was open. A little stone cottage to the right down some steps had a metal plate above its front door inscribed with the words “Porter’s Lodge”. As he neared it, ready to press the bell, a dark-suited gentleman sporting a well-tended moustache emerged.

‘Are you a fresher?’ he asked. Kweku seemed puzzled. ‘A freshman, that’s what we call first year students here?’

'Ah! Yes,' Kweku answered.

'Then this way please, sir. I'm the College Porter.' He motioned Kweku to enter the Lodge and helped him put his small bags down in the reception. Kweku hauled his suitcase in himself.

'Your name, sir?' the Porter asked, as he went behind the front desk to pick up a list clipped to a backing board. A bespectacled grey-haired gentleman sat poring over documents at another desk behind, ignoring the ongoing conversation.

'Kweku Mensah.'

'Come again?'

'Kweku Mensah.'

'So that's Mr Mensa then?'

'Yes.'

'Can you spell that for me?'

'M-e-n-s-a-h.'

'Ah, OK, with an 'h' at the end.'

'Yes.'

'All right, let's see now… Mensah, Mensah…'

After a few seconds, his eyebrows spiked upwards:

'There we are… gotcha! Mensah, Kweku!... That's a strange-sounding name. Can I ask where you are from?'

'Ghana.'

'Guyana?' Kweku had heard, for the umpteenth time since first coming to the UK twelve years earlier, his country's name confused with that of a well-known Caribbean nation with a similar-sounding name. He was nonetheless never offended by the misunderstanding as, with the exception of relatively small numbers of African slaves finding themselves transported to Britain during the slave trade, some of whom lived to be eventually freed, West Indians were the first black ethnic group to populate Britain in numbers. Most had been invited over to fill gaps in the labour market caused by two world wars, some around the time of World War One but the majority after World War Two.

'No, that's Ghana in West Africa,' Kweku corrected the Porter. Seeing him still looking stumped, he added: '… It used to be called the "Gold Coast" before our independence.'

'Oh, I think I remember now. You had a President… Kwame Nkrumah, I think it was?'

'Yes.' Kweku was impressed the Porter knew the name of his country's first President, although he hadn't himself been a big fan of Nkrumah – he decided he was too power-hungry after he declared himself President for life.

The Porter continued: 'Anyway, well done on getting in here, if I might say so. I know it's not easy to get into Oxford. Your parents must be really proud of you.'

'Thank you.'

'Oh, before I forget…' the Porter reached for a pile of large envelopes stacked on the right-hand side of the front desk. Flicking through, he found the one with Kweku's name on it. He removed it and handed it to him.

'There you go, that's your Welcome Pack. Don't forget to read through it – explains everything you need to know for now.'

'Thank you.'

'By the way, my name is Derek Walters … It says here on the list that you're in the garden quad. Don't forget you'll be sharing rooms with another student in the first year. You'll have your own bedrooms but share the sitting room.'

Kweku wore a slightly puzzled look on his face. It looked like, once more at a new institution, he would have to get used to new terms and slang:

'Garden quad?' he asked.

'Sorry, garden quadrangle.'

"Quadrangle" sounded like "rectangle" to Kweku, so for now he guessed it must be something similar.

'Anyway, you'll see when we get there,' Walters said. 'Is this all your stuff?'

'Yes.' He picked up Kweku's suitcase. 'Crumbs! What have you got in here then?' he asked Kweku.

'I'm sorry, I packed a few books to read.' Kweku gathered up all of his carrier bags.

'All right then, let's go.' He turned to his colleague as he left: 'George, mind the shop for me, will you? I won't be a moment.' 'Right you are,' his colleague answered, without looking up from his desk.

'This way, Kweku.' Walters led the way down a long drive, through two quadrangles and into a large one at the end. As they entered it on the south side, Walters pointed to the right. Kweku saw carpet-like lawns bordered by flower-beds dressed in beautiful colour combinations extending into the distance. 'That's why this one's called the garden quad,' Walters said.

He continued leading Kweku down the west side of the quad and into the hallway directly in front:

'You're on this staircase,' he said as they entered.

'Up the stairs?'

'Nope, you're in this room just here on the ground floor. There are other rooms going all the way up to the top of the staircase.' He set down Kweku's large suitcase, removed a huge bunch of keys from his jacket pocket and, jangling through them, settled on one. 'Here we go.' Like an impresario about to reveal the winning prize in a competition, he turned the key and opened the door. A towering reception room rolled into view, its ornate ceiling stretching almost as high as the grand reception room of a country mansion.

Chest puffed out, Walters helped Kweku move all his bags inside. As they walked in, there were two further doors to the right, one in each corner in front of them. Walters went to the one on the left first, opening it to reveal a spacious bedroom, wash basin along the wall on the left and lavatory in the corner. Kweku breathed a sigh of relief. Walters then led him to the last door. Pushing it open, he gestured to Kweku to go in first.

Kweku soon realised why. Between the bed on the right, a skinny-shaped cupboard alongside part of it, a small desk in the top right hand corner, a lavatory in the top left hand corner and a basin along the left wall, there was only a narrow, n-shaped channel to navigate solo. Two people couldn't be in this room at the same time without constantly bumping into each other. Kweku was perplexed by the naked disparity in size between the two bedrooms.

Coming back out of the room and standing between the two bedrooms, he asked, hoping not to be misunderstood as being presumptuous or ungrateful:

'Sir, how come the bedroom on the left is so huge and the one on the right so tiny.'

'Ah, there's an easy answer for that.'

'Yes?'

Pointing as he spoke, Walters said: 'Well, the room on the left was William Pitt The Elder's bedroom while he was up here… And the one on the right was for his batman. Not enough room to swing a cat in that one!' Seeing Kweku's jaw drop in shock, he let out a raucous cackle as he started back towards the entrance:

'Good luck sorting out with your room mate who gets to sleep where!... Most boys toss a coin for it!' He was still chortling and whistling away as he closed the door behind him.

For a moment Kweku was lost for words. He had of course heard of the famous Whig Prime Minister before in his history studies at Huntsmere. But he had no idea he would now be living in the same rooms he had once occupied, and was particularly apprehensive about how he and his roommate would determine the issue of who was to sleep where over the coming year.

Tossing a coin? The idea struck him initially as being surprisingly cavalier. But then he quickly realised that it was as good a method as any to resolve matters in such a case. And he comforted himself that whoever ended up in the small room for two out of the three terms wouldn't have to do so for long. Terms were only going to last eight weeks, a total of 24 weeks each year. So overall in each year there would actually be more holiday time than term time.

There were now 3 hours left before dinner in the College Dining Hall. For a few minutes Kweku paced around the imposing reception room, absorbing the museum-like history of his surroundings. He took out the Welcome Pack which he'd stuffed into one of his bags and opened it up. Sinking into the 3-seater on one side of the room, he started flipping through its contents. A sheet with the heading 'On Campus Accommodation' caught his attention. He knew that the course he had chosen, Classics, was a 4-year one. He now read that students would get their first 2 years on campus, the second year usually in their own room. But after that, unless they were scholars, they would have to make their own arrangements to rent digs nearby.

An hour had gone by when Kweku heard voices just outside the door, one of which he recognised as Walters'. There was a double knock on the door and it opened. In walked behind Walters a short, shy-looking student with pale white skin, reddish lips and long black hair. As he walked across the room, it struck Kweku that he was dressed like a pop star, a printed t-shirt under a brown leather jacket, flared jeans and platform shoes. Walters introduced them to each other:

'Kweku, this is Paul Rogerson. Paul, meet Kweku Mensah. You'll be sharing rooms for the first year… I showed Kweku around earlier and there might be an issue with the bedrooms?' He shot a teasing look at Kweku and winked.

'Oh yeah?' said Rogerson in an accent Kweku couldn't quite place yet.

Walters continued: 'What it is, is that the bedroom on the left is a fair bit bigger than the one on the right and, as I think you know, there are three terms in the year. Three's an uneven number, so obviously someone will have to lose out ...' Walters noticed Rogerson looking at him quizzically. He continued: 'And, just in case you're wondering, we don't allow people to swap rooms during term time – it's too disruptive. I mentioned to Kweku earlier that people usually toss a coin to decide who gets to stay in the big room twice, but feel free to decide if you can think of a better way – so long as you can both agree on it. Cheerio!'

With that, Walters was gone, striding through the quad on his way back to his Lodge and leaving the stranger freshmen gazing, cautiously sizing each other up.

Paul was first to break the ice. 'Have ya cum from far then?' he asked. Kweku found himself straining his ear to listen as Paul spoke. He was familiar with Cockney, Scottish, Welsh and Irish accents but hadn't yet come across the one Paul was using. He zeroed in on the word "far" to infer the meaning of Paul's question.

'No, just from London today. But actually I'm from Ghana.'

'Stone the crows! Ya coulda fooled me! Cum again? Ya sound so English.'

'Can I ask where you're from?... I mean, I know you must be British, but from whereabouts?'

'Sunderland, meate' he replied.

'Where exactly is that?'

'Way up north, Wearside, County Durham.'

'Oh, I see... Hey, by the way, congrats on that shock win over Leeds in the Cup Final a few years ago.' Kweku was always up to date with his football.

'Oh, ya know abote that then?'

'Yes, I do… And I remember now, you're called Geordies, aren't you?'

A deep frown suddenly came over Rogerson's face. Kweku knew he must have really put his foot in it and humbly awaited correction. It was swift in coming. 'Don't ya dare confuse me with a Geordie! Those Nyacassle lads and their Newky Brown Ale!'

'What's that? Newcastle?'

'Aye… Mind you, your accent's pretty posh eh? If I closed my eyes, I'd swear you were one o' them English toffs, like Terry-Thomas or sommat.' He let out a guffaw so hearty and infectious that Kweku found himself joining in. 'Did ya go to school here then?' Paul continued.

'Well, maybe I got the accent at prep school and then Huntsmere,' Kweku ventured tentatively, desperate not to sound patronising.

'Ohoo, oh yeah? Huntsmere eh?' Rogerson was intrigued.

'Yeah,' Kweku answered, trying to sound less stuffy in order to disabuse Paul of any notion that he wanted to show off that he spoke better English than someone actually born in the country, whose ancestors had lived there for generations. He had always felt that language should be spoken to be understood, not as a means of exercising one-upmanship over others.

'Ahh, that explains it.' Paul flashed a wide grin, tossing his hair back. 'Have ya not heard o' "Wearsiders" before then?'

'Nope, sorry.'

'What about "Tynesiders"? They're your Geordies. Ya've probably not heard o' "When The Boat Comes In" either then?' Paul asked, referring to the comedy drama which had just started airing on BBC TV that year.

'Sorry, no,' Kweku replied candidly. 'But I'll tell you what, try speaking some Wearside for me and let's see if I can follow you.'

'All right, yer on then Kweks… Canna call ya that? "Kweks"? Just seems quicker and easier to pronounce than Kwek-u.'

'Yeah, yeah, no problem.'

'All right then, how abote this one then?... "Where's wubbus?"'

'What?'

'Where's wubbus?... Ah, I'll tell ya… it means "where is our bus" in your posh-speak.'

'Oh, I see. Ha ha. Got it!'

'… What about "Ha'way the lads?"'

'"Away the lads?"'

'OK, that was too easy… Hey, try this one: it goes like: "R E murra?"'

'What?'

'Hahaha!' Paul was satisfied he had completely stumped Kweku. After a few embarrassing seconds of complete silence, he decided to put Kweku out of his misery.

Affecting his best attempt at a posh English accent, he elaborated 'OK, "R E murra?" means, "Are you all right, mate?".'

'Ah OK, got it now!'

Paul returned to practicalities:

'Anyway, shall we toss a coin then, to decide who sleeps where?'

'Yeah, why not?' Kweku took a coin from his jacket pocket. With a nod from Paul, Kweku flipped it. He lost. Rogerson cackled and began moving his things into the big bedroom on the left.

Kweku was left to reflect on a result he considered a perverse form of justice: his physique was almost twice the size of Rogerson's. After a couple of minutes sulking and feeling sorry for himself, he shrugged his shoulders, pulled himself together, and got on with it.

As they unpacked, they saw and heard boys entering their staircase and being shown to their rooms. When it was time for dinner, Kweku noticed, for the first time in his life while boarding in the UK, that there was no bell, no roll-call. At Johnston, at any time over a period of up to one and half hours, you could just turn up at the dining hall, pick up a tray and crockery, continue down the line choosing and being served from a huge variety of food and soft drinks, pay for them at the till at the end of the line, and find somewhere to sit down. The only thing you had to do was wear a formal gown before entering the dining hall – a thinner one in strips for "commoners", who formed the vast majority of the student population, and a full gown for "Scholars" or their more junior version, "Exhibitioners". You didn't even have to dine at College at all if you didn't want to. A full range of alcoholic and non-alcoholic drinks was also available in the Beer Cellar below.

***

Kweku found Oxford and its surrounding areas a place steeped in variety and excellence of every kind, academic as well as cultural. The beautiful architecture of its College buildings was complemented by pretty horticultural landscapes constructed and nurtured by teams of dedicated staff. He felt truly privileged to have the opportunity to go to Oxford, and his parents were so proud that he had gained admission to such a world paragon.

He soon learned that students were left to fashion their days however they liked, engaging in whatever activities they pleased; the only condition was that they should attend two one-hour sessions with tutors each week and do the requested essays to hand in at such tutorials. Lectures were entirely voluntary. Compared to the military discipline, supplemented by daily roll calls and other strictures, that he'd had to endure at boarding schools in his life up to that point, Oxford seemed like a passage to the terrestrial version of heaven!

Just as at Glenwood and Huntsmere however, it wasn't long before someone was so upset by Kweku's presence at an institution of such special privilege that they were driven to let him know directly how strongly they felt about it. In his first week at the College, Callum Bentham, a freshman Chemistry student living on the same staircase, was returning to the staircase as Kweku was on his way out. As they hadn't met before, aside from occasional brief exchanges outside the shower on the top floor, Kweku prepared to greet him as he would any fellow fresher. However, he noticed Bentham puckering his face at him disdainfully:

'I don't think black people should be allowed into Oxford,' Bentham told him directly to his face in his broad cockney accent.

Caught off guard by the casual nakedness of Bentham's racial slur, Kweku's instinct was to let him know that his own accent meant that by the same token he wasn't perfect either. Kweku reasoned that, as an adult, no matter how he had been brought up, under whatever parental or environmental influences, Bentham should have been able to think for himself. So this time Kweku didn't hold back:

'I don't think Cockneys should be allowed in here either,' he said, more in defence of his dignity than as part of an intention to insult Bentham.

Bentham blushed as red as a beetroot, clearly not expecting such a feisty response. Shell-shocked, as all bullies are when they get an unexpected taste of their own medicine, he entered the staircase in total silence, accelerating out of view as fast as he could.

At that moment, Kweku felt so grateful that his parents had sent him to boarding school in the UK. It had given him the chance to be able to answer Bentham's put-down with an immediate riposte. He deduced from Bentham's stunned silence that up to that point in his life, it simply hadn't occurred to him that, every bit as much as for black and brown people, against whom a colour bar had truly operated at Oxford up to the twentieth century – with the possible exception of major royalty – cockneys and other children from working class backgrounds had also traditionally been excluded from Oxford's intake in the "good old days".

As an meritocrat by nature, and one who understood the inequity of the lottery of birth – however much this should not stand in the way of a person using their best efforts to rise above the circumstances of their birth – Kweku certainly did not believe that cockneys should be excluded from Oxford. But he had already experienced too many instances in his life where he had bowed to pressure to rise above insults. He wanted to bring home to Bentham the hypocrisy of his jibe…

that the progression in social and cultural attitudes which had allowed his own class and also women to gain admission to Oxford was the same one which black and brown students like Kweku had benefited from, to his apparently deep resentment. Hypocrisy had always been like a red rag to a bull to Kweku, and now was no exception.

***

The first term raced by. In the second lecture on Virgil's *Aeneid* at Schools, Kweku noticed at a desk a few rows behind to the left of his favourite area of the hall a smart but casually dressed lady with auburn hair and a round, charitable face. He thought he would try to strike up a conversation with her. As the lecture wound up, he rose quickly to move towards the exit door. He stepped out in front of her, almost running into her and apologising disingenuously for his staged near-accident.

'Oh, I'm so sorry,' he said.

Breaking her stride to avoid running into him, she looked at him with large, soft, eyes and broke out in an engaging smile.

'Don't worry. I should have looked where I was going, too.'

A part of Kweku's heart melted, but he quickly held his emotions in check. Her accent sounded northern but, unlike Rogerson's, was easy to follow right from the start.

'Oh no, it wasn't your fault at all.' Kweku tried to keep the conversation going, but by now she was moving briskly ahead. For a few strides, he attempted to keep up with her. But she was walking too fast, and he lost sight of her in the crowds as the hall emptied.

He counted the days to the following Thursday's lecture on Virgil. Unusually for him, he made sure to get to the lecture hall 15 minutes before the start. He saw her enter with 5 minutes to go. His eyes followed her to see if she would notice him. He was sure it wouldn't be difficult for her. He had seen one black lady sitting near her at the previous lecture. Otherwise there weren't many Africans he had seen on that course in the weeks since the term started. As she got closer, her eyes locked on to him looking at her. He smiled as cheerily as he could and waved. She smiled, waved back and continued to her usual seat.

Kweku didn't want to rush this one. At the same time, he felt the need to strike while the iron was hot. As the lecture ended, he turned to move in her direction. She saw him coming.

'Hi.' She gave him that disarming smile of hers.

'Hi,' Kweku responded tamely. Then he suddenly remembered to ask her:

'Which College are you at?'

She was slightly taken aback by the forward nature of his question. After all, this was only the second time they had ever met. But she looked at Kweku's innocent expression and decided there could be no harm in telling him.

'Ormeron Hall, near the University Parks.'

'I've never been there before.'

'I would be suspicious if you had!' she winked teasingly. 'And you, which College are you at?'

'Johnston College.'

'Oh, I hear that's quite a pretty one, large gardens.'

'Yes, but not much of a chance to explore the College gardens now – it gets dark so early in England this time of year. But I hear they really come to life in the summer.'

They continued down the stairs and out of Schools.

As she headed briskly up the High Street, Kweku called out: 'See you next week!' A few moments later, he realised he'd forgotten to ask her name. It was too late… to call out now would create an unnecessary scene, to chase after her would be unnecessarily dramatic. He would see her next week.

***

The following Tuesday afternoon, Kweku had just finished a tutorial with his literature tutor. Once more, he had tried to get by in his essay just waffling, making vague, sweeping hypotheses unsupported by citations from the relevant texts. Something had gone awry. The sudden absence of martial discipline as an over-arching framework for all school-based learning to date in his life had left him disoriented. At the same time, he seemed for the first time in his life to be discovering what must be that thing called 'love', that irrational combination of feelings incapable of reduction to simple definitions. These two influences resulted in a lack of focus which was to plague the rest of his university days.

Instead of heading to the Bodleian or the College library to hunker down to some serious, focused study, in a bout of self-pity, he headed to the College Beer Cellar. He engaged in some chit-chat with the barman, sat down on one of the sofas near a TV in the corner and watched a couple of episodes of *The Fosters*. It was a hilarious sitcom of the day, close to home for Kweku as it explored the experiences of a black family in the UK. He identified parallels with his own current experiences and it straightaway put him in a better mood.

As dinner time approached, the place started filling up. People were playing darts on the board at one end of the room, on pinball machines in the opposite corner. Kweku went upstairs for dinner. He found himself sitting next to a rather kind-looking student, who introduced himself as Charlie Turner. Kweku introduced himself in turn and they shook hands. Charlie seemed fascinated to know where Kweku came from. They hit it off straightaway. Towards the end of the conversation, Charlie asked him:

'Do you know how to ride?'

'You mean horses?'

'Of course I mean horses!' Charlie laughed. 'What did you think I meant?'

'Sorry, no… I have a cousin who does back home, she loves horses…'

'Oh really… Does she have stables at her house then?'

'Oh no, not that. She goes down to the local army barracks. Her father knows the commandant in charge; there are always horses there that need exercising.'

'Oh OK.' Charlie looked Kweku straight in the eye before continuing: 'Is it something you would be interested in doing?... Riding I mean?'

'Why do you ask?'

'The thing is, a friend of mine and I are trying to put together an Oxford Polo team. At the moment it's just him and me. We need two more. Would you be interested?'

'Polo? Sounds interesting, why not? But how would I be able to play that when I can't even ride yet?'

'Never mind about that. The question is, are you interested? Do you really want to do it?'

Kweku reflected for a brief moment. He quickly concluded that his life was currently peppered with vacuums that needed filling. He had tried out rowing, but having to wake up every morning at 4:30 to make his way down to the College Boathouse and then breaking his back for an hour rowing before rushing back to begin a full day had proved a bridge too far. In the circumstances, he reflected that polo could be a workable alternative.

'Yes, I would, Charlie,' he said. 'I'll give it a try.'

'OK, if you're serious, my sister has just finished at a Swiss school. She has a few months before she starts work in the City in January. We've got stables up at our farm at Bicester, so she could teach you to ride... But mind you, it's only going to work if you're serious about it.'

Kweku felt very honoured by Charlie's offer. He was aware how expensive and exclusive the sport was. But, more than that, here was someone, a fellow student, who only knew that Kweku had been to a reputable public school and didn't know too much about him beyond what he had just learnt in their conversation. And yet he was prepared to give Kweku a chance like that? He was ready to go through the effort of training him up to play polo? He even added that there was the extra incentive, if Kweku made the team, of winning an Oxford half-blue and membership of the prestigious Vincent's Club on the High Street for sporting blues and half-blues.

Charlie swallowed a final mouthful of his fried chicken and chips. 'I'll have to check with my sister first and then get back to you tomorrow or Thursday. Is that OK?'

'Yes, that's absolutely fine. Thanks a lot.'

'All right then Kweku,' Charlie stood up. 'I've got to rush now. See you later.'

'Cheers Charlie. Thanks.'

With that, Charlie left Kweku to continue eating his cottage pie.

***

Carrie

Thursday's *Aeneid* lecture had finally come around again. Once more Kweku got to the lecture hall early, to continue the burgeoning pursuit of his new Ormeron Hall acquaintance. As he saw her walking in, he waved to catch her attention. She saw him and smiled. The smile progressed to a giggle and she waved back, blushing at the attention Kweku was giving her. He watched her all the way as she strode down the side of the hall in her beige overcoat, dark green polo neck sweater, grey skirt and knee-length zipped leather boots and went to sit down at her usual seat behind and to the left of Kweku.

The room wasn't too full yet. He summoned up the courage to go over to her desk. But as he got nearer, a student friend caught her attention and they plunged into an animated conversation. Already shy by nature, Kweku did not want to crash a conversation between two ladies uninvited. So he turned round and headed back to his seat: he would try again once the lecture was over.

The lecture went on for two agonising hours. Kweku was able to take notes but was constantly distracted. If a student asked or answered a question behind and to his left, he would look round, hoping to catch a glimpse of her. Twice, their gaze met. The first time, she looked quickly away again; the second, she smiled at him and their eyes locked. He seemed flustered, and after a few seconds it was his turn to look away in embarrassment.

As the lecture ended, he got up and walked towards her. She saw him coming and got up but this time waited for him. They walked out together, down the stairs and up the High Street. Kweku kicked things off:

'You know I never even got your name?'

'Well, it's actually Caroline, but everyone calls me Carrie. What's yours?'

'Kweku.'

'Quaker? As in Quaker Oats, you mean?', she giggled teasingly, knowing that couldn't be right.

'No, Kweku, spelt K-w-e-k-u. It's a Ghanaian name.'

'Where's that then?'

'Ghana, in West Africa.'

'Africa? You sound very English to me, very la-de-da. Where did you learn to speak like that then?'

'Well, I first came to boarding school here when I was six.'

'Six? Did you say boarding school at six?' She looked aghast. 'Poor you!'

'I got used to it after a while.' Kweku was trying to put a gloss on what had started out as a very tough experience for him but he felt had worked out for the best in the end.

'Those must have been pretty posh schools then? They don't talk like that at school in Lancashire, where I come from!' She beamed that full-cheeked disarming smile at him.

'You wouldn't want to know.'

'I might.'

Kweku felt encouraged to pitch that trite opening gambit for any suitor. It was now or never: 'Would you like to go out to dinner tomorrow?'

'Tomorrow? No, sorry. I'm off home for the weekend. It's a family engagement, someone's getting married.' She looked at Kweku, saw the look on his face of someone who had just had the stuffing knocked out of them. She felt sorry for him. She decided she did want to know more about him anyway. She added: 'But let me see now, I don't have anything happening next Tuesday evening at the moment …'

'Well, can we have dinner on Tuesday then?' Kweku hurriedly interjected as they turned right at the top of the High Street.

She elected to tease him a little: 'Oh yes, and where do you have in mind then?'

'Restaurant Elizabeth?' Kweku was trying to show off. The Elizabeth had the reputation of being the best restaurant in the city centre at the time.

She was impressed. 'Oh, you mean the Spanish one opposite Christ Church?'

Kweku nodded, adding: 'I've not been there before myself, mind, but I hear the food is really good – especially the seafood.' Kweku sensed some hesitation on Carrie's part. 'Or what about the Cantina di Capri? The Italian one, near the Randolph?'

'I've seen that one, looks very nice from the outside.'

'Yes, it's got that Blue Grotto look – like from the island of Capri, I hadn't thought of that before!'

'So, you've eaten there already then?' she probed provocatively. 'Who did you take? Am I just another one for you to charm?' She spoke half in jest and awaited his reaction.

'No, not at all Carrie! Never been. But people say it's got the lot – great food, wine, atmosphere.'

'Well it looks as if we have a date then, Kweku!'

'Great, Carrie! Shall we meet there then, say at 7?'

'OK, sounds good. But don't be late!' She giggled and continued down Cornmarket Street. Now taking longer strides, as if he had just found a new purpose in life, Kweku turned right on to Market Street on his way back to Johnston. He felt as if he was walking on air. Forgetting momentarily the narrowness of the pavement, he strayed on to the street right into the path of an oncoming cyclist, who swerved just in time to avoid him, ringing his bell and muttering curses under his breath, thankfully inaudible for Kweku.

When he got back to Johnston, there was a message in his mailbox at the Porter's Lodge. It was from Charlie, inviting him round for an informal dinner at their house in Bicester that evening. Charlie said he would be swinging by the College at 5:30 pm to pick him up for the drive down if he could make it. He added that Kweku shouldn't worry if he couldn't do it owing to the short notice.

At 5:30 sharp, Kweku was ready at the Porter's Lodge, dressed casually in Barbour jacket, light brown corduroys and brogues. Charlie came in and was about to ask Walters where Kweku's room was when turned round and saw Kweku already there, all set to go:

'Well done, chap! Let's go then.'

'Okey dokes.'

They walked out to Charlie's car parked opposite the College gates, a green Ford Escort. It looked as if it had seen better days, but who cared, so long as it got its occupants from A to B!

The traffic moving out of Oxford was slow but they were in Bicester by 6:30. They went up a long, tree-lined driveway. There wasn't much to see in the dark. The car lights illuminated some farm buildings as they made a right turn, lit windows here and there showing people at home in their cottages. Soon they were at the main house. Charlie parked up at the front. As they entered by a side door near the kitchen, Kweku saw a kindly-looking middle-aged lady with an apron, rinsing some greens in the sink. Charlie introduced Kweku.

'Mum, I'd like you to meet a friend of mine from Oxford… Kweku, this is my mum.'

'Hello, Mrs Turner, pleased to meet you.' Kweku extended his hand.

'Likewise you, Kweku,' she replied, shaking his hand. 'Don't bother with the "Mrs Turner", "Lucy" is fine. Charlie has told us lots about you. Apparently he's been seeing you around College, but it was only a few days ago when you happened to be sitting next to each other in the dining hall that he actually got to speak with you. He thought you were quite an interesting fellow.'

'Yes, we had a really good chat Mrs… Lucy.'

'I know, he's told me. They're looking for two more polo players and he thinks you could be one of them.'

Charlie chipped in: 'It's OK Mum, we'll get into all that a bit more later, once Scarlett is here.'

Lucy was fascinated by Kweku's accent. In a eureka moment, her eyes light up 'I know who you remind me of!' she exclaimed, beaming at Kweku. 'Oh, come on,

Charlie… someone help me out… that chap who reads the 10 o'clock news!'

'You mean Trevor McDonald, Mum?'

'Yes, him! Well, of course he's much older than you, but you talk just like him!' Lucy chuckled.

Kweku knew of and looked up to Trevor McDonald. A good-natured and industrious Caribbean role model, he had broken through an important glass ceiling by becoming the UK's first black national TV newsreader. Kweku was highly flattered by the comparison with this celebrity.

'Charlie's told us you're the only coloured student at Johnston,' Lucy continued.

'As far as I'm aware, that's true, Mrs Turner… Oh, I mean... I am sorry to keep saying Mrs. I think it's because of my natural inclination to respect age.'

'Hey, steady on!' Lucy fired back humorously, 'A bit less of the "age", if you wouldn't mind; there's a lot of life still in me yet!'

'I'm sorry, Lucy.' Charlie was laughing, shaking his head in disbelief as Kweku dug himself deeper and deeper into a hole.

Kweku's eyes began to wander around the kitchen. On a wall plastered with sticky notes and a full year calendar, he saw a silver rosette with "2nd" inscribed in large typeface in its centre, "Mrs Lucinda Turner" underneath and "Badminton Horse Trials" in an outer circle around it. Kweku was mightily impressed.

Lucy started up again: 'Now then, Kweku, how many Africans, I mean black students, are there at Oxford?'

'You mean in the whole University?'

'Yes.'

‘Well, I have no idea exactly… I can say that my sense is that over the years there have usually been more postgraduate than undergraduate black students… I’ve been to a couple of African Students Union Meetings – political debating groups. Only about 4 other students turned up to the first and 7 to the second… I’ve heard there are somewhere upwards of 20 black students altogether currently here… But a lot of famous Ghanaian politicians, lawyers and heads of government have been there, including our first Prime Minister after Kwame Nkrumah, one Dr Kofi Busia, who was a brilliant student. Many celebrated Ghanaians and other Africans have been to Cambridge too in the past.’

Just then, Charlie’s dad, William Turner, walked in. A distinguished-looking grey-haired gentleman, he was wearing a tweed jacket, grey trousers and brown shoes and had a book tucked under his arm. He had heard Kweku’s last sentence:

‘Kwame Nkrumah, yes, I remember the fellow,’ he said. ‘… One of the noisier members of that first generation of African leaders after independence…’

Charlie cut in: ‘Dad, meet Kweku.’

‘Oh yes, hello young man.’

‘Hello Sir.’ Kweku replied, shaking Mr Turner’s hand.

Mr Turner continued: ‘You know, I was out in Botswana, Southern Africa, for a number of years… They’ve got a very good leader out there, Sir Seretse Khama. He’s been working wonders on so many fronts for the past twenty years – the economy, education, infrastructure, indigenous rights. If you ask me, he’s set an excellent example for how African countries can administer themselves successfully as independent sovereign states. He's a very pragmatic and unhypocritical sort of chap, not so much of the waffle that you hear from some of the others. We could do with someone like that here too, I reckon!' Kweku's interest was piqued. He made a mental note to research more on the Botswana leader later.

'So, who's in charge in Ghana now then?' Mr Turner asked Kweku.

'Well, actually currently we've got military rule …' Kweku's tone was almost apologetic. As a proud Ghanaian, he was embarrassed to have to concede that, far from the boasts of competent, democratic self-government post-colonisation, an independent Ghana had already been through two coups d'état in less than 20 years. 'One of the Generals is in charge; but there's a lot of talk of their handing over to constitutional civilian rule soon. Let's see.'

'Oh, I am sorry to hear that,' Mr Turner sounded genuinely sympathetic. 'Oh well, good luck, I hope it all works out for the best!'

Turning to Lucy, he asked: 'So, dear, what do you have cooking in the aga then? Smells like a good roast.'

'Your favourite, William, roast venison.'

'Ah, excellent!' Mr Turner headed for the drawing room.

'I've added some roast chicken on the side in case it's not enough, as Charlie and Kweku are here …' Lucy turned to her son: 'Charlie, where's your sister?'

'I think she's upstairs.'

'Well, please tell her we're about to have dinner, so if she can come and help me set up the table.'

‘Can I help Mrs Turner?’ Kweku ventured.

‘No, no, don’t worry Kweku, that’s not your job. You’re our guest. And it’s Charlie’s job to keep you entertained while you’re here.’

Charlie went out to the bottom of the stairs and called out: ‘Scarlett! You’re wanted.’

A lady’s voice shouted from upstairs: ‘What?’

‘Mum needs a hand. Supper’s up!’

‘Oh OK, coming.’

Scarlett appeared, dressed casually in blue jeans and dark green jumper. She had the same light brown hair as her brother but looked as vivacious as her name suggested.

‘All right, Scarlett,’ Lucy said, ‘you go and stand on the other side of the serving hatch and I’ll pass everything through to you.’

Dinner was a masterful balance of protein, roast potatoes and home-grown vegetables – carrots and cauliflower, parboiled to retain most of the original flavour and nourishment, and loose-leaf lettuce. It was rounded off with a fresh fruit dessert and the accompanying peccadillo of a chocolate cake baked earlier, drizzled in hot chocolate fudge sauce with vanilla ice cream.

As they ate, Mr Turner indulged his curiosity about Africa’s modern political development. He wanted to know Kweku’s reaction to the whole colonial experience, and was pleasantly surprised to hear from Kweku a broad-minded take on the whole thing. They discussed country life with Kweku and arrangements were made for Kweku to come round the following Tuesday morning at 9:30 for his first riding lesson with Scarlett.

***

Kweku woke up on Tuesday morning with a sore head. He had overslept! It would take him an hour to get up to the Turners at Bicester for his first riding lesson. He thought about skipping it altogether. In the end he resolved that, for a first lesson, that would be just too discourteous; he should at least make the effort to turn up, even if very late. He was there by 10:30. Scarlett had gone out exercising with one of the grooms and hadn't returned. He decided the least he could do was to wait patiently for her return. Half an hour later, he saw them coming back up one of the lanes leading into the woods.

'Ah, Kweku!' she said, 'I can see you finally made it!'

'I'm so sorry, Scarlett, I forgot to set my alarm clock!'

'Never mind, it's the first day, so we'll just walk around the fields here.'

As they dismounted, the groom took the horses into the stables to unsaddle and feed them. She called after him: 'John, when you finish, can you go and saddle up Mildred for Kweku? I'll take Ralph. Turning to an apprehensive Kweku, Scarlett added reassuringly 'Don't worry, Mildred's a harmless old biddy, very patient – perfect for beginners.'

For Kweku the overriding emotion at that point was relief that Scarlett had not taken offence at his lateness, and that his journey hadn't been wasted.

She taught him all the usual things for beginners, how to mount and dismount, sit upright in the saddle, angling the knees properly with the feet in the stirrups, using the reins to steer or slow down the mare and control her movements, nudging inwards with the knees with encouraging words such as 'walk on' to set off and so on. They agreed to meet again the following Tuesday morning and, provisionally, every week for the rest of the term.

Kweku thought, what an attractive, even-tempered, affable lady. He told Charlie as much during lunch at College afterwards, prompting Charlie to look up suddenly from his plate. 'Hey, don't get any ideas, Kweku! She's like that with everyone.'

'Oh no, I didn't mean it like that! How could you think?... Anyway, I have a date tonight.'

'Oh yes, who with?'

'No one you'd know, chap... I met her during lectures.'

'One of the few you've attended then, eh?' Charlie said, gently poking fun. 'OK, I'm off up to Middleton Stoney to meet a friend.'

'Where's that?'

'North Oxfordshire. He's a car dealer. Someone's just given him a motor to sell and he reckons it could be just the thing for me. I'm not so sure, but he was quite insistent. Do you want to come along?'

'Er... no thanks, Charlie. Let's make it another time.'

'I'll bet it's because you don't want to take any chances with your date!' Charlie winked.

'Nope. Good guess, but I've got a tutorial on Virgil this afternoon at 3 and I haven't done the essay yet.'

'Crikey! You'd better get a move on then!'

'I know. See you later.'

Kweku managed to cobble together some literary analysis in an hour – enough to satisfy his tutor that he had made an effort. Once again, he was relieved he had dodged a bullet.

***

It was now 7 in the evening. Kweku sat nervously at the bar at La Cantina di Capri. To play it safe, he had phoned them last Thursday to book a table for two. In the ten minutes since arriving, he had already finished half a pint of cold lager while admiring the tapestry of photos of celebrities and beautiful landscapes of Capri in the Mediterranean on their walls. He was on his third cigarette. As he began sipping a second half, a huge picture of the island's Blue Grotto transfixed him. Blue was his favourite colour. Staring at the picture, he felt himself plunging into its blue waters, deep in thought.

He was jolted back to reality by a familiar voice he had been waiting to hear. 'Kweku, you seem lost.' He turned round and there stood Carrie, looking stunning in dark blue V-neck sweater under a fur vest, a pearl necklace draped below a light tartan silk scarf, black skirt and tights with knee-length zipped reddish-brown boots matching her auburn hair. As he gulped down the beer swilling in his mouth, he nearly choked:

'Carrie!' he managed to get her name out. 'Would you like a drink? ...' He stubbed out his cigarette.

But before she could answer, a frisky waiter emerged from the seating area of the restaurant:

'Your table is ready, Mr Mensah, *signorina*' he said, in Italian-accented English.

Kweku looked at Carrie. 'Shall we? ...'

'Why not?' she smiled.

'Then after you.'

'Thank you… It's nice here. I like the crystal blue and white theme, it's like being in an underground cave.'

'Yes, I think it's meant to evoke the atmosphere of the restaurant's eponymous island.'

'What?'

The waiter seated them at a cosy table for two along one side of the restaurant, an arched window giving them a clear view of the street outside. '*Benvenuti*! Welcome!' the waiter said. 'My name is Giovanni, and for this special evening with us, I will be your waiter.' He handed them menus. Kweku opened his up straightaway to check. The dishes were listed in Italian, but fortunately there were English translations in italics underneath each item:

The waiter seemed a little impatient: 'Would you like to order now, or should I give you some time?'

Kweku looked briefly at Carrie: 'We'd like more time please.'

'*Non c'è problema.* No problem, sir. I will come back later then.' He winked at Carrie as he turned to go. Kweku saw his gesture for the flirtatious act that it was. He reckoned it was a bit of a cheek but well, the fellow was an Italian after all, and a part of him loved Italians for their slightly theatrical behaviour. Carrie blushed and seemed flattered. They took it to be part of the 'service' to be expected when dining at an Italian restaurant. As Giovanni waved his hands and arms, it struck Kweku that Italians seemed as fond as Africans of using body language to get points across or amplify effects when putting on a show. Other Latins – the

French and Spanish – also used hand and arm gestures, but not to the same, almost exaggerated extent.

Kweku returned to Carrie's query: 'Aha, about the island of Capri, as I was saying…' He took out his pack of cigarettes, pushed one up in the sheath and offered it to her. She took it and he lit it up, removing and lighting another one up for himself. Looking at her, Kweku was intrigued:

'Are those real pearls? Is that real fur?'

'Of course not, silly! Who do you take me for, Elizabeth Taylor?' She giggled loudly.

Embarrassed, Kweku quickly returned to the topic of Capri:

'You know, I went to the island of Capri during my year off. It's not far off the coast, south of Rome. It's got this amazing blue grotto, I kid you not! ...' Kweku was narrating the story like an adventurer who had been to a magical world and was now back, trying to describe it. Carrie was fascinated by the boyish zeal in his facial expressions as he tried to explain it to her.

He went on: 'It's just like an underground cave, as you said, but the colour of the water there is an amazing blue, gifted by nature, and the ambient temperature in the summer a perfect, refreshing cool.'

'Really?'

'Apparently the Emperor Tiberius treated it as his private swimming pool.'

Carrie chuckled: 'You always have to bring it back to Classics, don't you?'

'No, it's just a coincidence. I wasn't even thinking of that, honestly …'

'I know… I was just teasing! Lighten up!'

‘Sorry… OK now, starters, or “*antipasti*” as they’re calling them here …’

Carrie began poring over the menu. ‘I rather like the look of this *bruschetta*, with tomatoes, basil and olive oil.’

‘And for mains?’

‘I think I’d like some seafood. Let me see now… Ah, the *tagliatelle* with bacon looks good.’

‘Great choices. I reckon to start I’ll go for the *gamberoni* and then for mains *ossobuco* with *polenta*.’

‘Sounds equally good.’ They exchanged smiles.

Kweku caught Giovanni’s eye. He sped over to their table.

‘Are you ready to order?’

‘We are, thank you. For the lady, *bruschetta* to start, followed by *tagliatelle carbonara*.’

‘Ah the carbonara! A very good choice, signorina, if I may say so. One of my personal favourites!’

‘And I’ll have *gamberoni all’aglio*, garlic prawns, to start; and then for mains, *ossobuco*.’

Giovanni looked up from his notepad: ‘Ah, just a minute… Did you say *ossobuco*?’

‘Yes.’

‘OK that one I will have to check with the chef. Just a moment please.’

He disappeared, returning after a few minutes:

‘I am afraid the *ossobuco* we cannot do it… Sorry signor but it’s too early. We like to do everything in the right way and with the ossobuco it takes time to cook it properly. If only you had told us earlier when you booked the table …’

‘OK, OK, no problem,’ Kweku re-opened the menu.

Giovanni leaned over, singling out an item with his pen: 'Then can I suggest you try this instead? The *vitello arrosto*, that is, roast veal, with potatoes, and then for both of you some *focaccia* bread with cheese and olives on the side?'

'That sounds great!'

'And to drink?'

'Sorry, I missed the wine list – here it is …' Kweku showed it to Carrie. Do you have any favourites?'

'No,' she smiled, I think I'll leave that to you.'

'Then red or white?'

'I think… white.'

'Let me see now… Shall we split a bottle of Pinot Grigio?'

'Settled.'

'Thank you very much, signor, signorina.' Giovanni spun round and headed for the kitchen. Now they could relax. Kweku looked into Carrie's eyes.

She started, genuinely curious: 'So what made you come over that second time at lectures and try to chat me up then?'

Kweku was caught slightly off guard. He decided to tell it like it was: 'Well, I actually tried to chat with you the first time I saw you, but you were in so much of a hurry and I lost you.'

She was flattered. Looking into his eyes, she said playfully: 'So was it love at first sight or something?... Oh, it's not fair,' she giggled. 'I can't tell if you're blushing.'

Kweku was relieved she couldn't: if he was pale, he would have turned bright red. To maintain his dignity, he tried to fudge the issue. 'Well, it was certainly attraction at first sight.'

Carrie seemed disappointed: '"Attraction" at first sight?' she said, 'What does that mean?'

Kweku didn't have an answer. He sensed that Carrie was obviously nowhere near confessing instant love for him and, though he thought it might have been love at first sight from his side, he didn't want to be ahead of her. Anyway, at that point in his understanding of the world, he didn't even know the difference between love and infatuation. He tried to change the subject:

'So, what drew you to Classics, Carrie?'

But she wasn't having any of it. 'Never mind about Classics, what drew you to me? Come on then, don't be shy! ...' She was using that cheeky tone again that Kweku found irresistible. He cracked:

'All right then, it was your kind face, coy mannerisms, big eyes and that charming smile. I don't know.'

'Oh yes? Anything else?'

'Your beautiful auburn hair too. That is your natural colour, isn't it?'

Carrie pulled up: 'What sort of a question is that to ask a lady on a first date?'

'Sorry.'

She burst out laughing. 'I'm just teasing,' she said, reaching over to pinch and toggle his left cheek between her thumb and forefinger. 'Cheeky, cheeky! You've got a round face too, and big eyes …'

Kweku interrupted 'But my nose is a lot bigger than yours. And I don't think my smile is anything like as sweet as yours.'

'Oh, don't say that… I think you've got quite a cute smile. I like it when you smile… but not so much when you're like this …' she pulled her hand down over her face, her smile morphing suddenly into a serious pose. Then she giggled.

Kweku loved her giggle; he found it so disarming. 'OK, but what about my nose, then? ...' he said. 'I have a sort of *Cyrano* complex about it.'

'A what complex?'

'Oh, it's from a play we had to study for French A-level, *Cyrano de Bergerac* by Edmond Rostand.'

'Ah, I didn't bother with French after O-levels.'

'Then what did you study alongside the Latin and Greek?'

'Art. I've always been fascinated by it.'

'Good for you, I'm impressed!' Kweku sensed Carrie suspected he was being disingenuous. He felt it necessary to emphasise: 'No, really, I am. I wish I'd had the sense to do something like that. It's so fulfilling to create or develop your own version of something.'

'No, but coming back to "love" …' Carrie was determined to finish her point '… women just don't fall in love at first sight. You can *like* the look of someone, but not love. You see, there's more at stake for us if we get it wrong, so even if we are ready for a deep relationship, we're more cautious about disarming ourselves too early, until we really get to know someone, their character, how serious they are… But it doesn't always have to be about love, anyway.' Her last sentence was more than she'd meant to say. She glanced at Kweku. He'd heard it, but it was anyhow too early for him to count his chickens.

By now the restaurant was half full, which Kweku found perfect: not so many customers that service was slow or confused, and not so few that waiters ended up being overly attentive to the ones that were there, staring at them or trying to eavesdrop on their conversations out of boredom.

Panna cotta and *tiramisu* for dessert rounded off an enjoyable dinner. The food and wine lived up to expectations and complemented the romantic atmosphere. When the bill came, Carrie wanted to go Dutch, but Kweku insisted on paying the whole amount. He told her she shouldn't feel she owed him anything. She could reciprocate by taking him out for a meal somewhere else on another day if she liked – no strings. As they rose from the table, Kweku moved over to lift Carrie's fur vest from her chair back and dress it on her. But he was beaten to it by an eager Giovanni, who had an extra spring in his step from the modest tip Kweku had just left him.

'Senorina, *per favore*, allow me… There you are, beautiful… Arrivederci, bellissima …' He was flirting with Carrie right up to the end.

'Thank you,' Carrie flashed a smile at him. Everyone likes to be pampered.

Kweku scratched his head, desperately searching for an apposite Italian sign-off phrase to use on Giovanni to impress Carrie. After an embarrassing hiatus, he could only come up with the excruciatingly mundane: '*Grazie mille, ciao.*'

'*Ciao senor*. Bye-bye.'

Giovanni held the door open, and they went out on to Magdalen Street. Kweku turned round to Carrie:

'Nightcap or coffee?'

'Where?'

'How about Emperors?'

‘OK, I think I know it. It’s that place directly opposite your College on Stuart Street, isn’t it?’

‘Yep, run by Monty MacLean, one of only a hundred MW’s.’

As they started off in the direction of Stuart Street, Carrie glanced at Kweku, an inquiring look on her face. Kweku was sure it was because of the acronym he’d just used:

‘MW?’ he asked her.

‘Uh-huh?’

‘It stands for Master of Wine. Apparently there are only one hundred allowed at any one time… a bit like the Knights of the Garter with their twenty-four member limit – excluding the monarch, first in line, and honorary members of course.’

The bells of St Mary Magdalen chimed the half hour. Kweku checked his watch. It was exactly 9.30. There was hardly any traffic on the street, little carbon monoxide to pollute the fresh evening breeze wafting down Stuart Street as they made their way to Emperors. When they reached door, Kweku held it open for Carrie.

‘Mr Mensah!’ MacLean shouted from behind the bar as they walked in. Kweku was embarrassed. He didn’t want Monty’s cordiality towards all customers he knew by name to be mistaken by Carrie to suggest he was a regular there. ‘I’ll have a large cappuccino, thank you Monty… And you Carrie?’

Carrie surprised him. ‘Do you have Irish coffee?’ she asked.

‘Of course we do, madam. Coming up.’

There weren’t many people left there and things were in wind-down mode. Monty came over to join them for a while. He expounded on the state of the wine trade and their elaborate preparations to receive a small consignment from the forthcoming Beaujolais run. They soon finished their coffees. Kweku hailed a taxi to take Carrie back to Ormeron Hall.

Once they reached there, he got down with her, asking the driver to wait. As they embraced to say goodnight, he kissed her on both cheeks, then looked into her eyes. He tried moving closer to kiss her again. But she pulled away sportively:

'Hey, you, take your time! This is just a first date.'

'Can I walk you inside then?' asked Kweku.

'Don't worry.'

'Then when do we meet again?'

'I don't know. Maybe Sunday?'

'Why don't we have lunch at the Cherwell Boathouse, near you?'

'OK, I'd like that. We can firm things up on Thursday.'

'I'll go ahead and book it anyway, just in case. They get quite busy at the weekend.'

'All right, Kweku, see you on Thursday then.' She blew a kiss in his direction. He blew one back at her, then watched as she entered and disappeared inside the College.

***

On The River

They firmed up the date at lectures on Thursday and at noon on Sunday he took a ride up to Ormeron Hall. She was ready when he got there, dressed casually in jeans and polo neck sweater. It was a sunny October day, so they decided to walk the three quarters of a mile to the Cherwell Boathouse. The place was packed with students and families. After a tasty lunch that didn't disappoint, Carrie insisted on paying the bill. Kweku kept his promise and didn't fight her: he realised it was early days and important for her to feel independent.

As they were leaving, he caught sight of a notice on the wall beside the exit: apart from being a Sunday, it was also the last day of the punting season. They decided to have a go. They went down to the river bank and hired a punt. Neither of them had done it before but, ever the gentleman, Kweku volunteered to do the punting from the stern. He gave the paddle to Carrie and asked her to sit at the bow and help steer the punt in case it veered off course.

What unfolded next was a disaster. The metal punting pole was much heavier than he had expected. Right from the start, he struggled to work out the effect that punting on either side of the boat would have on its direction. Carrie was rolling around in stitches, paddling frantically up front on one side then another in a vain attempt to keep the punt on course.

For the next 20 minutes, they mostly zig-zagged north up the River Cherwell, trying to avoid the poor swans tirelessly shepherding their cygnets around beginners like Kweku in their efforts to keep them safe. Kweku and Carrie weren't the only punters struggling on the river, but they presented a stark contrast to those who knew exactly what they were doing, lifting and dropping the pole as they swung it –

left to go left, right to go right, behind to steady the course.

Things came to a head as they approached a second bend in the river to the left. Trying too hard to dislodge his pole as it got stuck in the river bed, Kweku lost his balance and fell head over heels over into the river, disappearing beneath its surface! Carrie's peals of laughter quickly turned to shrieks of horror. But she was relieved when Kweku's head resurfaced moments later as he flailed his arms about, gasping for air.

Regaining his composure, Kweku swam after the punt as it drifted away, Carrie anxiously waving to alert oncoming punters to his presence. Eventually the punt lodged itself against the river bank not far down. He clambered out on to the bank, soaked through to his skin. Leaning over as he huffed and puffed, trying to get his breath back, he reached out his hand to help her out of the punt. They collapsed on the river bank, laughing, thankful to be on terra firma.

Of course, Kweku hadn't brought along any change of clothes with him. Falling into the river was the last thing he had anticipated in his complete underestimation of the difficulties involved in punting for beginners. They quickly worked out that no taxi would take him in his condition on their seats and have them muddied and steeped in river smells like that. The situation seemed hopeless. Feeling sorry for him, Carrie invited him back to her room at Ormeron Hall. They would work out what to do from there. Just then, it dawned on Kweku that in a strange way his luck might be about to turn.

As they entered the College, his drenched frame caught the attention of the Porter. He came out to stand in the doorway of his Lodge, gazing at them. A couple of other students on their way out of the College looked him up and down but walked past, one struggling to stifle a guffaw, the other turning her nose up in the air in a gesture of disapproval at the soggy, crumpled state of his clothing. They reached Carrie's room. She unlocked the door and pulled him in. They fell into the room, giggling and embracing, before she realised how wet he was:

'Ugh! Take off your clothes!' she said commandingly. 'I'll have to dry them on the radiators here.'

'All of them?' Kweku asked.

'Yes, all of them.'

At first, she made a show of looking away as he stripped. Then she realised that would be ridiculous, as he would have no male clothes to change into. She turned round to look at him standing there in her room, in his birthday suit. She blushed. 'OK, sit down on the carpet for now, just to dry a little.' She looked down at him sitting alone on her carpet, looking sorry. She wanted to hug him.

She sat down beside him. She told him she had met a lady from Jamaica at lectures who was also studying Classics. They had similar hobbies and had already become good friends. She had once let her touch her hair and she liked the feel of it. She asked if she could touch his. He nodded. She slowly ran her fingers through his hair. She loved the soft, silky feel of the tiny curls in spirals bouncing under the palms of her hands. Their eyes locked and he moved closer to her. This time she didn't pull away. Their lips met as they locked in a passionate embrace. They moved to her bed. Kweku was travelling on an amazing journey…

Hours later, for dinner, she went out to get some Chinese takeaway. By the time they had finished eating, his clothes were dry enough. He dressed up ready to leave. Monday she had a tutorial, Tuesday afternoon he had one, so they agreed to meet on Wednesday afternoon at Browns for a coffee. He gave her a bear hug at the door as he left her room, then walked quietly out of the College.

His lungs filled with the energy boost of love, in the cool of night, Kweku decided to walk the full mile back to Johnston College. He lit a cigarette and inhaled deeply. It helped him to think, to dream. He had lost his virginity during his year off before going up to Oxford, but this felt different: it was as if he had just started out on a journey with endless possibilities. He lay in bed re-living moments from the otherworldly experience he had just had with Carrie. That night, for the first time in years, he slept like a baby.

The following Wednesday afternoon, Kweku was sitting at a table by the window at Browns, lighting up one cigarette after another as he waited. He saw her coming up the street. He stared admiringly at her gait. As she got closer, she saw him staring at her and smiled. He went to meet her at the door, helped remove her coat and hung it on the rack in the hallway. She was looking beautiful, wearing a fresh-scented perfume, and Kweku was mesmerised. They pecked on the lips briefly but, as they sat down, Kweku noticed she had a serious look on her face.

He felt slightly unnerved: 'What's up?'

'Nothing.'

'Have I done something wrong? Did I get you into trouble at College that day? Did someone see us?'

'Noooo!' she laughed, 'nothing like that… It's nothing.'

'Are you sure?' Kweku persisted. She didn't answer, picking up the table menu and glancing over it. He decided to move things along: 'OK then, let's have some coffee, shall we?'

She looked up: 'Yes, I'm dying for a cappuccino.'

'Me too.'

She flashed a smile at him but, like her laugh, it wasn't sparkling with the usual carefree abandon. He suspected that she wanted to get something off her chest, but didn't know how to start. Just the day before, they'd had a wonderful time. Brilliant lunch; yes, he'd been clumsy on the river afterwards, but they'd laughed about it and the day culminated in an instinctively sensual experience together in her bed. Shouldn't things be getting better between them from there?

Part of him questioned whether he was just imagining that something had changed. Maybe she had got out of the proverbial wrong side of bed that morning? Or perhaps she'd received some bad news from home? So, for now, he should just stop worrying. If there was something, she could tell him, she would let him know, when the time was right?

He offered her a cigarette. She thanked him but pulled out a different brand from a pack in her handbag. She offered him one. He said he was OK with his brand. He lit both. They inhaled deeply.

The waiter brought the coffees. He watched her take a sip to taste and add two sugars. He added four to his own without tasting. He stirred his cup slowly. And then curiosity got the better of him. He was falling in love; if Carrie didn't feel the same way, that would leave him vulnerable to disappointment at any time of Carrie's choosing. He didn't like being left in suspense. He didn't want to be a burden to anyone. He had to know for himself.

'Carrie,' he began, 'if there was something, you would tell me, wouldn't you?'

She realised he wasn't going to let it go. 'Actually, Kweku, I'm worried about you.'

Kweku was dismayed. He could sense the direction the conversation was moving in. It struck him as such a patronising thing for Carrie to say: 'Worried about me?' he asked her, as if he hadn't a care in the world.

'Yes… I've seen the way you look at me sometimes. I'm flattered, and I really like you too. But it's just that I don't want you to think it means we're going to be an item or something like that… I mean, I'm happy for us to go out from time to time, but what happened last Sunday was a one-off; we both just fell into it and didn't really know what we were doing – or at least I didn't... I wouldn't want you to get the wrong idea.' As she spoke, she reached over and caressed his hand.

Kweku's balloon had just burst. He furtively glanced round the restaurant. Luckily for him, everyone seemed equally focused on their own little world, some sitting by themselves reading books, staring into blank spaces or out of the window at passers-by, others engaged in lively conversation. He assured himself that the spacious arrangement of tables and ambient BBC Radio 2-like easy listening music would in any case have made it difficult for any eavesdroppers to follow their tense encounter.

He shrank ever smaller in his seat as she continued, trying to let him down gently: 'It's not your fault… The thing is, I don't think I can be serious about anyone; it's just not where I want to be in life right now. I want to focus on my studies… And I can see in your eyes that you are looking for something I just can't give you.'

At that moment, Kweku wasn't actually looking at her, but through her. As he tried to recover from the shock of her let-down, he vacillated between appreciating her sympathy and feeling alienated by her pronouncements on the imbalance in their feelings for each other. Although accurate, these came across as uncomfortably condescending. He had spent the night and that morning dreaming of life ahead with an amazing partner… the places they would go to, the thrills they would share. Now it would all be taken away; well, now he was even being told it was never his to begin with, just an immature, impatient fantasy, constructed out of a giant misunderstanding.

As Carrie finished speaking, he looked away. He began lifting his hand from under hers to get up, but she held it down.

'Where are you going?' she asked.

'I don't know.' Kweku felt humiliated, he didn't want pity. Carrie felt guilty. She was fond of Kweku and didn't want to hurt him:

'Oh, come on Kweku! Look, at least stay and finish your coffee. I don't like it when you look so glum.' She pulled her cheeks down to mimic Kweku's sullen expression. 'I like it when you smile… like this.' She tugged at his right cheek, her full smile with all its usual sparkle was back. Kweku half-smiled – more at her tugging than in response to her urging.

As far as Carrie was concerned, she had now set the ground rules for their relationship going forward, provided Kweku was OK with it. But he wasn't. As he finished his coffee, he tried to convince himself that he should accept the limitations of their future relationship, however that would turn out. Just then the Eagles' *Desperado* came over the sound system. Kweku imagined the restaurant manager, spying at them through a cubby-hole behind the partition to the kitchen, had somehow synchronised airing of that track with the unfolding events in his world purposely to mock him.

So, Carrie had told him she wanted to concentrate on her studies. Shouldn't he be doing the same? Of course he should, he told himself! But the truth was that he wanted more and, try hard as he did, couldn't dispel a suspicion that Carrie had rejected a conventional relationship with him for unspoken reasons he wasn't as yet able to fathom. As they left Browns, there was no hug, no embrace; just strained smiles and brief parting goodbyes. They went their separate ways, she in the direction of her College, he towards his. No longer feeling airborne, his feet sensed the impact of each step on the stony ground as he trudged back listlessly to Johnston.

***

Thursday after lectures, Kweku and Carrie, without her friends, popped across the road for a coffee and slice of black forest gateau each. But the atmosphere was strained. Both realised that, after Browns, things were different. Physically and emotionally still in his late teens, Kweku wanted more from life. She didn't – or at least she had told him she didn't. He didn't know why, but couldn't bring himself to stay floating on the periphery of her life like a lost butterfly, waiting to unlock the key to the mystery.

He consoled himself with the fantasy that one day he would find an equally committed partner sharing the same dreams. But fantasies are by definition divorced from reality. In the ensuing weeks their relationship inevitably cooled further. For a while they still briefly acknowledged each other's presence whenever their paths crossed. But, as that too became increasingly difficult, eventually by the end of the following year they had become virtual strangers.

***

It was Tuesday morning. Time for riding lessons with Scarlett. Kweku's skills were improving, but by the fourth lesson he was having to be honest with himself that he was not a natural horseman. Riding proficiency was a baseline pre-requisite for playing polo, and he knew there wasn't the proverbial snowball's chance in hell that he was going to be able to do it well enough to be able to swing a mallet in hand while rotating this way and that, sprinting, stopping suddenly, making contact with the ball on both forward and reverse swings and the like in a way that wouldn't embarrass Charlie and the team in the Varsity match in the summer.

When he turned up for his fifth lesson, Kweku resolved that he had to put Scarlett out of her misery. She tried to convince him to soldier on, that there was more time for him to improve. She would be away working in London next term but they could get one of the grooms to help him continue learning. Kweku thanked her for trying, but wouldn't have it, so she understood.

Charlie was disappointed when Kweku broke the news to him but, following a subsequent discussion with Scarlett, realised that Kweku still had a lot of ground to make up in a relatively short time and, unless big sacrifices were going to be made on his part, would have no chance of being ready to play polo competitively by the start of the season. So they called it quits on the idea but remained good friends all the same.

***

In the last week of term, Kweku's old Huntsmere School friend Nick Ralston, who also got into Oxford that year but in another College, invited him plus partner to a fancy-dress Ball in London's Berkeley Square on the Saturday. Saturday had now come.

Kweku had earlier met Jenny, a lady in her twenties from Jamaica, in a one-night stand in South West London, where he had gone to a disco-party out of boredom. She was dressed in a figure-hugging satin suit and noticed him sipping his beer at the bar. He saw her staring at him while swaying in perfect sync with the music and was immediately attracted to her cute comportment and pert lips. There was no husband or boyfriend he could see hovering nearby signalling him not to try flirting with her, so he moved on to the dancefloor while swinging to the rhythm and linked up with her. It was an uncomplicated story of lustful looks exchanged and acted on in the style of the casual relationships of the day. They had exchanged numbers before he left her flat in the small hours to go home to Highgate.

When Kweku got the tickets from Nick, he decided he would ask Jenny if she wanted to go with him. Happily, she was up for it. His parents were both in Ghana, so the Highgate house would be available and he would be free to express himself, without feeling that his conduct or appearance was being observed and recorded for future assessment. Spurred on by the event's fancy-dress theme, it struck him that the combination of circumstances offered him a rare chance to act out his fantasy of playing the role of a brother "from the hood". He decided to go for it full pelt!

First he rang his barber in Kilburn to check:

'Eddie, hi. Hope I didn't wake you up?... Can I come over to your end at 10 this morning for a special job?'

'Who is this now, man?' the person at the other end of the line queried in a broad West Indian accent.

'Why, it's Kweku of course! Have you forgotten me already? I came to see you just three months ago, last September… You know, the one from Ghana with the unusual views on politics? ...'

'Oh, yeeeahhh! Ha ha! I remember ya now, man!'

'OK look, I'd like to get an Afro done …'

'An Afro?' Eddie was astounded. 'Ya mean, with ya hair all puffed out?'

'Yeah, that's right, puffed out bouffant-style, just like I've seen you doing for so many other customers.'

'OK now, man. But look, there's quite a bit o' work has to go into that. So look now, man, maybe it's better we start at 9 rather than 10, 'cause I already have an 11 o'clock booked for the same thing.'

'No problem, you got it! See you soon!'

He quickly packed, checked that he had his cheque book and card with him, and asked the Porter to order him a cab to the station. Using a chunk of his allowance from his parents, he took the Intercity fast train down to Paddington. From Paddington, a short run up the Bakerloo line to Kilburn and he was outside Eddie's on the High Street by 9. As he walked in, Eddie and an assistant were just finishing sweeping and cleaning up from the previous day's business.

As usual, Eddie's chatter reflected his analysis of the latest topical issues – sometimes surprisingly shrewd, demonstrating an enlightening, street-wise take on complex issues, at other times overly simplistic. Once he had a captive audience, like Kweku, who had a similar interest in politics, there was just no stopping him. It had the potential to make him tiresome, but he had such an affable, engaging personality that none of his customers dared burst his bubble by picking holes in his arguments, so long as he stayed focused on his barbering as he spoke, which he managed to do unerringly.

Two hours later, it was over. Kweku checked himself in the mirror… Thrilled with his creation, Eddie yelled 'James Brown, eat ya heart out now, man!' Rounding his £4.50 charge up, Kweku slapped a fiver into his palm and was soon back on the Tube, heading towards Covent Garden. Going round the many trendy fashion outlets there, he bought a psychedelic kipper tie, bell bottom trousers and platform shoes. At his last stop at a shop on Carnaby Street in neighbouring Soho, he settled on a slick black leather jacket with wide lapels and long-collared, satin fitted shirt. As he stood before the mirror in the shop's dressing room with the full set on, he thought to himself, 'Ohoo yes!'

He popped into the nearest phone booth to ring Jenny. She would be ready for him at 5. With that, he went home to shower and get a couple of hours' sleep. He was at her place in Brixton at exactly 5. She burst out in stitches when she saw him. She had just never pictured him like that. For her part she was dressed like a Jazz singer from the roaring twenties, which Kweku thought quite sassy!

***

The Ball in Berkeley Square lived fully up to its billing, but Kweku's experiment in assimilating a 'boy from the hood' didn't go quite to plan. Thrice while dancing he tripped over his platform shoes and had to be held up by Jenny to stop him crashing ignominiously to the floor. Some guests wore expressions on their faces which screamed 'what an idiot that guy is!', couched behind affected smiles and encouraging nods – followed by smirks when they thought Kweku was no longer looking. Others less hypocritically laughed directly in his face and pointed rudely. He was OK with either reaction.

Nick was dressed as a U.S. Navy sailor out on the town with a Gene Kelly mask. They weren't to recognise each other until late into the night, as heat and exhaustion gradually stripped partygoers of their disguises, revealing their true identities.

Looking over Jenny's shoulder as they smooched to Tony Bennett crooning *I Left My Heart In San Francisco*, Kweku was startled to see for the first time, sitting almost slumped out and looking the worse for wear, her cat mask upside down on the table next to a glittering cute turquoise-green buckled handbag, a black lady he had often seen chatting animatedly with Carrie at lectures. When the song ended, Jenny told him she wanted to powder her nose. At this, Kweku felt a window of opportunity open; it meant he would be on his own for a few minutes. His curiosity got the better of him and he sauntered over to the lady's table.

'Hi'. She raised her head, her initially glazed look focusing on the young man with an Afro and loosely hung kipper tie standing in front of her. She thought he looked familiar and squinted, trying to place him. Kweku now recognised her: 'I've seen you at Oxford, with Carrie, at lectures …'

'Oh, yeah… I remember you now!' she said in a Caribbean accent, sitting up in her chair. 'You're Kwayko or something …'

'Kweku.'

She began giggling at his appearance, then checked herself:

'Hey, what happened with you guys? Things seemed to be really taking off between you and then, just as suddenly, they died down again. You know she's my best friend?'

'Actually I didn't know that …' Kweku was a bit hesitant whether to continue.

'Oh yes, we share so much, but she was always very reticent when it came to discussing you. I mean, one minute she was saying she'd met this really interesting bloke called Kwayko – sorry Kweku – from Ghana and how you'd been to posh schools and all that and were cheeky and made her laugh …' She paused to look at Kweku's exaggerated hairdo and burst out laughing '… I can see why now!'

Kweku chuckled: 'I know… But you have to remember they did say fancy-dress. I couldn't think of what to wear, and it just suddenly came to me to go all the way!'

She looked him up and down. 'Oh my God! Look at your shoes, there must be at least 3 inches on those heels! No wonder you seemed so tall… Anyway, so what went wrong between you two? I may be wrong, but you don't strike me like the obsessive type, for instance?'

'I don't know what went wrong; I wish I knew… Anyhow, what's your name?'

'Roberta.'

Kweku was looking at her, and realised she hadn't taken her eyes off him. He thought he would try his luck: 'Where's your partner tonight?'

'Oh, don't take any notice of him. He's just a friend from London. He lost his job at a warehouse this morning and has been knocking it back since afternoon. For the first couple of drinks I tried to keep up with him – you know the sort of thing, trying to cheer him up, giving him a friendly shoulder to cry on – but he wouldn't stop. I told him he was being silly, and that even though we drove here, I hoped he wasn't thinking of driving back. In the end he was off his trolley. I said we should take a taxi home, but he got stroppy and told me to get lost. So I told him he knew what he could do. What's the time now?'

Kweku checked his wristwatch: 'It's just gone midnight.'

'Oh ok. Then that was about an hour ago now. But look, don't worry, it's platonic. There's nothing going on between us. I'll see him again tomorrow – that's if he hasn't driven himself into a ditch…' The thought suddenly hit her: 'Oh, my goodness! God forbid he's actually tried to drive home!'

Kweku guessed he wouldn't have long before Jenny returned – or that Roberta got up to look for her guest. He quickly got to the point. 'Are you in London?'

'Yes.'

‘Do you have a phone number?’

She looked into his eyes, unsure for a moment. She couldn’t recall anything negative Carrie had had to say about him; she had only told her once, when they were discussing him, that he wanted more from her than she could give him and that, as the first person from her family to get into Oxbridge, her priority was her studies. Roberta mulled over whether she could she trust Kweku. She wondered: didn’t Kweku feel any loyalty towards Carrie, trying to chat up her best friend like that? But at that moment there wasn’t any man in her life. She was intrigued to find out more and curiosity got the better of her, too.

She unzipped her handbag and pulled out a pen, looking around for something to write on. Kweku reached for the cigarette pack in his pocket. Only four were left, so he ripped off the flip-top and gave it to her. She scribbled down her number, checked it over and handed the top back to Kweku. He read it to check that all 7 digits were there, then quickly stuffed it into his breast pocket.’

***

‘Hello.’ Kweku recognised Jenny’s voice behind him.

‘Oh, hi Jenny. This is someone from Oxford. Hey, fancy that! Meeting someone from Oxford here!’ Kweku was desperate to change the subject and slip off.

But Jenny sensed that something was up and didn’t want to let him off the hook that easily. She turned to Roberta, eyeing her with deep suspicion: ‘Oh yes, and you are?’

Kweku intervened: 'Oh, we've just met at lectures a couple of times here and there.' Roberta looked at Jenny, then both looked at Kweku.

Clasping Jenny's hand, Kweku tried to guide her gently away, but she pulled her hand abruptly from his grasp. He had to find a way to wind things up quickly. Turning to head for the main exit, he said: 'OK Roberta, then see you next term at lectures?'

Roberta said nothing, just staring at Kweku and nodding silently once.

For a moment Jenny stood directly in front of Roberta, facing her squarely. Then she realised she looked silly, as she actually knew very little at that point, however much she suspected. She turned and caught up with Kweku, the alcohol they had consumed emboldening her to confront him right away:

'I saw her give you that piece of paper. It had her number on it, didn't it?'

***

Kweku didn't answer. He continued walking briskly towards the exit. Thankfully at that moment he spied a mask-free Nick Ralston sharing a cosy chat with a lady friend. It was the perfect distraction for Kweku.

'Nick!' he said. 'Been looking for you all evening!'

Nick turned round. Seeing Kweku's Afro hairdo and exaggerated bell bottoms and platform shoes, he burst into peals of laughter: 'Hey, Kweku!... Don't worry, I understand! That's the problem with these fancy-dress do's. Another thing that's tricky about them is that, unless you arrive together or there's a seating plan and people stick to it, no one knows where anyone else is!... Anyway, good to see you at last… Meet Alice.'

Kweku and Alice shook hands. Nick continued:

'And who's that there with you?'

'Oh, Jenny, meet my great buddy at Huntsmere and Oxford, Nick.'

Jenny was torn between the temptation on the one hand to make a scene in protest at Kweku's earlier flirtation and a desire on the other hand not to blow her first impressions with someone Kweku had just described as his best friend. She decided to keep things formal, shaking hands curtly with Nick and Alice.

Kweku was anxious to move the discussion on, to conceal any hint that anything was up between him and Jenny. 'It's been a real blast, Nick! Thanks a lot for the invite. Great food, music, a tombola, magician and …'

'Did you win anything on the raffle?'

'Nope, but it's all good for charity.'

Nick flashed two air tickets at him, a twinkle in his eye, then folded back the covering letter stapled to them. Kweku made out in caps at the top of the covering letter the words: "A Christmas Weekend Skiing In Klosters". He was genuinely surprised:

'So you're the one who got the second prize then?'

'Yep!' Nick gave his tickets another wave in front of Kweku's face.

'How did I miss that then? I must have been in the gents or something.'

Nick chuckled: 'Easy to miss, Kweku, there must have been over a thousand people here at one point, not counting all the staff on hand… So where will you be spending Christmas?'

‘I’m off back to Ghana for the hols.’ Now it was Kweku’s turn to try to make Nick jealous: ‘Think of all that warm tropical sun you’ll be missing...’

Nick was up to the unfolding Punch and Judy banter. He began by giving the impression of conceding: ‘I know. I sort of envy you in a way, with the weather and beaches and all that …’ But then he quickly followed this up with a teaser of his own: ‘On the other hand, I definitely won’t miss all the diseases I’d probably catch down there!’

‘What do you mean?’ Kweku asked, rising to his country’s defence as a travel destination.

‘I mean like malaria, yellow fever, meningitis and all that sort of stuff – you know what I mean.’ Nick was tilting his head to one side, arm playfully outstretched in a gesture asking Kweku to acknowledge the obvious.

Kweku knew that the concern Nick had expressed was a valid one for any first-time European traveller to the African tropics. However, he had the perfect answer:

‘But you can get jabs against nearly all diseases, and there are prophylactic tablets you can take to prevent malaria… And then, what about all the flu and other bugs you can catch here in England, too?’

‘OK fair enough …’ Nick chuckled.

‘Yes! 1-1’ Kweku said to himself.

‘So, are you guys leaving now?’ Nick asked.

Kweku didn’t want to risk the embarrassment of looking at Jenny and her returning a scowl, so he decided to answer promptly for both of them. ‘Yes, we’ve had a fantastic time, but well, as the saying goes, all good things must come to an end.’

'OK, then see you next term, old boy!'

'Yeah, see you Nick! All the best – and don't break a leg in Switzerland!' Kweku waved politely at Alice as well. Then he and Jenny left, through the exit to queue alongside the taxi rank.

The taxi dropped Jenny home first. She said nothing to Kweku for the entire journey. As they reached her flat, he offered to walk her to her front door, but she slammed the door shut in his face, almost taking his nose off.

***

Early evening the next day, Kweku rang the number Roberta had given him. She seemed pleasantly surprised he had kept it. They arranged to go out on Tuesday. Kweku was dying to see *The Mousetrap* at St Martin's Theatre on West Street. The great novelist and playwright, Dame Agatha Christie, had passed away earlier in the year and there had been renewed interest in her long-running play which had caught Kweku's attention. Roberta was just as keen to enjoy a bit of whodunnit, for the thrill of a ride trapped in a world of nightmarish uncertainty, secure in the knowledge of emerging at the end with all mysteries resolved, returned to the safety of familiar surroundings. She lived in Kensal Rise, so they agreed to meet for an early dinner at Le Caprice in Piccadilly and go on from there to West Street.

They felt relaxed in each other's company. For Kweku, even though he hadn't planned it that way, there was the added benefit of not having to be concerned, or to pretend not to be concerned, that others were judging the mere fact that an interracial couple was going out together at all… He knew that what he felt on such occasions would have been the same for Carrie the few times they had been out together. However hard she might try to block it out of sight, out of mind, there was always the impulse to check the reactions of others nearby – black as well as white, men and women – to seeing a mixed-race couple socialising. Some would purposely stare, faces squeezed, long enough for their disapproval to be noticed, and only then look away, noses in the air. Reassuringly however, whatever their true feelings, most acted or tried to act as if they were witnessing nothing reprehensible – that the mixed relationship was nobody's business but hers and Kweku's.

But there was a chemistry between Kweku and Roberta stemming from their easy-going personalities that made them click. It was an evening to remember, from the stylish early dinner in Piccadilly to the walk up Shaftesbury Avenue to West Street and a classic piece of West End Theatre to round off the evening. From the theatre they took a taxi, first to West London to drop Roberta. Kweku got down to walk her to her front door and they embraced before, still heady with the enjoyment of a fun-filled evening, they briefly shared a French kiss. They both had commitments on Wednesday, so they agreed to go out again on Thursday, this time for a disco night at the other end of the culture spectrum. The taxi continued on to Highgate to drop Kweku home.

Thursday's dinner at a fast food joint in St John's Wood left plenty of time before the discotheques opened. So they strolled back up Wellington Road to the Odeon Swiss Cottage, where *Silver Streak* was showing, a comedy action film starring Gene Wilder, Jill Clayburgh and Richard Pryor. It was uncomplicated gut-busting stuff and teed them up perfectly for a frank evening where there would be no competition about how well they had understood Virgil's *Aeneid* or Homer's *Iliad* in their first term at Oxford.

They finally ended up at the nearby Indigo Bear discotheque on Finchley Road. The place was quite busy, but not packed. Time flew by as they laughed while exchanging stories about African and West Indian life.

Only once did Kweku feel the tension that normally lurks in the background undermining interactions between Africans and those shipped from Africa against their will, in chains, first to the Caribbean and later directly to the United States, as slaves to work on plantations and earn their owners wealth beyond imagination. This was an old tension Kweku was already aware of: the feeling that those left behind in Africa had not fought hard enough to save them from the slave trade. Worse still, that their fellow Africans from a leadership level down had even participated – on an extensive scale in the case of swapping prisoners of war for goods from the merchants – in the trade which left those who survived the perilous transatlantic journey with little human dignity thousands of miles away from their homes.

So Roberta and Kweku drank and boogied the night away, letting themselves go at the start of the holiday season. Well after midnight, towards the end, the DJ started playing slow numbers, giving Cupid a chance to let his arrows fly.

As they smooched to the sound of The Commodores' *Just To Be Close To You*, her left hand resting on his shoulder, his right arm around her waist, Kweku teased her closer with his left hand as they stared into each other's eyes. It was as if the music had stopped. They had a long, lingering kiss and didn't even notice at first when the music really did stop. Kweku hailed a taxi back home to Highgate and they continued there into the early hours of the morning…

Later that morning he was up to ring for a minicab to take Roberta home to Kensal Rise. He told her he was flying down to Ghana early the next day for the Christmas break, so would see her next term. But, as they waited the 30 minutes for the minicab to arrive, she wasn't so sure. The euphoria of the previous evening had evaporated with the realisation that they would only next meet back at Oxford. She started to feel guilt, obsessing over what Carrie would think if she ever found out. Betrayal by her best friend? Surely that would be too much of a cliché? Kweku tried hard to reassure her that he and Carrie were history. She accepted that, but somehow both of them realised that things would be tricky going forward.

Even Kweku now started to doubt his motives. Had he only pursued a relationship with Roberta because he was still hung up over Carrie? Was that her real attraction to him? For now, neither would have to over-analyse these concerns. The Roman poet Horace's advice, *carpe diem* – seize the moment – had won out. They had consensually enjoyed a fantastic time and were young, single and free in the 70s. Who knew what troubles lay ahead for either of them, and so who could begrudge their taking advantage of these few moments of self-indulgence?

***

Holidays in Ghana

December 1976

Kweku arrived back in Ghana with the harmattan season well underway. The desert winds sweeping in from the Sahara Desert to the North of the country had overpowered the moisture sweeping in off the sea to the South. Days were hot but dry, humidity very low, dust clouds covering the sun for most of the time. Nights were cold.

Kweku's parents sensed that their son, at eighteen, had moved beyond the self-questioning and inexperience which characterising adolescent life. He had now embarked on what was sometimes termed 'young adulthood', no doubt to distinguish it from the mature adulthood of twenty-five years so perceptively alluded to in Anstey's *Vice Versa*. Kojo and Deborah were anxious that their son should be mixing with the 'right crowd', to make it less likely that his good nature and easy-going manner would be readily exploited by unscrupulous chancers.

Partly out of boredom, and partly in hope of meeting new friends, Kweku willingly tagged along with them to daytime social events hosted by their friends for their children – christenings, birthday parties, Christmas parties, weddings and the occasional funeral.

But he couldn't shake off a nagging urge to find out what had become of his old Nursery School friend, Kwesi Osei. During a lull in the seemingly endless round of supervised social functions, he decided to break free and give him a ring. By the end of the call, he wished he hadn't. Osei took the opportunity to offload on him everything that had gone wrong in his life in the year and a half since they had last been in contact. He began by asking Kweku if he had time to listen to the whole story. When Kweku replied yes, the floodgates opened:

'Hmmm, then where do I start?... Well, while I was at secondary school, that is, when you were at Huntsmere,' he added, in a tone that came across as being laced with envy, 'my father was made redundant from his job as factory supervisor at the shirt-making company where he worked – you remember?...'

'Er, yes,' Kweku quickly added.

Osei continued, in words that would later prove prophetic in his own case:

'Some people get sacked and immediately resolve to bounce back in life and prove the person who sacked them wrong. Others allow their dismissal to crush them. My father fell into the latter category. He descended into a downward spiral of drunkenness and self-pity. There were no funds to pay my school fees any more, so I was withdrawn from the school. Mum asked everyone she knew, but no one would help. I even suggested she should ask your mum, Auntie Deborah, but she slapped me down pretty quickly on that one, saying the two of them hardly knew each other and weren't really on those sorts of terms.'

'Well, that is true,' Kweku affirmed, relieved that Osei's mum had chosen not to put his own mum in an awkward position.

Osei went on:

‘Eventually Mum swallowed her pride and visited her well-to-do but stingy mother, Grandma Grace, to appeal for help.’

Kweku interrupted:

‘I didn’t know your grandma was still alive? I thought she passed away long ago?’

‘No, I don’t mean my mum’s mother, I mean her mother’s sister. Didn’t you know? By custom here in Ghana, my mum’s sister is also my mother. If that useless father of mine had a brother, he would also be my father.’

‘I see.’ It was an idiosyncrasy of Ghanaian culture which had escaped Kweku during all his years schooling in the UK.

‘Anyway look, let me finish. Grandma Grace had always warned Mum against marrying my dad, saying it would come to no good. When my mum went ahead and married him anyway, she strongly advised her not to put all her faith in him: he just seemed to her the weak and unambitious type. So you can imagine, when Mum finally went to beg Grandma Grace, she milked the situation for all it was worth, repeatedly crowing “I told you so” and all that!’

‘OK, go on.’

‘Knowing my mum, I am sure she kept her cool and just sat there listening patiently, looking chastened. What’s important is that, at the end of her lecture, Grandma Grace said she would give Mum the investment money she was after to try to start a new business from home, but would only pay my school fees up to the end of secondary school. She said she had to make sure she had enough money for herself in her old age and that money didn’t grow on trees.

So at least the school re-admitted me and I was able to complete my secondary education. Meanwhile, as for Mum, first she set up business in the living room as a seamstress. But competition was fierce for a basic trade like this. She couldn't charge enough to cover her costs, so she just couldn't make ends meet.

When that business failed, she rented a stall in the market to sell cakes baked at home to a special recipe in a book she had bought. Here too, business has been slow, but at least it has allowed her to make barely enough money to pay for our food and basic necessities. However, she wasn't able to afford university admission for me and I wasn't smart enough to get a bursary.'

'So, what are you doing now then?' Kweku asked.

He sighed. 'Well, I've been applying for jobs here and there, looking out for government youth employment programmes and the like… With these too, you sign up, everything looks great and you start doing something practical, but then they never pay you. They promise they will pay next month, then the following month, and on it goes. In the end you run out of money even to pay for transportation to the job site and have to stop going in.

So I'm still looking for work. Whenever I see an old newspaper that's been discarded, I go straight to the jobs columns and comb through to see if there is anything I can apply for and have hope. Mum has been trying too, ringing round old friends. When she tells them what's happened, some are genuinely sorry but complain of their own struggles with daily life. Others shed crocodile tears in *schadenfreude* and waffle on, giving useless advice to mask the fact that deep down they don't really care – as if that advice was any substitute for money. Others still suddenly become harder to contact, frightened that her new state of penury might be contagious. She is at her wits' end and can't do any more for me than she's already doing.'

'Hmmm, I see.' Kweku pondered. He had no idea how to help. He couldn't suggest to his dad to hire Osei at the factory in Mim. Osei was a good friend. What if it didn't work out? Wouldn't that sour their relationship for ever? And then, what would other staff think, if someone without any relevant experience was parachuted into employment over the heads of better qualified applicants?

Impatient with the silence, Osei decided to jump in:

'Kweku, can *you* help me out? I mean, can you lend me, say, two hundred pounds. You can even think of it as your Christmas present to me.'

Kweku was taken aback: 'Pounds, you said, not cedis?'

'Yes, pounds. This our clueless government have been keeping the cedi artificially strong for years now. Its official value against hard currencies like pounds, dollars or deutsche marks makes no sense, when you compare what you can buy with it and what you could buy if you had the same in hard currency at the official exchange rate. But there's a thriving black market for foreign currency exchange at a place near the market in central Accra called 'Zongo Lane' or 'Cow Lane'. You know, northerners always seem to have a ready market for foreign exchange outside official channels. I reckon the military government know that it's going on but are turning a blind eye – maybe because they're changing money there too! Anyway, there are makeshift hidden foreign exchange booths there where you can get a proper market exchange rate for hard currencies several times the government's own artificially overvalued rate.'

'But then why doesn't the government just allow the cedi to be exchanged at market rates for these currencies?'

'Why? You mean you don't know? Then, Kweku, you have been away for too long! It's because the previous government's devaluation of the cedi – which they said they were doing to boost exports so their value would exceed that of our imports – well, this devaluation of our currency was the very excuse used by the senior army officers to seize power in a coup, without waiting for the people to express their vote in a general election scheduled in less than two years.

And so, even though for a long time now everyone's been telling the military government to bring the cedi back into line with real market exchange rates for any number of reasons to help the economy and stop the widespread black market *kalabule*, they are stubbornly refusing to do it. That's the kind of thing that goes on down here – it's all about shim-sham, spin and holding on to power, not doing things that will really benefit the average person.'

'I see.'

'So then, will you be able to lend me the two hundred pounds?'

'I don't know. I don't have it with me right now, I can probably only spare a hundred right now. Maybe I can get the rest in two weeks' time from my allowance… But then what about me, what will I use for my own treats and entertainment for the rest of the holiday?'

'You are talking of treats and entertainment, when things are so dire for me and my mum?'

'Whoa, just you hold on right there! Look here, Kwesi, it's not my fault you and your family have found yourselves in this situation!'

'I know. I'm sorry, I didn't mean it like that …'

After a pregnant pause, loaded with tension, Kweku said: 'OK, I'll do it.'

'Oh, thank you so much, Kweku. I'll never forget it.'

'But, as I said, you'll have to wait.'

'Can I at least get the one hundred pounds now?'

'OK, I'll see. It'll have to be on my next visit. I'll tell my mum I want to meet you tomorrow to catch up.'

'Thank you so much, Kweku. Then I'll look forward to seeing you tomorrow.'

'OK Bye… Oh, are you still there?'

'Yes?'

'Kwesi, I am helping you this time, but please don't expect me to be doing this again for you. I am not your mum or dad.'

'Please, don't even mention that man. He is no dad to me, and no husband to my mum either!'

'I know, I know. Sorry. OK, forget that. What I mean is, I'm just starting out on life myself. I don't have any dependants and I don't need any.'

'Is that how you see me?'

'What?'

'As a "dependant"?'

'Well, maybe I didn't put it very well, but that is essentially what you are asking me to do… To stand in because other family members are unable or unwilling to help.'

There was silence the other end. Kweku thought he could hear Osei starting to sob. He was sorry he'd felt compelled to put things so bluntly to him. For his part, Osei so desperately wanted to tell Kweku that he should forget it, that he could go and stick his two hundred pounds where the sun didn't shine. But he was desperate for the money, so he bit his tongue. All he could bring himself to say, after he had pulled himself together was: 'OK, I get it.'

'OK,' Kweku replied.

'OK thank you. Bye.' Osei hung up.

***

Kweku got the one hundred pounds to him the next day, a further fifty pounds the following week and the last fifty the week after that. It meant that for the rest of the holiday he had to spend more time tagging along with his parents for their functions rather than being able to sneak out partying on his own. He was OK with that, but very worried for Osei's future and his own relationship with him going forward.

He resolved that he would give Osei whatever emotional support that he could for as long as he could, but that if the time came when that was not appreciated, then he might have to let Osei loose. If there were to be no limits to Osei's requests for charity, he wouldn't be able to sacrifice his own life and career prospects for Osei's. He had too much loyalty and appreciation for his parents' sacrifices for his own welfare.

The episode gave Kweku the opportunity to reflect that Lady Luck did not deal evenly with all living beings in this world, from the lottery of birth and onwards through later life, although along the way people sometimes had their own choices to make to improve their destiny. He could only interfere with the vicissitudes of life up to a point. Simply put, for him as much as anyone else, life was too short.

***

After his friend Kweku had gone back to England, one day in Accra, larking about in the neighbourhood, Osei saw a discarded newspaper and decided, as usual, to flick through the classified section on jobs. He noticed a quarter-page advertisement for army recruits. The banner screamed out from the page "Join our proud military, defend the nation and be somebody!" He had hit rock bottom. Here was a potential lifeline to being somebody, to proving wrong all those who had encouraged his mum to give up on him, to leave him to his drunken father and try to save herself. They said no one would blame her if she did that; she could always come back for him later, once she had made it in life, and he would accept her. After all, they assured her, no child ever gives up on their mum. For her, that was just unthinkable. It never crossed her mind.

He checked the date at the top of the newspaper. It was just a week ago. He prayed it wouldn't be too late. He rushed over to the advertised location for the army recruitment office to find out more. He was given a form to complete. He dashed home to tell his mum.

She was so excited that, after two years of drifting and keeping ever seedier company, he had latched on to a dream worth pursuing, one that could make an independent, grown man out of him. She helped him hurriedly complete the form.

Early the next morning, he returned to the recruitment office. He handed in his form, together with a photo and other requested identification documents. He was given a short interview and a test checking his basic skills with reading, writing and arithmetic. They told him they would let him know in a week to a month's time.

His mum, who had the key to their post box, was checking it twice weekly, on Tuesdays and Fridays, as she always had. Two weeks came and went with no response. When a third, then fourth week passed by, Osei feared the worst. On the Friday of the fifth week, his mum returned home, anxiously clutching an envelope. It had been stamped on the outside "Army Recruitment Office" and was addressed to her son. She handed it to him, unwilling to usurp his right to open it for himself. He snatched at it, tearing it open at the side and read out its opening lines:

"Dear Mr Osei,

We are pleased to inform you that your application to enlist in the Army has been successful, subject to passing a medical examination …"

That was all Kwesi Osei wanted to see. He tossed the letter into the air in jubilation, hugged his mum, tears now streaming down her cheeks. She picked it back up off the floor and gave it to him to read out the rest:

"... You are to report at Tolman Barracks on Monday 4th April for your medical examination.

Yours sincerely

T.K. Asare-Acquah

Recruitment Officer"

Monday 4th ... Osei worked out that gave him just over a fortnight. For the next two weeks he fretted constantly and made sure he stayed in good physical shape. When the medical exam came, he passed with flying colours and was enlisted as an infantryman with the 5th Battalion based in Accra.

***

First Hilary Term

January 1977

Kweku returned from Ghana in early January. The next term at the first Aeneid lecture, he saw Roberta with Carrie. Watching their interactions from a distance, he presumed Carrie had no idea. He felt guilty. After the following week's lecture, Carrie invited him to join them for a coffee. She thought it was time she introduced Kweku to her friends Roberta and Louise properly beyond smiles and waves.

There were a couple of moments during the conversation at the café when Carrie was sure Kweku and Roberta had exchanged furtive glances. But she made the assumption that, as they didn't know each other very well, they were just trying to size each other up. She couldn't imagine it was anything more complicated than that. She decided to think no more of it.

Kweku generally hibernated during the rest of Hilary Term's harsh wintry weather from January to March. Shamelessly scrapping around for a justification, he consoled himself that, after all, he was an African; the intemperate seasonal British weather was not his natural environment, so he could be excused!

Apart from the odd social function, going to church on Sundays was one of his few reasons to come out of hibernation for the rest of term. Baptised a Catholic by his Roman Catholic mother within months of his birth, Kweku was still by then making an effort, not always successful for different reasons, to attend weekly Mass

– in Ghana at his local parish church in Cantonments, and in Oxford at The Catholic Chaplaincy on St Aldates. Especially in Ghana, he preferred the evening Mass, as it tended to have a smaller congregation. That meant it was usually less showy, with shorter, more punchy sermons, and the priests were less inclined to feel they had an audience to perform to. Most importantly of all, evening Masses were consequently the shortest of the weekly Masses. In a sense, it was: box ticked, job done for the week – excluding of course holy days of obligation, which were extra.

According to Kweku's rather simplistic analysis, it all came down to whether we believe we are being watched by a timeless presence continually judging our conduct – whether we call this presence God, Jehovah, Buddha, Allah or otherwise – or, if we don't believe this, whether we care how we behave. He at least decided that he cared, and beyond that thought it better to hedge his bets!

In Oxford, as the plant world blossomed again in Spring, the warmer weather and longer, brighter days brought hibernating fauna and previously hidden colours back out into the open. People moved about dressed attractively to look their best, hoping to catch the lingering look of an admirer and receive a boost to their self-confidence. Kweku too was out of his shell and back to the land of the living in Trinity Term, in April.

***

Near Miss

April 1977

His first weekend away in Trinity Term, Kweku was at Oxford station awaiting the train to London Paddington when he spotted his ex, Carrie, looking happy with a young man on the platform on the opposite side of the tracks. His heart missed a beat. In the weeks and months since they had split up, he had tried to convince himself that he was over her. But was he? Really? Deep down, he couldn't be sure.

Against his positivist, forward-looking instincts, he found himself speculating: Could this man she was with have anything to do with why she had cooled on him, or why in truth they had never really got going, after that idyllic first evening together? Or was the man just a relative, a platonic friend with no love interest in her nor she in him? They hadn't spotted Kweku yet, but that was OK with him: you are always at an advantage when you have spotted familiar faces in public but they are yet to see you. It allows you to control the ensuing narrative – to go somewhere you will be invisible to them, to try to catch their attention, or to stay where you are and leave it to fate to determine whether they will notice you.

Acting on impulse – against the dictates of a better judgment calling for him to avoid reviving any romantic interest in Carrie with unknown consequences – he found himself walking up the stairs to the connecting bridge, wanting to know more. On reaching the top of the stairs, he noticed an intercity train approaching the station from the left. He looked to their platform. He saw them interrupt their conversation to look up at the train and then move down the platform, closer to the edge. It must be their train. He slightly quickened his stride. The train ground to a complete halt as he reached the other end of the bridge.

He went down the stairs on the other side into the climbing flood of passengers just disgorged from the train. He eventually reached the area of the platform where he'd last seen them, but then lost his bearings in the jostling crowds. To make matters worse, from what he could see of the carriages that was not obscured by those on the platform, the carriages were packed with rush-hour commuters. That made it virtually impossible to distinguish anyone, unless they were almost pressed up against the windows.

One by one the carriage doors slammed shut. Kweku had almost given up when he caught a glimpse of Carrie, still chatting animatedly with her companion. She hadn't seen him yet. The guard blew his whistle to sound the all-clear, and with a jolt the train resumed its stealthy consumption of the tracks in front of it, the engine at the rear purring mockingly as it passed Kweku.

***

Never Feel Sorry for Yourself

May 1977

It was now late May. As Kweku made his way along the north side of the front quad at Johnston, still caught up in the rapture of Pimm's No. 1 consumed while cheering on the Johnston Eights from the balcony of the College Boathouse at the annual regatta, he spotted one of the two Classics scholars in his year, Nathan Chalmers, approaching from the opposite direction. The look on Chalmers' face evinced simultaneously sympathy and puzzlement. Chalmers slowed up as he reached Kweku, deciding to confront him directly.

'Kweku, you know they were considering giving you an Exhibition at the end of this first year? But you've just blown it. You've taken things too easy this term.'

Kweku was stunned. He had entered College as a "Commoner", the title for the vast majority of students not awarded Scholarships or Exhibitions prior to entry. He had no idea that academic awards could be made after courses had already started, less still that he had been under consideration for one. After entry, he had thought that was it.

Sometimes in life, in our reaction to disappointment at not winning something, we hide under cover of a shell constructed out of self-pity. A better response is to let others feel sorry for you, if the majority of those informed about your circumstances think you deserve their sympathy. Sometimes you will deserve it, the victim of circumstances beyond your control, such as the lottery of birth, an accident or a natural disaster. Most of the time you will not deserve it, the victim of choices for which you were entirely responsible, made from a pool of options with predictably different likely outcomes, at least one of which would have been better for you than the one you chose. Best of all is to learn not to seek the sympathy of others any more than of yourself. That way, if it doesn't come, you won't miss it.

Self-pity is therefore more often than not an immature choice, rooted in a belief that others have been insufficiently perceptive about your virtues or unfair in judging you. The mature reaction to the disappointment of failure is a determination to prove the doubters wrong. At that point in his life, Kweku made an immature choice. He withdrew even further academically, and was later in life to regret this.

CHAPTER ELEVEN

Off Campus

October 1978

Near the end of his second year at Oxford, Kweku caught up with Charlie again at a College lunch. Charlie's course, Chemistry, like Classics, was a 4-year one. He told Kweku that he and his friend Giles wanted to rent out a place on South Parade up the road in Summertown and there was room for one more. Kweku knew he had to find digs somewhere soon. His 2 years on campus would be up at the end of term, so he was interested. Charlie ran him up there to have a look.

It certainly wasn't the Savoy, but it was fine for students. Charlie's friend Giles was there when they arrived. Kweku had heard a lot about Giles, but this was the first time he actually met him. Now here was someone who was fascinated by cars, loved racing them, working on them, knew everything about them. His passion for racing was infectious: when you're shown the inner workings of a craft by an expert, it's easier to love it. Kweku's enthusiasm for racing was born that day. It didn't extend to a willingness actually to race cars – spectating knowledgeably gave him enough of a thrill.

From the flat, Giles took him for a spin in his Triumph Convertible to the White Hart pub in Wolvercote. Before ever laying eyes on Giles, Kweku had thought he was fine with speed. Little did he know, as he stepped into Giles' car, that he was about to embark on the most frightening car journey of his life to date. Giles chortled and grinned like a 2-year old in a toy car as he raced round harpin bends at breakneck speeds, the bonnet of his car never pointing in the actual direction of its movement even on straights. Immediately he was through one corner, he was preparing for the next, tyres screeching and skidding all the way.

Kweku gasped as Giles waxed lyrical about left-handers and right-handers, adrenalin pumping faster through his body than he had ever experienced before. Seeing his apparent panic as the car kissed the kerbs and edges on either side of the road only made Giles grin and chuckle all the more. 'Hold on to your seat, chap!' he would say as he sped on. Kweku found himself being frightened and thrilled in equal measure. He held on to his seat for dear life, only relaxing his grip as they finally pulled up outside an inn with the White Hart sign emblazoned aloft. He had made it! He asked Giles for a Valium, but Giles took it as a joke and laughingly told him his first pint would work equally well to settle his nerves!

***

With his digs for his last two years at Oxford now nailed down, Kweku's remaining priorities during the summer holidays were to learn how to drive and buy a small secondhand car of some sort to get around, especially between College and Summertown. Walking and cycling weren't going to be enough any more.

The process took much longer to finish than he'd hoped. He found a driving school in Muswell Hill. The lessons were sometimes weeks apart because of his studies and travelling schedules, then there was all the time it took to arrange the driving test. Something went wrong on his first test which he never was able to ascertain; but he sailed through his second one.

The next hurdle was to get a car. Knowing that Kweku always loved speed as a child, as he had to some extent himself in his younger days, Kojo was worried. As usual, Deborah supported Kojo. He tried to persuade Kweku to carry on cycling and walking, using the bus if necessary, but Kweku staged a virtual strike on any conversation. He immersed himself in exaggerated self-pity, like an actor in a Greek tragedy waiting for the ground under his feet to open and swallow him up. Recalling this conduct years later, Kweku was not proud of this phase of his life.

After almost a month of seeing his son moping around, Kojo reluctantly gave in to his emotional blackmail and agreed to buy him a small secondhand car. Kweku had his heart set on a blue Mini Clubman. His new flatmate Giles, a used car dealer himself, rang up contacts and flipped through auto magazines looking for one. Kweku did his own searching. After four weeks, Giles located a beautiful blue, well-kept one with a full service history. He brought it round to the flat and Kweku fell instantly in love with it.

Deservedly or not, Kweku now had his independence in all but a financial sense – he was still reliant for money on allowances from his parents. It was his first car and he nursed it like the family pet. On blizzard-hit days in the worst of the English winter, he felt vindicated in the bolshy tactics he had used to get the car. On other days, he struggled to forgive himself:

he had behaved like a spoiled brat and, after all the sacrifices they had made for him over the years, his parents deserved better.

***

Living further out of town, Kweku's life became even more unstructured. Term-time was already less than half of the year, contrasting with the term-time lasting three quarters of the year he had been used to at all his schools in England before going up to Oxford. The idea behind a year consisting of three 8-week terms was that a more mature student would exhibit the required self-discipline to do most background study preparation on their chosen area of the curriculum during the holidays, then apply this accumulated research, supplemented by further study and lectures, directly to answering questions in the field during the short term-time.

For a variety of reasons, the key one being inadequate self-discipline, Kweku struggled to put into practice in his home environment the necessary routines to facilitate the basic accumulation of research. Instead, he habitually returned to College rudderless at the start of successive terms, hoping to "wing it" on the job.

Meanwhile political instability back home had seen an internal palace coup led by generals within the ruling military council in 1978, followed by a bloody overthrow of that entire council in June 1979 by junior army officers led by Jerry Rawlings. Within weeks, the new military council had summarily executed eight senior military officers, including three former heads of state and members of the deposed council. These grim events thwarted plans by Kweku to return home to Ghana for the last holidays before his final year at Oxford, although constitutional rule was returned to the country in September that year and a President was democratically elected in free and fair elections.

***

By the start of his final year, Kweku had belatedly reached the conclusion that it was impossible to "wing it" at Oxford – unless in the case of a genius, which he certainly was not. He made a determined effort to turn things around during term time, but always found himself chasing his tail due to lack of adequate planning and discipline during the preceding holidays. During the holidays, he spent too much time at concerts, plays and sporting events and too little time visiting the local library. Stubbornly flippant, he considered spending time in the library to be a boring and unproductive pastime in a morgue-like environment. All this was combined with an obstinate belief that the key to any written discourse would be revealed to him in a flash of inspiration after the most cursory term-time study.

And so he continued fecklessly to engage in a whirlwind of social outings in the countryside and in Oxford, attended debates of the university's African Society to slake his persistent thirst for the politics of the day – something he was convinced was down to a 'politics' gene he had inherited from his father – and shied away from the drudgery of painstaking analytical research, the much-maligned true foundation for all "eureka" moments.

In his last term, Kweku finally brought a desk into his bedroom at the flat in Summertown. He was back to believing in miracles, to praying that it wasn't too late and that he still had five weeks to rescue an almost forlorn endeavour. Sadly for him, but in hindsight in an outcome probably no better than he deserved, his water-based soft contact lenses had imperceptibly been absorbing over an extended period tobacco ingrained into the same yellow, nicotine-stained index finger which he had been using to massage the lubrication solution into them daily. It eventually sparked off a massive allergic reaction in his eyes, which increasingly blurred his vision for the whole of that term, with matters coming to a head during his final exams.

CHAPTER TWELVE

School's Out

June 1980

The Invigilator bellowed, staccato for each monosyllabic word, 'Time! Put your pens down now!' Kweku's ordeal was over. It was a merciful release, so inflamed were his eyes. His problems with his sight had peaked just before the toughest paper of all with the biggest weighting, "Logic". It covered partly formal logic but mostly epistemology or the theory of knowledge. He could hardly see the paper in front of him for virtually the entire exam. Would it have made any difference if he had? He didn't know, and thankfully didn't have to explore this. In a variation of the Alice Cooper hit, his finals had ended, "[Schools were] out for summer… out for ever!"

He joined the throng weaving its way down the stairs, spilling out on to the street in front of Examination Schools. As he came out into the open, the realisation hit him – it was over. The resulting adrenaline rush was a perfect antidote to the inflammation in his eyes. It was a sunny Tuesday afternoon. Champagne corks popped all around, as police struggled to separate partying students – past caring at this once-in-a-lifetime moment at the end of Schools – from frustrated motorists, cyclists and pedestrians given added incentive by the insouciance of the students to resent their privileged circumstances. For 10 to 15 minutes sheer bedlam reigned in the tensions between town and gown, as car horns honked, abuse was shouted by 'townies' at students and returned with interest.

'I'm going to get absolutely arsed tonight!' yelled one of Kweku's fellow-classicists, Jules Barrington, popping open his second bottle of Bollinger and spraying its contents around randomly before guzzling with bacchanalian abandon.

'Oh boy, me too!' said Kweku, struggling to see through his watery eyes where another fellow-classicist Ed Dover was. Spinning round, he made him out, standing right behind them, looking subdued, deflated.

'Ruddy Logic paper!' Dover moaned ruefully. 'I reckon that's definitely blown my chances of a 2:1 and getting a shot at merchant banking!'

'Oooh, listen to him – clever clogs!' Barrington chipped in, before adding dismissively: 'I don't care if I get a third. So long as it's an honours degree, I'll get an MA in 3 years' time anyway – more than enough. Don't you just love traditions!'

Just then Dave Rayburn, another classicist from Johnston, joined them:

'Yeah, it's all right for you, Barrington! Your dad's some kind of big shot corporate raider in the City, isn't he? Championing conduct that's all part of the unacceptable side of capitalism, if you ask me!' Rayburn was repeating almost verbatim a slur famously thrown some years earlier in the direction of a well-known corporate raider by a conservative prime minister in Parliament.

'My dad's an investor,' Barrington retorted. 'It's all about shareholder wealth maximisation, but hoi polloi like you wouldn't understand that sort of thing.'

Rayburn had had enough: 'Blah, blah, blah!'

'Hey, come on you guys!' Kweku interjected. 'So, where's everyone going tonight? I hope my eyes will be ok to move around.'

'I don't know about you lot,' said Barrington, 'but I've got a train to catch, the 5:30 to Paddington. Quick shower, then dinner at Langan's Brasserie and on to Annabel's. Time to partayy! Party time, suckers! See you in another life!'

'Not if I see you first!' muttered Rayburn. 'What a pillock!' he added, as Barrington strode off out of earshot back up the High Street towards Catte Street.

'Isn't he staying for the College Ball this Saturday then?' asked Dover.

'Oh, leave him be,' said Kweku. 'He wouldn't be the only one giving it a miss… Ahh, freedom!... Hey, how about we meet up at Browns at, say, half six and take it from there?'

'Boooring!' Rayburn commented cynically.

'Well, what do you suggest then?'

'Don't know, but not that!'

By now the crowds outside were fast thinning, harassed by local and Schools authorities to move along.

Kweku signed off: 'Anyhow, I'll see most of you on Saturday then, if not before.' Because of the trouble with his blurred vision, he had come into town with a taxi that day. He walked carefully and slowly up the High Street, then right at the top, down Cornmarket Street and on to Magdalen Street where he caught a taxi back to his digs in Summertown.

***

When he got there, he saw Charlie's car parked outside. He was sure he would be prepping for his own final exams on Thursday.

Carefully navigating around a hole hidden under the carpet just inside the front entrance at the bottom of the stairs – a relic of a previous Scotch-soaked tenant's hapless stumbling entry into the flat three years earlier – he made his way to the landing at the top. He popped his head around the door to Charlie's room.

Charlie pushed his chair back and looked up from the layers of opened books and files on his desk:

'So how did it go?'

Kweku shrugged his shoulders, pointing to his inflamed eyes and shaking his head. Just then the scent of white wine following Kweku hit Charlie's nostrils: 'Poo, you stink of wine or bubbly!'

'Well, what do you expect? Everyone was just spraying it around outside Schools… Not saying I didn't swig any, mind.'

'Lucky you! I've still got one more exam left. Arrghhh, two more days and then I'm free forever! Can't wait!'

'I know, old boy… Look, I don't want to be in the way… I'm thinking of going down to London tomorrow. I'll be back up on Saturday morning in time for the College Ball.'

'Oh, you're going to that are you?'

'Well, yeah, in the end I decided I might as well… Actually, I was sort of pushed into it by someone. She's never been to an Oxford Ball before – not that that's different from any other kind of Ball. Anyway, she wanted to go. So, I know I'm sort of being used but hey, she seems quite special, so I'm happy to be. Who knows?'

'Someone I know?'

'Oh no, you wouldn't know her. She's just someone I met in Highgate.'

'Oh yeah, bit of a dark horse then are we, Kweku?' Charlie suddenly realised the unintended double entendre. He added quickly: 'Oh I don't mean it like that of course!'

'Don't worry, chap, no offence taken.'

'Actually, come to think of it, I reckon that's quite a good one, "A bit of a dark horse!"' Charlie chuckled, pleased with his unplanned pun. 'Anyway, chap, I'm not sure I'll be there. One of my three trained polo ponies is still down with some sort of flu bug, so I'm already skating on thin ice. There's a big charity match at Kirtlington Park this Saturday and Prince Charles might be coming, so I'll definitely need to borrow at least one more, ideally two from somewhere.'

'Have you tried asking Hugo Fry?'

'No point. I know he wants to use all four of his that day, he's been training them for ages. He's already going to have to rotate two of them to get through the match. But I hear another Kirtlington Park member, Tom Morton, has had to travel with his dad to the States at short notice for an urgent business meeting. So I reckon I'll try and borrow at least one of his. Anyway, I've got to get back to work… By the way, I bought a loaf of bread and a tasty sponge cake for everyone.'

'Really, where's that then?' asked Kweku, stepping into the kitchen and looking around. '… In the fridge?' He swung open the fridge door, expectantly.

'Nah, I ate it!' Charlie roared with laughter as an empty fridge stared back at Kweku as usual, yellowing sides and shelves the only colour visible inside.

'You!' Kweku half-laughed, shaking his head, upset with himself for falling for yet another of Charlie's practical jokes.

Eventually recovering his composure, Charlie added:

'Anyway, if you're not sure what to do, you might want to stick around. I know Stanton said he was meeting one of the Directors at Snetterton this morning.'

Kweku seemed confused. Charlie went on:

'You know, the race track near Thetford.'

Kweku was still unclear. His patchy mental geography of the UK didn't extend far.

'You probably only know Silverstone,' Charlie said, rolling his eyes.

Kweku smiled wryly.

'Anyway, apparently this Director chap wants to sell his TVR sports car. He's arranged with Giles for him to take it round the track for a spin this morning and then try it out for a couple of days. Giles said he'd be passing through here afterwards to pick up some stuff on his way to The Bear in Woodstock to meet up with an old friend.'

'The Bear Hotel?'

'Yep, that's the one.'

'Yeah… I remember there. I think you guys took me there in my first summer here? Lovely spot. Really quaint and colourful in the summer.'

'Anyway, you decide what you want to do, Kweku. I've got to get back to swotting. See you later.' With that, he pulled his chair back up to his desk and refocused on his work. Kweku went to his room, lay on his bed and dozed off.

An hour later, the screeching of tyres and ever-louder revving of a sportscar engine woke him up. The vibration of the flat's creaky timber frames and wooden floorboards meant the car must be right outside. A couple more revs and the engine went off. Moments later, a key turned in the front door. Kweku had a good idea who it must be. He got up and went out into the corridor. Sure enough, it was Giles, his face flushed red with the exertion of a long, adrenaline-pumping ride. As he lit a cigarette and started climbing the stairs, he looked up and saw Kweku on the landing.

He froze momentarily, as if he had just seen a ghost: 'Hey chap, I didn't expect to see you here then… I thought you'd finished your exams?'

'I have, but I got talked by someone into taking them to the Johnston College Ball on Saturday. Don't worry, you don't know her. Anyway look …' Kweku was anxious to change the subject: '… I hear you're going to The Bear in Woodstock.'

'Turner told you that, I'll bet.'

'Yes.'

'That's true, old boy. But I'm going to The Trout first for some grub. I don't know about you but I'm starving.'

'That sounds great. Have you got room in your car? It's only that my eyes are still playing up and I don't want to risk driving.'

'Er… Well I've just got this TVR from one of the chaps at Snetters. He wants to sell it and he's let me have it for a couple of days on trial. It's a two-seater, so I've got space at the moment, but well… not sure about the way back …' He winked knowingly. Kweku thought that probably meant Giles would be trying his luck. But he was desperate to escape from Oxford somewhere right then, so he stayed on message:

'Don't worry, chap. I can always get a taxi back or something. And the bill at The Trout is on me.'

'Good man!' Stanton said. He went to pop his head round Turner's door.

'How did it go?' Turner asked him.

'The visit went a treat! And I mean that! You should have been there! I tell you, old boy, I haven't had so much fun in a long, long time. The track was in really good nick too. No, but it was amazing. You can't beat a TVR I reckon. She was purring beautifully, great handling round corners too!'

'The engine sounds a bit loud though – I heard you coming all the way down the street.'

'No! See, you want the engine to make all that noise when it's running. That way you know it's a proper sports car.'

'All right, go on then, let's get a closer look.' They both rushed downstairs into the yard. Kweku, keen to know more about racing, followed them. He listened in as the two of them chatted briefly outside the car about how it had performed on the different corners and straights round Snetterton. Turner and Stanton sat in the car. Stanton turned the ignition key, revving the engine up a few times while explaining the dashboard and controls to Turner.

Turner gave his verdict as he climbed out. 'Pretty impressive!'

‘It’s just the ticket, I tell you, old boy!’

‘Are you going to buy it then?’

‘I’d love to, but I reckon I might have to wait till I’ve sold a few more cars!’

‘Anyway, dreams, dreams. Got to get back to work, chap! I hear you two are off to The Bear in Woodstock?’

‘Yep, just got to run up to Middleton Stoney first to get something from the house.’

‘So look, then let’s catch up on Thursday evening, yes? I’ll be done with my finals by then.’

‘All right, let’s do that.’

‘Good one!’

Stanton sprinted back upstairs to get his stuff. He waited 10 minutes for Kweku to spruce up and Turner watched from his window as they left together in the TVR, with the usual screeching Stanton-style start, the car pointed every which way before finally settling in a forward direction and rapidly accelerating down the road out of sight.

***

By now it was almost midsummer, the sun shone as brightly at 6 o’clock in the evening as if it were midday. Giles was literally taking the borrowed TVR for a spin – in fact, several spins – round hairpin bends, under bridges, over bridges, grinning with enjoyment. His passenger Kweku held on to his seat for dear life, his teeth chattering as the tyres skidded and smoked through country lanes. He cursed himself for not remembering to take a Valium before climbing into Giles’ car. It was almost like boarding a flight.

The Trout Inn was at its glorious best on a clear June day. Giles was spotted as he walked in by an old friend wearing a tweed flat cap. The friend looked slightly the worse for wear as he teased: 'You old goat, what are you doing here? Up to no good, I bet!' As they glad-handed each other, catching up on the latest talk of the town, Kweku noticed behind them how busy the place was.

He spied a solitary free table by the river and walked briskly over to bagsy it. Lighting a cigarette, he sat down to absorb the inn's quaint surroundings, a gentle breeze refreshing the atmosphere as the waters of the River Thames rippled by, trout leaping through the weir under Godstow Bridge. After some minutes, he saw Giles waving his friend off and making his way towards the table.

'What will you be having then, chap?' Giles asked. 'Do you need a menu?'

'Nope, if they have a sirloin or rump steak, medium-well, with chips and salad or something, that would be great. Don't need any starter.'

'I wasn't going to offer any!' He laughed.

'Look Giles, everything here is on my tab. It's the least I can do.'

'Don't worry about it, chap.'

'No, I meant what I said earlier.'

'Well all right then, if you're sure?'

'I am.'

Giles appreciated the gesture, and it made Kweku feel better that he wasn't freeloading. 'What about drinks?' he asked Kweku.

'I reckon a nice chilled lager would be just the job on a day like this, Giles. None of that premium beer mind, just a regular pint. Harp if they've got it, otherwise Carlsberg will do.'

'You need to get a pint of Hook Norton inside you, old boy, proper British beer – none of that Scandinavian stuff.'

'It's actually Irish, Harp. Carlsberg's Danish of course, but Harp's Irish.'

'Yeah, yeah, whatever. I still say you can't do better than a pint of Hookie!'

'Warm beer in hot weather? Not where I come from!' Kweku retorted facetiously.

'No problem, old boy – your loss, not mine.' Giles lit a cigarette and disappeared inside. He re-emerged ten minutes later with a pint of bitter in one hand and a lager with a nice head of froth in the other, the outside of the glass sweating beads of condensation. He lit another cigarette as he sat down. 'So tell me, now that all that College stuff is over, will you finally be getting down to some proper work?' he asked, a provocative smirk running across his face as he spoke. 'I mean, will you be going back to Ghana or doing more studying or be looking to get a job here or something?'

'Nah, I'll be going back home to try to help grow the family business.'

'Is that your dad's confectionery business?'

'Yep. It's all up to me, you know, I'm free to decide. I mean, apart from my dad and his partner, a Swiss friend, there are already managers in there running it. So my parents have left it entirely up to me to find a career doing something else if I want, at least for now… But, as I said, my choice is definitely to go back home and help expand the business further.'

'Well, it's nice of them to give you the choice. Then again, maybe they gave you the option as they wouldn't want you coming anywhere near the factory to mess everything up, and they were hoping you'd choose to stay out!' Giles winked mischievously, then burst out laughing.

Kweku as usual could see the funny side, but continued, more seriously, 'The thing is, people often won't be fully committed to a business, unless they have a stake or some level of ownership in it. And my dad has been let down by other managers before. So, even though they're not saying it, I know that ideally in the long run both my parents would want to keep the business in the family for future generations rather than just sell or give it away when they get old. I mean, it's quite a big business – not that big – but it's been their life's work building it up and for all my sins I have a loyalty or gratitude gene – I don't know which of the two it is. It would be the least I could do to help pay back the sacrifices they've made over the years and the constant care I've benefited from.'

'Future generations, did you say?' Giles was picking up on one phrase in what Kweku had just said. 'Oh yes? When are you going to be settling down then?'

'What do you mean?'

'Well, you're an only child, aren't you? … I'm sure they'd be wondering about that more than anything else.'

'You mean grandchildren?'

'Well, yes.'

'Steady on, old boy! I've only just finished uni. Let me live a bit first.'

'Well, I reckon that's the main thing they'll be wanting to know as they get older.'

'I know, I know. You're right. They've even been conspiring gently to do some not very subtle matchmaking for me on and off for a while now – usually with a daughter of close friends, people within their establishment social grouping. But I just naturally rebel against things being set up for me. It's meant that I don't take much time to explore in any detail whether their choice might be right for me. Just the fact that they are doing the choosing is what makes it wrong: I want to be able to choose for myself.'

'Yeah, I know what you mean, chap. It was a bit like that here in England, too, not so long ago. But there are all sorts of ways parents can still give you a nudge and a wink about who they think would be suitable for you. Over time you get an idea of the sort of person they'd like you to be with. If they really think your choice is mad, they wouldn't have to show up for the wedding and you and your partner might not want them to be there anyway – I mean, you could just do a quickie at a Registry Office or something… But they usually come round, once they realise their kid is serious about going through with it. I mean, I've never personally known of a parent being expected and not turning up to a wedding.

'Well anyhow, at least it means nothing is forced in England, as it still is in some parts of the so-called "developing" world.'

'Are marriages forced in Ghana?'

'No, not nowadays, except maybe that the list of potential suitors or brides can be very limited in areas of the country practising Islam, especially in the north.

But the usual hypocrisy of those pretending to follow religion dogmatically means that they think the rules they profess to be sacrosanct don't actually apply to them – you know, a case of "do as I say, not as I do". Hey, did you know, some in the south even say they have a funny rule up north?... If a brother dies, his brother can inherit his widows too, provided the widows agree to it.'

'Really?'

'Well at least that's what I've heard. I can't imagine it's true though. But you know Ghana is traditionally a polygamous society. I mean, before Europeans came to colonise the region, polygamy was the norm: it wasn't only Muslims practising it. It's like, traditionally, you weren't limited to one wife. The main thing is you had to be able to look after any woman you were calling yours – you know, provide them with accommodation and financial security. But on the emotional side it was one-way. Women always had to be ready to receive you any time you felt like their company and wanted to visit. But they weren't free to find sexual comfort elsewhere without suffering scandal and sanction.

It was with the influence of Christianity – more particularly the teachings of Jesus Christ under the New Testament as part of the colonial legacy – that monogamy (more often than not with paramours or casual affairs on the side) gradually became the practice among non-Muslim communities. But polygamy – having more than one customary wife – is still to this day fully OK provided you haven't married any of them in a Christian Church: that's because, as you know, all Christian denominations forbid marriage to more than one woman at the same time.'

'Well, I don't know, chap, that sounds like too much information. I just thought there are many of us on this side of the world that would envy you lot being able to have more than one wife like that. You know, just in case you get cheesed off or cheese them off for some reason, you could just go and visit another one – a bit like in one of those *Carry On* films …'

'Oh yeah, I know the one you mean… *Carry On Up The Khyber* I think it was, where that princess gets into a harem with Bernard Bresslaw as the sultan or something? …'

'That's the one!' Giles chuckled.

'Anyway, old boy, it's not quite like that in real life – at least not in Ghana any more. Don't get me wrong, it's still OK to have different 'customary wives' in different accommodation you're providing for them; it's just that they're not forced to be at your beck and call whenever you want to visit or take them out anywhere. The sole condition under customary law is that you can only have one person officially registered as your wife at a time – unless you're a Muslim, in which case you can have up to four at a time officially registered as your wives, provided you can look after all of them. At least that's how I think it works.'

'What's a customary wife then?'

'Oh, it's like the two families just have to go through different rituals at progressive stages recognising the union and exchanging promises.'

'Well what about Church weddings then?'

'You mean ordinance marriages? ... Oh yes, as I indicated earlier, those are very much the norm today in most parts of the country. My own parents were married in a Catholic wedding in London in the early

50s… that was after a customary wedding to get the consent of the traditional families first to the union.'

As Kweku finished speaking, the waiter brought in two sizzling dishes – the steak and chips he had ordered, and what looked like a huge piece of cod with chips and peas for Giles.

'Let's get stuck in!' Giles said. They picked up their cutlery and set about the food in front of them.

Giles savoured it: 'Mmmm… Just the job, I tell you!'

'As good pub food as you'll find anywhere,' echoed Kweku.

Pausing occasionally to sip at their beers, they made short work of their meals. After eating, they lit up and strolled along the riverside for a few minutes, each lost in his own thoughts, before returning to the car parked across the road. The engine roared as Giles started the car, revving it up a few times on the spot to clear the pipes, and then they were off to the races again, up to his parents' house at Middleton Stoney.

As they went through the gate up the short driveway, Kweku was a little apprehensive. He didn't know if Giles' parents were at home. He mulled over basics such as whether he was dressed decently enough.

'Are your parents in?' he asked.

'I don't think so. They told me they'd be going round to the neighbours for dinner… I can't see my dad's car here… Anyway I won't be long, chap. Just getting a bag.'

'A bag?'

'Yeah, a rucksack, just in case, you know.' He winked and grinned impishly at Kweku before trotting into the house.

***

Kweku was reminded of the awkward position that he had put himself in. He wasn't going to be having much fun at the Bear Hotel if Giles would be romancing his date there overnight! His suspicions confirmed, he now chided himself for being so slow on the uptake!

Moments later, Giles re-emerged with a small rucksack. He threw it into the boot and they were back on their way. As they raced down through country lanes heading for Woodstock, there was an awkward moment as they passed a pub sign sporting the name "The Black's Head" above an unflattering image of a negro's head. Startled at the nakedness of the presentation as of 1980, a time when he thought such things belonged to the past, Kweku felt a lump in his throat and cleared it. He could see out of the corner of his eye that Giles was hoping he hadn't noticed the sign or, if he had noticed, hadn't let it get to him.

But Giles realised from the sudden change in Kweku's demeanour that he had indeed spotted it. In an attempt to console Kweku, tossing his head backwards in the direction of the sign, he told him with a twinkle in his eye:

'It could have been worse, you know.'

'What, you mean they could have used the n-word?'

'Well, yeah. Things don't change that fast in the countryside, you know, it takes time ... I'll give you an example. My dad fought in the war, was mentioned in dispatches. But even with all that, when he and my mum moved up from Pimlico in London to Middleton Stoney at the end of the war, I remember him telling me once that for the first two years no one at all spoke to them – not even their neighbours. They would just stare or peer warily at them through windows or gaps in the curtains. If they passed them in the street, they would reply tersely to any greeting or query if they had to.

I got to understand that it happens because in that time they're trying to size you up as newcomers – to see if you believe in the same things they do; whether you have secrets, whether you'll keep their secrets if they open up to you or as you get to find out more about them with time; whether you or anyone in your family will rock the boat, making loud noises or leaving strange smells or untidy waste, building unauthorised structures or generally behaving in a highhanded manner.

It's like an examination with no time limit, until one day everything falls into place: people who before would brush past you without giving you the time of day now stop to chat idly in the street, discuss the latest gossip and developments in the village with you and seek your opinion about all sorts of things you never even knew were going on there. My dad said it took a full ten years for them to be fully accepted by the village as belonging there.

Kweku didn't really know how to respond. He knew that resistance to change in the status quo was an instinctive reaction in many parts of the world, not just in England or 'white-dominated' countries. As broad-minded as he tried to be – often at the expense of others' misunderstanding that meant he was weak in standing up for his black ethnic grouping – he knew that racial and ethnic discrimination was not something exclusively practised by white people but was indeed practised, wittingly or unwittingly, by all groups everywhere on the planet.

Indeed, he considered it the height of hypocrisy when other races, who had suffered from colonial oppression, continued during the course of such colonisation and even after the colonisers had left to practise religious and ethnic discrimination against other tribes or ethnic groups within their countries and even against those following different religions within the same ethnic groups, while at the same time stridently lambasting white people as racist. He knew that discrimination of all kinds – gender-based, ethnic, religious, age- or disabilities-based – coexists even within the same tribal and smaller social subgroups and that the only effective antidote for it over time is education.

So he did feel offended by the proud display of the pub's sign. But he wasn't looking for any sympathy; others had over the years suffered far more, not from minor emotional hurt such as he was experiencing at that moment but serious physical injury and even death. He resolved not to allow this sight to dominate his evening. He simply parked it in a corner of his memory and left it there.

***

As they entered the reception at The Bear, Giles looked round, clearly seeking out a familiar face. His eyes settled on an elegant-looking blonde, sitting cosily cross-legged in an armchair, thumbing her way through the pages of a glossy magazine on her lap.

'Catriona!' he called out.

'Giles!' She rose to approach him, revealing a white top with marine chiffon dress, which her tall, leggy frame carried as effortlessly as a model's.

'Sorry I'm a bit late… It's his fault!' said Giles, motioning in Kweku's direction, with a trademark grin and wink. Kweku flicked his head backwards to one side, rolling his eyes and chuckling quietly as he looked on. They embraced, pecking each other on the cheek. Then Giles pulled away, eyeing her up and down:

'You look a million dollars!' he exclaimed. 'Anyway, meet a friend of mine from Oxford, Kweku.' She shook Kweku's hand politely. 'Can I get you a drink?' Giles had started weaving his magic.

Catriona smiled: 'Why not?'

Kweku could read the tea leaves. Giles and Catriona had clicked and he had to extricate himself from the situation as soon as possible:

'I'm sorry, I forgot to get more eye drops,' he told them. 'I've got to get back to Summertown and rest my eyes ahead of some commitments this weekend.'

'At least stay and have one beer – on me this time.' Giles urged.

'Well all right then, just the one.' Kweku gulped down a half-pint, rushed his goodbyes and slipped away into the street outside, hailing a taxi back to Summertown.

***

The next morning Kweku packed for London. He had rested his eyes and the inflammation was better with the medication he'd applied. It was the first time he'd used in his car for days and he was in no hurry, so he drove down carefully down the A40 and on to the North Circular Road. On reaching Highgate, he rang Susan. They had first met a year earlier through the local tennis club opposite his parents' house in Highgate. They had chatted idly there at the occasional function. He hadn't ever met her parents, but she told him her mum trusted her judgment and she was an adult. He learnt her parents had separated twelve years earlier, when she was nine. She hadn't seen her dad since. She wasn't ever specific about what had happened. All she did say was that after what saw her mum go through with him, she didn't want to feel committed to another man ever again.

Kweku suggested they should get to Oxford slightly earlier on the Saturday. His flatmate Charlie had invited him to a polo match at Kirtlington Park in the afternoon, so they could go to watch that, change into evening wear and continue on to the Ball. He would pick her up in the morning around half past ten. He had booked a room for her in Oxford at the Randolph Hotel, so they could check her in there first. Meanwhile he wanted to use up to Friday to rest his eyes so that he could be in better shape for the weekend.

Saturday morning, he got to her house on time. She saw him arrive from the window of their front room downstairs. She came out half way and waved at him to come in, told him her mum wanted to meet him. He straightened his collar and followed her into the house. Her mum was standing in the hallway. She smiled gracefully at Kweku, but seemed nervous, coy:

'Hello, Kweku, please come in,' she said. 'Would you like a cup of tea?'

Kweku looked at Susan, unsure how to respond. She jumped in:

'Oh no, thank you Mum, we need to be setting off now. Kweku's friend is playing in a polo match before the Ball, so we need to get there quite early.'

Kweku started: 'Well, actually, Mrs Johnson …'

'You can call me Angela.'

'… All right sorry, Angela …'

Susan interrupted again:

'He's just trying to be polite, Mum. We really need to be going. Come on, Kweku.'

Kweku nodded. 'But thank you so much, Mrs… Angela.'

'That's OK, maybe another time then?'

'Yes, I would like that, thank you.'

Kweku picked up Susan's suitcase from the hallway and began walking back out. Susan turned to leave but, as she was following him out, Angela called her back into the house. Kweku continued to the car, loading her suitcase into the boot. He went to sit in the car and wait for her. After about 5 minutes, Susan re-emerged from the house, hurrying. Her mum stood in the doorway and waved them off.

'Sorry, Kweku. Mum always tends to stress herself.'

‘Can’t say I blame her. She must be worried seeing you go off like that with me, and me being… you know …’

‘You mean because you’re black?’

Kweku shrugged his shoulders.

‘Don’t be so silly! There’s good and bad in every race. She knows that too. She was just fussing, you know. She even told me, the little she saw of you, she was quite impressed. She asked me where you learnt to speak English like that. She said your accent… you sound just like Trevor McDonald …’

‘Trevor McDonald?’ They both giggled at the incongruity of Kweku, a student with no professional career, being compared with the distinguished journalist. For a moment, his mind flashed back to an occasion four years earlier, during in his first term at Oxford, when Charlie’s mum had also compared him to the prominent journalist.

Susan continued:

‘I told her about Huntsmere and she was pleasantly shocked actually. The rest of the time I was just saying ‘Yes, Mum’ to everything. You know how it is.’

‘Yes, I know. Mothers, eh?’ He sparked the car up.

‘Anyway, Kweku, let’s focus on the fun weekend we’re going to have, I hope! Never been to an Oxford Ball before. Huntsmere and Oxford, eh?’ She giggled again, turning to look at him and leaning forward slightly.

‘Get away!’ He playfully pushed her away and they laughed together as he drove off.

***

The day turned out to be even more fun than Kweku had anticipated. Prince Charles did come to the match at Kirtlington Park, at the wheel of a beautiful azure blue Aston Martin Vantage convertible with white leather trimming. As Kweku emerged from the marquee before the start, glasses of Pimm's in hand for himself and Susan, he nearly bumped into the Prince as he strode across purposefully, his equerry alongside him, in the direction of his ponies to saddle up. Kweku had fun explaining what he knew of the rules to Susan. She caught on very quickly and even corrected Kweku a couple of times. Oxford were on good form and the match ended in a draw. Tom Morton made his ponies available and Charlie Turner was relieved his team hadn't disgraced themselves.

Immediately after the trophy presentations, Kweku and Susan made excuses to Charlie and a couple of Charlie's other friends from Kirtlington, then slipped off. They didn't want to be late for the Ball, Susan's main reason for coming to Oxford.

The Ball Committee did full credit to the College and put on a lavish affair, the centrepiece of which was a huge marquee on the lawns off the garden quad at the back of Johnston. It was almost midsummer, so it was still broad daylight at 8 pm on a balmy evening when things really got underway.

Guests were ushered in with a glass of chilled Taittinger to the sound of a live classical ensemble playing tripping baroque compositions by Vivaldi. This was followed, in between charity raffles and tombola events, by jazz and easy listening, with professional singers covering a variety of favourites, from the incomparable Ella Fitzgerald to the legendary

Sinatra. The background music moved up in a crescendo as a rock and pop band came to the fore, eventually peaking decibel-wise with disco tunes like Donna Summer's *I Feel Love* and the Bee Gees' still-infectious *Saturday Night Fever*, before decelerating at the end to dreamy songs like Aznavour's *She* for the romantics. The College chef and under-chef displayed the full panoply of their skills with a 5-course culinary exposition. Most of the dons were there at the start but began peeling off as the music turned to noisier rock and disco sounds.

Only half of Kweku's Classics year group turned up. It was their last chance to meet and, with finals out of the way, they were more uninhibited than Kweku had ever seen them. Kweku shared their relief. The wide world beckoned. Goodbyes were exchanged, but not tearfully – they were too grown up and cynical for that. There were promises to catch up at a Gaudy reunion for old boys one of these days, if not before. The reality for many was that it was the last time they would meet for 25 years.

Susan drank, ate, and danced her feet off. She had the time of her life and Kweku was glad. He loved making people happy – especially those who appreciated that everyone has a choice and no one is forced to do anything.

When they got back to her room at the Randolph, Susan asked Kweku to stay. They shared a passionate night there together. The next morning, after freshening up and a light breakfast at the hotel, Kweku swung by his digs in Summertown for a change of clothes and got Susan back home to a grateful Angela. They kissed in his car before she got down. He walked her to the door. For the second time in a row, he had to turn down Angela's offer to sit down for a cup of tea – this time because he instinctively preferred not to allow her to get a whiff from his breath of the remnants of stale tobacco and alcohol from a night of fun. Susan for her part had come equipped with Fisherman's Friends and sucked on them for the last 10 minutes of the journey.

CHAPTER THIRTEEN

Honey & Love

July 1980

After the Johnston Ball, Kweku was anxious to get down to real life. The day after his exams, he had called his parents to confirm to them that he had set his heart on returning home to help grow the family's confectionery business.

The reality was that the fig leaf of academia, his shelter for so many years from the harshness of the world outside, had vanished, leaving him exposed to the necessity of a stark choice – to sink or swim. Now back home in Ghana, sixteen years of schooling in England behind him, he was bent on atoning for the folly of a lack of focus at Oxford.

The timing was fortuitous. Adrian's wife Eva, a delicate lady who had never joined her husband in Ghana for fear of falling sick with some incurable tropical disease, had grown increasingly tired of his long absences from their home in Zurich. He had tried to balance these out by holidaying four times a year with her at home, sometimes combining such trips with trips to machine suppliers with Kojo. But after twenty years the strain had become almost unbearable. Besides, he would soon be sixty-five, retirement age in his country. With each passing year, he saw greater validity in Eva's favourite question to him since he turned 50: When was he going to be able to slow down enough for him, for both of them together, to check the remaining items off their bucket lists before mortality caught up with them?

With the pressure from Eva intensifying, the time was now. On Kojo's next trip to Mim, Adrian found time to make a proposal to him. He was sure they would be able to come to an agreement on a fair price for his fifty percent share of the business. He trusted Kojo implicitly and wouldn't mind spreading payment over, say, five years to allow him time to seek additional funding for the purchase, if he needed it. Meanwhile the current factory production manager, a Belgian called Pierre Rousseau, was now in his fifth year with the company. Adrian said that, with the exception of the company's first two production managers, one Swiss, the other Dutch, who had chosen to return home at the end of their first two-year contract, Pierre was the best at the job he had seen in terms of the key skills of resource planning and co-ordination, technical understanding, including quality control, and product costing.

Pierre was now settled in Mim with a Ghanaian wife, and had no plans to move anywhere anytime soon. So Adrian was satisfied that continuity would be achieved in terms of production and above all quality assurance, even if he was no longer there.

Furthermore, from what Adrian had seen of Kweku over the years, he was confident that he would be able to step into the administrative aspect of his job with a short handing over period – no more than, say, six months. It would probably take a little longer for Kweku to get to grips with the material planning and resource requirement aspects but, provided Pierre continued on his current path of personal development, he saw no reason why Pierre couldn't eventually be promoted to General Manager and take over those aspects of the job as well, with Kojo's permission.

In the context of their close relationship, Adrian had some final words of advice for Kojo himself, advice he knew he was the only one capable of giving him with the certainty that it would be taken in the right way:

'Kojo, you are not that far behind me in age. You'll be 60 in three years, yes?'

'Yes, Adrian, and still fighting fit. I'm in good shape, you know,' Kojo shadowboxed with a few jabs at waist height to reinforce his point.

'I know that,' Adrian continued, 'but isn't it time you started to take a step back and enjoy some of the fruits of your lifelong industry? And all that shuttling between our offices in Accra and Tema, the factory in Mim and overseas trips with me? Eva tells me all the time: "What's the point of working to make all that money, if all you ever do is work?" Take Deborah on a cruise, see some of the real world outside business – before your eyesight goes!' He meant these last words as a joke, but wanted to get Kojo's attention. Kojo didn't take any offence. 'You can even visit me in Switzerland; Eva and I would love to host you both at our lakeside villa.'

'OK, I'll think about it,' Kojo responded, a little shell-shocked at the idea that it might soon be time for him to retire from day-to-day administration and feeling slightly deflated that it was his own best friend who had just delivered such a message to him.

Pushing home the point, Adrian went on:

'And at least, if we get Kweku involved now, as you told me recently he said he is now keen to put his shoulder to the wheel after finishing at Oxford, we will have six months of overlap to see whether he's up to it. You won't get that chance if you wait until after I've already left.'

'OK OK, Adrian, I get you. Just… just give me a few days to think over it all with Deborah. I promise I'll get back to you within a week.'

'OK.'

***

Kojo had always been a bit of a micro-manager in his business style, a legacy of his incredibly industrious nature and close attention to detail. Always punctual, neatly dressed and organised in the old-fashioned way, he was in the habit of listening to both sides of every argument, but had no time for humbug. He was happy to delegate responsibility, once he had confidence in the appointee, but would then immediately follow up with requests for updated reports to assure himself that things were still on track. At the same time, he reflected that Adrian had made a valid point about a life beyond work, which the success of the business had given him an opportunity to contemplate.

On his return to Accra, Kojo discussed with Deborah Adrian's proposal, and the additional words of advice he had for him. To his surprise, she was all for it. Now that Kweku had finished at university, she felt they had done their part and should think of themselves a little more, spend more time together. Bringing their son into the business would be a great way to help him settle down in life. He needed to be doing something, and if this was what he had told them he wanted to do, and he was ready especially for all that commuting, particularly between the office in Accra and the factory in Mim, then why not? Two days later, Kojo signalled his agreement to Adrian on all points. He called Kweku in for a discussion.

Kweku was thrilled with the news. Finally, he would have the independence and feeling of self-fulfilment which only earning his own income could bring, and not be answerable to anyone for how he spent any of it.

Welcoming into the practice of his daily life the re-discovered gems of his parents' childhood advice, their significance at last understood, he was now punctual and neatly dressed for virtually all his appointments. It was the symptom of a return to the discipline that had been missing from his life since Huntsmere.

Crucially however, this time the discipline was self-imposed. It marked the onset of personal maturity for him. The unwarranted self-pity was gone. He was no longer hurting, but helping, himself and others. It was a new lease of life, and he was extremely grateful to get a second bite at the cherry.

***

Kweku threw himself into the business, working 16-hour days and making himself available for work 24 hours a day, 7 days a week. Kojo introduced him to the local buyers and distributors of Honimo and their other confectionery products and from then on Kweku kept in close and regular contact with them, prioritising accurate feedback to improve performance. Within a year, and with the help of a re-motivated Pierre, production and sales records were set and quality control standards further improved.

Kweku became more analytical about all aspects of his life. To help sharpen his skills in time management, for instance, he considered that there are 1,440 minutes in a day. He counted out a minute and thought of all he could achieve in that one minute. He then multiplied that out by 1,440. A day became a gift of time full of possibilities; a year, 365 of such days with extraordinary potential for meaningful achievements.

***

Now that the career side of his life seemed to be falling into place, it stood out for Kweku's parents that what was missing from his life was a family. They were eager for his own well-being that he should be properly settled in life. It would also give them a chance to have grandchildren and be assured about the continuation of the family line.

They had been trying to fix him up with a young woman, the daughter of close family friends who were well established and had a good reputation in the society. They had been closely following her progress. Kweku had always felt something was afoot whenever his parents would visit hers. There were occasions during such visits when he would enter a room where the four of them were chatting and all four would suddenly fall silent, staring at him, one or two smiling nervously. A new subject would then be hastily introduced by one of them leaving the others struggling to infer continuity and relevance. In fact, he was sure that the main point of common interest between all four of them that year was matchmaking between their children.

But Kweku had an independent streak he couldn't shake off. He viewed marriage as a long-term commitment, as it is meant to be. If he was going to share the rest of his life with someone, he wanted it to be on his own terms and at his own timing. No one knew himself better than he did, or so he thought.

However, in answer to Kweku, do we really know ourselves when so young? ... Yes, we have a rough idea that we do, or want to do, things differently from others – better or in a more innovative way, given the starter package of our own peculiar circumstances, the complexities of which we convince ourselves that others are not as well positioned as we are to understand properly. But are we really doing things better, given that starter package? Or do we sweep under the carpet failures stemming from a rush to favourable or unfavourable judgment of things and people, based on secondhand information or worse, without investing the necessary time to conduct honest, direct enquiry and reach properly validated conclusions? Is that even too mechanical a way to approach such a major decision with long-term emotional consequences? Kweku avoided exploration of such awkward questions. He was in too much of a hurry to succeed in business.

***

Another Takeover

December 1981

Kweku was at home in Accra with his parents, preparing to see in the New Year on the last day of 1981. Out of the blue, another military takeover was announced on the radio, overthrowing the democratically elected, although badly performing, civilian administration in power. Constitutional government was suspended and replaced by rule by an unelected military council, led once again by Jerry Rawlings, supervising a civilian administration.

A year-long period of curfews followed. No one dare roam the streets or be caught driving from dusk till dawn. Officially that meant from 6 pm to 6 am, but it was best to err on the side of caution and leave plenty of time on either side: bad timing, intentional or otherwise, could have fatal consequences. So-called "curfew parties" became the fashion – parties that began in the late afternoon and lasted all night until well after daybreak. Seeing who made it in and out and when, or had close shaves at improvised military road blocks, added to the excitement of the evening and made easy talking-points. For obvious reasons, such parties were popular with young, single people like Kweku.

But it was a period when keeping a low profile, and showing respect for others, as you usually had no idea who they were or whom they knew in a position of power, could go a long way to helping you stay out of trouble. An exception was if you were unlucky enough to be already personally targeted as a result of a grudge held by someone with a newfound ability to cause you harm.

Soldiers of any rank suddenly held immense power, simply because junior military officers were in charge of the country's government. Ordinary Privates and Lance Corporals effectively passed themselves off as card-carrying members of the ruling party in a dictatorship. They used the power of their badge and uniform over civilians to exact revenge and mete out their own versions of unsanctioned justice to settle personal scores, sometimes relatively trivial ones involving money or perceived romantic slights: a beating here, an unauthorised arrest and detention at a military camp there on a trumped-up charge, extortion of money under false pretences. For some time, events like these became normalised.

Beyond the score-settling and intoxication with power of a rank and file which the ruling council was struggling to control, particularly in the early months following the coup, there were reports – among other unsolved crimes and stories of summary justice handed out to coup plotters – of top government involvement in the abduction and gruesome murder of three High Court Judges and the personnel manager of a state-owned company, a retired Army Major. Constitutional government would not return to the country until January 1993, when the leader of the ruling military council became a democratically elected President, whose popular mandate was repeated in an election widely acknowledged as free and fair four years later.

The early years of the military government's eleven-year rule from December 1981, paradoxically described as 'provisional', were nevertheless characterised by a resort to propaganda and populist sloganeering typical of all governments – military, civilian and every possible mixture of the two – promising citizens a coming utopia of plenty for all following their accession to power.

However, the lack of pragmatism in policy development and implementation in this early period continued the pre-existing years-long downward spiral in productivity for many of the country's manufacturing industries. Sonimo was unable to buck the trend. It had to continue laying off staff and was now operating at less than fifty percent of production capacity, despite the strenuous efforts of Kweku and Pierre.

By 1983, the damage caused by the deteriorating economic position was compounded by a drought and near-famine, leading to worsening political instability. Essentially in an act of self-preservation, the military council began siding against voices of more radical socialist-leaning elements in the ruling administration, aligning itself instead with the voices of pragmatists favouring rapprochement with western governments and institutions. Government policies were reversed to embrace market reforms, enabling access to much-needed international multilateral and bilateral financial support to revive the economy.

Key reversals occurred in terms of exchange control liberalisation, adjusting the national currency, the cedi, to international exchange rates more reflective of its true market value. Foreign currency retention accounts were also allowed to fund importation of key production equipment, spare parts and other foreign expenses. And then, in order to boost rural development and employment, substantial corporate tax rebates were given to companies establishing or operating outside major cities, in rural areas such as Brong Ahafo where Sonimo operated.

Kweku discussed with Adrian and Kojo approaches to markets in Europe, particularly for Honimo with the uniquely attractive flavour of its dark Ghanaian honey and other ingredients. Adrian said although he was now retired, he would try to call some contacts and follow up. Pierre said he knew one of the purchasing managers of a large Belgian wholesaler with blue-chip accounts in the retail confectionery market. They had studied at technical school together. He rang the person up and an appointment was fixed to coincide with his upcoming leave.

Meanwhile for Kweku the timing was perfect, as he had a conference in London the day before on value-added processing and marketing on the African continent. The invitation letter had actually been addressed to Kojo, according to an old mailing list the conference organisers had for Sonimo. Kojo thought it would be a good idea for Kweku to attend and check the market's potential to support increased production. It would also give him an opportunity to rub shoulders with other captains of industry, and who knew where that might lead? So Kweku and Pierre would link up in Brussels for the meeting with Pierre's export buyer on the Wednesday.

***

Joanna

March 1984

Kweku flew business class to London and checked into the hotel where the conference was to be held. Still drowsy from jet lag the next morning, he had a cold shower to try to jolt his nerves back into rhythm. He put on his usual dark grey suit and took the lift to the ground floor. A short stopover at the breakfast room for some cold cuts, a croissant and coffee, then he made his way to the lobby for registration.

As he stood in the queue, he heard a voice call out from directly behind him:

'Stephen!'

He turned round to see a beautiful woman, smartly dressed in navy blue jacket and slacks, with white blouse and shiny black shoes. Her smile quickly turned to embarrassment as she realised Kweku wasn't the Stephen she thought he was.

'I'm so sorry... You look just like someone I know from Ghana.'

'Actually I'm from Ghana too,' said Kweku.

'Really?'

'Yes, but not Stephen, Kweku.'

'I feel so silly.' She patted his arm in apology as she spoke.

Kweku felt a chemistry igniting in his body. He smiled: 'Don't worry, I wish I was Stephen.'

She smiled shyly, looking right back at Kweku. She knew he intended his words to be a compliment, but was torn between their humour and audacity. She tried to work out whether they represented just the hackneyed pitch of a seasoned Romeo or he meant them sincerely. She decided that for now she would remain sceptical.

They registered and collected their handouts.

'Shall we find somewhere to sit?' Kweku asked, expectantly.

'Actually I'm here with two other colleagues from our business.'

Kweku tried to keep up the conversation as they set off from the lobby towards the main conference room:

'What business is that then?'

'Consolidated Beverages Ghana. It's part of a multinational conglomerate.' She reached into her handbag. 'Here's my card.' Kweku looked closely at the details under the company logo. They read: "Joanna Forson – Regional Sales Manager, Greater Accra".

'Wow! I see.'

'What about you?' she asked.

Kweku reached into his inside jacket pocket and pulled out a card: 'Oh, here's mine.'

Joanna recognised the company's name straightaway, and was surprised to see Kweku's position. 'Oh, you're with Sonimo, are you?'

'Tell me, what have you heard about us?' Kweku asked, adding playfully 'And don't lie.'

'Who hasn't heard of Sonimo? It's not the biggest company, but it has a strong reputation for being a high-quality, well-run operation… And I see you're the managing director, no less?'

'Yes, for my sins. It's a family business. My dad founded it twenty years ago with a Swiss partner. He's the executive chairman – the ultimate decision-maker, if you like. But he leaves me to run it with a colleague based in Mim and I just report to him on the big issues – you know, sales, new markets, profits, charitable projects. Actually he's really big on the last one – putting something back into the community… I think I might take that to the next step myself one day, you know, become a politician or something. The local community already want me to be an assembly member for the area, but up to now I simply haven't had time even to entertain the idea.'

They were now inside the main conference room. Joanna looked round and saw her colleagues. Waving, she caught their eye and they beckoned her over.

From the way Kweku seemed to be following her around, she sensed that he was very attracted to her. She was flattered. Although she didn't yet feel quite the same way, as she first wanted to get to know the real person behind the appearance, she thought he was OK looking. She found him intriguing: he seemed on the outside to be a perfect English gentleman and she liked that in a man. He had an air about him that was different from other Ghanaians she had met up to that point in her life. In general, she hadn't been that enthused about men in any romantic sense. She'd had a bad experience in her late teens falling for someone and being two-timed. She had vowed never to let her guard down again.

For his part Kweku sensed that she wasn't at all intimidated by him or put off by his public-school English accent. That appealed to him.

As they caught up to where her colleagues were sitting, she told Kweku diplomatically:

'I'm sorry. Maybe we can catch up later then?'

'What about lunchtime?'

‘Let’s see.’ She turned to her colleagues and began engaging them in conversation.

Kweku walked further up and sat down on the right, closer to the front of the room.

As conference speakers addressed the gathering and patiently answered questions, Kweku found himself turning round impulsively several times to glance at Joanna. Their eyes met on two occasions and she smiled. It took him back to the lectures on Virgil’s *Aeneid* he attended in his first weeks at Oxford and his infatuation with Carrie.

During the mid-morning coffee break, he went over to join her. She introduced him to her colleagues but he only feigned interest briefly in what they were doing. Calling her to the side, he tried to invite her out to lunch. She declined, but asked if he would be back in Ghana by the weekend. He told her he had an important meeting the next day in Brussels but was scheduled back in Accra by Thursday. She suggested they meet for dinner on Saturday. He said he would give her a call on Friday to confirm and it would be his treat. She agreed.

Kweku’s mind was buzzing for the rest of the day. He took notes and did some networking with Ghanaian government officials and colleagues from other private sector companies he spotted at lunch and during the tea-break. He even managed to conjure up one pertinent question to ask in the final session of the conference. But in truth there was little in any practical sense that he learnt from the conference that he didn’t know already from the extensive market research he had conducted in the preceding months in his efforts with Pierre to find effective ways to grow the business in the more liberal macroeconomic climate.

His most significant takeaway from the conference was the meeting with Joanna. Long since over his crush on Carrie, he was ready to settle down and bring an end to the meaningless casual encounters he was falling into from time to time. Could she finally be "The One"? Only time would tell, and he desperately hoped the answer would be 'Yes'.

***

From that day on, Joanna would never be far from Kweku's thoughts, no matter what he was doing. On Wednesday he and Pierre travelled to Brussels loaded with enough samples, not only of Honimo but of all their other brand flavours, with accompanying price lists complete with quantity discounts. They didn't think anything could be guaranteed, but were quietly hopeful. In the end their meeting with the buyer went much better than even they had dared to dream. She took straight away to the samples she was given and singled out the Honimo for special mention. She said she had never tasted anything so uniquely pleasurable. She found the price offers reasonable but warned they would be subject to approval by head office, who would draft a standard agreement. They gave her a selected pack of samples to return with. She promised meeting their purchasing director on it the next day and getting back to them as soon as possible.

Terms would be agreed the following week. A month later, she would revert with a trial order for a full twenty-foot containerload, with a make-up of fifty percent Honimo and the balance in equal quantities of assorted flavours. The consignment was well received on the European market and a huge bulk order followed, which would occupy the factory at full capacity for four months. Sonimo re-engaged laid-off staff and production, sales and profits soared.

With surplus funds being generated by the business, the company would later resume significant investments in corporate social responsibility. Government policy at the time was focused on educating young girls to engage in higher-skilled professional careers away from traditional domestic roles in the home or on the farm. Sonimo would use a portion of its free cash flow to build local schools at nursery and primary level, construct boreholes and community buildings, and sponsor many deprived children from Mim town and surrounding local villages through primary and secondary school.

***

Back from the London conference and the very successful meeting with Pierre and the buyer in Brussels, on Friday Kweku rang Joanna at work to invite her to dinner at one of Accra's swankiest restaurants, La Chaumière in the Airport Residential area. On the one hand he wanted to avoid the nouvelle cuisine which had by then become all the rage. He viewed it as fashion tool used by clever chefs to save money by presenting shavings of food in pretty formations and slices so thin that they were transparent: you could even discern the patterns on the plates supporting the food. He preferred honest, hearty, rustic portions to urban pretence. At the same time he wanted to impress Joanna. La Chaumière perfectly combined both qualities – excellent French cuisine and decent portions.

Joanna sounded happy to hear his voice. She responded 'OK' when Kweku mentioned the name of the restaurant. She gave him directions to her house in Ridge for the pick-up. "OK" was a middling, not superior or superlative adjective. It left Kweku wondering whether he had made a mistake. If he hadn't and she was familiar with the restaurant's cuisine, it would be great news, as it would suggest she disliked pretence every bit as much as he did.

When he got to her house on the Saturday, she came out as soon as she heard the sound of his car approaching on the gravel. Fortunately, her parents – her father David, a senior civil servant, and mother Irene, an author of children's books – were out at a function of their own. That conveniently eliminated the need for any awkward introductions so early in their courtship. Kweku had been in that situation before: a girl's father suspecting he was only after their daughter to satisfy a lustful urge, the mother scrutinising his appearance and both of them interrogating him about his family's history and assessing whether he was good enough for their daughter before giving their blessing even to a simple getting-to-know-you dinner outing. Thankfully this time he would be spared that kind of examination.

The dinner went down a treat. La Chaumière didn't disappoint with their Michelin Star-motivated presentations. But, most importantly, Joanna and Kweku both discovered they had far more in common in terms of their approach to life than either had imagined at that first meeting in London. He discovered to his delight that, in addition to her natural beauty, Joanna had a wicked sense of humour, a genuine smile and hearty chuckle to go with it, and a thick skin. Kweku was looking for someone that he didn't just find incredibly attractive, but who could be at the same time a best friend and confidant. Someone to share musings with over life's ironies and vicissitudes. Someone whose company he would enjoy, watching a film, sitting next to each other chatting, walking side by side or exploring new spots together.

They didn't always have to agree, but that other person should be someone who shared his values and views about human relationships. Above all someone as willing to give respect as to receive it. For Kweku, most of the problems in life as well as relationships came down to an imbalance between the two. Many difficult people are happy to receive respect – indeed they often insist on getting it – without feeling under any reciprocal obligation to give respect.

But the reality is that no one but a masochist enjoys being taken for granted. A religious or otherwise metaphysically-inclined person may tolerate it but will not enjoy it. Indeed, people are more happy to help than is often realised; but they invariably resist being taken for granted – whether that resistance is expressed openly or not. Kweku did not count himself among those too shy to express their resistance to being taken completely for granted, but in the case of those reluctant to express their resistance, the proof – for the education of the respect predator – is to be found in their actions, when words are absent.

***

From that first dinner, Kweku was thrilled he had finally met a soulmate, someone who understood the importance of reciprocal respect, which was for him the foundational and vital lubricant of any lasting relationship. Joanna understood that and warmed to him, lowering her self-defensive guard further with each successive meeting over the weekend for the next several weeks.

The last dinner in the series came at the end of a day spent visiting the hydro-electric plant at Akosombo and taking a pleasure cruise on the Volta Lake with its spectacular scenery. Afterwards, instead of driving back to Accra, they checked into the Volta Hotel. They laughed at the irony of having to sign in as Mr and Mrs, although Kweku didn't use his real name. It was an unforgettable experience, enhanced by the feeling of reciprocated respect. Neither had the sense of being judged by the other in silence. If either had a problem with anything the other had said or done, they would express their disagreement and make an effort to understand the other's point of view. If they couldn't agree, they would end the discussion respectfully, not quietly harbour resentment as some do for months or even years, only for it to eventually boil over unexpectedly in a furious rage of retribution against an unsuspecting partner.

CHAPTER FOURTEEN

Tying The Knot

Summer 1984

Back in Accra, Kweku's first priority was to slip out of his office at lunchtime on the Monday into a jewellery store on Osu Oxford Street to buy Joanna an engagement ring and invite her to dinner that evening at a French restaurant across the road from the Dutch embassy. The first great bit of news for him was that, despite the short notice, she could make it. As they waited at the bar for their table, he pulled the little box containing the ring out of his pocket. He opened it.

Her eyes widened. She raised her hands momentarily to cover her face, peeked through her fingers, then slowly lowered them. 'What are you doing?' she said. She looked at the ring: 'And what's that?'

Kweku didn't want to do anything dramatic like getting down on one knee. Before she could utter another word, he looked deep into her eyes and proposed to her.

'No!! Really? Me?' She was genuinely stunned.

He held her hand tenderly and slid the ring on to her finger:

'Yes, you.'

'Oh, my goodness. Yes… yes I will.'

Her answer sent Kweku spinning in a whirl. The barman extended his congratulations and the atmosphere in the restaurant changed, as other customers realised what had just happened. The waiter came round, grinning from ear to ear, telling them their table was now ready. The manager, who must have just been informed, suddenly appeared from the kitchen, promising them a bottle of wine on the house. Slightly embarrassed that they, or more particularly Kweku, had brought everyone in on what was essentially their private moment, they moved shyly to their table as scattered applause went up around the restaurant.

Fortunately, everyone soon went back to minding their own business and they could enjoy their first lunch together as an informally betrothed couple. They couldn't wait to tell their parents.

***

To say that both sets of parents were elated at the news would be an understatement. In their own old-fashioned but pragmatic way, although neither Kweku nor Joanna were thinking like that, they thought the marriage had a much better chance of succeeding because their children came from similar backgrounds in terms of ethnicity, religion (both were Catholics) and class. They set about arranging the formal ceremonies to validate a union. These began with the traditional or customary ceremonies.

Knocking and Other Customs

First the parents informed their extended families, including grandparents, uncles, aunts and cousins, and set a date for the "Knocking" ceremony.

On the agreed date in mid-June, representatives of Kweku's family visited – or figuratively knocked on the door of – Joanna's residence on his behalf. In a theatrical ritual, one of them presented gifts, including drinks, some cash and an official engagement ring (different from the one Kweku had personally put on her finger at the restaurant), and asked one of the representatives of her family present for her hand in marriage.

Kweku didn't have to be there for this Knocking ceremony, but Joanna asked if he could come and he wanted to. Her eyes lit up when she saw him arrive. The formalities had their humorous moments, as when her representatives made out at the beginning, as part of the drama, that his people must have got the wrong house, as there was no lady at home by that description. The two of them smirked occasionally, spurred on by excitement that things were really happening for them. But they were careful not to show disrespect. Joanna's acceptance of the gifts in the presence of the two families marked the equivalent of what would be their engagement in western culture, and a date was set for the full Customary Marriage.

Kweku and his family were back at Joanna's residence for the Customary Marriage in August. This time it was a much grander occasion, and numbers were swelled by a fuller family complement, invited guests and well-wishers. The dress code was white – not only for the bride, as in western culture. Most attended dressed in an array of costumes with a white theme, or combinations of white with other colours. Women and young girls wore tight, sequinned dresses in western styles, some wearing looser, more expansive tops, and elaborate head-dresses. Meanwhile clothing for the men and boys came in various combinations reflecting the transition between pre-colonial traditional cloths and western suits and tops.

The quantity of gifts and bride price brought by Kweku's family for this final customary ceremony naturally dwarfed those presented by them for the Knocking ceremony, including ladies' jewellery and fabrics, and of course cash. But the principle was the same. The gifts comprising the bride price were negotiated and handed over after a longer theatrical process between the families over what was fair.

Next, Joanna's family had to fulfil their part of the exchange by producing her for Kweku to confirm that yes, this is the woman he wants to marry. For Kweku, this was the funniest part of the ceremony, as Joanna's sister and two other friends of similar height and build stepped forward and came down the stairs impersonating her under identical veils, and his family had to reject all of them before insisting that the real Joanna step forward, which she did under a similar veil, which Kweku could only lift to confirm her identity after she had been picked by his representatives as the woman he wanted to marry.

He was never told what would have happened had his family representatives made a genuine mistake and selected her sister or a cousin as his bride. Surely, he – or more accurately his representatives – would have been allowed to have another go and not have him embark on married life with the wrong girl? Out of natural curiosity, he wanted to ask. But they had got it right, so he left things at that!

The tables were then turned as Joanna's family demanded to see their prospective son-in-law. However, without the disguise of the veils, the suspense this time was more contrived and the possibility of mistaken identity easily avoided.

Joanna's acceptance of the bride price, marking the final confirmation of the union, was followed by advice on married life delivered loftily by family members whose own track record with it was highly debatable.

To round things off, celebrations kicked off with a huge party, to the sound of celebratory music, with sheep and goat roasted on separate spits, a wide range of Ghanaian and European food and drinks galore. Both sets of parents danced with delight. Their children were on their way and they prayed for the success of their partnership amid the ups and downs of life.

***

Kweku and Joanna were now prepared for the final stage of their union – a Catholic ordinance wedding. Indeed, the Catholic Church had insisted they must first be customarily married according to tribal tradition, signifying full acceptance and validation of their union by their two families, before they would in turn conduct and certify an ordinance marriage in Church. They explained that this was required to forestall the possibility of any member of the traditional family of one of the parties claiming in future that the family had not consented to the union, which if true would render the union invalid according to customary law, no matter what the Catholic Church had certified. It was another example of the concurrent application of pre-colonial customary practices and adopted colonial western practices, the two sources meshing to form the hybrid structure of updated customs and regulation in post-independence Ghana. A wedding date was set for mid-November.

***

The next morning, as Kweku sat in the living room of his parents' home in Cantonments awaiting breakfast, Tina told him his mum and dad wanted to see him upstairs in their bedroom. Thinking to himself 'Oh no! more boring family advice,' he trudged slowly up the stairs. When he entered their bedroom, he saw beaming smiles on their faces. They handed him a key: it was the key to a new house in the Airport Residential area. Now that he was finally settling down to family life with Joanna, he would need his own space. Kweku gasped and covered his mouth, overcome with a mixture of astonishment and excitement. He couldn't believe it! He was so grateful.

After breakfast, they took him along to show him. It was just twenty minutes away, in a great location. When he saw it, he felt an instant connection. Pretty and perfectly-sized, it was a dream house. They told him they had been quietly building it for two years, praying that the day would come when he would at last want to lay down to roost with a partner. That day had now come.

Immediately he returned home, he rang Joanna to tell her. It was news she had been dreaming of. She wouldn't be able to move in permanently with him until after the church wedding, but she had already started fantasising and asking Kweku for every detail about it.

Everything seemed to be on the up for Kweku, but a dark cloud was about to return.

***

A year earlier, Kweku's childhood friend Kwesi Osei had been cashiered from the army for physically assaulting an officer's wife during her attempt to intervene in a dispute between her husband and Osei over a gambling debt. Osei decided not to tell his mother about it. She had put her whole store on his dedicating himself to a career in the Army. When he was given a second chevron to mark his promotion from Lance Corporal to full Corporal, she was so proud she let all her extended family know.

Now that his army career was over, he knew it would break her heart to tell her. So he avoided going home, hanging out on street corners outside familiar bars and restaurants in Accra patronised by the rich and famous, hoping to sweet-talk someone into offering him a job. He had come close on a couple of occasions, but so far no one had taken the bait: a festering body odour and haunting look of desperation in his eyes weighed heavier than his silver tongue.

Reluctantly he rang his boyhood friend Kweku to ask for help. But, out of sympathy for his situation, Kweku had already lent him sums totalling thousands of cedis of his own hard-earned cash on and off over the years, money which Osei had squandered in an ever more dissipated lifestyle gambling at casinos and on any other platform available. When Kweku had first helped him with money more than seven years earlier, he had warned him he wouldn't be able to do so again. However, against his better judgment, Kweku had gone on lending further amounts in response to desperate pleas from his friend. The last time he had lent him money was six months earlier, when he let him know, this time in no uncertain terms, that he would never be able to help him again. And now this.

Kweku told him he would need a long time to think about it, but that as far as the present and immediate future was concerned, he was sorry but he couldn't help. He had met someone and wanted to start a family. So he had new responsibilities. Kweku's mention of a family triggered something in Osei. He suddenly starting shouting down the line, swearing that he would one day get even with Kweku and banged the phone down.

Get even for what? Kweku pondered as he put the receiver down. He no longer recognised the person he had just spoken to. He began to regret all the times he had loaned Osei hundreds and thousands of cedis to help him out of a hole, without ever once complaining that he had never repaid him a single pesewa.

***

Eventually, more than three weeks after his dismissal from the Army, Osei's compass reunited him with the magnet of home. At least at home he would be able to get a square meal and a shower before deciding what to do next, he thought. Maybe his mum could even give him some spare cash to finance his frantic job-hunting in a slowly improving economy.

When he got home, there was no answer at the door. A neighbour, trying to make out if she had seen him somewhere before, finally recognised him under his unshaven stubble and dishevelled looks. She told him his mother said she was going to the Post Office to check her mails and see to one or two other things. She was sure she wouldn't be long. Osei decided to sit on a bench outside the house and wait for her. The neighbour, shocked at Osei's appearance, couldn't bring herself to invite Osei into her own flat. Keeping Osei at a distance, she limited her hospitality to offering him a glass of water, which he readily accepted and guzzled down, asking for and getting a second glass.

Meanwhile at the Post Office Osei's mum Sheila had seen in the mail an envelope from the Army addressed to her son marked "Urgent". She was elated. Perhaps it was news of another promotion or some other boon? She asked a clerk if she could use their telephone to call her son. She was eventually put through to someone in the army recruitment office, who gave her news she never thought she would hear. They said they had written formally to Osei about a week ago to confirm his dismissal. Sheila realised this must be the letter she was holding. She hung up. Feeling suddenly unsteady on her feet, she looked for a place to sit down. She saw a free space at the edge of a bench just inside the main door. One of those seated, a young man, who noticed her flustered state, gave up his seat for her.

Her heart was racing. Against her better judgment, she decided to open the letter. She could no longer trust that her son would tell her the truth. She wanted to know for herself… There it was, in black and white. Her beloved only son was being discharged from the army dishonourably for an offence under the organisation's code of conduct. The victims of his offence had decided not to pursue the case criminally, as would have been their right.

She folded the letter and placed it back in the envelope. She bit her lips and began sobbing. A staffer saw her and came over to comfort her, asking if she could help, but she was inconsolable. She put the envelope, together with other mail – demands for money from the electricity and water companies – into her handbag and walked slowly outside. There was no bench in the yard outside, so she just paused there. Deeply religious, she gazed up at the expanse of the sky, looking for a sign, asking for divine help. But no sign appeared: the sky simply became overcast. Distraught, she caught the *tro-tro* public transport van back home.

The van pulled up at her stop and she walked the last five minutes to her flat. She made out her son Kwesi Osei, sitting outside. She walked towards him, arms outstretched. He saw her and stood up. She embraced him, sobbing. Osei instinctively sensed that she must have heard something. She led him into the flat. As they entered, she sat down in her two-seater, beckoning him to sit beside her.

She reached into her handbag, pulled out the envelope and handed it to him. He straightaway realised from its serrated top edge that she had already opened it and read its contents. He wouldn't be able to spin his way out of this one. But how could he complain that she had tampered with his personal mail? He knew he had been dismissed from the Army, and yet hadn't told her. Worse still, he had no plans to tell her and, if he'd had his way, would have kept it from her for the rest of her life. He had no explanation and nowhere to hide. He got up and went outside the flat towards the bench.

'Where are you going?' she asked.

'Nowhere.' He sat down.

She pleaded with him to come back inside, at least shower up and have something to eat. She offered to make him his favourite fufu and light soup with grasscutter meat and smoked fish. Disconsolate, he shrugged his shoulders. She went ahead anyway and started cooking.

Osei enjoyed his meal, wiping the bowl clean with his fingers. But he went to bed that evening crushed with worry. The next morning, he sneaked out of the flat early without a word to his mum. He went back to hanging around the fringes of popular haunts of the rich and famous, more determined than ever to catch an opportunity. By default, he fell into the company of other runaway souls who had fallen by the wayside and were desperate to find a way back on to the ladder. They were full of stories of how to make quick money. There weren't really any victims, they told him, because ultimately everything would be paid for by insurance companies or banks, and institutions like these were making so much money at the expense of ordinary people that they deserved it. Effectively they argued that, by engaging in fraud or theft, they were acting as instruments of the equity of wealth redistribution from the overpaid to the underpaid. God, and Christians, should be proud of their work.

At first, Osei was hesitant to buy into this logic, tantalising as it sounded. Even though he had got into some bad habits, he really wanted to put that all behind him, to find regular work somewhere, at least a job in between the normal registered taxpaying world and the demi-monde of his new associates. He sent out applications for work in response to various advertisements in the papers, turning up randomly at construction sites touting his skills, living by the skin of his teeth through begging.

Unluckily for Osei, one night one of the go-betweens for some old gambling creditors spotted him and sent word back to his principals. They asked him to 'invite' Osei to an urgent meeting. A couple of hours later, Osei was laughing heartily at a crude joke of one of his group when he felt the cold steel of a knife pressed against his back through the thin fabric of the tattered shirt he was wearing. The sudden silence and palpable sense of panic among the rest of the group confirmed to him what was going on; he didn't have to turn round to check.

He was hurried by three people into a small car, where the one holding a knife gave another a blindfold to put on him, pushing his head face down on to the back seat immediately afterwards. In less than 15 minutes he was going down stairs in a building somewhere – he didn't know where. At the bottom of the stairs was what seemed like a dank basement. As his blindfold was removed, he found himself sitting at a small rectangular wooden table opposite a panel of three people: one at the head, the bright light of a large lamp positioned beside him to shine directly into Osei's face and obscure his vision; the other two at the sides.

As the person at the head of the table started speaking, Osei realised it was a man with a gruff, croaky voice. Beyond the edge of the lamp Osei saw in the dim surrounding light a sliver of a pock-marked face. The man explained that Osei had been a naughty boy: he had failed to pay his debts despite being given ample time to do so. Now, on pain of death, he would have to join their outfit as an "employee". The head added that, on the bright side, Osei's new job had fringe benefits as, unlike the case with the Army, there would be no retirement. At that he let rip a loud guffaw, the other two and the goons who had abducted Kweku laughing along raucously in unison.

When he had recovered from laughing at his own joke, the boss explained to Osei that he would be given back ten percent, shared equally between all those directly participating in the relevant job, of any cash he brought to the pot. If he tried skimming any of the income "off the top" before reporting it, he would lose parts of his body, ending with his head. By now the sweat was streaming down from Osei's forehead. He was shaking like a leaf.

The boss then motioned to the goons behind him. One came forward. Osei recognised it was the same one who had stuck the knife in his back half an hour earlier. He approached and put a small open bag on the table. He then grabbed Osei's left wrist, turned it face up and drew smartly across it with his knife in three directions. As blood spurted from the open wound, Osei shrieked in pain. Bursting casually into an evil cackle which sounded as coarse as uncut granite scraped on timber, the goon then pulled out gauze from the bag, wound it round Osei's wrist several times and taped it to close the bandage. The boss explained that he had just been given their distinguishing gang-sign.

By the end of the "job interview", apart from the debilitating pain in his wrist, Osei's clothes were soaked through with perspiration. The boss welcomed him to the fraternity and then told him to get out of there and bring home some money. He was taken to one of the gang's apartments in Osu to await further instructions.

So began a life of crime for Kwesi Osei. He joined other members in a series of bank raids, robberies, burglaries of big houses. Using skills learnt in the army with land navigation and weapons handling, he quickly gained a name in the organisation for proficiency, for getting the job done. More money passed through his hands than he had ever seen. There was an honour among them as thieves which he respected. He loved the adrenalin rush of hold-ups, escaping capture at speed, changing vehicles, hiding in bushes. He was glad to be in a fraternity where rules were simple: loyalty to each other and respect for the chain of command. It was just like being in the Army, but with the potential to make a mint, if luck smiled on him.

And after all, he reasoned, everything in life was based on luck anyway. No baby ever chose ahead of their birth to be born a boy any more than a girl, to rich parents any more than to poor parents, to an ethnic Chinese father any more than to an ethnic Swede, Afrikaner or Negro mother.

In truth, we are all dealt the cards that will have the greatest influence on our lives before we are even born. The exercise and influence of choice comes into play after we are born. But how much of that is conditioned by parental education, genes, astrology and other influences as yet dismissed as humbug because as humans we must believe that we make our own choices, otherwise no one is responsible for anything, and ultimately, once all the charts and genetic and biodata are in, everyone's actions are predictable to a high degree of probability?

Osei's new life of crime was however turning him into something unrecognisable even to himself in the few quiet moments of honest reflection which forced themselves into his thinking despite his determined efforts to avoid them. He was becoming more like the father he hated than the mother he loved. The change happened quickly, but imperceptibly, as for the sniper whose first hit was a nervous experience full of self-doubt but whose fourth killing weeks later was just like drinking a glass of wine.

It always takes much longer to build something up than to knock it down. Osei was changing rapidly for the worse while, despite appearances, the world around him went on changing, more slowly, for the better.

***

The housekeeper, the calculatedly obsequious Johnson Boakye, had gone quietly to unlock the front gate. He lifted the bolts at the bottom securing the gate to the cement floor and opened it gingerly, leaving a small gap in the middle which was invisible to the naked eye unless from close up. Electrified fencing had been strung above the walls all round the house, but the wires had the design flaw of being attached to the gate and parted without triggering any alarm, breaking the flow of electricity, whenever the gate was opened. The assumption was that intruders would not be able to open the gate from outside. That left security vulnerable to an inside job, but the elderly couple living there were both of a stubborn disposition and had placed their full trust in the unctuous Johnson.

Their home was beautiful, built like an ancient Roman villa with solid foundation and structural pillars, walls made of concrete, granite and marble. But for all the house's robustness and aesthetic beauty, the alarm system had been switched off. As the couple kept forgetting the 4-digit passcode, setting off false alarms, the local police response had become haphazard. And there were no dogs: the lady of the house had a huge, fluffy male cat that had been a big part of her life in her years as a widow before she met her new husband, and she didn't want to take any risk of dogs who had not grown up in tandem with him bullying him. Johnson had carefully studied all the house's security weaknesses and fully briefed his co-conspirators. He told them the job would be like a picnic – a walk in the park.

So there was no advance warning as Osei and his two associates slid up to the house in their van in the small hours of the morning, switched the lights off and parked it outside. Pulling down their masks, locally-made pistols holstered at their waists, they sneaked through the open gate. The automatic compound lights came on; but these always came on, even if an innocent pedestrian was walking by in the street outside. So the temporary extra glow of light did not disturb the couple's deep sleep beyond generating an extra grunt or twitch here and there before the alternating rhythm of their snoring was resumed.

As the burglars tiptoed across the compound, they saw Johnson, their inside man, peering at them through the *jalousie* windows of his adjacent servants' quarters. They jimmied the sliding door to the main reception room, shone their torches on the paintings, ornaments and sculptures hanging on the walls and nested cosily in alcoves, and began removing these to their van. From there they moved to a second reception room and dining room. Once all the walls had been stripped bare, they crept up the hardwood stairs. One creaked loudly under the weight of Osei's feet. They stopped and waited to see if any lights came on or doors opened. All they could hear was a cat starting to meow. After two minutes, they decided to continue climbing.

They opened the door at the top of the stairs using the skeleton key the safecracker had brought along with him. Johnson had told them the safe was located in a study at the end of the corridor to the right. The homeowner was a wealthy retired businessman. His place was a popular stop for politicians of all persuasions seeking cash donations to bolster their campaign war-chests and feed their burgeoning payrolls of pseudo-ideologues and flunkeys.

The owner kept all his cash in the safe. Johnson's furtive espionage during the two years he had been working for the couple, slowly gaining their trust, had established that the design of the safe was nothing sophisticated – just a combination-style spinning tumbler. There was a keylock beside it, but he had never seen the old man using it, and the old codger was anyhow useless with keys, always misplacing them and asking him to look for them. A professional safecracker would be able to get the job done easily, and one of the gang was an expert.

The door to the study was unlocked. They slinked in and closed it quietly behind them. Seeing the safe in a far corner, the expert got to work. He went up to kneel beside it. Pinning his ears back, he spun the tumbler clockwise and anti-clockwise in several iterations… Now he was sure he had cracked it… But when he swung the handle to open it, it didn't move. All three of them started sweating, panicking, their pulses racing. The safecracker must have got the combination wrong. Maybe he simply wasn't up to it after all and had conned the "sponsors" of the job? Osei shone his torch directly into his face. He and the other burglar now stood menacingly over him, asking him to try again… and again… But the door wouldn't budge.

In desperation, the safecracker brought out his skeleton key again. But he already knew that the one he had brought was only meant to open doors. There was a special one for safe keylocks, but he would have had to hire that from an associate in the neighbourhood. He hadn't bothered because Osei had assured him, based on information from Johnson, that he would only have to deal with a spinning tumbler device. For the same reason, he also hadn't brought along any power-drill or oxy-fuel cutting torch. The noise from these would have woken the couple up anyway.

Shining their torches all round in a panic, checking to see if the key had been discarded nearby, one by one the intruders banged the safe door in frustration. They fiddled over and over with the skeleton key… Nothing worked. Then they heard the cat start meowing again, this time without pause, ever louder. Pointing their torch in the direction of the study door, they realised the cat was right behind it. A light went on in the corridor, visible in the gap under the door. The cat darted off, still meowing. They pinned themselves against the wall, Osei standing closest to the entrance, and waited. The sound of slipper-clad feet could be heard shuffling closer and closer. The door swung open. A bespectacled man appeared in the doorway, a revolver tightly gripped in his outstretched right hand, his left arm swinging back over his shoulder to turn on the light switch on the wall behind to his right where the burglars stood.

Osei knew they were about to be exposed. In a karate-chopping manoeuvre, he tried to dislodge the revolver from the old man's grip. The old man bent over, pulling the trigger as he fell to the floor, still gripping the gun tightly with a strength and determination for his age that Osei simply hadn't anticipated. A bang went off and the bullet ricocheted off three walls, lodging in the thigh of the safecracker. He screamed in agony and fell to the ground, blood pouring out from his wound.

Osei drew his pistol and callously shot the old man as he struggled to get up from the floor, once in the back, then twice in the head at close range to make sure. He helped the safecracker up, but he could hardly move. So he dropped him and ran out into the corridor, heading for the master bedroom… he had to stop the old lady from doing anything foolish.

However, unknown to Osei and to Johnson, the weekend before, while Johnson had gone to his hometown in the Western Region to visit his sick mum, one of the politicians who had passed by earlier that week, concerned that the couple were keeping so much cash in their house, had engaged a private security firm to visit them. They came round on the Saturday when Johnson happened to be away and had installed a panic button in the couple's bedroom linked directly to the Police Headquarters.

The cat had by now vanished to safety – somewhere out of sight that only cats can find. Osei tried the bedroom door, but it was locked. He had just started shooting at it when he heard the sound of approaching police sirens in the distance. In a moment of panic, he turned back and shouted to the others that they had to get out of there fast. Slinging the wounded safecracker's arm over his shoulder, he dragged him down the stairs, the other man helping on the other side.

As they reached the foot of the stairs, they saw Johnson. His eyes were stretched wide in horror, fear written all over his face. He raised his arms as if to ask 'What the hell happened up there?' He daren't ask out loud in case his voice was recognised by the old lady. But there was no time for any recriminations; the sound of police sirens was now much louder. Moving at a gallop, Johnson helped them through the sliding door, across the yard and back through the front gate. By the time they reached the van, the first two police cars had turned into the street, their tyres screeching as they raced up.

Dropping the safecracker, Osei and the other burglar fled back inside the house and sprinted to the rear of the compound. Johnson gestured frantically for them to leap over the wall at the back, helping to launch them over, one by one, using his shoulders as support. He then rushed back to his quarters, praying he hadn't been spotted by anyone, so that he could play the innocent and emerge only now, as if awoken by the gunshots.

But unfortunately for Johnson he had been spotted ... by the wrinkled eyes of a heartbroken old lady aghast at his treachery. She had seen him darting to and fro across the compound, helping the robbers to escape. For a moment she thought she must be having a nightmare. Then she realised she wasn't mistaken: it was him.

Four policemen entered the compound. Two rushed across the yard and into the house. The other two stayed outside to search for the robbers and secure the place. As the two policemen inside reached the upstairs corridor, shouting out to the old lady and her husband, she came out of the bedroom to lead them to the study. Seeing her husband's body lying motionless on the floor in a pool of blood, she let out a piercing scream and threw herself over him, desperate to will him back to consciousness. The policemen struggled to pull her away. One of them got closer to check his pulse. An ambulance was already on the way… But there was no pulse. The policeman shook his head: the poor old man had already gone.

They asked her who else was in the house. Sobbing constantly as she spoke, she narrated everything she had seen and heard, including her shock at realising that, of all people, it was their Judas of a housekeeper, Johnson, who had masterminded the robbery.

By now the ambulance and two more police cars had arrived. A small crowd of onlookers, many still in their pyjamas and nightgowns, was gathering outside, keeping a safe distance. Others peered from lit windows in houses nearby. Leaving his colleague to console and watch over the lady, the second police officer rushed down the stairs, radioing for his colleagues to arrest Johnson, get the wounded burglar to hospital and help him check the compound for the missing two robbers.

A neighbour came forward to the front of the house to tell the police she saw two men jumping over the wall at the back of the house some 25 minutes earlier. Seeing that behind the house were woods and wasteland, the police realised it would not be easy to try to locate the remaining burglars until daybreak, by which time they would likely be long gone. They decided for now to prioritise securing the house and comforting the grieving widow.

***

Kweku had just sat down to a mid-morning brunch of kenkey and snapper fish with mixed red and green *kpakpo shito* pepper sauce and onions, black *shito* chilli sauce and a hard-boiled egg. He was about to swallow his first mouthful when he glanced at the front page of a newspaper beside him. A picture of a man looking just like Osei jumped out at him, alongside photos of another man under the banner headline: "WANTED!"

He put his food back down and picked up the newspaper to read the article. He straightaway lost his appetite. It was indeed Osei. He had committed a horrific crime and was now on the run with another armed robber. Kweku moved to sit down in his armchair. He put the rest of his day aside and spent it listening to media reports and answering calls from people who knew of his friendship with Osei. His mum and dad were first to call. He told them he had no idea what had happened and was finding out himself. He had not told about them about the strange call from Osei a year earlier, which had ended with Osei cursing and hanging up on him.

After a while he asked Tina not to put any more calls through to him. He was fed up with people rather calling him to find out more. He himself now wanted to read everything about this man he had grown up as best friends with, to see if he could glean from somewhere in the multiple stories and sourcing clues as to why and how this shy, cheerful boy had turned into such a monster. His thoughts went to Osei's mother Sheila. Such a dedicated, innocent woman.

This was the last thing she deserved for all the sacrifices she had made in her life. What an ungrateful son! So he had never really known Osei at all.

***

By the next day Kweku's focus was back on the immediate priorities of his own life, the promise of new beginnings and a family life of his own. Over the years, he had heard so much spoken about the joys of family life in the round, beyond ephemeral tensions. He was happy and so grateful to have the parents that he had, but he had no idea if that happiness would carry over into his own marriage and possible parenthood later… How would it be on the other side of the fence, when the boot was on the other foot? He was keenly aware that his parents were anxious to see him settle down while they were still alive, so they could witness it and give him any support he needed as he embarked on that phase of his life.

And he was under no illusion that there would indeed be challenges along the way. But life was meant for challenges, reaching for solutions, for perfection. He was excited at the prospect of having a life partner who seemed to enjoy his company as much as he enjoyed hers, while sharing his understanding that everyone still needs their own private space from time to time, above all that respect is a two-way street. Osei had turned out to be such a disaster. Joanna held out promise of the complete experience.

***

Charlie and Anne Visit Ghana for the Wedding

November 1984

Kweku rang his old friend Charlie Turner to ask him to be best man at his wedding. He'd spent more time with him than with anyone else in his university years and they always got on somehow. So, even though he knew it was a long-shot, Charlie was first on his list. He would take it from there. To his shock, Charlie told him a friend at the Ham Polo Club, retired army major Nicholas Chalmers-Duncan, had rung him the week before to ask if he would be interested in joining a Polo trip to Accra being sponsored by British Caledonian Airways in the third week of November.

Charlie was very interested, so he had actually cleared his diary and was planning to get back to Chalmers-Duncan and surprise Kweku while down there. Now, with the wonderful news he had just got from Kweku, the timing was fantastic and he would like to bring his wife Anne along too. Kweku was thrilled and insisted they stay with him while in Ghana. He now had his own cook, Rockson, doubling as a house help, and Tina had trained and sent over a cousin, Maria, to help them as well. He had two company cars at his disposal, so would assign his driver Justin plus one of the cars to take them around during their stay.

***

The British Caledonian flight from Gatwick Airport touched down in Accra on Tuesday night, 30 minutes late. Charlie and Anne were no strangers to long-distance travel, but the blast of hot air they felt as they emerged from the plane told them right away that they were in Africa. It took longer than usual for them to clear immigration and customs, as the plane's delayed arrival meant that it clashed with other flights.

As they came outside, Anne, not seeing any lady with Kweku, asked if Joanna was at the house. Kweku explained the wish of both sets of parents to do things the traditional way. Even though Joanna and Kweku were now customarily married, it was decided she wouldn't move in with Kweku until the night of the full church wedding. Kweku and Joanna were willing participants in this, even though it was slightly hypocritical, as they were already man and wife according to customary law and their parents were fully aware that Joanna was already spending weekends in the house with Kweku and that they were travelling elsewhere together. But it was everyone's way of salvaging some novelty for the church wedding, to enhance the significance of its ceremonies.

Joanna had been up to her eyeballs in preparations for the wedding for several weeks now. She would be at the house mid-morning the next day to take Anne out sightseeing at Makola Market, while Kweku took Charlie to Tema to show him round Sonimo's export warehouse and Tema office. With the wedding now just 3 days away, things were quite hectic.

At the airconditioned house, Kweku showed them to their ensuite bedroom. No expense had been spared to make them feel right at home. It was late, so they only wanted a light supper. Kweku asked his new cook, Rockson, to sort out some cold cuts from the fridge with salad and toast. Maria was on hand to assist. He called Joanna to let her know they had arrived safely. He then shared a couple of beers with Charlie over supper, while Anne had a vodka and coke. Then it was straight to bed for everyone.

***

The next morning Kweku had pulled out all the stops to arrange a full English breakfast to help settle their digestion. Internal discomfort often results from a plane journey – whether from the plane food, plane sickness due to buffeting by the clouds during ascent and descent, cabin pressure variation or a combination of all three.

There was an assortment of breakfast cereals to start, accompanied by servings of diced mango, pawpaw and sweet Cape Coast pineapple. Three large jugs stood on the table – one of ice-cold water, another of freshly squeezed orange juice and a third of fresh water melon juice, the pips removed before blending. Finally came platters of fried eggs, fried tomatoes with onion rings, and rashers of back bacon and pork sausages beside stacks of white and brown toast, a large bowl of baked beans and a bottle of tomato ketchup.

As they tucked into the feast in front of them, Charlie turned to Kweku:

'Anne was saying she thought she heard a cuckoo this morning. I don't know, I was fast asleep. I told her she must have been dreaming, you don't get cuckoos in Ghana!'

'No, Charlie, she probably really did hear a cuckoo,' Kweku replied. 'In fact, did you know that the cuckoo you hear in summertime in England is the same one that can be found warbling in Africa or even Asia that same year?'

'No, you've got to be kidding!' said Charlie chuckling, genuinely shocked. 'Really?'

'Yep! It's almost like they're taking return tickets twice a year migrating out to and back from hot weather destinations without the need for border checks.'

Anne turned to Charlie 'See, I told you!'

'Well I never!' Charlie conceded.

Kweku continued: 'To tell you the truth, I feel a bit like a cuckoo myself …'

'Oh yes, and how is that then?' Anne was intrigued.

'Well, you know how I always like to time my visits to the UK for the summer and get back to Ghana before the onset of the British winter?'

'Oh, hahahaa!' Charlie had worked it out. 'Yes, come to think of it, you do always seem to be around in the UK in the summer for business meetings or conferences – and then we don't hear anything from you again till the next summer!' As they all giggled wickedly together, Kweku reflected that it always cheered him when he could make people laugh – not politely to flatter a story-teller, but at a comical twist in language or a situation that hadn't previously occurred to them. It indeed was an entertaining reminder of what great travellers birds are.

But Kweku sensed that there was something else that Charlie was itching to ask him. He looked at Charlie, cocking his head slightly to one side and raising his eyebrows to invite the question.

‘Kweku, honestly thank you for asking me to be your best man. I shall try not to mess things up.’ Charlie started.

‘Thank you rather for agreeing, old boy. I’m sure you’ll do just fine.’

‘Listen Kweku, I hope you don’t mind my asking… I mean, I hope you don’t take this the wrong way, but I was wondering… in Ghana, are you allowed to have more than one wife?’

Anne cut in swiftly: ‘Charlie! How could you ask Kweku something like that at a time like this just days before his wedding? That is sooo rude. Don’t take any notice of him, Kweku.’

‘No, I mean it,’ Charlie went on, winking mischievously. ‘You know, in England we think men in Africa are lucky, because you’re not limited to one wife, are you?’

‘I don’t think I want to hear any more of this,’ Anne sighed, dropping her cutlery and elbowing Charlie gently in the ribs.

Kweku was sure Charlie hadn’t meant that he personally had any ideas. He knew Charlie was just playing devil’s advocate. He hadn’t taken any offence either. He quickly intervened:

‘No no, Anne, I’m sure Charlie’s just joking. Look, I don’t mind answering at all. It’s quite interesting actually… The traditional or customary marriage ceremony – you know, the one Joanna and I went through in August – is the only marriage ceremony we had here before the Europeans arrived. And then, particularly when the British came, indigenes in the region now called Ghana started willingly adopting not just Christian religion but, beyond religion, rules of

English common law and equity where they felt these evidenced greater fairness in the dispensation of social justice than existing local customary laws.

Charlie interjected: 'Crikey, you're going into some detail, Kweku. But actually, I'm interested in hearing more, so long as were not boring you, darling?' He turned to Annie.

But Annie too now seemed interested. 'No no, go on,' she said.

'OK guys, it's the only way to explain it. So, if you do have a moment, now is as good a time as any to let you know whatever little I know about it all …'

'Yes, yes, don't worry, carry on,' said Charlie.

'OK, now, as far as customary marriage is concerned, a man can customarily marry any number of women, provided the woman and representatives of the two extended families agree. But even on this point note that, in a sign of continuing inequality between the sexes according to customary law, a woman can customarily have only one husband. So polygamy is allowed, if you like, but only for the man.'

'But that's not fair!' said Anne.

'Indeed it isn't, and it certainly means that women don't have the same rights as men when it comes to customary law marriages…

But the playing field is levelled out when it comes to ordinance marriages – that is, civil unions registered under the Marriages Act. Here, in the case of non-Muslims, the man too can only have one person at a time registered as his wife under the ordinance. The woman is still limited to one man, as is the case for all marriages where women are concerned. But at least in the case of ordinance marriages there is equality between the sexes.

Now, for those following Islam, who live principally in the north of the country – where there are also some Christians, mind you – but also in many communities elsewhere throughout the country, the number of customary wives is limited to four. But the Mohammedan's Ordinance allows all four to be registered simultaneously as wives. So for Muslims in Ghana there is no equality in this respect for the woman at either customary law level or ordinance level.'

'I see,' said Anne.

'That's interesting,' Charlie chimed in.

'Anyway, I think that's enough on Ghanaian customs for one day. You'll get to know others as you go along – most of them unwritten codes of behaviour, I might add. As in every culture, you learn as you live among them – you know the old saying, "When in Rome …"'

'Yes, yes,' Charlie said. Anne nodded and smiled.

***

After breakfast, while Anne went back upstairs to her bedroom to finish unpacking and pick one of the books she had brought to flip through while waiting for Joanna to arrive, Kweku set off with Charlie to Tema Harbour. They went via the Accra – Tema motorway. In just over half an hour they were at the company's warehouse near the harbour. Charlie looked on in amazement at its size.

As container-laden flatbed trucks moved in and out of the yard, Kweku explained:

'We plan on building another warehouse over there, to the right, to keep up with export demand for our Honimo honey sweet. Oh, I've just realised I forgot to offer you and Anne some yesterday. It's our best-selling product: people just seem to love the distinctive darker, richer flavour of Ghanaian honey. I'll get some for you now.'

They got down from the car and were first given a quick presentation by the export administration manager. Charlie was given a bag of Honimo and popped one into his mouth. He savoured it as the despatch managers took them on a quick tour of the warehouse. Charlie listened attentively and seemed genuinely interested, asking pertinent questions on matters such as security in transit.

From there they drove up to the entrance of Tema Harbour itself, just to give Charlie an overview, without actually going in too far and getting caught up in all the bureaucracy and traffic queues. There wasn't really any time for that, and Kweku was sure Charlie had seen all that sort of thing before in the UK anyway. After that, they decided to head back to Accra. Traffic was much heavier on the way back.

By the time they got back to the house, Joanna and Anne had just returned from the market. Kweku introduced Joanna to Charlie. Charlie embraced her, nodding in Kweku's direction to signal that he'd made a good catch. Joanna and Anne had already introduced themselves in their absence.

The visit to Makola Market had been a real eye-opener for Anne. Recounting her experience, she said she was shocked how hectic it was. She had never seen anything like it. People selling large tomatoes and other huge fruits on the pavements; the formidable market mammies – Joanna had told her they were the key drivers of the country's substantial informal economy – parading in front of their stalls in huge straw sun hats, tugging arms of passing shoppers and shouting 'Buy something for me', by which they actually meant 'Buy something *from* me'. The noise, the colours, the smells, the heat; she had found it all so overwhelming – especially coming from a cold country where modern markets such as her beloved Bicester market could also be large but were much more clearly organised into sections.

'The fabrics, shoes, handbags, so beautiful and creatively styled… really interesting combs too,' Anne continued. 'But as soon as Joanna saw that I was interested in buying anything, she quickly tipped me off.

Joanna interrupted: 'Yes, I told her never take their first offer. When they see an *oburoni*, a white person, they immediately triple their normal selling price.'

'Why is that?', asked Charlie.

'Because they're convinced you can afford it. To use the old expression, they still think the streets of London are paved with gold! So I told Anne, if they say 20 cedis, tell them you will pay 7, and so on. It won't always work, because some of them gamble right up to the limit and can overplay their hand. Others have a false sense of pride and think, when you go too low, it implies they wanted to swindle you rotten with their first offer – which, sadly, is often exactly the case! Such types would rather lose the sale than have their ego punctured. So, if you really want to buy something, I told her, continue playing cat-and-mouse with them until the discount reaches at least half if not the full two thirds of their original offer. They will usually accept.'

'But the place is so huge,' Anne added.

'I know,' said Joanna. 'We didn't get the chance to go all the way round. You'd probably need a full two days to be able to get round to all the stalls.'

Anne continued:

'Oh, and I loved the African fabrics with colourful mysterious print designs which all have names and meanings. Joanna explained it all to me. I jotted them down here on this notepad on our way back – like flowers representing the name Felicia to mean "happiness", another design referring to famous Ghanaian proverbs such as *Gye Nyame*, meaning only God can do things or God is all-powerful… My favourite was *Sika wo ntaban*, which Joanna said means "money has wings"!' Anne laughed out loud, glancing at Charlie, then at Joanna and Kweku. 'It's so true though, isn't it? Money does fly where it wants to go: if you don't handle it well, it *will* fly away from you.' Charlie seemed momentarily embarrassed, before realising Anne had only intended it as general wise counsel.

Joanna quickly added:

'And Anne was really impressed with the beads.'

'Oh yes, such beautiful African beads! … I love the one that said *Ahwene pa n'kasa*, meaning "Good beads don't talk" – i.e. your actions will speak for you. I thought that was brilliant! … Anyway, in the end I bought these necklaces and this handbag.' She lifted them out of a bag to show Charlie.

'Gorgeous, aren't they?' she said.

Charlie was impressed: 'No doubt about it. And I've never seen a handbag like that before.'

'I know,' Anne said, 'It's wonderful. The beige cloth speckled with polished glass beads, a blue stone covering the centre buckle in front.' She turned to Joanna, pointing to the blue stone: 'Is that lapis lazuli? ...'

'I don't know,' Joanna replied, 'but it looks absolutely exquisite. Lucky you!' She couldn't help turning to Kweku. 'Hint, hint!' she teased, fluttering her eyelids at him.

'All right, darling,' Kweku said. 'Don't worry, I got the message.'

Not wishing to be outdone, Charlie shifted the conversation to how his own day had gone: 'Well, Kweku took me on a fascinating tour of Sonimo's export warehouse and offices. We even went to the port area... We didn't actually go very far in, as we didn't want to get caught up in all the traffic and queues, but it looks like Tema is being developed into a huge, modern container port... And the Sonimo warehouse! So many trucks going in and out and so neatly organised. It was like a well-choreographed parade.'

'Thank you, Charlie. I'm glad you liked it,' Kweku appreciated the compliment. He knew Charlie loved making practical jokes but was never one to make throwaway comments when assessing things.

'Sounds interesting,' Anne chimed in diplomatically.

'Uh-huh,' Joanna added. Anne and Joanna both knew that for them the trip to the market had been considerably more fun than a trip to a warehouse, offices and port area would have been. On the other hand they had no idea which of the two trips men would genuinely find more appealing. So they opted to take Charlie and Kweku at their word that they'd had equal fun.

After a brief lull in the conversation, Charlie looked at his watch and piped up. 'OK anyway, we need to get ready to welcome the main tour party at the airport tonight.'

'The driver and car are fully at your disposal, Charlie and Anne,' Kweku reiterated. 'So make the most of them.'

'Thanks, that's so nice of you,' Anne said, looking at Joanna and Kweku. Charlie smiled and nodded.

***

The flight bringing the rest of the tour party led by Nick Chalmers-Duncan landed on time. They spent Thursday unpacking and checking over their ponies stabled at the Accra Polo Club. At the first match of the tour on the Friday, the Club captain, the famously mercurial Arsen Karadian, caught the British contingent unawares by fielding a young Argentinian 6-goal prodigy, who was in the country for a month to visit an uncle engaged in the construction industry. This was done deliberately, with no prior warning to the British team, and it ensured that the tour kicked off with a major controversy.

The visitors were down 4-0 by half time, before being convinced from the Argentinian's exceptional playing skills that something was awry. During divot-stamping, they raised strong objections, after which the young prodigy was switched to the role of umpire for the last three chukkas. The match ended 5-4 to the Ghanaian team, with Charlie scoring one of the British team's goals.

During the trophy presentation ceremony and speeches after the match there was strained applause, with red faces everywhere – for those members of the Ghanaian team and Club Committee with pale enough cheeks to show it – and facial expressions betraying varying levels of embarrassment for the other members. Only a small section of the Club's social members propping up the bar cackled noisily at the controversy, earning disapproving stares and shushing from others.

It took all of Karadian's legendary charm and infectious humour, and a massive poolside banquet laid on at his mansion that evening, complete with a huge pig roasted on one spit and a sheep and goat on another, with copious wine and champagne, to calm tempers down and leave everyone laughing at the end of the day. Charlie secretly thought the whole thing was hilarious, but had to hide his feelings from his teammates until they had loosened up at the party.

***

At noon the next day Kweku and Joanna were married at Kweku's local Catholic parish. A smart, well attended fashionable occasion, it was an emotional moment for the couple, their parents, and sentimental sympathisers reliving their own weddings. Some younger guests dreamt it would be their turn one day to be standing at the altar; they stole glances around the congregation in spare moments during the service to see if any likely candidates were present.

There was the usual moment of high tension during the pregnant pause after the priest asked anyone aware of a reason that the couple could not be married to step forward. It was not that either of them thought there really was a reason, just that control over the service was at that point temporarily surrendered to anyone willing to step forward or making a feint to do so. At that moment, how many brides or grooms weren't afraid some misguided prankster or mentally challenged person would step forward and temporarily steal the limelight. Worse still, if there was any real basis for such an intervention.

In the end, everything passed off without any major hitches. Crucially, Charlie played his part in not forgetting to bring the wedding ring for Kweku to place on Joanna's finger. The only small irritant was the long delay when it came to the photography immediately following the service, because of the large number of family members attending and insisting on being featured in studied poses for posterity. The bride and groom got to the wedding reception half an hour late as a result.

The reception was a huge one at a nearby hotel, complete with marquees, tasteful furniture and crockery, and colourful floral arrangements. The highlight, for good or ill, was Charlie's best man's speech. It contained all the elements of a classic British best man's speech, calculated humorously to heap embarrassment on the groom by recounting tales of wild mistakes committed by him in his youth. For many in the crowd, Kweku's dad included, it was side-splitting fun. Joanna laughed nervously at some parts of the speech, and looked distracted at others.

Out of the corner of his eye but avoiding looking directly at her out of a sense of guilt, Kweku saw his mother growing increasingly embarrassed as the speech progressed. He felt like disappearing under the table during some anecdotes – as when Charlie mentioned Kweku visiting Emperors wine bar in his orange coloured socks and pyjama top to deliver a message to someone, or when he was sent packing by the nurses from the Radcliffe Infirmary after being dropped there by Charlie and other friends as a joke.

A part of Kweku was impressed at Charlie's memory retention for trivia he had thought long forgotten, and suicidally actually wanted him to continue refreshing him about some of the outlandish things that had occurred during his Oxford days. Another part of him was dying for Charlie to propose his toast to the newlyweds to bring the curtain down on his ordeal. When it did end, Kweku inwardly breathed a huge sigh of relief.

So many guests came up to him afterwards, saying Charlie's speech was the highlight of their day, that they had never heard such a string of fantastical tales and what a comedian Charlie was. The first time it happened, Kweku laughed out loud along with the guest, mightily relieved for the second time in minutes. Similar subsequent feedback from guests confirmed that they had absolutely no idea that everything Charlie mentioned had actually happened. What saved Kweku was that it was all so implausible that none of them believed that any of it could be remotely true.

It was the perfect outcome for Kweku to the most nerve-wracking moment of his day, and he was certainly not going to correct their misapprehension.

The only person who realised it could all easily be true, and never asked him to confirm things either way, was the person who knew him best – his mum. She took about an hour to recover from the speech but several weeks to forgive Charlie. In the end she did see the funny side. When the bride and groom reached their hideaway at the end of the day, Joanna, with the instinct of a woman who understood the man she had married, asked him if it was true. Kweku told her some of it was. In truth, all of it was, but it wasn't then a lie to tell her, as Kweku had just done, that some of it was. Joanna never followed up, as a trial lawyer would have done, to ask about the truth or otherwise of the rest. And so the full, embarrassing truth somehow crazily survived as a secret between him and Charlie.

CHAPTER FIFTEEN

Married Life

Honeymoon

December 1984

Exhausted and slightly intoxicated, Kweku did not have the energy or strength to carry Joanna over the threshold into their new home. It was a western tradition anyway, and even then a custom more honoured in the breach than the observance. As Charlie and Annie were still their guests for the duration of the British polo tour, it would be the following weekend before he and Joanna would be able to fly to Europe on their honeymoon.

The morning after the wedding, Joanna was keen to start putting her own individual stamp on the house's character. She needed to banish the presence of imagined competitors for occupation and make it her own creation as inseparable from her as a child. She asked Kweku to join her in visiting the main art gallery in Accra central. Together they chose six paintings. The choices were mostly Joanna's preferences, as Kweku saw how important this was to her and was already engaged in the practice of compromise that so many older extended family members had advised was the bedrock of any successful marriage. He reflected that for those who always want to get everything their own way, staying single would be better than deceiving a hopeful partner and themselves about their ability to compromise. For his own part, for better or worse, he had decided to attempt a partnership.

From the Sunday afternoon to the middle of the following week there was an extended roll-out of polo matches, parties and barbecues, including one adjacent to the beach further east along the coast at Prampram. After the tour was over, Kweku and Joanna took Charlie and Anne on a private trip to Elmina Castle. It was built by the Portuguese and was the first outpost in West Africa for European colonisers seeking riches trading in gold, slaves and ivory. The centrepiece of this trip was the descent to the Door of No Return, the last point for slaves boarding ships during the horrific transatlantic slave trade. Charlie and Anne got very emotional reflecting on the possibility, however remote, that during the years the Castle was administered by British colonisers one of their ancestors could actually have been involved in such a ruthless business, for all they knew.

Kweku tried to reassure them that those were different times, when different principles were commonplace. Horrific things were also being perpetrated between local tribes at the time and within tribes, with chiefs serving as absolute monarchs with the power of life and death over their subjects. Even though white slavers were the ostensible drivers of the trade, it could not have gone on without the support and acquiescence of local chiefs and entire tribes. Racism and discrimination on ethnic grounds was a universal human mischief, not one restricted to groups of people with a particular skin colour.

From Elmina they travelled up country to the Sonimo factory in Mim, via Kumasi, where they toured the museum of the Asantehene, part of the Asante chief's palace at Manhyia. Mim was like an oasis in the middle of a desert, so alluring were the facilities there for nature-lovers. In the short time they were there, Charlie and Anne didn't encounter any cobras or alligators close up, but they did see stark, bright colours of plants, insects and birds that they had never laid eyes on anywhere else.

Before they left Mim, they were given by Pierre on the company's behalf two large boxes of assorted confectionery, including the firm's flagship Honimo tasty honey sweet, to take home and show friends a little something about Ghana. Back in Accra, they did a little souvenir shopping at the Arts Centre on the High Street – mainly wooden carvings in the form of miniature stools and some kente stoles. By the time they flew out, the fuss over Charlie's best man's speech was a distant memory and they were thankful for an unusual holiday. They insisted that Kweku and Joanna must get in touch whenever coming to the UK, to give them a chance to reciprocate, or they would not forgive them.

***

Finally Kweku and Joanna were free to enjoy their own company, on honeymoon. They flew out for a magical fortnight on the Greek island of Rhodes. Out of reach of business colleagues and family, they renewed the relaxed interactions of their courtship, more laid back than ever, with the formalities of marriage and all those prying eyes out of the way.

Nobody knew them in Rhodes, so they could spend long, guilt-free hours on the beach, in the surf or by the hotel swimming pool, sipping cocktails, reading books and enjoying brilliant fresh sautéed seafood. It was the unsustainably self-indulgent backcloth against which an ideal married life begins, before the return to a familiar home and office environment restores connections to altruistic sacrifices and commitments.

During the honeymoon, they discussed not having children for a few years. Joanna was still a rising star at her company, Consolidated Beverages. She was anxious to try to break the glass ceiling there, with the help of her father's contacts in the industry, and climb to the level of Sales Director before she could entertain any thoughts about ending her career in favour of child-rearing. With her husband a full-time employee spending half of his time outside Accra, if she was going to have a child, she wanted to be able to look after her or him for most of the time, not have to pass them off to the care of others on her way in to work and only reconnect with them in the evenings after work.

They didn't want to use contraceptives. Instead they preferred the clock method to help them avoid pregnancy, as all their friends swore by its efficacy.

***

Meanwhile business was continuing to grow in a favourable economic cycle for Sonimo and other exporters, a more pragmatic macroeconomic environment allowing them to expand their businesses into international markets and employ more labour.

Apart from improving economic indicators, the military government acted with the speed that only military governments or respected determined civilian administrations can, to right certain wrongs in society. They encouraged formal female or "girl-child" education from primary school age and introduced a more equitable intestate law to govern the situations, still all too prevalent, where people died without making a formal will. Prior to 1985, under customary law, when for instance a husband died without leaving a will duly sealed at court, traditionally the husband's family could, and sometimes actually did, throw the widow and the children out of the house and on to the street. A new Intestate Succession Law gave rights to the widow and children to carry on living in the matrimonial home, as well as to inherit the majority of the deceased husband's assets.

Kweku felt the same deep irony that many would have felt at the time – that it took a military government, which had overthrown a democratically elected government and suspended the country's Constitution, to enact in Ghana this and other legislation guaranteeing such basic human rights.

***

Man or woman proposed, God disposed. One Saturday morning in December 1985, at the start of their second year of marriage, Kweku and Joanna were at the dining table catching up with the latest news in Accra, as they waited for Maria to bring their usual weekend brunch of kenkey and ground red pepper with fish, when the scent of the fish now being fried came through from the adjacent kitchen. All of a sudden Joanna got up from the table, covering her mouth and showing signs of wanting to vomit. Kweku asked:

'What's up, darling?'

But she waved him away with her other hand and rushed to the toilet. From a polite distance, he could hear the sounds of her retching inside. Minutes later, she re-emerged looking weak and exhausted.

Moving closer to her, Kweku asked, 'Are you feeling unwell, my love?'

She responded, almost in a whisper, 'I think I'm pregnant.'

He could see the shock on her face. He was equally astonished – they had been following the clock method religiously. 'We need to get you to a doctor right away,' he said.

'No darling, it's OK. My usual doctor won't be available till Monday. I'll go and see him then.'

'All right, I'll come with you.'

'OK.'

He helped her back upstairs to their bedroom.

'Can I get you something, love, anything that'll stay down?'

She waved him away:

‘Don’t worry, love, I’ll think of something. Right now, I just want to cool down for a while… Can you switch the air conditioner on for me?’

‘Of course, dear.’ He went to switch it on as she lay down on the bed and sighed. ‘I’ll ask Maria to come up and maybe she can suggest something for you?’

‘Thank you, love. Nothing right now.’

‘OK dear, you rest and I’ll be back later.’

***

They both monitored her condition closely over the weekend. Thankfully it didn’t worsen. She was able to keep some food down which she didn’t have adverse reactions to, but she continued to retch in the mornings and to feel awful and drained.

On Monday morning Kweku drove her to the clinic to see her doctor, a conscientious professional, Dr Susan Gantey. She did a thorough consultation, asking her all the relevant questions and took a sample of her urine for testing. She asked her to return the next day for the results.

Kweku was back at the clinic with Joanna mid-morning on Tuesday. They sat nervously in the queue in the waiting room. When her turn came, as they walked into Dr Gantey’s consultation room, she looked up at Joanna from the report she had been reviewing on her desk:

‘Congratulations,’ she said, ‘you are two months pregnant!’ Diplomatically, Dr Gantey quickly turned to Kweku, adding: ‘Congratulations to both of you!’

Joanna and Kweku looked at each other. They felt simultaneously amazed and overawed by the confirmation. In front of the doctor, they agreed what great news it was and lied that they had been planning for a child. Well, what they said was partially true: they had been planning for a child, only they had been planning, using the clock method, on having a child in 5 years' time, not now – the growing foetus obviously hadn't read the script!

Back inside the privacy of their car, they allowed their expressions to reflect their real apprehension. Joanna in particular was tearful. In one sense, these were happy tears; in another, the child, if it carried to term as they both hoped, would spell the end of her dreams to rise to the top at her organisation. A big company like that would not wait a year and a half, two years, and then kick out whoever had replaced her during the months when she had rightly prioritised her baby's well-being. At the Regional Sales Manager level, no one was going to come and work on a temporary basis only.

Mentally, Joanna was in turmoil. The life she had planned was now over. At the same time she had been blessed. But, from all the stories she had heard, pregnancy and childbirth themselves held out prospects of so much risk and painful endurance. How was she going to cope? At least Kweku had been supportive so far in their married life. She comforted herself with the hope that would continue.

Although also apprehensive, Kweku was much more upbeat. But seeing Joanna's agonised state, he didn't want to show it. He was as happy as Joanna that she was pregnant per se. But in his case the happiness of childbirth would entail no unpleasant sacrifices – or so he thought at the time.

In the event, Joanna had to resign from her job six months into the pregnancy. She was given a warm send-off by her colleagues at a brief function before she left but, despite her dad's frantic lobbying of the directors, no promises of being re-hired. Their excuse was that the company was an international conglomerate applying group policies globally. They regrettably had no power to bend group policy, even for Joanna.

***

The pregnancy carried to term and a big healthy bouncing baby boy, named Kofi as he was born on a Friday, came into Kweku and Joanna's world in September 1986. They were thrilled and excited. Kojo and Deborah were overjoyed, as were Joanna's parents, David and Irene. Days after his birth, the baby was "outdoored" or presented at a family gathering and named after his paternal grandfather, Ampoma Owireku, in a traditional naming ceremony. The rites included dipping the baby's index finger into a concoction of *akpeteshie* (distilled palm wine) and water – both signifying purity – and putting the finger straight afterwards into his mouth, so that the baby could know what is purity or truth and distinguish it from a lie.

Both sets of grandparents fussed over Joanna and the baby for the next eight months, visiting regularly. Kofi was baptised at the local Catholic church. His given name was Alexander. Both naming ceremony and christening were followed by generous refreshments at Kweku and Joanna's house in the

Airport Residential area to welcome the new arrival formally.

***

Meanwhile, looking past the disappointment of the enforced domestication of Joanna's career, Kofi was a healthy child with a big appetite, growing fast, and the confectionery business was booming. Everything seemed right in the world. But destiny would determine otherwise.

CHAPTER SIXTEEN

Away Game

January 1987

After Kofi's birth, the cliché Kweku feared but thought unlikely happened: Joanna lost her appetite for sex, a victim of postnatal depression. He hadn't lost his. Added to this condition or doubtless worsening it, she struggled to shed the extra pounds she had put on while eating for two during pregnancy.

She breastfed Kofi from birth, but after 6 months, as his appetite increased, he would grow impatient of waiting to be fed. Under pressure from his increasing demands, Joanna would supplement her breastfeeding with SMA bottled formula milk and baby foods. That would work better for a while. But less than two years later, as soon as his milk teeth had formed, he would reject baby foods entirely and be tucking into adult solid foods, chopped up small enough for him to eat and digest.

For a while, Kweku managed the deprivation he was experiencing due to Joanna's PND, relieving himself in an act once described to him during a one-off class at Huntsmere about the "birds and the bees" as 'semi-sex'. Huntsmere had felt obliged to pick up the tab on this issue, so to speak, as part of the boys' education alongside peer group gossip, as parents in those days felt extremely uncomfortable about schooling their children personally in such matters. This is not to say that parents don't still feel very awkward about discussing such topics with their children even now. But with "Google it!" being today's instinctive response to anyone seeking answers to anything, the relative anonymity of the internet means that this responsibility is nowadays more often than not conveniently contracted out to unknown online third parties.

Kweku was a warm-blooded human being. Tired of having to engage in semi-sex for months on end, he was ripe for distraction. He had been subconsciously putting out signals for weeks that he was 'available' for a touch of adventure. There was no forethought or planning involved, but he now felt free to "window-shop", to flirt, with his eyes, in casual conversation – instincts he had intentionally shut out of his life from the moment he and Joanna had decided to tie the knot.

He had just spent a few days in Accra and Tema in productive discussions with logistics companies based there. There was talk of expanding sales of the company's prestige Honimo sweets elsewhere in the West African sub-region, a potential market size many multiples of Ghana's. On his way up to the factory in Mim, he stopped off in Kumasi for a lunch break at his usual Chinese restaurant. His favourite meal was shrimp fried rice with mixed vegetables. The same waitress, Lisa, had served him many times. She always served him politely. He never noticed that she had the habit of caressing the last dish she would put in front of him – until today, when she did it again and saw that he had finally noticed it. There was an extra swing to her hips as she left to get his beer; she sensed that he was watching her and smiled.

She had long taken a fancy to him. He seemed to her to have the kind of ambition, drive and purpose that she liked to see in a man. Of course, it helped that he was the young managing director of a large and successful business, and Kweku was not so naïve as to ignore that this was likely his main attraction to any single woman showing an interest in him.

Their eyes met a few more times as he ate his lunch hurriedly. When he finished, he signalled her to bring the bill. As she came to clear the table, he lifted his plate towards her to help and she caressed his hand as she collected it. He smiled. Lisa knew that at last, today, she had landed Kweku on her hook.

He wrote a nearby hotel address and room number on the back of a serviette and slipped it to her. He told her he would be there in thirty minutes, for one hour. She could guess the rest, that there would be no commitments, hopefully a thank you and a promise of a future encounter. She made a flimsy excuse to her manager, Joe: her mum had just sent her sister with a message that something had happened at home. It was an emergency, so she should come immediately.

Lisa knew how to work her way around Joe from the day of her interview for the job. She knew that was the reason he had hired her and she humoured him with her graces from time to time. Joe saw no reason to question her; he only asked her to let him know if he could help in any way. She thanked him but said for now, no.

With that she left, feeling a little guilty, but giggling at Joe's naivety as soon as she was inside the taxi on her way to the hotel. When she got there, Kweku let her in. Within an hour, after a shower, she was on her way back to the restaurant and he was on his way to Mim. It was the first time he'd had extra-marital sex, but because it involved no commitment, no promise of deeper ties, just satisfaction of a natural instinct with a willing partner, he felt it was nothing to dwell on or be ashamed about. He wouldn't tell anyone, least of all Joanna, and he had the feeling Lisa wouldn't talk – at least not in these early days when she, unlike him, would definitely have been hoping their relationship would grow into something more meaningful. He paid her taxi fare both ways, with something extra for her mum's emergency (they both smirked about that).

***

Carrie Calls

It was a Monday night. Kweku was on his way to Brussels again, via London, for a meeting on Thursday afternoon with Sonimo's Belgian buyer. Pierre was to fly into Brussels on the Wednesday and hook up with him the next day for an update over lunch ahead of the meeting. On arrival at Heathrow Airport on Tuesday morning, he took a taxi up to his parents' house at Highgate. Walking through the front door, he set his bags down in the corridor. As he opened the door to the drawing room on the right, he noticed a red light blinking on the answerphone machine next to the phone. He went over to check.

There were eight messages. He decided to go through them in case there was an urgent one from Pierre rescheduling the meeting, or one from Joanna in Accra. The first message was from a department store Joanna had ordered some dresses from, advising that her items were now in. The next a cold call from a telemarketing company offering life insurance – how did they get his number, he wondered? The third was a blank recording. The fourth message was from a week ago. His heart skipped a beat as he began listening to it. He recognised the voice instantly. It was Carrie. She said she was now in London working for a firm of solicitors in The Strand and would like to meet up with him soonest, so he should give her a call. He allowed himself a couple of minutes to calm his nerves and reflect. He had moved on from Carrie years earlier. In the circumstances, did he have to ring her back at all?

He quickly dismissed the idea of ignoring her message completely. He rang the number she had left. It was a solicitors' office. He asked to speak to her. She came on the line briefly and said she would call him right back from another line in a couple of minutes. He waited patiently by the phone. When it rang again, she sounded hurried. She said she'd had a hectic day and was still working on a letter to a client. But she had the afternoon off tomorrow: it would be great if they could meet at a café in Charing Cross near her workplace. Kweku knew the one. It sounded urgent, so he agreed.

Instead of taking the Tube all the way to Charing Cross, he decided to alight at Leicester Square and take a walk down to Charing Cross, soaking in the sights along the way. Sauntering past the Garrick Theatre on the left and National Gallery on the right, he entered Trafalgar Square. He looked up at that symbol of Empire and dogged British resistance, Viscount Nelson's column, towering over it to remind witting tourists of the huge debt owed Britain's most famous admiral by a grateful nation. Leaving Trafalgar Square, he turned left past St Martins-in-the-Fields Church and started up The Strand to the café.

Once inside, he quickly cast around: she wasn't there yet, but he was a little early anyway. He sat down, ordered a coffee and waited for her, just as he had done a decade earlier at Browns in Oxford. Only this time he was in a contented marriage which had just been blessed with a child. He wouldn't be as vulnerable to Carrie's whims as he was on that day. Gone was the emotional insecurity of a late teen adolescent.

He spotted her as she entered. He waved. She saw him and waved back. For a moment, as their eyes locked, he felt a spark. She was looking at him the way she used to when they first dated. But he felt differently now, as if all that belonged to a lost world behind a closed door that he no longer wanted to open.

As she sat down, she ordered a *café au lait* and asked for a menu.

'The desserts are great here,' she said.

'I know.'

‘Let’s indulge ourselves then, shall we? You’re not on a diet, are you? Although maybe …’ she saw Kweku had put on a couple of pounds, his cheeks had grown slightly chubbier, a small pot belly developing. She wasn’t put off though, she found that quite attractive in a man, comforting, homely. She chuckled: ‘I see the love handles are coming on.’

She lit a cigarette and offered him one.

‘No thanks, I’ve given up.’

‘Really, when was that?’

‘Since just before I got married.’ Kweku noticed the shock on her face.

‘Married?’

‘A couple of years ago.’

‘Oh, good for you!’ She was smiling, but he could see she wasn’t expecting to hear that. Maybe it was because he wasn’t wearing his wedding band; not all married men did in Ghana – maybe she didn’t know. She quickly followed up: ‘Any children yet?’

‘Yes, a beautiful boy who’s growing nicely. He’s a bit of an early starter – a little impatient, like me. Only six months but he’s already standing, with support of course.

‘But that’s wonderful!’ There was a polite hollowness about her words, but Kweku understood.

The waiter brought her coffee and asked: ‘Have you decided if you would like to order a dessert, or something?’

She looked at Kweku. He held and glanced at the menu. ‘Can you give us more time?’ she said.

‘No problem. Just give us a shout when you’re ready.’

Kweku saw that Carrie wasn’t wearing a ring on her wedding finger, but had to ask her too:

‘You?’

‘Me?... You mean anyone in my life?’

‘Uh-huh?’

'No. Well, there were a couple of times I came close but …' she looked down into her cup '… nope, still looking for Mr Right!' She laughed nervously and took another sip of coffee, took a deep drag on her cigarette, exhaled and flicked the ash into the ashtray on the table.

He was slightly embarrassed for her. He knew that only the fullness of time could tell whether anyone had found their Mr or Mrs Right, including him.

'You're absolutely right not to rush into it, Carrie,' he said. 'Marriage really does entail proverbial lifelong commitments. I only pray that Joanna and I have got it right.'

'Don't worry, Kweku. I'm still young, so I'm not at all worried.' She laughed, but Kweku detected a hint of self-pity in her laughter. Putting on a brave face, she added: 'For now, Anderson's the only company I need.'

'Who?'

'Anderson, my pet cat …'

'Oh, I see.' Kweku chuckled.

'No seriously, he's better than any man I ever met… Well, maybe with one exception.' She was now deadly serious. She looked him in the eyes, then looked away for a moment, tilting her head slightly upwards to look into the space behind him, anywhere except at him, biting her lip.

She took a last drag from her cigarette, then tossed her head back as she exhaled a long plume of smoke. She stubbed the cigarette out. Almost immediately, she lit another:

'Do you mind?' she asked.

'No, not at all. Go ahead.'

'Shall we order some red wine?'

'Sounds good.'

'How about a Rioja?'

'Perfect.'

The waiter brought a bottle and poured some for Carrie to taste. She rolled it around in her mouth and passed it on to him. He did likewise. They both liked it.

They reminisced about times past, swapping notes on what they had heard of old friends. Kweku had fallen out of contact with most of his fellow students, except Charlie and friends from Huntsmere who had gone up to Oxford in the same year he did. As he was living and working in Ghana for most of the year, and they had their own schedules, they'd hardly had a chance to catch up since graduating.

She opened up about Roberta. The conversation went dead for a moment, before she looked him in the eye and told him:

'Don't worry, I know what happened between you.

She told a mutual friend, Louise Berriman, I don't know if you remember her? ...'

'Er… was she the one who joined us for coffee a couple of times after lectures when we were cooling?'

'Yes, her. Anyway, she and me both had our suspicions. I asked Roberta, but she denied it outright. It was about six months later that we were all at a College do. Roberta and Louise were in stitches laughing about something, and then their faces suddenly changed when they saw me watching them. At that moment a bell just went off in my head. The next day I decided to corner Louise about it. She said she had pressed Roberta on it a couple of weeks after that first coffee meeting that term and she admitted it. She told me the two of them couldn't believe I still hadn't cottoned on months later. That was what they were laughing about. She apologised for not telling me sooner, but after that I stopped talking to both of them. I mean, I know you and me were finished and that was my fault, but I couldn't handle the fact that they had just been laughing about me behind my back like that all the while. Real friends don't do that, do they?'

Kweku agreed:

'No.' But he still felt guilty.

Carrie saw the remorse on his face and tried to set his mind at ease:

'Look, as I said Kweku, I couldn't blame you – you were just acting on the same impulses I had… I'm sure you just felt more comfortable being with one of your own? ...'

For a moment, Kweku was speechless, looking at Carrie as she continued:

'Times have changed. I wouldn't care today what other people, black or white, thought about mixed relationships. I'm even ashamed I let the stares and snide comments get to me in the short time we were together.'

Kweku refilled her glass, then his: 'To be honest, Carrie, that wasn't the reason Roberta and I got together. We met by chance at a Ball in London after the end of term. It was pure coincidence, it wasn't planned at all. Anyway, we got together after that and one thing led to another. You are absolutely right that it made things more comfortable that we were both black. I can't deny that. But it wasn't the reason for either of us getting together in the first place. That just wasn't in my mind at the time – I don't think it was in hers either. Maybe it rather started for me as a way of getting closer to you after you had shut me out. I don't know. If it's any consolation, she felt so badly about it later because of her close friendship with you. She felt she'd betrayed you. I felt a bit guilty about it as well, as it had only been a few weeks since we'd split.'

'Anyway Kweku, as I said, after I found out, I cut them both off. Maybe it was a bit petty of me to be so final about things like that, but I'd had let-downs in the months following our split and by then I just wanted to focus on my studies …'

She widened her eyes and lit another cigarette:

'Talking of let-downs, Kweku, in fact that was the reason I wanted to talk to you again after all these years. I felt I owed it to you to explain why I behaved like I did when we first got together. I should have told you ages ago.' She poured another glass for each of them, pointed to the bottle and looked at Kweku.

'Another?'

Kweku nodded. She signalled to the waiter to bring another bottle of the same, then continued:

'As I said, when it all went wrong, I just didn't have the guts to tell you. And, thanks to Louise, I knew we were already history. What happened was that, even before I came up to Oxford, a boyfriend I'd known since school days …'

'School days?'

'Yes, we were dating even then… he was 17 and I was 16. We'd slept a couple of times but swore to our parents that we hadn't yet and they believed us. The thing is, he's from the same hometown and both sets of parents know each other really well. You remember that crazy day we had punting on the Cherwell? ...'

'Carrie, how could I ever forget it?'

'No, I mean the very next day – on the Monday – he rang me at College to say he had something important to tell me and I should be sure to come home that weekend.

The way he said it, I half suspected what it could be about. It turned out I guessed right.'

'Well?'

'He ended up proposing to me over dinner! But when I spoke to you at Browns, I thought it was time to tell you we weren't going to be an item, as I was already spoken for. You seemed like a really nice guy and I didn't want you to find out one day and think I'd been leading you along.' She looked at Kweku, realising he had become distracted and was squinting as if trying to recall something:

'You know, Carrie, some months after we split, I saw you at Oxford station with someone.'

Carrie blushed. 'When was that?'

'Oh, I think it was the following summer… Yes, I remember now! It was the first weekend of Trinity Term, in April. I remember it because I tried so hard to find out who you were with.'

'Yes, that was him.' She looked at Kweku to see his reaction. 'That was before he showed me his other side …'

'How do you mean?'

'I didn't realise it at first, kept giving him the benefit of the doubt. But he was so possessive. It just got worse and worse; no man could even talk to me when we were out together without him getting the hump.'

'But you seemed so happy together, he seemed so normal?'

'I know. Don't worry, he fooled me too.' She looked down at the table and shook her head. 'No, no, well rid. Just too obsessive. Anyway, forget about him, I don't want to talk about him any more.'

She leaned back in her chair, relieved to have got a load off her chest:

'So there, now you know what happened and I'm really sorry.'

'Don't worry at all, Carrie. Honestly, I really appreciate your telling me all this. You didn't have to.'

Half of the second bottle was left. She lit another cigarette and split the rest of the bottle evenly between their two glasses, filling them almost to the brim.

'No, but I'm really, really happy, Kweku, for you and your family.'

‘Thank you. I’m settled now, and count myself lucky to have what I have.’

‘You are.’

As people in all relationships, Kweku kept mum about problems in his own marriage with Joanna that he was still trying to resolve. She had made great strides in recovering from her post-natal depression, but things weren’t perfect yet by any means.

They called for the bill. Kweku insisted on settling it, but Carrie snatched it and paid with her debit card. They took the last gulps of wine.

‘Anyway, I’ve got to get back to Anderson …’ They both smiled. ‘… And I’m sure you’ve got loads of things to do before you go… When is that?’

‘I’ve got a meeting with a buyer in Belgium tomorrow. I’ll fly back home on Friday.’

‘I see. Well, thank you, Kweku, for making the time to do this at such short notice. For me, it was some unfinished business and I’m glad it’s all sorted now.’

‘Thank you, Carrie. It was really nice to see you again, I mean that. And you’re looking better than ever.’

‘Really? You mean that?’

‘Yes.’

‘Thank you.’

She was looking as attractive as ever, but Kweku wanted to give her an extra boost as they left. He was now settled, she wasn’t yet. She would make her Mr Right a happy man one day. They got up and walked towards to the door.

‘We’ll probably catch up at an Oxford reunion one of these days,’ she said. ‘Pity we weren’t at the same College though; there won’t be any year group gaudies or College concerts or memorial events for us to maybe bump into each other. Never mind. If it was meant to be, it was meant to be.’

As they left the café together, they embraced, pecking each other on both cheeks and keeping their gazes on each other as they pulled apart, momentarily holding their shoulders before dropping their arms to the side.

'I'm taking the Tube back to Highgate,' he said.

'I'm taking a bus, to Holborn.' She gestured to the bus station across the road. 'Then see you.' She waved, adding teasingly, 'Until we meet again.'

He smiled and waved back: 'Bye.'

***

On his way home, Kweku reminisced over how they had first met, the punting disaster that paved the way for a magical evening… Then his puzzlement at her sudden distance afterwards.

At least now he knew what had happened. She too had now had her own moment of closure on Roberta. His thoughts went back to Joanna and Kofi. He would call this evening.

***

Strike Next Door

April 1987

There was an industrial strike at the country's biggest timber company, which lay adjacent to Sonimo's factory. They employed almost 2,000 workers, dwarfing Sonimo's 300 staff roll. The strike was over several grievances, including the usual ones of pay and conditions of service. Negotiations between Management and Unions had been at a standstill for months and in the vacuum more intransigent members of the unionised staff were in the ascendancy. The Deputy Minister for the Brong Ahafo Region had visited the town to try to mediate in the dispute. Sadly however, he and his team had completely underestimated the strength of feeling among the workers. On arrival of his convoy at the factory gate, his security detail had barely begun opening his car door when, seemingly out of nowhere, they were set upon by a livid, stone-throwing, machete-wielding mob. They leapt back into their cars, slamming the doors shut, and barely escaped with their lives as their convoy fled, the tyres screeching and smoking on the road.

Kweku first received word of the strike in Accra that evening. Shortly after this incident, police arrested and detained at the local station the four most violent rabble-rousers among the striking workers. But the next day a group of workers attacked the police station and sprung them free from their cells.

As the group escaped, they were confronted by a policeman outside the station armed with an AK-47 assault rifle. He fired three warning shots in the air in an attempt to stop them leaving. They began scattering in different directions, each man for himself. And then one of the group recognised the policeman. He was married to a cousin of his. He knew him to be a devout churchgoer. He was sure there was no way this man would actually use his weapon to kill anyone. Hearing this, the main ringleader among the freed prisoners, a scar-faced ruffian with bloodshot eyes and bushy hair, strode up to the policeman, staring him down. As he approached, the policeman fired more warning shots over his head, shouting at him to stay where he was. But the thug continued, wrestled the policeman's rifle from his grip, turned it on him and riddled his upper body with several rounds until he lay motionless on the ground.

Meanwhile the rest of the police officers posted to the station had long since fled. Waving his arms in the air, his hand still gripping the rifle, the killer urged the rest of the group back towards the station. By now a larger mob had gathered. They torched and razed the police station to the ground, delirious with their new-found unchecked power.

Usurping the position of custodians of law and order for the vicinity, they erected a barricade on the main road at the only roundabout controlling entrance to the town. Tying red bandanas around their heads and necks to signify that they were on the warpath and no one should try their luck with them, they danced with wanton abandon, chanting war songs. For Dutch courage, they swigged *akpeteshie*, the very strong local gin made from the distilled fermented sap of palm trees – popularly named 'VC-10' after the Vickers jet engine, as it gets you where you want to go very fast in terms of intoxication!

The Deputy Minister, on his return to the regional capital, Sunyani, had sent an urgent message to central government in Accra. Kweku received a radio message in Accra from the factory informing him of developments. He was told that Sonimo's workers were not themselves on strike, but as the timber factory was adjacent to theirs, the unrest could eventually spill over to them and there were imminent security concerns. Kweku informed his driver Justin and immediately packed for Mim with the aim of reassuring Pierre and his senior staff, who were holed up in their bungalows with their families, terrified of what might happen next, now that the town had descended into anarchy. Sonimo's Mim staff only had one satellite phone and one Motorola radio device to share between them.

Kweku informed his parents. They agreed that he had to travel urgently, but they pleaded with him, instead of journeying overnight, to wait until dawn before setting off. He knew they were right. He was well aware of the dangers of travelling at night in Ghana: the darkness of roads due to lack of street lights, the over-speeding, reckless and drunk drivers and motorcyclists, the broken-down vehicles abandoned on single-lane highways with no triangle warning signs, the potholes or missing sections of road, the overloaded charcoal trucks swaying dangerously from side to side as they struggled under the weight of their cargo, the heaps of sand or stones left halfway across highway lanes by careless house- or road-builders.

For all of these perils, there would be little or no warning for any approaching motorist before they're at the spot and must swerve to avoid them – God forbid that should be straight into the path of an oncoming vehicle or other obstacle. Ghana certainly had an ignominious reputation among the top twenty countries in the world for road fatalities. So Kweku resolved to set off at daybreak instead.

Meanwhile expatriate and Ghanaian senior staff at the timber company were barricaded up in bungalows on their senior management estate, awaiting rescue. They were equally stuck for communication, with only one satphone and two radio devices between all twelve of them and their families. The only functioning external phone line was in the managing director's office, which had been overrun by the strikers.

With power-drunk thugs in charge, the whole town was gripped by fear that evening. Women, children and law-abiding men huddled behind closed doors, peering anxiously out of windows and doorways, reacting to the slightest unusual sound as an indication of impending terror.

***

At daybreak, a lone Jeep was spotted on the horizon by strikers manning the barricade at the roundabout. Realising, as it got closer, that it was an army Jeep, the same gang of terror who had been boldly threatening anyone who defied them with death and destruction, tossed their crude weapons aside, loosened their bandanas and took to their heels, melting away into nearby woods and forest huts.

As the lone, small Pinzgauer 4-wheel drive army Jeep passed through the roundabout to climb the hill into the town, they found the place totally deserted. In fact, things seemed so hushed and peaceful that the four soldiers on board – a captain, corporal and two privates – wondered at first if they had come to the right town. They had been given instructions first to secure the estate housing the timber company's senior management, with a focus on protecting the twelve expatriate staff and their families. The latter were considered to be more vulnerable to attack, as they were thought to be close to the unpopular managing director, a harsh German disciplinarian.

On reaching the managing director's bungalow, they informed him that the town was calm and, apart from the burnt-out police station, they had seen no indications of any hostile activity at all on their arrival.

The managing director explained to them what he was sure must have happened. The country in 1987 was still under the military rule of the Provisional National Defence Council or PNDC. (In fact, constitutional government, suspended at the time of the 31st December, 1981 military overthrow by the PNDC led by Jerry Rawlings, was not to return until January 1993, when Rawlings became the first constitutionally elected President of the country's Fourth and current Republic.)

The striking workers understood very well that, while police officers work within and are known by the families in a community, especially a relatively small community such as Mim, members of the armed forces are merely deployed to a trouble spot: they don't actually live there. As they are unknown strangers, if they are obliged to take lethal action while following orders of their superiors, they will do so and no one in the community will know the identity of those who did the killing, still less be able to target them for retribution.

And so the thugs knew that, had they decided to do to the four soldiers what they had done to the policeman, a bigger army detachment would have been sent to the town, and the massacre that would have followed would likely have been indiscriminate. It was proof that the ringleaders of the civil unrest, as crazed and intoxicated as they appeared, were still sufficiently in control of their mental faculties to be able to infer the likely outcomes of their actions.

The managing director of the timber company told the soldiers he was convinced that it was for this reason that the same rioters, who so boldly were able to chase a Deputy Minister from the town and murder a principled police officer in cold blood, had scattered to the winds after seeing a single army Jeep approaching on the horizon.

***

Kweku had left Accra at dawn. By mid-morning he was in Mim. He had received no update en route and was consequently surprised to see no sign of any barricade at the roundabout or trace of hooliganism anywhere except the police station, which had been razed to the ground. After checking with Pierre on staff at Sonimo's senior management compound and confirming that they were all still safe and accounted for, he joined Pierre and a couple of other senior managers to the Mim industries' common clubhouse, where he met and spoke to the timber company's management staff and the four soldiers.

The soldiers were enjoying refreshments and expressed their surprise to Kweku that, after readying themselves for a difficult assignment to restore order to a town in turmoil, they had arrived to see a community completely at peace. Representatives of staff unions were also present at the clubhouse for informal conversations, and meetings were scheduled between national union leaders and the company's top management to resolve all issues moving forward in a collaborative manner devoid of mindless violence.

Kweku took the incident as prima facie evidence that, in some situations, it is only the threat of force or, if necessary, deployment of actual force, that can deter a minority from taking the law into their own hands against the wishes of the law-abiding majority of a community.

CHAPTER SEVENTEEN

Representing The People

As he learnt over the ensuing days more and more details about the origins and motivations behind the costly strike next door, Kweku was presented with a dilemma. He had spent most of his life up to that point focusing on his personal educational development, followed by a professional career trying to expand the family business. He had been a willing supporter of many of his dad's philanthropic causes, including substantial donations to the Church and broader society. But such support was more in the form of extra-curricular activity fitted around priorities of keeping the business going.

There was nothing wrong with that, as the continued employment of the 300 plus staff at the factory, and the foreign exchange generated for the country by the company's exports, had a positive impact on the regional and national economy. But his years of experience so far in charge of administration at Sonimo, having to handle all the local protocol issues involving chiefs, assemblymen, district and regional political appointees, as well as discussions on politics from an early age with his dad, had opened his eyes to the significant impact that political decisions could have on people's lives, for better or worse.

Pierre now had the factory running like clockwork, and the more often Kweku repeated his own work routines, the less time he needed to complete them. It was creating enough space in his schedules to allow another pursuit. Why not politics, he thought?

On his next visit to Accra, he raised the matter first with Joanna. She was caught off guard. She told him she had no idea he had been entertaining ambitions of that nature. He told her he hadn't been, that the idea had only come to him as he reflected over the recent strike at the company next door. She warned him that politics was a double-edged sword: it could be their making reputationally, if they were lucky, but it could also be their undoing, if they upset important people or spent a fortune on it.

She went on to remind him that they had a young child who was barely seven months old. How would she be able to accompany him on campaign trails or help him with the female vote? He tried to reassure her: things were nowhere near that stage yet, and, even if it came to that, she shouldn't worry. He would be able to carry things off on his own, and people would of course understand why she had to be at home with her baby instead of at his side.

Joanna told him she needed more time to think about it. But by the following day, she recognised that look of determination on his face. She suggested he sound out his parents: if it was OK by them, she told him, then it would be OK by her. Secretly she hoped Kweku's parents would immediately express strong reservations about the idea, that that would make him ditch it.

She decided to consult her own parents. She took Kofi along with her. At first, David and Irene avoided commenting. Stealing glances at each other that made clear their discomfort at being handed a hot potato, they used Kofi as a distraction. As Joanna dilated on her concerns, they took turns holding him, cosseting him with baby talk, then passing him back to her when he wanted more breast milk or just to snuggle up to his mum and catch forty winks. When Joanna, frustrated by their apparent reluctance to get involved, eventually pressed them directly for advice, they initially expressed concern about the unwelcome publicity and noise the career shift would introduce to their young family's lives.

However, as they were very traditional and conservative in their thinking, they gave vent to their preference that Joanna should support her husband in his ambitions. Besides, they said, Kweku's motives for getting into politics must clearly be altruistic. He was not the exhibitionist type, and even though still relatively young, they already had enough money to guarantee a very comfortable life for years ahead. The same could not be said for all politicians, particularly in Africa and the developing world. So they told their daughter that if her husband wanted to go into politics, at least for a change he would be doing so for the right reasons. In conclusion however, they did not wish to dictate Joanna's life for her and she would have to make her own decision.

With these words of advice still ringing in her ears, Joanna returned home with Kofi, head down in thought. Essentially her parents had shied away from getting entangled in a major decision that they felt was one for their daughter and Kweku to reflect seriously on and make for themselves as a married couple. It was above all their own lives and that of their baby and any future children that the decision would most impact.

Meanwhile, unaware of the strength of Joanna's feelings against his plans, as she had chosen to gamble that Kweku's parents would discourage him from them, Kweku was under the mistaken impression that she had given them the green light, subject to his parents' OK. As such, he was wallowing in the blissful ignorance that husbands sometimes allow themselves to fall into when taking a wife's voiced consent literally, in isolation from the tonal and facial expressions which accompany her words and indicate the exact opposite! He now prepared to meet his parents on the issue as the last hurdles to clear. He chose to see his dad first. Over the years since his childhood, they had excitedly shared long conversations about political developments locally and internationally. He was sure Kojo would have particularly useful insight to impart on the issue. He would see Deborah afterwards.

When Kweku called asking to come round to discuss something important, at first Kojo assumed there must be a problem with the business or the marriage. Kweku clarified no, it was something personal, well – he would explain when he came over.

At Cantonments, Kojo's interest was piqued the moment Kweku revealed an eagerness to get involved in politics. He listened intently as his son explained his strategy, beginning with a campaign for the post of member of the district assembly incorporating Mim in forthcoming elections under newly evolving local government structures. He would base his eligibility not only on his father's sterling reputation established over many years of social investment in the community, but on his own successful assumption of the mantle and subsequent painstaking interest shown in local issues.

From there he could graduate to seeking election as presiding member for the district assembly, and who knew where that could lead, once constitutional government was one day restored, as everyone believed it inevitably must soon be?

As Kweku spoke, Kojo sensed his genuine enthusiasm for the career shift, and himself grew excited. He had always dreamt that his son would one day explore the possibility of a career in politics, using the financial security of a successful business. He couldn't wait to discuss it with Deborah. Kweku told Kojo he had originally intended to discuss the issue privately with his mum first. But seeing his father's enthusiasm, he changed his mind and decided they could go together.

On their way to see Deborah, with an eye still on the health of the business, Kojo reminded Kweku that, apart from Deborah, he would also have to discuss the issue with Pierre in Mim to get his take before making any final decision. This was because, if the business was to suffer from his absence politicking, that would be counter-productive, as it was only the business that could generate enough surplus funds to sustain the costs of his political campaigning. Kweku agreed. He didn't want to be beholden to any special interest group or foreign entity. Consequently, only self-financing, or more accurately financing through the family business, would allow him, if his campaign was successful, to make political decisions in office as he saw fit rather than in the interests of his financiers. That would apply unless he was to double-cross his financiers, or to have a plan to finance himself, once in power, from exercise of that political power, as unfortunately was all too often the case in the developing world, including right across African continent.

In the event Deborah was far less keen on the idea than Kojo – for the same reasons her husband had himself originally baulked at it when it was first broached by the District Commissioner in Goaso more than 20 years earlier. She asked Kweku to give her time to think about it and come back the next day.

The following day, when Kweku returned, she told him she had concluded that she would go along with whatever he wanted to do. It was his life after all. But she asked if he had discussed it with Joanna. He said he had, that she was fine with it if his parents were. He then mentioned in passing Joanna's original remarks about politics being the proverbial double-edged sword, that it could go either way. This elicited an immediate response from Deborah:

‘She is so right. I am glad you married such an intelligent woman… Make sure you talk the whole thing over fully with her again before reaching a final decision. Don’t forget that whatever you decide to do will affect her and the child you have together.’

Kweku knew his mother was right. He returned to Joanna with the final feedback from both his parents. It was only now, on seeing Joanna’s disappointment at the news that his parents would not stand in his way, that Kweku realised that her mind hadn’t been made up after all. It was all too clear that she was still pondering over things, unable to reach a final decision. Two days later, she told him she had made her mind up. In the end, she said she wanted him to be happy, so whatever made him happy, she would try to go along with that.

So effectively, Kweku would now have to make the final decision on his own. He was OK with that, provided he wouldn’t ever get the sole blame if things went wrong. But, if things did go wrong, why shouldn’t he get the blame? Surely an agent of change to the status quo had to accept responsibility if the result left things in a worse state than they were in to begin with? Well, that too was fine, he thought, so long as he got the credit if things turned out well – not that he needed any. And at what point should blame attach to the agent of change? If things went well for over 10 years but awry after 15, should an agent, him or herself, get praise for 10 years and more and then be pilloried if problems surfaced after 15? It was a moot point, but he had the opportunity to get into politics now to assist his community, district and beyond, and felt inspired to help.

***

On his next trip to Mim, Kweku met Pierre to raise the issue with him. In response, Pierre shrugged his shoulders: his job was complicated enough already, without having to worry about local politics. Pragmatically, he said that if Kweku was going to go down that road and switch to being a part-time boss, he should make sure either to promote someone he could trust among the company's current administrative staff or to recruit someone he knew with the requisite experience and qualifications to be able to vet and approve recurrent financial and administrative expenditure. Pierre emphasised that for his part he just wanted to continue focusing purely on production and marketing issues.

Kweku emerged from his meeting with Pierre knowing the way was now clear for him to make a decision. He decided to go for it. He called to speak to a nephew of the main local chief, one Kenneth, who was also one of the company's senior managers. He was personally popular in the town and a highly effective networker. When Kenneth heard about the idea, he thought it was brilliant and couldn't wait to get started: 'For you, boss, the sky will be the limit,' he said. 'I will get my uncle involved, and I will personally support you because I know the kind of person you are. Looking at all the useless people involved in Ghana politics today? Hmmm. I tell, you, it will be like a breath of fresh air. The people won't know what hit them.'

The Mensah's excellent name in the community provided considerable clout and, with the solid backing of profits from the business, Kweku began campaigning earnestly for the post of assembly member for the area as an independent with no historic party affiliation. Combining a sense of pragmatism with an ability to sift the feasible from the implausible, and deploying the local nous of Kenneth in networking and event planning, Kweku made sure that he was seen and heard in the right places, delivering realistic messages of hope based on what he, and his father before him working with Adrian, had demonstrably achieved in terms of job growth and exemplary strike-free labour relations over the decades.

Kweku made use of his natural facility for mixing and communicating with people from different backgrounds, from dining with chiefs in their palaces to sharing palm wine with the poorest families in their village huts. This distinguished him from his principal rivals backed by the main left- and right-leaning traditions dominating the political landscape in Ghana. They preferred to focus on power meetings with the prime influencers in each area, kissing babies on the way to and from rally platforms, but not actually taking time to sit down and get to know ordinary people and the difficulties they experienced every day trying to get by, delegating such painstaking "dirty work" instead to lower-ranking officials.

Despite his own wealth and social status, Kweku treated everyone with humility and respect. As a result, he rapidly gained a strong network of hardworking volunteers. He took time to visit all corners of the electoral area, no matter how obscure, so that no one felt left out. Many willing to listen to him understood what his plans were, his vision of how they would benefit them individually and the society at large. Others too weren't actually very listening closely to what he was saying but were positively influenced by his empathetic manner, which gave them a general feeling that his speeches and focused posters, flyers and messaging were addressing their concerns.

The running costs of the campaign were debilitating, but Kojo could think of nothing better for the family's surplus dividends to be spent on than launching his son's political career. Kweku won his first plebiscite and was elected assembly member for the area in a landslide. The win gave him impetus and confidence that he could be successful in politics. As the son of a successful family business couple, inheriting a valuable advantage in life was one thing. Building on that legacy by finding a way to expand the business sustainably was a challenge of a different order. But forging a political career had the potential to leave a lasting positive social impact on a much broader scale than family business alone could ever achieve.

His parents shared in his joy, Joanna more cautiously so. However, she did her best to support him as the politician's wife, while remaining in the background, as was her preference with a growing child on hand and to avoid being targeted. During the day, she typically networked with school-age friends and neighbours; some married or in long-term relationships, others not yet; some divorced already but keen to use lessons learnt to help them choose better next time around; still others divorced and sworn off long-term relationships altogether – for now at least.

It helped to relieve the boredom in her life during Kweku's long absences campaigning. It also allowed her to feel alive by staying up to date with the latest gossip in Accra and to keep her husband abreast of anything she thought relevant to their welfare. On rare occasions she travelled up to Mim with Kofi, to organise the minutiae of bigger entertainment functions with volunteers and influencers which Kweku had to host. She had her own driver now, Sampson, and Maria would go along to help. Event planning for smaller functions was adequately handled by the highly competent Augustine at the Mensah family bungalow.

Kweku's focus while in office was on realisation of his manifesto commitments. He was so successful in delivering on his promises that, at the end of his first term, he easily won election as presiding member for the district assembly.

By the time plans were implemented in 1992 for the return of constitutional government in Ghana, to take effect from January 1993, with institutions including a national Parliament, Kweku was well recognised across the new Mim constituency incorporating most of the old district. With the support of his father, he decided to run as an independent on a manifesto platform mixing market economics with social intervention for those left behind. He promised an administration based on merit and objectivity, devoid of corruption and mismanagement. With the traditional parties thinking it not worth challenging the name recognition and financial resources of his father in the constituency, Kweku had a comfortable win and was elected as an independent member of Parliament for Mim.

CHAPTER EIGHTEEN

Chocolate

Around the time of Ghana's independence in 1957, the country was producing almost one half of the world's supply of cocoa beans, the raw material needed to produce all chocolate confectionery, drinks and desserts. Cocoa was the product which Ghana was most famous for internationally, apart from the eponymous commodity which gave the country its colonial name, the Gold Coast.

After independence, through different colours of political administration, whether civilian or military, that share of global supply gradually dwindled as production in other tropical countries, notably Ivory Coast next door to Ghana, surged.

Prior to 1984, all shades of post-colonial government in the country – whether ascending to power through constitutionally held democratic elections, then holding on to power through less democratic means, or seizing power by military force – had kept a tight control over the production and marketing of cocoa.

The government, through the Cocoa Marketing Board, later renamed Ghana Cocoa Board or Cocobod, was the sole licensed buyer of cocoa beans wherever farmed across the country. They fixed the producer price to be paid to farmers in respect of each cocoa season, running from 1st October of one year to 30th September of the following year, and monopolised export sale of the beans. Even domestic further processing of the beans for very limited local sales of chocolate confectionery was controlled by the Board's subsidiary Cocoa Processing Company.

Ironically it was the self-styled 'provisional' military government of the PNDC that first liberalised the cocoa sector in 1984, allowing licensed buyers to buy from farmers but at prices still fixed by the government – both the price by weight which the licensed private buying companies had to pay the producer farmers whose beans they were buying and transporting to government warehouses for quality control by government assessors, as well as the price at which the licensed private buyers then had to sell the approved beans on to the government. Marketing – that is, local and export sale of the dried beans – was still entirely controlled by the government.

Initially, Sonimo, as a believer in value-added manufacturing, decided not to get involved in what was essentially a business of making margins on transportation of the dried beans in return for financial incentives and subsidised provision of inputs to cocoa farmers such as fertiliser and pesticides against common diseases like black pod and swollen shoot.

But, in a further surprise move for a military administration, ahead of democratically-held elections at the end of 1992 the government widened the pool of licensed buyers. The new regulations permitted any qualified company to become a licensed buyer of Cocobod, bring to Cocobod depots the dried beans purchased from farmers at the fixed producer price and, after quality checking by Cocobod's assessors, be refunded that producer price plus a margin for evacuation and transportation costs.

The crucial change was that any licensed buyer was now allowed to buy beans from Cocobod at international market price FOB Ghana port and the buyer could then take the beans away for further processing themselves at their factory, instead of having to sell the beans only to the government.

In a win-win for Ghana, this opened the door to any Ghanaian licensed buyer to buy the beans at export price and process them locally into intermediate products for sale directly to the big confectionery houses on the international market at negotiated prices between private Ghanaian seller and private international buyer. It brought an end to the system of Ghana continuing to export almost its entire crop of raw beans overseas to international middlemen or intermediate producers for them to add jobs and value to the products before selling them on to the confectioners.

Seizing the new opportunities available, Sonimo quickly expanded manufacturing capacity at its existing site in Mim, investing in cutting-edge roasters, peelers, grinders and other processing equipment to make the cocoa liquor, cake, solids and butter for which there was huge demand from the big international organisations manufacturing chocolate confectionery for the wholesale and retail markets. Further processing machinery on a limited scale – melangers to refine and mix the liquor and butter with sugar, milk and flavouring, tempering equipment and moulds – were added to enable full bean-to-bar production to cater for the much smaller domestic retail market for finished chocolate confectionery.

Pierre supported the expansion using his ever-growing network of strong contacts among Belgium's international chocolate confectioners. Adrian too, even though he had long since retired, used his old connections in the confectionery business to help market the company's intermediate chocolate products to Swiss buyers. They were always interested in receiving Ghanaian cocoa, due to the acclaimed high quality of the country's beans.

In the meantime, with developing international trends putting increasing pressure on the big overseas buyers to limit their purchasing to ethical and sustainable suppliers adhering to fair trade principles, Sonimo invested in the audit personnel and documentation required to ensure attachment of full chain of custody logs validating responsible sourcing of all the beans used in their manufacturing processes. This, together with achievement of the latest international quality standards accreditation, allowed the company's products to fetch additional premiums on the international export market and significantly boost profitability.

***

Meanwhile Kofi was a growing boy. Kweku discussed with his dad that he wanted his son to have at least as good an education as he had been able to benefit from, thanks to his and Deborah's sacrifices. But he and Joanna had decided that, unlike Kweku, their son would start boarding school at eight, not six. Kofi's early exhibition of a similar independent streak to the one Kweku had displayed as a youngster gave Kweku the confidence that he would be able to blend in with first year boys at his old school, Glenwood, who would likewise be eight years old.

To Kweku's delight, at Glenwood Kofi did not wish to ride on his father's coattails but was anxious to succeed on his own merit. He didn't end up as head boy, but managed to get into the first team for cricket, where he opened the bowling – right arm fast – and built a fearsome reputation for the accuracy of his line and length. He also made it into the hockey 1st XI, where his vision for the killer pass proved vital in midfield.

Towards the end of his time at Glenwood, Kofi won a scholarship to Huntsmere, entering his dad's old house, The Mount. Kweku was overjoyed that a silver-haired Ventham was still Housemaster there, and Ventham was in turn delighted to be able to welcome to the House a new generation of Mensah. Kojo and Deborah proudly attended the new boys' reception, where they had a long chat with Ventham and his wife Marjorie, reminiscing over changes at the school in the twenty-eight years since Kweku had first arrived there as a new boy.

At Huntsmere Kofi distinguished himself academically, as he had done at Glenwood, but narrowly missed getting into the Cricket 1st XI in a year when the competition was fierce. He could only make it into the 2nd XI. But after four successful years at Huntsmere, in the last of which he was appointed a school super, he left with an entrance exhibition to Richardson College at Oxford. There he used all the skills learnt in life as a child growing up in a political family to rise to the position of President of the Oxford Union, the University's debating society, and graduated with a first in Politics, Philosophy and Economics (PPE).

Alongside Kofi's ambitious nature was an altruistic disposition, but one that didn't suffer fools gladly. Joanna and Kweku both doted on him. He appreciated two bits of advice from his parents while growing up. From Kweku, to keep his feet firmly on the ground whenever he risked becoming overly impatient or too dismissive of others' points of view. From Joanna, to take nothing for granted and to thank his lucky stars every day for what he already had.

Like his father before him, from university Kofi wanted to return straight home to Ghana. But, unlike his father, his career interest was in politics, not family business. Against this background, Kweku happily got him involved in politicking from an early age, without any objections from Joanna. He took his son with him on the campaign trail whenever Kofi was in the country and free. By the time Kofi graduated from Oxford, he had the entry-level experience necessary for Kweku to appoint him administrative secretary at his Parliamentary office in Accra.

Kofi understudied his father, acting as his virtual deputy through five more terms that Kweku served as MP for Mim, beating in the last election to his great satisfaction the new presiding member for the Mim district assembly, one Arthur Kyereh. Kyereh was a brash, iconoclastic, quack pharmacist-turned-politician epitomising the worst in modern post-truth politics. He shamelessly held the belief that any means were acceptable so long as you win.

***

Kofi and Kweku both agreed that it was now time for him to step up to the big stage. Joanna didn't want to stand in the way of her son's ambition: Kofi had got so much right up to now, so she was prepared to trust his judgment. Kweku would retire his seat at the next general election in just under a year's time and throw the full weight of the family's contacts and financial muscle behind his son's campaign for the Mim seat.

CHAPTER NINETEEN

Joe

January 2020

In Kumasi, the restaurant owner Joe had fallen on desperate times. Almost thirty years earlier, one day, while his lead waitress Lisa was in the shower, he had checked through her list of contacts and was shocked to see Kweku's name there. When he confronted her with it, she saw the rage in his face and assumed he had found out about everything. Panicking, she denied ever dating Kweku, hoping her denial would draw a line under the developing nightmare. But her denial wasn't emphatic enough. She delivered it too hesitantly and it reeked of guilt.

He began slapping her around. Eventually, under pressure, through bruised cheeks and bloodshot eyes, she broke down in tears and admitted sleeping with Kweku on and off over a period of 4 years. In an effort to paint herself as the victim and gain Joe's sympathy to save herself from further beatings, she quickly added that she had even had to abort a child under pressure from Kweku, and that was why in the last year of the affair there were two months when she kept calling in sick. She was right that the affair had gone on for four years, before Kweku suddenly cut her off and stopped coming there, feeling guilt as his son was growing and Joanna was slowly winning her battle with PND, exercising in yoga groups at her local gym. However, there was no truth at all to her accusation about his role in an abortion. Still, her lie about this succeeded in its intended purpose of deflecting Joe's anger away from her and on to Kweku.

As the years went by, Joe watched with envy as Kweku's family's business expanded. He had seen

Kweku entering politics, smiling and glad-handing all and sundry wherever he went. He became filled with a sense of loathing for him because of what Lisa had told him, cursing the Mensahs' name, and Kweku's in particular, whenever he saw advertisements for Sonimo products in the newspapers or heard political campaign messages for Kweku on the radio.

All the while his restaurant business faced declining patronage with the inexorable collapse of the timber industry in Kumasi, propelled by steep but unfair competition from the Far East and dwindling local forest resources. Eventually the bank moved in to threaten foreclosure, giving him six months to pay up on his mortgage. From hating Kweku for the great strides he and his family were making in business and politics, he had now shifted his focus to viewing him as a possible lifeline to save his business. He wrote to Kweku appealing for assistance.

After four weeks there was still no response. In fact, Kweku had seen the letter, but had stuffed it into a part of his briefcase he reserved for sensitive documents, out of sight of Joanna, while he mulled over how to respond to it, if at all.

Impatient for a response, Joe had decided to take a bus down to Accra with the sole mission of meeting Kweku to persuade him to invest in the restaurant to save it. Acting on information he had been given about Kweku's address, Joe knew he was now at the right house.

***

Kofi was in his father's study overlooking the front of the house. He had seen a man entering earlier, looking rather scruffy. The visitor was also sweating and red-eyed, as if from a sleepless night or a long journey. Kofi didn't recognise the security guard on duty that afternoon. He thought he must be new, but as he had let the man through the gate into the house after signing the visitors log book, and Kofi knew that his dad was open to meeting all sorts as part of his political work, he didn't think anything of it. He continued reviewing the campaign literature in the study. The security guard rang the visitor's name through to the cook, Rockson, who emerged from the staff quarters behind the house.

Rockson asked his name again, Joe confirmed it and claimed that Kweku was expecting him. It was of course a lie. Joe was the last person Kweku was expecting to see at his house. But with that, Rockson led him into the reception room, gave him a seat and told him he would let Kweku know he was there. Meanwhile Kweku, watching TV upstairs with Joanna, had heard someone entering the house. He saw the person shuffling in down the driveway, but couldn't make out who it was.

Kofi heard his father coming down the stairs with his mother, engaged in conversation as they walked into the reception room. As soon as Kweku laid eyes on the visitor, even though Joe had aged, with thinning, grey hair and more wrinkles at the corners of his eyes, he recognised him instantly. He began panicking. Joanna was standing right beside him. He had to think on his feet:

'Don't worry, love,' he quickly said. 'I can handle this one.'

'But who is it?' Joanna asked.

'Oh, just someone… you know, one of my constituents, he's following up with some information for me… I'll be up soon, darling, don't worry.'

Joe was standing by, his hand outstretched ready to shake Kweku's. He saw Kweku squirming as he spoke. He smiled with satisfaction at his discomfort. At that moment, he knew he had the power to wreck the scene of family tranquillity he had just intruded on. But getting money to save his ailing business was his priority for now. So he would keep mum about everything, provided Kweku was going to help him out.

Joanna lingered, looking suspiciously at the man's demeanour and dishevelled state, and starting to have doubts about why Kweku should be meeting such a person at home and not in his office:

'Are you sure, darling?' she asked.

'Yes, yes, my love. I can handle it. Go back upstairs and continue with the film. Let me know what happens, I'll be up in a few minutes, I promise.'

'All right, love.' Joanna was still unconvinced, but Kweku had given her that firm look which said 'Please, love, do as I'm saying. I shall explain.' So she left and started back up the stairs. But when she reached the top of the landing, instead of continuing to the TV room, she stopped. She had a sixth sense that her husband was being evasive, and was intrigued. She decided to try to eavesdrop on their conversation.

As they sat down, Joe began calmly enough:

'It's been many, many years since we last saw you at the restaurant, sir, too long ago. Is everything all right?'

'Oh yes, Joe, thank you, there's no problem at all… It's just that er… they constructed a road, a new detour, you see. The new road cuts out so much of the traffic and means I don't have to come into Kumasi any more.'

Joe pouted wryly, sceptical about Kweku's answer.

'By the way, Lisa sends her regards. She said she's missed you all these years and wondered whether she did anything to upset you.' By now his eyes were like daggers spearing Kweku's.

'Me? Why should she be missing me?' said Kweku, playing the innocent.

Joe said nothing in response, continuing to stare at Kweku in silence for upwards of a minute, knowing full well what torture that was for him. Kweku meanwhile knew from Joe's provocative attitude that the secret of his and Lisa's liaison was out. Right then, he understood that the current equilibrium in his family life was Joe's to either maintain or shatter in an instant. He had lost control; Joe was now in the driving seat.

Kweku started sweating, his pulse racing. Joe continued in a matter-of-fact tone, confirming his awareness that he had Kweku exactly where he wanted him:

'Anyway, you know, what with the timber business being so down nowadays, I've lost so many customers, you know. Things just aren't the same. I've been bumping into old customers here and there over the years. Whenever I ask, they always tell me the same thing… The Chinese are spoiling their business, in their export markets in Europe, in neighbouring West African countries, even in Ghana, supplying their buyers at half price.

Meanwhile the government just keeps jacking up prices of fuel and taxes. Everything's going up all the time. I've already had to lay off most of my staff. Nowadays I'm running a skeleton team, with Lisa, an assistant cook – his boss had enough and left last year – and one other waiter.'

'I'm very sorry to hear that, but how is it you think I can help? I'm not in the restaurant business.'

'I know that… Cigarette?'

'Sorry, I gave up smoking long ago, thank you.'

'No, I mean, do *you* have one or can you get one for me?'

'Well, I don't have any, but if you like I can ask my staff to get you one?'

'Yes, I would like that. Thank you.'

Kweku shouted for Rockson. He stuffed a 10 cedi note into his hand and asked him to buy a packet of cigarettes for the visitor.

'Thank you,' Joe said, disingenuously affecting courtesy. 'Now, Mr Mensah, what I came to ask is, can you help me out?' Kweku looked at him quizzically. 'You know, save my business?'

'But what's that got to do with me?'

'It's got everything to do with people like you.' Joe started raising his voice. He began to lose his cool, his rage re-surfacing with the apparent rejection by Kweku. 'Do you know what sort of a state you've left Lisa in?'

'Lisa? But? ...'

'Oh yes, she told me all about it. You dirty old man!'

Kweku felt like saying, 'What about you?' but he knew he couldn't. He was desperate for Joe to shut up… But he wouldn't, he just got louder:

'It's because of people like you… that's why everything's wrong with the world nowadays!' He was jabbing the air repeatedly with his index finger, pointing it excitedly at Kweku as he spoke.

Kweku tried to calm him down. 'OK look, how much are you after exactly?'

'Oh, "how much" is it now then? Not even so much as a "How is Lisa doing since I just abandoned her with a problem like that?"'

Kweku thought he heard someone gasp on the upstairs landing. He stood up:

'Darling, is that you?' he asked. Joanna was there, dumbstruck at what she had just heard. Kweku, her dutiful husband, who everyone said was a saint, this popular MP, had got a restaurant waitress pregnant, then abandoned her? Is that what she had just heard? No, she had to hear the rest of this! Without answering Kweku, she quietly squirreled herself away into a corner of the landing, within earshot but out of sight of the first few steps.

Meanwhile Joe was getting more and more agitated. He stood up, yanked out a knife from his waist and approached Kweku, who tried not to flinch.

'What's that you've got there?' Kweku asked, the hairs bristling on the back of his neck.

'You know what it is.' Joanna came forward and started down the stairs to try to glimpse what was going on. She saw the flash of steel in the reflection of the sun through the windows and shrieked. Hearing this, Kofi opened the study door and came rushing out. He saw the visitor threatening his dad with the knife. He shouted for Rockson, who came running in, then stopped when he saw what was going on and ran back out again, reaching for his mobile phone and shouting to the security guard at the front gate to come and help and call the police.

Acting instinctively, Kofi dashed back into the study. He knew that his father kept a pistol in the top right-hand drawer, now that he was a politician, precisely in case his life was ever threatened by an angry constituent or member of the public. He rummaged around and felt what seemed like a pistol near the back of the drawer. He pulled it out. It was an automatic. He had seen many – in films and in real life. But he had never fired one before... He knew there was a safety catch that had to be released first. He saw a red button and slid it, praying that would activate it.

'Don't be silly!' Kweku shouted, as he kept ducking Joe, by now lunging frenziedly at him with his knife in wild, slashing gestures.

'It's a bit late for that, isn't it, eh? A bit late for that, you la-de-da bastard!' Joe exclaimed.

'OK look, I'll get you what you want.'

Kofi stalked up quietly behind Joe, pistol in front of him, both hands gripping the handle tightly:

‘Leave my dad alone!’ he shouted.

Joanna screamed when she saw her son.

Joe swung round. Seeing Kofi, he couldn’t believe his luck. There was no way this young posh-boy would know how to handle a gun, he thought. He charged straight at Kofi, his knife raised high over his head and starting a downward swing. Kofi moved his right index finger to the trigger and pulled. A shot rang out. Joanna let out a blood-curdling shriek and came running down the stairs. Joe was stopped in his tracks and froze, the knife slipping out of his grasp as he fell like a stone to the ground.

As Joe lay on the floor, bleeding profusely from the neck, Kofi, sweating, his hands shaking, felt something weighing down his right hand. He saw everyone staring at him, then saw the gun in his hand. He came to his senses and tossed it to the floor in horror. He looked down at his blood-spattered white shirt. Joe’s head collapsed to one side, his eyes frozen wide-open in an expression of shock.

Kweku came closer, as Joanna rushed to hug Kofi. He checked Joe’s pulse but couldn’t feel anything. Then he saw what looked like a complimentary card on the floor beside his body. He assumed it must have fallen out of his pocket when he snatched his knife from his waist to attack him. He bent down to pick it up and was stunned to see the name on the front, “Arthur Kyereh” and underneath that name “Presiding Member – Mim District Assembly”. He couldn’t believe it. This man had been his rival in the last general election, a lawless fraudster. How did Joe get himself mixed up with someone like that? He turned the card over. There, right before his eyes was a handwritten instruction, reading: “Joe, this is the address in Accra Airport Residential area of the man you need to visit for justice in your case: 42 Lawson Street. Good luck! Arthur.”

Suddenly realising the card could be vital evidence pointing to motive, he replaced it on the floor, as near as possible to where he had picked it up from.

By now they could hear police and ambulance sirens wailing in the distance. Within minutes they were at the gate, then speeding down the driveway. Three police officers and two paramedics rushed in. Rockson, then Maria, followed them in. The senior paramedic, seeing Joe lying still on the floor, feared the worst. He went through the formality of checking Joe's vital signs, then closed his eyelids, confirming his death and recording the time. One of the police officers now shouted to warn all present:

'This is a crime scene. Do not touch or move anything. Stay away.'

'It was self-defence, officer …' Joanna began explaining in defence of her son.

'Yes,' Kweku quickly added, pointing to Joe's knife on the floor. 'The man was trying to kill me with that knife. Who knows who else he would have attacked after that? Thank God my son shot him as he was about to stab him, too, and saved us all.'

The police officer gave no reaction, saying only: 'We will need you all to stay around so that we can take statements from everyone here. In the meantime, stay away from this area.' He started marking out the area.

Kweku picked up his mobile phone from a side-table in the front porch and began making calls.

Joanna started to go upstairs, still hugging Kofi, who was listless and still in shock.

But the police officer shouted after her: 'I'm sorry, madam, you can't go up there.'

'Why ever not? That horrible man never came upstairs.'

'That may well be, madam, but we still have to lock the house down. The whole house is a crime scene and we'll now have to do our work painstakingly. For a start we will have to take into evidence the gentleman's …'

'My son's …'

'OK sorry, your son's shirt and other clothes, as well as his shoes. Mr Mensah's too, as I have already been told he was also involved in the altercation and that in fact it started with him. A forensics team and detectives from the homicide division are on their way. We'll need time here to do our work.'

'How long?'

'I'm afraid I can't say, madam. It depends. We always want to move as fast as possible, but we can't leave anything to chance. Maybe the detectives will be able to tell you more when they get here …'

'It's ok, love,' Kweku interjected. 'I just spoke to my dad. He was frantic and told us to pack and come over to Cantonments right away. So let's pack up everything we need.'

The officer cut in again:

'I repeat, leave everything as it is. And you won't be able to pack anything up, I am afraid. As I said, we'll be needing to take statements from everyone, including Mr and Mrs Mensah and your son. Afterwards Mr Mensah and your son will have to accompany us down to the station. Fortunately for you, it seems there are a lot of witnesses who are saying it was self-defence, but we will still have to take your son in.'

Joanna's jaw dropped:

'You mean you have to lock up my son? But why? He was only trying to protect himself and everyone else here?'

Kofi didn't react. He just stood there staring into an empty space in front of him.

The officer continued: 'If all goes well at the station, we'll release your son on police bail pending further enquiries.'

The officers began taking statements from all the staff and Joanna. About half an hour later, two detectives arrived – a chief inspector and a sergeant, in white short-sleeved shirts and dark trousers. They flashed their warrant cards while introducing themselves: detective chief inspector Dan Tetteh and detective sergeant Andrew Sackey. Tetteh, a bald moustachioed man with spectacles, put on gloves. Kneeling closer to the body, he asked:

'Has anyone touched or moved anything since he died?' With an experienced eye, he spotted Kofi looking at Kweku.

Kweku turned to his son, their eyes met, then he turned to Tetteh:

'Only the complimentary card to the right of the body on the floor there… I picked it up without thinking. But I put it back in exactly the same place.'

Tetteh walked around to the other side of the body and picked the card up. He saw a name on it he recognised instantly: Arthur Kyereh, the forceful and well-connected Brong Ahafo politician, a member of the ruling party, always in the news for making provocative, headline-grabbing statements. He turned the card over and saw the handwritten instruction. He was visibly stunned. He looked back up at Kweku. They gazed at each other, then he looked away. This time he asked Kweku directly:

'Have you touched anything else?'

'No, only that, detective chief inspector… But you can clearly see now who is behind all this. I hope you can take immediate action and bring him in for questioning as soon as possible.'

'Please, Mr Mensah, do not tell me how to do my job. Just make sure you don't move anything else in here… We're taking statements from everyone, so if you and Mrs Mensah and your son… his name?'

'Kofi.'

'… If you and Mrs Mensah and Kofi can wait for me in the garden, I'll be through shortly. And then afterwards I would like Mr Mensah and Kofi to accompany me to the station.

Kweku was quick to add: 'I've called my lawyer to come round urgently. He said to give him an hour.'

'OK. It might be more convenient for you all to stay somewhere else tonight, maybe longer. Just make sure you don't leave Accra without telling us. We'll let you know when we're done.'

Kweku remembered his driver Justin had closed from work at lunchtime. He called him to come back in urgently. Joanna's driver Sampson had the day off.

A pathologist arrived with forensics and a cameraman. He examined the body and noted the time of death. Then he gave instructions to the paramedics to seal the body up and stretcher it away. Forensics bagged and logged into evidence the knife, gun, clothing and other items from the scene. They also recovered one spent shell casing from the floor.

The lawyer was last to arrive. When the time came for Kweku and Kofi to join the car to the station, Joanna insisted on joining them. At the station, Kweku and Kofi were photographed, fingerprinted and interviewed separately under caution by Tetteh and Sackey. For Kweku, there were awkward moments when he had to come clean for the record about his affair – if anyone wanted to call it that – with Lisa. Kofi remained distracted throughout the ordeal, but both Kweku and Joanna emphasised to him before his interview that he should just tell the truth.

Detective Sergeant Sackey explained to Kofi that, once they had a positive ID of the victim, it was possible charges could follow but, provided he could show he used reasonable force, he might be able to claim self-defence. He said it would not be up to him to decide. That would be up to the prosecution services and possibly the courts to determine, including ruling out murder or manslaughter.

Kofi was eventually released on bail and Justin took them all in Kweku's car from the station straight to Kojo and Deborah's home in Cantonments.

CHAPTER TWENTY

The Present Time

Kojo and Deborah came down to the front porch to welcome them. They straightaway threw their arms around Kofi, ushering him inside to sit down, Joanna following right behind, then Kweku. Kojo briefly asked Kofi about the police interrogation, but he was listless, completely disinterested, still numb with shock at what he had done and what he had seen. He had just shot a man, seen the life ebbing slowly out of him until he was motionless.

Deborah intervened:

'Kojo, leave him alone. Can't you see what he's just been through?'

'Yes,' Joanna chimed in.

'I'm sorry D, Joanna, you're both right.'

Kweku nodded sombrely. Deborah called Tina. Joanna took Kofi by the hand and, holding him tight, followed Tina upstairs to the bedroom reserved for him by his grandparents. As Joanna climbed the stairs, she turned to give Kweku a withering look which told him two things: first, that she would thrash everything out with him about this Lisa tart on another day; but, more importantly for now, it was time for him to think long and hard about the whole politics thing. Kweku had no answer. Feeling full of guilt, he looked away, wondering what the future would hold.

***

Kojo motioned to Kweku:

'Come on, Son. Let's go and sit outside on the verandah.' He asked Tina to bring them a bottle of his best Scottish pure malt whisky from the drinks cabinet, with two glasses and ice.

As Kweku sat down, he held his head in his hands. It all hit him. Tears began rolling down his cheeks.

‘Politics, Dad. Will you look at where politics has landed us?’ He was angry, not with Kojo but at himself. Kojo had chosen to be just an observer of politics, a commentator from the sidelines. Why did he actually have not only to dip his toes but to plunge his entire body into politics and swim in the morass of such a treacherous profession? Worst of all, why had he allowed his son to join him in the same profession, instead of advising him to look for another career.

Kojo had no answer. He was kicking himself for ever encouraging his son to get involved in politics in the first place, for giving his blessing to something which now risked causing the family such scandal. At the same time, he was still and had been for many years a fighter.

He asked Kweku if he felt OK to talk about the whole incident. Kweku started narrating everything to him. He left nothing out. Kojo tilted his head and raised his eyebrows when Kweku mentioned the Lisa connection. He gasped as Kweku narrated the quick and brave action Kofi took in the emergency which had saved his own life, Kweku’s, Joanna’s and likely the lives of many others. Finally, Kweku explained about the complimentary card he had seen by Joe’s body and the message on the back from Kyereh.

Kojo sat bolt upright in his chair: ‘Oh no! Him? You mean *he* is involved in this? ...’

‘It seems so, Dad.’

‘Well, I’m going to make sure that’s the last time he messes with us. Who does that fellow think he is? Ever since your call, I’ve been ringing round my friends, retired senior police officers and experts in the legal profession on self-defence. I’m going to straighten all this out. Don’t you worry, son. Huh! Kyereh! Why, he wasn’t even a sprat on the horizon when we were supporting the whole district with jobs, charity projects and income from the taxes we were paying! We’ll see who's got influence in Mim all right!' Kojo asked Tina to bring him his diary. He knew just the person to call.

He continued:

'And Kofi's actions were a clear case of self-defence. Would people have been happier if that man – Joe or whatever you said his name was – had stabbed our grandson, son, daughter-in-law and who knows who else to death and then escaped? Nonsense!'

After recounting the events, Kweku was now himself feeling tired and slightly distracted. As Kojo began flicking through the pages of his diary and making and receiving more calls, Kweku took a long gulp of whisky from his glass and set it down again. He realised it was politics that had complicated his life and rued the day he had decided to enter into it. There had been minor bumps in the road up until then, but now politics had brought looming scandal to his house – possibly done irreparable harm to the career of his and Joanna's precious and dedicated only child, Kojo and Deborah's only beloved grandson. Why had he done it? What drove him to risk his smooth-running life, and for what? To help others who can't help themselves?

The longer he ruminated on the state of politics in the world generally, but more particularly in post-independence Africa, the more angry and frustrated he felt. Switching to deep political analysis in an effort to make sense of his obsession for politics, he tried to gather together his thoughts on an array of issues and organise them into some kind of coherent tour of key issues constantly niggling at his political thinking.

His mind went back to the rugby game against Arkley in his last year at Glenwood, when he was deliberately punched and left winded on the ground by his grinning opposite number. Even though the offender's team lost, the efficacy of fighting asymmetric warfare with the use of intelligence and special operations targeting, as compared with the open-plan lambs-to-the-slaughter approach, accompanied by breaks for tea, of British contingents fighting the Crimean War in the nineteenth century and the suicidal stubbornness of trench warfare in the Great War, was demonstrated. The fact that Kweku scored no more tries in the rest of the match and that Arkley outscored Glenwood in the second half were vindications of the argument that there is no 'fairness' or 'cricket' in war or politics for that matter – that methods used seem to be less important than winning.

Kojo had just finished a long call with a close friend he had arranged to meet early in the morning. He turned to Kweku, whose thoughts were still raging. Kweku continued, now speaking out loud, forgetting that Kojo would not understand the premise of his question, which he had articulated only in his own thoughts while Kojo was on the phone:

'So, Dad, is it then the case that what we are left to reach are subjective judgments about the superiority of the value systems of the protagonists? Surely not.'

'Eh?'

'I mean surely, in an objective assessment of the superiority of contending political value systems, superiority can be tested by analysing what would be preferred destinations for the majority of humans in a borderless world? The only condition is that, in assessing the superiority of one political system over another, we equate its superiority with its popularity or long-term sustainability.

'OK, I think I am with you now.'

'Such a test would currently unquestionably see a flight to political systems where there is more transparency, more respect for the rule of law, than others where there is only a semblance of democratic institutions established for the benefit of a fictitious 'people'.

After the Second World War, during the height of the Cold War, the balanced observer did not need detailed ideological explanations to be able to understand which of the two political systems – the one to the east of the Berlin Wall or the one to west – was superior. The argument was won and lost by the fact that the wall was constructed at all by the powers to the east of the wall dominated by the Soviet Union, in order forcibly to keep their citizens behind it and stop, by murder if need be, anyone trying to flee to the Western sector.

The phrase "people vote with their feet" says all you need to know about who is making a better job of running their country: you just need to see which direction the majority of the people flows are in, in a hypothetical situation when all barriers to entry and exit – physical and administrative – have been removed.'

'True, Son. I'm on the same page.'

'Now of course, the biggest constraint on the receiving end is that countries that are better-run cannot simply throw their gates wide open to receive anyone who wants to come in. Governments have a responsibility to manage their resources for the benefit of those already resident in their jurisdiction and to avoid destabilising delicate cultural and ethnic balances established in their countries or societal groupings over a number of painstaking decades and sometimes centuries.

All parties in any national political system are aware of this. The phoney battles around the issue are the ones waged by those on the left of the political spectrum to show that they are more charitable and welcoming to immigrants than those on the right, and by those on the right to show that they are more aggressive towards immigrants than those on the left.

Refugees from war are an exception, but not ones ignoring or passing through several safe countries to land themselves at a cherry-picked destination of their choosing, unless by invitation from the receiving country's government or following an invitation by a close family relative already resident in the jurisdiction which has been approved by the receiving government.

All sides – left, right and centre – of the political spectrum in the receiving country destinations know that there are limits to the realities of their positions. Direct evidence of this is the fact that deportations of illegal immigrants from the United States grew at a faster rate under a well-respected, sagacious and balanced Democratic President Obama on the so-called left of centre than they had under the immediately preceding Republican administration on the so-called right wing of politics under President George W. Bush.

Such realities render redundant the easy tags of left-wing and right-wing as far as honest debate on this topic goes. The key difference between the so-called left-wing and right-wing – and it is a crucial one – is that there seems to be a better understanding on the left-wing of the fact that suspending engagement with the immigrant source countries or, worse still, encouraging political instability in those countries, is most decidedly not the best way of encouraging their indigenes to stay put!'

Kojo took a sip from his glass, as Kweku paused to sigh before continuing:

'For almost 60 years now, Dad, the African continent has for the most part comprised fully independent sovereign states free to decide on their own development strategies, direction and policies – not, as many still seem to be in the habit of repeating, partly independent states still ruled under so-called "neo-colonialism".'

'Yes, I always thought that stuff about neo-colonialism was in essence an excuse to do nothing and feel sorry for yourself instead of rolling up your sleeves and getting to grips with the issues.'

'Exactly, Dad! Those attempting to excuse the slow pace of infrastructural development across the continent by scurrying under cover of the increasingly implausible fig-leaf of continuing neo-colonial rule by the West as an excuse are doing their countrymen and women a great disservice. This is firstly because you cannot begin to solve a problem, unless you recognise both that it exists and that you are responsible for solving it; and secondly because continuing lamely to hang on to such excuses, which did once have a measure of validity, many decades well into your capacity and operation as a fully independent state, precludes any serious attempt at evidence-based, rather than ideologically-rooted, analysis.'

'No doubt.'

'The almost universally applicable driving cause of continuing sub-standard development across the

African continent, as in many other more slowly developing regions of the world, is corrupt and incompetent administration in the government sector, grounded in political patronage. In almost every instance, this displaces by far the most efficient driver of development, which is impartial decision-making in the government sector, centred on merit-based recruitment, and selection and award of government contracts to organisations and people based on objective performance criteria.

Speaking more generally about the need to control greed as a natural human tendency not limited to any segment of the global population or geographical area of the world, the fact is that, in the normal course of business, large multinational companies will always exploit market and regulatory inefficiencies wherever they can, for the benefit of their shareholders – or of the senior managers controlling the company. Witness the infamous proclivity of the pharmaceutical industry in the United States for overcharging and avoidance of price regulation. Identical medicines are reported to cost up to 10 times as much there as they do across the border in Canada – all down to intense political lobbying by pharmaceutical companies at the highest levels of government in the US to allow the practice to continue.

Kweku paused for another sip, before continuing:

'Even this whole thing with China began when large US corporations holding considerable political clout as political donors during the late 1960s, facing decelerating sales growth or market saturation at home and in other western markets, began greedily eyeing up the huge Chinese consumer market as targets for their sales.'

'Really, Son? I thought the welcoming of China was all part of Cold War re-alignments – you know, the US taking advantage of tensions between the Chinese and the Soviets to align with China and put pressure on Brezhnev and his cronies.'

'I know, Dad, those were the headlines, but I'm telling you the story behind the headlines was more complicated than that. The big companies were major donors to the political parties – the Republicans under Richard Nixon were in control of the country's administration from the beginning of 1969 – and they started sizing up the Chinese market, a population of almost 800 million, four times the size of the US's, although of course with far lower disposable income per head. But think about it, one dollar of sales of a product per person would have got you 800 million dollars in those days. You can imagine what that would be worth now.

The thing is, their grand strategy all went pear-shaped, as they massively underestimated Chinese competencies and cunning. The Chinese, you see, through enforced technology transfer agreements as part of allowing American companies access to their markets, were able to learn how to produce copycat items at far lower cost to sell back to US consumers in even greater quantities than they – the original Chinese target customers – were buying. Cue the start of growing US trade deficits with China.

In realities presumably concealed from the US investing companies, labour costs were said to be sometimes further depressed by the Chinese manufacturers' use of labour provided by minimally paid prisoners or army personnel already receiving salary on the government payroll. Such collaboration would not have been possible without the active co-operation of China's government with the Chinese manufacturers, most of them state-owned or otherwise government-affiliated in those early years.

The sharply lower production costs available in China then enticed US companies – under pressure or incentives from their shareholders or stock market investors to maximise shareholder value – to shut down manufacturing in their own countries and boost profits by getting the same goods made at far lower cost in China, without at the same time feeling obligated to reduce selling prices correspondingly all the way down to reflect the much lower production costs, i.e. without passing on all the gains to the US consumer.

So there was some benefit for US consumers – but not as much as there could have been. The bulk of the benefit went to the US companies' shareholders and to top management recommending for themselves and receiving from happy shareholders higher remuneration from the much larger profits.

Again, forced technology transfer – forced transfer to the new Chinese manufacturer of most of the secrets and science behind production of the goods – was an integral part of the deal. As mentioned, it led to theft of intellectual property and copycatting by the Chinese, but the result was an explosion in profit margins for the companies transplanting production from the West to China and elsewhere in the Far East.

And so, just to emphasise again that, even where retail sales prices were brought down in a proclaimed win-win for US consumers, corresponding production costs had actually fallen much further. For the western companies involved, it led to huge hikes in profits – and consequently in share prices, which are fundamentally a reflector or multiple of future earnings or dividend flows.'

'OK, got you.'

'The same phenomenon was repeated elsewhere in the West. This is how manufacturing in the US, UK and other traditional manufacturing hubs in the West was displaced to the Far East on a large scale. Consumers bought goods in the stores cheaper, shareholders – entrepreneurs and their families, pension funds, speculators and savers – got richer with the bigger profits, as selling prices did not fall as fast as production costs. Who lost out? Those in manufacturing jobs in the West.

The driving forces behind these developments were the very same business leaders revered as paragons by many in their local communities in the West. Incomes of those able to hold on to their jobs in sectors less vulnerable to displacement by Chinese production, such as in the higher-skilled engineering sector – were in turn hit by the collapse in Union collective bargaining power following aggressive action taken by Ronald Reagan in the US and Maggie Thatcher in the UK at the start of the 1980s to "free up" the labour sector and make hiring and firing easier. The gap between pay at the top and pay at the bottom of the employment ladder widened significantly.

To ignore the importance of governments leading the way in encouraging re-training in ever-newer technology or higher-level skills for employees in displaced industries is as nonsensical as, for instance, the ostrich-like behaviour of the climate change deniers, the modern equivalent of the ever-shrinking minority of flat-earthers of the last two millennia.

But in making that original miscalculation about bringing China in from the cold in the late 1960s, business leaders and politicians in the West seemed to have forgotten their history: China was a culture and civilisation which had invented gunpowder at a time when Europeans were still using comparatively low-technology bows, arrows and catapults as advanced weapons of choice in their warfare. So China was not a technologically backward culture that would take a long time to learn any tricks it was shown, so to speak.

Within a short space of time, manufacturing capacity at all but the highest levels of precision engineering was hollowed out not only across the West but in lower-cost producing countries in Latin America and Africa, including Kweku's home-country of Ghana. By way of illustration, the development had a direct and brutal impact on businesses in Ghana engaged in the manufacture and exportation of processed timber to the same hard currency-paying markets in the West targeted by the Chinese government for Chinese producers.

Meanwhile African countries, as former colonies mostly of British and French empires, and to a lesser extent of Portuguese, German and Italian expansion, had incorporated into their own labour laws many of the hard-won regulations on human rights and employment of labour of the colonising countries. Full compliance with these labour laws was usually made a strict conditionality of access to both multilateral and bilateral investment finance, under the umbrella of World Bank and International Monetary Fund rules.

Investment funds, even if obtained by national governments in Africa on concessional terms, were – according to terms imposed by the multilateral or bilateral lender or guarantor – lent on to businesses at fully commercial bank rates. Such rates comprised a base of interbank rate as the lending bank's cost of capital, plus a huge country risk premium and the bank's profit margin on top of that. This culminated in a cost of funds for businesses so high as to make net profit almost impossible to achieve for all but the most lucrative enterprises generating abnormally high operating margins.

State financial support or subsidies for private businesses were in practice almost universally prohibited. Ostensibly the insistence on funds being on-lent at fully commercial rates was to prevent government corruption in picking favourites to allocate the limited cheap funds to. This would have given the favoured producer an unfair advantage in terms of a below-market cost of capital, enabling it to sell at lower prices undercutting competitors who had to finance their business using funds obtained at fully commercial bank rates.

So the market allocated the limited funds to business borrowers at commercial rates corresponding to the perceived risk of default – with slightly lower rates applying to corporate borrowers considered to have a lower risk of defaulting on the loan and higher rates applying to borrowers perceived to have a higher risk of defaulting.

The idea was for government to let the market work independently and not interfere – the old principle of laissez-faire capitalism, a kind of survival of the fittest or, if you like, an extension of Darwinian natural selection. Kweku however considered it to be the height of irony – indeed hypocrisy – that the countries effectively controlling the multilateral and bilateral lending institutions imposing such conditions were simultaneously protecting their own agricultural producers through a mix of subsidy and state purchase on a massive scale.

Against this background, manufacturers in a largely self-reliant China – far less bound by such restrictions imposed by lending institutions in the West, as they were only borrowing very limited sums from them – were effectively given a free hand to undercut the competition in every sector of global manufacturing, supported by closely coordinated targeted intervention by their government in a highly successful synergy which continues right up to the present day.'

***

'Wow! OK, Son. But are you sure you can ever give up politics? I mean, you seem to have researched everything in such detail.'

'I don't know. We'll see, Dad… The point is that strong political leadership, motivated by the desire not to accumulate personal wealth from particular resource transactions but to maximise long-term strategic benefit for the nation as a whole, will minimise the scope for exploitation. If a political leader, in return for promised cash or asset-based incentives by a large multinational company, makes agreements extending 20 or 30 years into the future, guaranteeing fixed input costs way below current market prices – for instance for power supply, as was agreed in Ghana with Kaiser Aluminum in the 1960s – or tax benefits assessed as being extraordinarily generous by independent analysts, the fault is not "neo-colonialism", as some are fond of claiming, but greed, poor negotiating skills, incompetence – or a combination of all three – on the part of the leadership negotiating on behalf of the host nation.

The key is not to sell assets cheaply. The Botswana government, for instance, is a rare example of an African government pursuing policies bound to inure to the benefit of its citizens in the long term by insisting on at least 51 percent ownership by Botswana of all natural minerals. In many other African countries on the other hand, rights to the majority of profits in extractive industries – up to 90 percent in some cases – are sold for decades in advance to large multinationals. Such a practice inevitably works to the long-term detriment of the country's citizens, whatever incentives might be reaped from lopsided agreements like these in the short term.

Again militating against uninterrupted steadily expanding national development is the tendency of each new administration from an opposing political party to cancel, delay contractual payments or withhold permits or licences for, projects and ventures initiated by their predecessors or individuals or entities perceived as being close to the predecessor government. This is invariably done on the pretext of thwarting corrupt benefit by the predecessor government or individuals and organisations perceived to have close links to it. Even projects nearing completion are not safe from this recurrent practice, with consideration of the immediate interests of the end users whom the projects were actually intended to benefit of secondary or no interest to the incoming government.

Political parties of all persuasions, both those believed to be capitalist-oriented as well as those considered mixed market or socialist-oriented in name, are equally guilty of this shabby, disruptive practice and it continues to prevail across the continent to Africa's great shame.

Endless complaints about or attempted prosecution for corruption of preceding administrations of an opposing political party are easy to trumpet, as the responsibility for such past corruption can easily be avoided by the incumbent administration on the basis that they were not in power at that time. That does nothing to prevent the continuation of discredited practices by the new administration once it has taken over at the steering wheel of government. Moreover, almost unheard of are complaints or prosecutions of ruling party officials, unless where they have openly challenged the authority of the ruling party leader.

Such conduct, ridden with internal inconsistencies and corrupt partisanship, contributes to the perpetuation of a poisonous political atmosphere militating against uninterrupted development and is a symptom of the most deleterious aspects of political management across post-independence Africa.

Mind you, Dad, I am not trying to say that African independence has been a failure. Every experiment can take years, decades or even centuries to crop and mature. For instance, the first body resembling a modern Parliament in England was assembled by Simon de Montfort in 1265, adding local borough officials to advisory councils to the monarch which up to then had comprised noblemen only. However, rights to vote in elections to choose local and national governments – in the case of men without any pre-condition of property ownership, were only extended to all men above 21 years, and most women above 30 years – more than 650 years later, in 1918 amid the radical social upheavals catalysed worldwide by the Great War. It then took a further decade, until 1928, for universal suffrage to be extended to all men and women in England above 21 years irrespective of property ownership (the age limit was later lowered to 18).

And so the concept of self-determination or self-rule, involving government by representatives of the majority of votes, with protection for minorities under a system of agreed rules, is as valid today as it ever was, although I of course hope it doesn't take African countries 650 years to develop accountable democratic systems of government! At issue rather is the length of time taken to reach agreed goals in infrastructural and scientific development.'

By now, Kojo was feeling drowsy. He excused himself and left. After getting so much off his chest, Kweku was also calmer. He decided to pour himself one last dram of the single malt.

***

Sticking to Africa, Kweku reflected that even the leadership of the ANC in South Africa engaged in acts of political sabotage and media manipulation similar to those which many organisations have undertaken in the past to win the day against domestic rivals – although they should always be answerable under the law for any criminal wrongdoing. The well-constructed documentary, *Tainted Heroes*, was on point in highlighting the ANC's focus on ruthlessly eliminating rival domestic black political organisations in order to establish itself locally – and particularly in the eyes of the international community, the source of the strongest political and economic pressure on any national government – as the only legitimate voice of the struggle for black empowerment in South Africa.

Kweku understood that, when the record of any political group was analysed critically, there were no saints. What the mass of people hoped for with the passing years was improvement. In most of Africa, that was not happening.

However, in a glimmer of hope for Africa's future, the new leadership of the ANC under Cyril Ramaphosa had recently surprised many observers, taking a huge leap forward in post-apartheid race-harmonisation by not excluding a white person from appointment to head the management of the nation's key power utility, Eskom, purely on the basis of his skin colour. Ramaphosa did this in the face of strong opposition by many in his party who were insisting on continued 'positive' or reverse discrimination in order to 'redress the balance' of centuries of disenfranchisement.

But the often-overlooked central fallacy of whataboutism is that two wrongs do not make a right. In support of his argument for non-discrimination, Ramaphosa quoted the former Chinese leader, Deng Xiaoping, who once famously said:

"It doesn't matter if a cat is black or white, so long as it catches mice."

Whether the exemplary decision-making processes undertaken for this appointment would be sustained and extended to decision-making in other sectors of South Africa's economy, or turn out to be yet another false dawn in a long line of many for independent Africa, was open to question. Time would tell.

The same country had recently won the Rugby World Cup, with a black person as its Springboks captain for the first time. This appointment subsequently met with the willing acknowledgement of almost the whole nation – black, white, and everything in between – that he had been promoted to the post by the coach on merit. The capture of the Webb Ellis Trophy by the team was the ultimate vindication of the coach's judgment.

In Kweku's disillusioned mind, Africa as a continent had long ago reached the stage of development where appointments should be based purely on merit – on applicants' competence in addressing the relevant task, rather than their colour, class, rank or political affiliation. Indeed, he felt strongly that the same criteria should be used in all societies, not just African ones.

He finally went upstairs just after midnight, locking the doors and being careful not to wake Joanna as he slipped, disheartened, into bed. Amid the chaos of his day, his reflections on politics were now made stark by one simple illustration:

The Accra – Tema Motorway was opened to traffic in 1965, just six years after Britain's own first motorway, the M1, and seven years into Ghana's independence. More than 50 years later, as of January 2020, it remained Ghana's only motorway.

In the view of an overwhelming majority of the continent's population, including Kweku, its post-independence political leaders had a lot more doing to do, and a lot less talking to do. His final thoughts went to an imaginary future era for Africa, where performance would be evaluated based on useful tasks completed instead of useless speeches made. He thought it unlikely he would ever live to see such a day, but he had not given up hope – yet.

***

Printed in Great Britain
by Amazon

63283776R00284